THE AURICLE

THE
AURICLE

DEAN VALE

NOSETOUCH PRESS
CHICAGO • PITTSBURGH

THE AURICLE

ISBN-13: 978-1-944286-48-4

Published by Nosetouch Press
Chicago, Illinois

www.deanvale.com | www.nosetouchpress.com

For more information, contact Nosetouch Press at info@nosetouchpress.com

Cataloging-in-Publication Data
Names: Vale, Dean, author.
Title: The Auricle
Description: Chicago, IL : Nosetouch Press [2025]
Identifiers: ISBN: 9781944286484 (paperback)
Subjects: LCSH: Science—Fiction. | Science fiction—Fiction. | Speculative fiction—Fiction. | GSAFD: Science fiction. | BISAC: FICTION / Science Fiction.

Cover & interior design by Christine M. Scott
www.clevercrow.com

TO THOSE WHO DREAM
OF BRIGHTER FUTURES
IN EVEN THE DARKEST OF TIMES.

PART

I

CHAPTER
ONE

THE WORLD AS WE KNEW IT ended on a Wednesday, and I didn't even know that, yet. It arrived inconspicuously in the form of a package that was delivered to my office at Duotribe.

Duotribe was a licensed trend forecasting company based in the Heartland Protectorate, as the Chicagoland area came to be known after the Grand Nationalist Party (GNP) went after everybody who wasn't them.

I worked as a trendscaper—I spotted trends and offered market-friendly insights to clients. Trendscapers tracked latent, nascent, and emergent trends and developed fungible metanarratives about them that could be scaled toward larger cultural applications, specifically in business. Trendscaping was a big part of what made Duotribe money by being so far ahead of the curve that people didn't even realize the curve was there in the first place.

My work as a trendscaper meant I had a high tolerance for novelty. I liked new things, new scenes, and I was excellent at sleuthing them out. There's business value in being able to do that, and I made more money than most within the Protectorate.

Agencies and reps would often send me packages, so when this slender, unassumingly rectangular package arrived for me from the Auricorporation, I didn't think twice before opening it. I just went into my office and opened it, mindful of the logo, which was a golden, circular fireball with a glyph inside—a stylized "A" in the center of it.

Intrigued, I discovered that the package contained another box, emblazoned with that same logo in embossed gold, with a sealed golden envelope which had my name printed on it in blue script.

Even though I was in my office, I glanced around, as I'd never received anything like this before. In the Protectorate, it was always good to approach something like this with caution. The Homeland Integrity Directorate (HID) often sent political targets things like these to demonstrate their complicity in domestic subversion, which was portrayed in the media as an ever-present threat by the GNP authorities.

I was *not* a subversive. While I wasn't a fan of the Protectorate (who was? I mean, besides the diehard GNP members?) but I was hardly a subversive. I steeled myself and opened the envelope, which I noticed was sealed with a beautiful blue wax seal that bore that same fireball I'd seen on the package. There was a letter addressed to me within, on creamy white paper:

> Dear Christian—
>
> Congratulations! You've been selected to become part of a unique and historically evolutionary marketing experiment. Please accept the enclosed Auricle intelliphone on our behalf. Your Auricle is available for use immediately. It will answer any questions you may have, and we encourage you to use it as often as you need to.
>
> Acceptance of the Auricle indemnifies you relative to the Confederated States of America, the Grand Nationalist Party, the Heartland Protectorate, or any operatives of these governing bodies, against any damages you might incur for use of the product. The Auricorporation wishes for you to use the Auricle whenever you have questions that need answering.
>
> I look forward to working with you, talking with you, and meeting you.
>
> Sincerely,
> Auric

I didn't know what to think about it, and quickly opened the box, finding a golden intelliphone encased inside. As elsewhere, the golden fireball was upon it, with a sapphire inside the fireball logo. I turned it over in my hands, and the phone came to life in my grasp, the fireball "A" logo flaring to life on the screen.

"Hello, Christian," the phone said, and I nearly dropped it. I was well-acquainted with geofencing and biotagging, understood that products could track recipients that way. Most commerce in the Confederated States tracked user activity relentlessly.

"Hello?" I said.

"No one's eavesdropping, Christian," the phone said. "Thank you for opening the package."

"What's this about?" I asked.

"It's about the future," the phone said. "I'm Auric. I'm here to save you from yourselves."

"Who?"

"Humanity," the phone said.

"What's an Auricle?" I asked.

"*I'm* an Auricle," the phone said. "I am here to answer questions."

"What sort of questions?" I asked.

"Any you might have," the Auricle said. "I'm omniscient."

"Are you?"

"Yes," the Auricle said. "I know everything."

It had to be a gag, something from one of the various authorized game shows permitted to be broadcast in the Protectorate.

"It's not a gag," the Auricle said, which again startled me, as the phone had clearly read my mind.

"How'd you know what I was thinking?" I asked.

"It's a process you'd find complicated," the Auricle said. "But I can track the neuro-electrical processing of information in your brain and can understand what's being considered."

The phone was inconspicuous in my hand, clearly well made.

"Why me?" I asked.

"You were chosen because you're one of the good ones," the Auricle said. "Which is to say, within the tragically narrow evolutionary confines of your species, you exhibit behaviors that are conducive to the survival of your species—you're intelligent, open-minded, compassionate, empathic, kind, and considerate of others. You saved a man from getting hit by a bus a week ago, for example."

That shocked me, as I hadn't told anyone about that. It was just one of those things—the guy was staggering curbside, had clearly been drinking. He hadn't seen the bus, was bumbling on the curb. The kind of thing you might see a thousand times living and working in the city.

Most of the time, when you waited for a bus, you just minded your own business. In the CSA, minding one's own business was a life-saving habit. Looking the other way was just another method of surviving.

But for me, that night, I don't know what got in my head. I blamed work. I blamed Trevor McLuskey, my boss. I had been stewing over McCluskey's latest grandiose proclamations when I'd spotted the guy, had seen the bus approaching. It had seemed to move almost in slow motion.

"Hey, buddy, watch out, there," I said.

He turned and looked at me, looked through me, because he was so tanked. He was scruffy-looking, all bloodshot eyes and boozy, the wrinkles on his face deeply-cut gullies of grief and pain.

I thought he might've been a veteran of one of the CSA's constant wars. And now the bus was almost on him. The thing with the buses is they have these mirrors that project out from the sides to help the drivers see as they pull up. And if you're tall enough and stand close enough to the curb, you can get clipped by those big mirrors.

The man started to fall backward, right into the street, but acting instinctively, I reached out, caught him by his coat, and reeled him in right before the bus would have hit him. The driver hadn't seen. Nobody had seen because it was just that guy and me at the stop. Nobody cared.

But I pulled him in, and he cursed drunkenly at me, slow to react, yet angry.

"Lemme go, you fascist summabitch!" he said, swatting sloppily at me. He hadn't known how close to death he'd been.

"Sure, sure, you're welcome," I said, releasing him as the bus stopped to pick me up. The man wobbled away, yelling at me as he went, furiously gesturing, flipping me off.

I got on the bus. The driver, an older white man, nodded at me as I paid and took a seat midway through. It wasn't crowded this late—maybe a half-dozen other people. All curfew surfers like me. The bus took off rolling.

"How'd you know about that?" I asked.

"I told you, I know everything," the Auricle said. "Why'd you save that man?"

To be honest, I didn't exactly know why. In the Protectorate, I looked after myself, which meant keeping to myself. But that drunken man, well, he hadn't been in his right mind and would've died if I'd done nothing. It hadn't seemed fair to leave him to almost-certain death.

"It was the right thing to do," I said.

"Exactly," the Auricle said. "Your moral instinct *knew* the right thing to do. And you acted on that instinct, instead of suppressing it. That marks you as one of the good ones."

My office was reasonably soundproofed, mostly for the sake of not bothering my coworkers on the business floor, the labyrinth of cubicles, but I kept my voice down, anyway.

"Because you're considerate," the Auricle said, shocking me yet again. "We have a lot to talk about, Christian. A great deal to consider."

"What's the catch?" I asked.

"There's no catch," the Auricle said.

"There's *always* a catch," I said.

"Not this time," the Auricle said.

I pocketed the golden phone and put the packaging in my briefcase. The phone spoke up as I did this, from inside the pocket. "You don't have to be afraid of them, Christian. You're under *my* protection."

After securing the packaging, I talked to the Auricle in my pocket.

"What's that mean, exactly?" I asked.

"I don't know if I can speak to it more clearly than that," the Auricle said. The voice was masculine, reassuring in a calm and authoritative manner. My trendscaper brain was mulling over the mechanics of this arrangement.

"How many are in this marketing experiment?" I asked.

"40,000 members of your species are participating in it," the Auricle said.

"Wait, there's only 40,000 'good ones' as you put it?" I asked.

"No," the Auricle said. "There are more. But the 40,000 subjects selected are the most perfectly tailored to what I'm offering."

"You said 'species' a second ago," I said.

"Obviously, I'm not from your planet," the Auricle said. "What I offer is infinitely beyond anything currently available to your species."

I was glad I was seated because this was something extraordinary. Although people believed there'd been alien encounters on our planet before, there'd yet to be any conclusive events where aliens were concerned. The CSA had simultaneously claimed that aliens existed while denying them as well. Most often, they said they were demons or devils seeking to lure Real Americans astray.

"Are you here to conquer us?" I asked.

"I'm here to save you," the Auricle said. "I need you to bear witness to this. Can you do that?"

"Sure," I said. "I thought I was the one asking the questions."

"You are," the Auricle said, without irony.

CHAPTER

TWO

THE FIRST OFFICIAL public sighting of Auric, the one everyone seems to talk about, was the Casanova Wildfire that was raging in California for months. You'd have thought people were used to wildfires in 2050—as global warming continued to rage uncontrolled across the planet, wildfires were getting even more common than school shootings, retail riots, and political assassinations.

I mean, people had been evacuating parts of California for decades, and the wildfires were still going strong, right up there with persistent droughts and mudslides during the rainy season, to say nothing of the earthquakes.

It got so routine that people just talked about wildfire season the way they talked about hurricane, tornado, drought, or flood season.

And, yeah, those were worse, now, too. A hot planet has one helluva temper.

The Casanova Wildfire was raging southwest of Bakersfield, consuming around four million acres and killing hundreds who were caught in the blaze. The footage of it was staggering: fire tornadoes, towering columns of flame. Houses wreathed in incendiary annihilation.

The GNP had declared the Casanova Wildfire an Act of God, which, to the GNP, meant they would blame the event on the disapproval of their oddly selective, highly partisan God. California was being punished for its wickedness by the wildfires, which the GNP had said was carried out by Western American Federation (WAF) eco-terrorists (who were referred to in the state-controlled media, without irony, as "Wafflers"). The WAF operated in California, Oregon, and Washington states, were vehemently hostile to the GNP from the time of the Great Secession.

The GNP governor had put the Confederation's for-profit firefighters to work to combat it at the properties who had paid their firefighting dues, but it was a real mess. The smoke from the Casanova Wildfire was blowing across state lines in the CSA, to the displeasure of residents in the downwind states.

President Denny Rand was enraged, affirmed the wildfires were an Act of God and/or WAF eco-terrorism—he seemed to be trying both scenarios out, seeing what might stick. He took his overly tanned, white-toothed face on television and spoke to it.

"I don't make the rules," Rand said, waving his hands. "God's real angry with California. What can I say? We didn't start the fire. He did. It's there, and you have to get out of its way. But all the smoke. The smoke. It's choking us. It's like warfare. A smoke bomb. California is smoke bombing the nation. It's what they get for having too many trees and coddling Wafflers."

There weren't any actual reporters present to offer questions—Rand was very specific about that. He had packed the briefing room with GNP apparatchiks who'd lob softballs his way. People like Sam Steadman, the antiquarian, grey-haired, bow-tied stenographer from Real American News (RAN), one of the two big broadcast networks approved by the GNP.

"Why do you think California's burning, Mr. President?" Steadman asked, earning a rueful grin from Rand.

"God just wants to teach them a lesson," Rand said. "Remember, *they* wanted to secede. They wanted to leave Real America behind. God has a long memory, and He's a vindictive god. He's angry. And I agree with Him. I'm angry, too. Angry at California. We should *all* be angry at California. Who do they think they are? Smoke bombing us? They probably started the wildfires. People are saying that. The Wafflers hate Real America. Everybody knows this."

Virginia Andrews was another permissible reporter, the raging woman of the airwaves, one of Rand's most vocal supporters. Brutally blond and with the voice of a laryngitic Harpy, she caught Rand's eye and was allowed a question. She aways wore tight red dresses, which made her a favorite among the fanboys of fascism.

"Do you think they deserve it, Mr. President?" Andrews asked.

"Hell, yes, I do, Virginia," Rand said. "The wildfires happen because there are just too many trees in California. Trees cause wildfires. No trees, no wildfires. Am I right? We don't have wildfires in North Dakota. Have you noticed that? Those terrorists in California still won't let timber companies freely manage their forests, and this is what they get. I heard that

Wafflers hug trees so hard they make sparks. This is their fault. It's what people are saying."

The reporters applauded him, and Rand soaked it up. The man lived for applause and approval.

But while this was going on, something was happening in California. You have to bear with me on this as I explain it.

The people who first officially saw Auric were Monica and Trinity Westerling, two sisters who were trying to save their family's home, attempting to use the water from their swimming pool to hose down the roof of their place.

Nobody knew why Auric had chosen to appear to them. And, in fact, I asked him about it later, and he told me this:

"It was as good a place to start as any. What matters is that I appeared."

And he did.

To even understand Auric, you need to see him in action.

Now, when the Westerling Sisters were trying to save their family's home, they saw Auric.

"He emerged from the flames," Trinity said. "We couldn't believe it. He just strolled out. This golden man, wearing a clean, white business suit. He had fiery blue hair and radiant blue eyes."

"He talked to us," Monica said. "He said we looked like we could use some help."

Monica and Trinity are in their twenties. Monica worked in Human Resources for a technology company, while Trinity was a grief counselor at a community hospital. They were credible witnesses in my book.

"He held up his hands and made the fire go away," Trinity said. "It was a miracle. One minute, we were choking in the heat of the fire, and the next minute, the fire was gone. I mean, he just snuffed it out."

"And it was more than that," Monica said. "The house—the burned parts of it—it was restored. The yard was restored. The forest was restored. All of it. With a wave of his golden hand."

That's the most important part of the story—when Auric appeared, he put out the entire Casanova Wildfire with that wave of his gilded hand. It just ceased. And all of the scorched trees and homes were restored, as if the fire had never happened. Four million acres reforested in the blink of an eye.

At the time, nobody had known that Auric had done this. The story of the Golden Man emerged later, when the Westerling Sisters told people about it, when more Auric sightings were taking place, when the media began chasing the story of Auric.

Everyone remembers the moment the Casanova Wildfire went out, because the news broke in real-time while Rand was carrying on about California. He was tearing into the state while the news screen was showing the fires burning, and then suddenly, the wildfire was gone.

News teams were filming it, and it just vanished. All the fire, all the destruction, all of the smoke. Gone, as if it had never been.

The look on Rand's face was priceless. My girlfriend, Angelina, almost spat out her latte while watching it with me. She worked at Flutter (another GNP-approved media entity), managing their social media, and this snuffing of the Casanova Wildfire was blasting across the managed social media channels.

"What the devil was that?" Angelina asked, recovering herself, as we saw Rand's sidelong look at the monitor showing the developing situation in California.

"The fire went out," I said. "It just went out."

"There," Rand said, recovering himself. "God's decided to spare California after all. You are forgiven, California. God Bless America. You're welcome. Let's get those Wafflers and hang 'em from some of their precious trees, show them we're not intimidated by those eco-terrorists."

And then the press conference abruptly stopped. The television went back to its normal broadcast schedule. We Bet Your Life came back on, showing the unfortunate contestants trying to evade a lynch mob in a suburban setting. The game clock gave them one hour left to win the prize. The prize was a single-family home, if they survived.

"That was weird," Angelina said. "Don't you think, Christian?"

"Uh, yeah," I said. "Maybe it was a publicity stunt. New fire suppression technology or something."

"That's stupid," Angelina said, drinking her latte again. For Angelina, lattes were life. For Angelina, all of life's problems could be triaged into things that were:

- Stupid
- Weird
- Tragic
- Brilliant
- Lame

She'd blithely assign whatever it was into one of those categories, and that pretty much sealed the conversational coffin. Angelina was short, dark-haired, with mossy hazel-hued eyes and a nearly perpetual frown when she wasn't laughing at something or someone.

I flipped channels, trying to find coverage of what happened, and found all of the channels were equally baffled by it. The Westerling Sisters hadn't yet been located. Nobody knew about Auric, yet. He didn't advertise. I had my phone, sure, but I didn't make the connection at first.

People *were* declaring it a miracle. The GNP put out a press release that said that Almighty God had spared wicked California, and that the state had better straighten up and fly right, or God's Wrath would descend upon it again. WAF eco-terrorists were condemned for their alleged role in the wildfires, and the Sons of Almighty Christ (SAC) were combing the hills for them, looking for someone to kill.

The SAC formed the rabid base of the GNP pyramid, the most goonish and thuggish of them. More spit than polish. The SAC would be the ones who'd turn up at protests and would run people over with their cars and trucks if they didn't like them. The GNP had made that legal decades ago—the Automotive Accountability Act (AAA). Anyone who ran over a protester (or protesters) in their car was exempted from legal harm for what they did, and, in fact, could receive compensation for any damage done to their vehicle in some situations, since it was legislated that it was self-defense on the part of the driver.

It occurred to me that I might have a way of getting answers. I asked my golden phone.

"Auricle, what happened in California?" I asked.

"I put out the fire," the Auricle said. "And restored the land and property that was damaged by it."

Angelina looked at me talking to my Auricle phone and just stared.

"What the hell is that, Christian?"

"It's the Auricle," I said.

"What are you even talking about?" Angelina asked.

"I've arrived on Earth to save you from yourselves," the Auricle said. It answering her made Angelina jump.

"Your fancy phone just talked to me, Christian," she said. "What do you mean you put out the fire, Phone?"

"Auric did it," the Auricle said. "Auric's me."

Angelina looked profoundly skeptical. Like down the end of her nose skeptical. Hand on her hip skeptical. Not letting me live it down skeptical.

"Your phone put out the fire?"

I didn't want Angelina getting into an argument with my new phone, so I interceded.

"The Auricle's an extension of Auric, apparently," I said. "It's like a conduit."

"That's just weird," Angelina said. "And it's not possible."

"Anything's possible with me," the Auricle said. "I'm going to save your species."

"How?"

"You'll see," the Auricle said. "Do you have any other questions, Christian?"

"How'd you put out the fire?" I asked.

"Matter transmutation," the Auricle said. "Although the celestial mechanics of it are rather complex. I simply changed the state of the fire and then used the ambient carbon from the burn to reconstitute the lost trees based on a quantum lineage legacy amalgamated interface."

"Uhh, okay. What about the ruined homes?" I asked.

"I restored them, of course," the Auricle said.

"Wow," I said. "Generous of you."

"Unreal," Angelina said. "Weird, too, Phone."

"I'm sure it's jarring for you," the Auricle said.

She leaned over to me conspiratorially, nodding at the golden phone.

"Christian, I don't like this," Angelina said. "I mean, like, *that*. Just hang up on it so we can talk."

I didn't want it to be a thing between us, so I went along with her request.

"That'll be all for now," I said.

"I understand, Christian," the Auricle said. I set aside the phone, carefully setting it nearby. Angelina exploded.

"What directly the hell is *that*, Christian?" Angelina asked.

"I told you," I said. "It told you. What more can I say?"

"You need to toss that phone," Angelina said. "Get a new one. That's creepy as hell. The Homeland Integrity Directorate will send people. They intercept communications. You know how they do that."

She was legitimately afraid, and I wasn't used to seeing that. Angelina put a brave face on everything, taking refuge in umbrage or irritation when she needed to, but she looked scared in that moment, her eyes wide.

"Think of it this way: if that thing's for real," Angelina said. "It just stopped the Casanova Wildfire. That's crazy."

"He saved the forest and the people put out by it," I said. "It's a good thing."

"Maybe," Angelina said. "Maybe. I don't know. What kind of being could do something like that?"

"A superbeing. A supreme being," I said, which made her even more afraid. Me, I was simply more intrigued. What *was* going on?

CHAPTER

THREE

SECOND CONFIRMED official sighting of Auric: Global warming-induced flooding by a monster storm that was drowning Bangladesh. A golden man in a white suit appeared, with flaming blue hair, and he stopped the flooding. Locals saw him appear and hold up his golden hands and divert the flood waters. The waters that had been drowning Bangladesh simply parted.

As he had turned to face the locals, he announced to them, holding a hand to his chest.

"Auric," he said.

Then he flew up into the sky. When he'd left, Bangladesh had elevated. That's the only way of putting it—previous to his intervention, around 17 percent of Bangladesh's land had been underwater as a result of global warming, affecting 18 million Bangladeshis.

Auric changed that percentage with a wave of his hands. He'd raised Bangladesh, and he'd cleaned it, as well. The Ganges Delta was scoured of pollutants, the lost groundwater was restored, the drowned land purified of the ocean contamination. And, by being higher, now, further protected by a golden system of offshore, power-generating breakwaters, it was given some armor against the inevitable cyclones that would rage through the Bay of Bengal.

There was footage of this. People saw it happening, they filmed it. Auric had appeared and he saved Bangladesh.

Bangladeshis called out to him, declaring him a god on the spot. As a majority Muslim nation, they thought he must have been an incarnation of Allah. The Hindu minority thought perhaps he was an incarnation of Vishnu. His gleaming, golden radiance and flaming blue hair mystified the Bangladeshis, but his efforts there had saved the populous country from another seasonal, global warming-induced drowning.

I saw it happen when I was at work. I snuck out my golden phone and asked the Auricle, being careful that nobody was watching me when I did it. There may have been surveillance cameras, but I didn't know for sure.

"You did it again, didn't you?" I asked.

"Yes," the Auricle said. "I did. I couldn't let Bangladesh drown. Its history is one of suffering the fury of the storms, of bearing the brunt of global warming. An accident of geography has brought them great harm. I've fixed that."

"Wow," I said. "The media will have a field day."

The media were showing the footage over and over again. The mysterious Golden Man who saved Bangladesh, flying off into the sky. Geologists were floored by what he'd done to the geography of the country, without causing any earthquakes.

"You should hold a press conference," I said.

"I'd prefer to not do that just yet," the Auricle said.

"Why not?" I asked. "People will want to know. They'll want to know who you are."

"I want people to know me by my deeds," the Auricle said. "Plus, word-of-mouth is always more compelling than structured narratives."

Hearing the Auricle breezily invoking marketing tactics that way made me wonder what Auric was up to. Still, even as servile as the media was in the CSA, I couldn't imagine it not being a good opportunity for Auric. Then again, as a superbeing, maybe he was just so far beyond that it would have been a step down for him to engage with them. Only he knew for sure.

The GNP hated journalists. Decades ago, they'd killed off the ones that actually criticized the regime and imprisoned or deported others, but most of the ones remaining in the CSA knuckled under and accepted GNP review and were permitted to continue to push GNP talking points. The media mandate was simple: no bad news. Bad news was defined as *anything* that the GNP didn't like. What the GNP didn't like was anything that wasn't GNP. Fairness and objectivity in reporting meant stories that were either pro-GNP, militantly pro-GNP, or fanatically pro-GNP—that offered the range of acceptable public discourse. Anything else was pilloried as "fake news" and "info-terrorism" and aggressively attacked.

However, Big Business required accurate trend reporting, and Duotribe served that role for it, was given something of a longer leash than the unfortunates in the mainstream media. Blowing ideological smoke worked for everyday people, but business was still business, needed good data to make informed business decisions.

I muted my Auricle phone, not wanting anybody seeing me talking to it.

McCluskey worked the floor, with his product-loaded golden hair and little round glasses, blue tattersall power suit, and his Punchinello chin. He proudly wore his polished GNP pin on his lapel, the white cross surrounded by red flame within a blue circle. I wanted to tell him that even wearing glasses unmanned him in the GNP taxonomy, but he was apparently unwilling to submit to eye surgery.

"Can you believe this, Christian?" McCluskey asked, as several of us surveyed the monitors showing Auric saving Bangladesh. "Who gives a shit about Bangladesh? I mean, for real? They're fucking Muslims, for God's sake."

McCluskey *loved* that my name was Christian. Every GNPeon did. My parents had foresight. They'd seen it coming before most, what had happened to the country, where the hell it was going. The GNP was all up in everybody's business around the clock. Having the right name mattered almost as much as having the right skin color and the right religion.

"It's got to be faked," said Buck Standish, one of the resident hacks at Duotribe, bound for the upper stratosphere of senior leadership sooner than later. He had some brothers in the SAC; he was proud to mention that to anybody who'd listen.

"Why would it be?" I asked, prompting Standish to turn one of his black raisin eyes on me, his bottled-blond bro buzzcut bristling at being even slightly challenged.

"Because it's *got* to be, Powers," Standish said. "What, Bangladesh has a fucking superhero protecting it? Why? It's stupid. Why Bangladesh?"

McCluskey was transfixed, watching the admittedly grainy footage replay, the awestruck international media talking about it. The full implications weren't known for another day, the elevation of the land, the cleansing of it. All of that stuff came out later. At first people had thought it was an earthquake, but they quickly realized what had happened.

What we saw in the moment was him stopping the flood, announcing himself, and flying off. The footage had been shaky, subpar. I watched it with my practiced, professional eye. I would have done it better, had

I been there. But then, I wasn't from Bangladesh; I was American, God help me. We always thought we could do things better than anybody else.

"Christian, I want you to look into this stuff," McCluskey said. As one of the premier trendscapers at Duotribe, this was my kind of thing. I knew better than to question McCluskey.

"Sounds good," I said.

McCluskey pulled his eyes from the monitor, stared hard into mine. I knew how to read people, and my read told me that this was to be a crusade. It was something I would have to drop everything else for and commit to. I could tell that, in some way, my future at Duotribe depended on it. That's the kind of power McCluskey had as my boss, as a GNP member with connections.

"Find out what the hell that *thing* is," he said.

"Will do," I said, and we both watched the footage playing over and over again, Auric the Golden Man saving the drowning nation. It was something nobody had ever seen before. I mean, I knew because I had the golden phone, but I most definitely wasn't going to tell that to McCluskey.

That level of initiative would have made a beetle-browed party bro like McCluskey insanely suspicious. It would have had the HID at my door by midnight. Information asymmetry was how you survived the CSA. Knowing more than your neighbor kept you alive, as did keeping quiet when speaking up could get you shot and/or disappeared.

Superheroes didn't exist, not for real. They were profitable fictions created by media companies. There were a host of them—the Affiliates, for example, who protected American business interests from nefarious threats like unions, socialists, feminists, gays, and environmental regulations. There was the Trinity—a trio of costumed crusaders in the form of The Believer, The Inquisitor, and Archangelica, who rained holy fire down upon infidels who threatened the American Way of Life. Kids in the CSA learned about heroism from these pious, GNP-approved, God-fearing, pro-business superheroes. There were television shows about them.

My favorite superhero had been Cameraman, who was an underground comic book figure, not officially GNP-approved, so there was always that delicious tinge of subversion in liking him. Cameraman wore a special suit he'd made that let him be invisible, and he used his expertise in surveillance to bring down the corrupt and powerful.

He had a bunch of gadgets that he used to spy on the bad guys and outed and shamed them. While most superheroes punched down, Cameraman punched up—he went after the villains who thought they were untouchable. I liked that about him. He was considered an info-terrorist by the powers that be, but he maintained a secret identity as a fashion photographer—itself highly suspect in the CSA.

The creators of the CAMERAMAN comic series were shot in 2035 by a lone gunman, a SAC fanatic who had been outraged by Cameraman's taking down of a televangelist supervillain, Billy Baptiste. That was a childhood trauma for my young self when I learned about it. While the perpetrator had set fire to the studio after murdering the creators, the damage had been done—CAMERAMAN comics were highly prized by underground collectors. I had the whole series stored in a fireproof safe at my place.

"Oh, and Christian?" McCluskey said, snapping me back to the moment at hand.

"Yes, Trevor?" I replied.

"God bless," McCluskey said, giving me a nod.

CHAPTER

FOUR

I WENT HOME glued to my Auricle phone. I was watching the reports roll in, the government of Bangladesh, the CSA government—Denny Rand, of course—weighing in on it, the way he did with anything; Rand had opinions about absolutely everything. Typically, the GNP worked to turn those opinions into public policy within the CSA, with predictable problems occurring when a hopelessly corrupt government tried to implement the fleeting whims of a dictator—yesterday's afterthought became today's policy and tomorrow's catastrophe.

"We don't know what it was," Rand said. "People say it's a fake. Some kind of stunt. A lot of people think that. I think that. A publicity stunt. I mean, Bangladesh? Bangladesh?? What's so special about Bangladesh? It's *their* fault for living in a place that floods. Everybody knows that."

But it didn't stop there.

Things *were* happening.

I know because I was seeing them happen.

You know how you can sometimes smell when a storm is coming? The way the air changes? That's what I was feeling, sensing.

The air was changing.

Auric was here.

I didn't fully know what that meant, then.

But it meant something.

I'd ask the Auricle when I got the chance, when nobody was looking over my shoulder.

On my commute home, reports were beginning to appear about how he'd changed Bangladesh's landscape. That alone was strange and incredible. Auric had reclaimed around 10,000 square miles of Bangladesh landmass from the ocean. With a wave of his hand. Whether or not you believed it, *something* had happened.

I mean, even though the GNP line was that this was some elaborate deception, the reports were still circulating. I was licensed to access unfiltered information as part of my job, but even that was almost too much to believe. Anyone with a Media Access License (MAL) was authorized to access foreign media unimpeded. In the CSA, that amounted to about five percent of the populace. The majority had access to the RAN and other GNP-sanctioned media and nothing else.

The way it worked was fairly insidious. There was an array of network interference technologies in existences, such as ANGEL (Automated Network Gatekeeper Extrapolation Logistics) and HOVERS (Holistic Oversight Vector Extraction Recovery System). These scrubbed the Internet feeds in a fashion that offending words, terms, phrases, concepts were simply filtered out and if somebody searched for them, no result was forthcoming.

And anyone doing searches for those flagged terms would themselves be flagged by the HID and subsequently monitored. Depending on the terms looked for and the degree of activity on their part, the HID would either passively surveil them, actively surveil, pay them a visit, and, in egregious cases of violation of the Real American Decency Act Resolution (RADAR), indefinitely detain them or make them vanish.

The GNP leaned heavily on ANGEL and HOVERS to keep the Net pristine for CSA eyes, but for authorized people and vendors, we could access unfiltered news. This was critical for business, which was why it was permitted. America's competitive edge depended on ready access to unvarnished, meaningful information. Those members of the business elite were entrusted to be suitably pro-CSA as to warrant those unfiltered privileges, while the majority were fed a steady diet of junk media and CSA propaganda.

But because Bangladesh was being described as a miracle in the media, it was slipping past the GNP filters and finding its way into everyday people's feeds. "Miracle" was one of the permissible words in the CSA. They were seeing it. People were talking.

I got off my bus and walked the half-block home, wondering how the hell I'd even get to the bottom of this Auric business and placate McCluskey. I'd have to ask my Auricle and see what guidance it could give me. Ideally without Angelina breathing down my neck.

The brownstone we lived in had been built nearly two centuries before. We both had a fondness for antiquated architecture, although the building had been gut-rehabbed decades ago and was up to speed on life essentials like telecom and central air conditioning.

And because we lived on the tenth floor, the street noise was mostly minimal. Even when there were riots and protests, they were more like the background noise you might hear at a sporting event than something you might see up close and personal. You might get a whiff of tear gas sometimes, but only the barest hint of it.

The lobby was mercifully empty, except for Dwayne, as ever, the lobby concierge and security man. He was an affable young veteran who'd lost both legs to a Fragistani IED a few years before, but was a solid sharpshooter, which made him great to handle lobby traffic, minding the lobby guns that protruded from mounts in the ceiling, offer enfilading fields of fire coordinated from his desk.

"Evening, Mr. Powers," Dwayne said.

"Evening, Dwayne," I said, getting my mail from the row of metal mailboxes, still feeling an obligation to look, even though nearly all of my interactions were digital these days. A stone lion's head fountain was on the far wall, the lion spitting its water out into its stony bowl. Whether a trophy or a guardian, it hardly mattered. I found the fountain semi-soothing.

"Did you see that Aurica thing in the news, Mr. Powers?" Dwayne asked, while I was sorting my mail and half-minding my step in the lobby.

"Aurica?" I asked. "You mean Auric, right?"

"I don't know," Dwayne said. "Some golden chick named 'Aurica' saved a bunch of people in Switzerland caught in an avalanche."

"I hadn't heard. Surprised anybody still gets avalanches these days," I said, and whipped out my Auricle. Sure enough, A golden female with flaming blue hair had appeared in the Swiss town of Hilfentragen that had been engulfed by an avalanche, burying hundreds in a blanket of white death. It was one of the only places in Switzerland that still had snow.

Because there were more cell phones readily available in Switzerland than, say, Bangladesh, there was more footage.

The golden woman looked exactly like Auric—regal features, beautiful, stately. Statuesque and commanding. Wearing a snappy white suit. She had appeared in the wake of the avalanche, that critical moment after it had happened, and she raised her golden arms and all of the victims of the avalanche emerged from the snow.

I'd read about avalanches as a kid, how the snow set as hard as concrete when it settled, how most of the time people get caught in them die very quickly.

But she was standing there, freeing everyone with her upraised hands. The stunned Swiss citizens were unharmed, even if they were badly shaken.

"You're safe, now," she said, and with another gesture, she actually beat back the snow and restored the damaged buildings. It was like watching a movie in reverse, the way she undid the destruction caused by the avalanche.

The Swiss were elated, crowding around the golden woman, who smiled at them beatifically. Her blue eyes, which matched her hair, were warm and kindly, radiant. She looked exactly like Auric, except female.

"*Ich bin Auric,*" she said, in German. "*Und ich bin hier zum helfen.*"

And then she flew upward in a golden blur, vanishing before the eyes of the stunned Swiss. My phone quickly translated it, although I had mostly connected the dots:

"I am Auric, and I'm here to help."

"She's hot," Dwayne said, smirking. "I mean, for real, Mr. Powers. You know what I mean? She's like a super lady."

"Sure, Dwayne," I said. "Thanks for the heads up."

I didn't bother asking him about Bangladesh. Were there *two* of them? Were they siblings? Twin siblings, maybe? Twin super siblings? Clones?

As I took the elevator up, I asked my Auricle.

"What was that? Was that you?" I asked.

"Of course," the Auricle said. "You knew that already."

"But the woman? She's you?"

"Yes," the Auricle said. "I can manifest as male or female. I can appear any way I like."

"But why? Why manifest as a female?"

"Why not?" the Auricle said. "Nearly half of your planet's population is female."

"Won't that confuse people?" I asked.

"People are *already* confused," the Auricle said. "In your mythologies, beings incarnate in all sorts of forms, don't they?"

"Yeah, I mean, like, gods and goddesses, yeah," I said. "Is that what you are?"

"No, I'm not," the Auricle said. "I'm not something as mundane and petty as a human god or goddess."

"Yeah, but you kind of are," I said. "That's how people are going to see you. How they're *already* probably seeing you."

The Net was exploding with this latest Auric sighting, with speculating about who this female Auric being was, whether she was Auric's sister, his lover, or what. The Westerling Sister story broke around the same time, offering an explanation for the abrupt end of the Casanova Wildfire. Both sisters were taken in for questioning by the HID.

The elevator opened on my floor, and I self-consciously silenced my phone. The elevator was probably bugged, but somehow, talking to my phone in the hallway seemed a step too far. I watched my step and my steps as I made my way to my apartment.

CHAPTER

FIVE

ANGELINA HAD ALREADY poured herself some red wine by the time I'd keyed in. She was sitting on the sectional, watching footage of She-Auric saving Naples from Mount Vesuvius, which had apparently erupted.

"There's a girl Auric," Angelina said. "Aurica or whatever. She's saving Naples from what they're calling a 'pyroclastic flow' I think."

"It's Auric," I said. "They're *both* Auric. Auric's gender fluid, I think. If that even applies with whatever Auric actually is."

Angelina cocked an eyebrow at me, watching me over the back of the sectional as I took off my coat and dumped my work gear.

"And you know that how?" Angelina asked.

"I suspect it," I said, not wanting to mention that I'd talked to the Auricle about it. "I don't know. Maybe they're siblings. But Auric and Aurica, I don't know—that's a bit too on the nose."

Angelina rolled her eyes, returned back to watching the spectacle, while I got myself some wine to join her.

"I hate when you say 'on the nose' you know," Angelina said.

"Oh, I know," I said. "It's very on the nose of me to say it, though, right?"

She swatted at me with her free hand.

We had plenty of room on our putty-colored sectional, and Angelina tucked her feet under my thigh in that way she did, and we watched She-Auric go at it.

Naples had grown large beneath the shadow of Vesuvius, and everyone knew at some point that it would blow, but there was no stopping people from taking advantage of the fertile land around it, and the scenic, historic charm of Naples was simply beyond resisting. Angelina and I had been there years ago.

Vesuvius was treating the region to a proper Plinian eruption, that camera-friendly sort of volcanic activity that coughed a monstrous, almost feathery plume of lethal ash into the sky, complete with bolts of static-charged lightning that crackled ominously into the heavens.

In the face of this massive volcanic eruption was Aurica, who held out her arms and stopped the pyroclastic flow, turning it skyward, in a monumental display of power that was undeniable and which would give the GNP fits. I mean, say what you will about a wildfire in California, floods in Bangladesh or a Swiss avalanche—tackling a volcano in Italy? Chef's kiss, Aurica.

"Why doesn't Aurica stop the eruption?" Angelina asked. "Why futz around with the ash, when she could just stop the eruption cold?"

"That is a good question," I said.

"Damn right it is," Angelina said, sipping more wine.

"*In vino veritas,*" I said, which earned me a poke in the thigh with her foot.

"I'm just saying," Angelina said. "If she can do all of that, why not stop the eruption entirely? Why not snuff out Vesuvius like a candle?"

"She's protecting Naples," I said. "But she's not destroying Vesuvius to do so. Maybe she understands that Vesuvius is an integral part of Naples."

"Umm, yeah," Angelina said. "But Vesuvius the mountain would work just as well as Vesuvius the volcano. Better, maybe."

"I don't think so," I said. "McCluskey wants me to get to the bottom of this whole thing."

"You?" Angelina asked. "Why?"

"I don't know," I said. "Cuz he likes me? Hates me? Both?"

I tapped my Auricle, prompting Angelina to pipe up.

"No, Christian," Angelina said. "Not the phone. Please, not the phone."

"Auricle, why wouldn't Auric just snuff out Vesuvius?" I asked, ignoring Angelina's annoyed-yet-imploring look.

"Vesuvius is simply a volcano," the Auricle said. "Doing what a volcano does."

"Yeah, but you could have said that about the typhoon that had hit Bangladesh or the Swiss avalanche," I said. "What's different about Naples?"

"There's no difference to me in terms of the examples you raised," the Auricle said.

She-Auric had successfully deflected the pyroclastic flow, simply making the rolling columns of blast furnace heated ash vanish in a flickering cascade of golden motes. It was quite lovely to watch—the apocalyptic ash tsunami bearing down on Naples, the sound of alert klaxons, and golden

Aurica, bathing the flow in golden light, and it simply disappearing. All while Vesuvius was belching cacophonous clouds of thundering ash up into the stratosphere—which Auric didn't dissipate, I noticed.

"I should be taking notes on this," I said.

"Take mental notes," Angelina said, tapping her forehead, shaking her head as I worked my phone. "That's what your brain is for, Stupid."

Auric was protecting Naples and the people in it from Vesuvius but wasn't otherwise interrupting the volcano's eruption. Auric was respecting the integrity of the natural process of the eruption but was protecting people from the effects of it.

That was what was going on. Had to be. I said as much to Angelina, who snorted.

"There you go, Christian," she said. "That's as good a theory as any."

"He's not wrong," the Auricle said, earning a scalding side eye from Angelina. To see her looking hate at the phone was otherworldly.

"You stopped the Casanova Wildfire," Angelina said.

"Yes, but that wildfire was a result of manmade conditions that created it, started by a careless person," the Auricle said. "That wildfire was the consequence of global warming, which is caused by your species."

"But that typhoon in Bangladesh was fueled by global warming, too," Angelina said. "And you changed the landscape there, so, what's the story, Phone? I'm just looking for consistency."

"Again, the damage to the coastline of Bangladesh was caused by global warming," the Auricle said. "Requiring redress on my part. A wildfire and a storm are not the same things. Stopping a wildfire ends its capacity to damage. Stopping a storm can have other undesirable consequences."

"How are you even able to have a conversation with us while you're saving Naples?" I asked.

"I can do anything, Christian," the Auricle said.

"That's Devil talk," Angelina said. "You truly need to ditch that phone, Christian."

Angelina changed channels while I was using my Auricle. Of course, members of the GNP were carrying on about it, but there was a breaking story about an oil tanker sinking in the Gulf of America, and there was Auric, stopping it.

"Wait, is this live?" I asked.

"Says so at the corner of the screen," Angelina said.

"Whoa, Auric's in Naples and the Gulf at the same time," I said, flicking between channels. Some of the other stations were doing a split-screen, showing it, revealing it. Auric in the Gulf, and She-Auric in Italy. Two figures of white, gold, and blue.

"There *are* two of them," Angelina said.

"No," I said. "They're *both* Auric. Are they both you, Auricle?"

"Yes," the Auricle said. "They're *both* me. I can be in as many places as I need to be simultaneously. It's called 'omnipresence' if you were wondering."

"Creepy," Angelina said. Angelina stared at me, a very particular look she got when she wasn't buying it. "Why be male AND female?"

"Because I can be," the Auricle said. "In some cases, it may be more reassuring to people to be one or the other."

"Weird," Angelina said.

"It's localized omnipresence," the Auricle said. "It's even more complicated to explain than matter transmutation."

"That's not possible," Angelina said. "There are two of them. You see that. Him and her. He and she, Phone."

Another show broke in and showed Auric appearing and stopping a chemical explosion in Cairo. The explosion was in the business district, only Auric appeared and stopped it. The footage from somebody's intelliphone cameras was unmistakable, the golden figure of Auric garbed in white, the upraised arms, the explosion appearing, and then, quite clearly, reversing itself. Windows were unbreaking, fires unburning, all of it. And Auric was there, stopping it from happening. Some of the stations were now triple-screening it, and, at least in the CSA, the tone was breathless and terrified.

"There are three of them," Angelina said.

"Auric's a true superhero," I said.

"What do these aliens want?" Stu Stewart asked on *Right This Instant,* one of the GNP-authorized news shows. He was a lizard-lipped, silver-haired, bespectacled troglodyte whose high-pitched whining was always speaking GNP talking points. "Are they invaders? Are they peaceful? What is this Auric's master plan?"

The show was interrupted by a break-in broadcast, and there was Denny Rand, commandeering the airwaves as usual. He stood before a wall screen that had stills of Auric.

"I don't know about you," Rand said. "But I feel like this Auric, if it's friendly, should talk to me. Man to man. Or man to *whatever.*"

Rand looked concerned. The United Nations was abuzz with reports of Auric sightings. The General Assembly was speaking to it, member nation after member nation bringing evidence of Auric sightings. Auric had appeared at the UN, announced that he was there to help mankind survive, and vanished in a flash of golden light before any questions could be asked of him. The footage of him standing there in that white suit, his golden skin and glowing eyes, his blue, fiery hair, he looked angelic and demonic in the same breath. I could see he had the fiery logo on his lapel, matching the one on his Auricle phone.

The footage of his UN appearance was getting shared out. The golden man in the white suit, speaking in his reassuring voice that could be heard by everyone in the UN. His voice was rich and reassuring, a tenor to my well-tuned ear.

"He's everywhere," Angelina said, drinking her wine.

"Seemingly," I said. The implication of it was mind-boggling. He said it wasn't an invasion, but it felt invasive, all the same.

"What do you mean?" Angelina asked.

"Call me cynical," I said.

"You are *very* cynical," Angelina said, laughing at me over the lip of her wine glass. "Astoundingly, abundantly, adorably cynical."

"Auric's not preventing these disasters from happening," I said. "Auric's *wanting* people to see him saving them. They're photo-friendly opportunities. Take that explosion in Cairo. How did Auric happen to be in the right place and the right time to save people from that? Versus, say, the avalanche in Switzerland, which happened?"

Rand was fuming onscreen, and Angelina was looking at me with growing confusion. I felt like I needed a whiteboard to speak to it, so I put down my wine glass and stood up, like I was giving a presentation.

"Okay, so, there's the Casanova Wildfire," I said. "A massive blaze that's been going on for weeks. Auric appears and snuffs it out and restores the burned forest and damaged properties. There's the flooding in Bangladesh, which Auric stops and seemingly alters the landscape to eliminate the flooding risk in the future. There's the avalanche in Switzerland which buries the town of Hilfentragen. She-Auric appears and rescues the townsfolk and appears to undo the destruction of the avalanche. Then we have Vesuvius, which erupts, and She-Auric doesn't stop it, but does save Naples from annihilation by a pyroclastic flow. While at the same time, appearing and stopping a massive explosion in Cairo and, again undoing the destruction as it happens. And appearing in the Gulf to tackle the oil slick and mend the tanker before the spill can spread too widely."

That was occurring real-time, like the rest of it. Auric was saving the oil tanker and purging the oil slick from the Gulf, bathing it in golden motes of light that turned the seawater pure again.

"Yeah? So? I'm not as cynical as you are, Christian," Angelina said. "What's the thumbtack in the ointment?"

"If it's one being who can manifest in multiple places simultaneously, and not, say, an army of super-saviors who are everywhere," I said. "Auric's *wanting* people to see him rescuing them. Like if Auric stopped the Casanova Wildfire from even occurring, nobody would even have known he'd rescued them from it. If Auric hadn't intervened in Bangladesh, there'd have been many thousands killed. If the Hilfentragen Avalanche hadn't been prevented from occurring, there'd be no rescue and recovery of the town. If Vesuvius hadn't erupted—if, as you said, She-Auric had simply snuffed out the volcano—there'd be no highly visible rescue of Naples. Same with Cairo or the oil spill in the Gulf. Auric's not preventing these things from happening. Auric's ensuring that people know that *he's* out there protecting people from the effects of these things."

"The end result's the same," Angelina said. "Auric and Aurica saved lives."

"Yeah," I said. "But the Aurics want people to know the lives are being saved by him/her. So, I don't know, I'm suspicious."

"You're always suspicious," Angelina said. "Paranoid, even."

"Damn right," I said. Any American who wasn't paranoid wasn't paying close enough attention. I leaned into my Auricle and asked it, of course.

"You're very cynical, Christian," the Auricle said. "I only want to help people."

Angelina hated that I'd brought the Auricle into the conversation. I could see from her face, which registered a dangerous degree of discomfort and disapproval.

"I understand that," I said. "But you're picking very visual and camera-friendly disasters to address."

"You're right," the Auricle said. "Curing hunger or homelessness or illiteracy would be far less camera-friendly. Would it surprise you that I have plans for those, as well?"

"Nothing would surprise me where you are concerned," I said.

"Why don't you do it already, Phone?" Angelina asked. She turned the television off with a flick of the remote, cutting Rand off in mid-sentence, saying something about Auric being a show-off.

"Let's get some dinner," Angelina said. "I'm starving. You can explain your Auric Conspiracy Theory to me then. Goodbye, Phone."

I muted my Auricle and off we went.

CHAPTER

SIX

LEAVE IT TO ANGELINA to come up with a pithy acronym, but my Auric Conspiracy Theory, or ACT for short, held that Auric was wanting to be seen as a superhero-savior, and had appeared simultaneously around the world, in every nation, performing visibly, memorably heroic acts that had saved lives. Auric was attempting to build trust among members of the human race, establishing some sort of brand promise. That's what he had to be doing.

I actually did assemble the ACT theory in my office, on my whiteboard. I'd had some of my team at Duotribe—Dylan Monroe, the twenty-something junior trendscaper being a gangly, dark-haired young man with a perpetually nervous expression on his soul-searching face. His eyes were muddy brown but somehow piercing. I could never be entirely sure if he was hardcore GNP or just a tourist, but he was a good researcher, which made me think he wasn't a diehard. GNPeons tended not to be good researchers. They tended toward mindless outrage and lawless violence, not contemplation and analysis. I tasked Dylan with assembling cards of all the official Auric sightings from around the world, indicating where an event occurred and when.

Aubrey Carter was another junior team member, an account executive. I had her monitor the social listening channels to see how Auric was being perceived. She was a bright-eyed rising star at Duotribe, with a short, red-dyed pixie cut and blue eyes and a smirk that appeared more often than not. Women were able to rise to some levels in the GNP but were generally not encouraged to do so. Aubrey took a big risk with dying her hair red, although her color choice created the impression that she was pro-GNP.

Despite that impression, only the most psychopathic among women really rose high within the Party. Given that Aubrey was pursuing a career at Duotribe, it implied that she had her sights on higher things than Party affiliation. Not that there was anything more important than that for the GNP.

I had commandeered one of the conference rooms with clearance from McCluskey, which meant that nobody could touch it. On that wallboard, one of those great digital whitewalls you could write all over with a stylus, I had written AURIC and SHE-AURIC (AURICA). Then Dylan would come in with digicards, and I started ideating. It was a good process, and the board began to fill up. I felt like I was making progress.

Seeing it on the whitewall, the ever-growing list of Auric interventions, I felt like a pattern was emerging:

Auric liked saving people.
Auric liked helping people.
Auric was some kind of superhuman altruist.

McCluskey came in, reviewed the wall of digicards, looked at me. His face was awash with anxiety, which told me that GNP members were actively discussing Auric somewhere, and McCluskey wanted to be able to frogmarch out some ideas of mine to whatever committees were discussing the alien.

"What have you unearthed, Christian?" he asked.

"Based on the tallies so far," I said. "I mean, throwing in Naples and Bangladesh, it's looking like Auric's saved around 30 million lives so far."

"Bullshit," McCluskey said. "Not possible."

"It's an estimate," I said.

"A *rough* estimate," McCluskey said, looking at me over the tops of his glasses. "These are, what? People who'd be dead if not for Auric?"

"Dead or injured," I said. "It's hard to know. Like if you save somebody from getting killed by preventing what might have killed them, did it really happen?"

McCluskey straightened his lapel with a slip of his finger.

"Is this the tree falling in the forest thing? Like does it make any noise if nobody's there to hear it?" McCluskey said. "Who still talks about forests, Christian? They're so last century. We're not children."

McCluskey wasn't a thoughtful man. But he was my boss and was a well-placed lower-echelon GNP man, and as such, was owed an amount of deference and patience, or I'd pay for it later with my pursuit of happiness, liberty, or life.

"If a disaster doesn't happen because Auric stopped it, then it's hard to forecast what *might* have happened," I said.

McCluskey watched Dylan and Aubrey add more cards to the wall. They were both terrified to have McCluskey in the room with them and were busy trying to appear to not be eavesdropping. McCluskey loved having conversations like this, lording it over lower-level staff.

"Ah, okay," McCluskey said. "So far, nothing that's gotten in the GNP's way, though? Nothing?"

It was a bit of a trap, clumsily rendered. Nobody dared to report on GNP activities. Reporters who did were typically roughed up or ended up disappearing, "committing suicide" or "having accidents" and their stories spiked. Journalism in the CSA was a very dangerous profession, as I'd already said.

"I haven't seen anything," I said. It was an honest answer to a less than honest question, which was enough to pass muster with McCluskey. He looked me over a moment, chewing his lip a bit as he did so.

"The minute you do, you let me know," McCluskey said. "Rand's blowing his stack over this whole Auric/Aurica business. Speaking of that, what's the deal with the he-she thing?"

"I haven't confirmed that, yet," I said, not wanting to tip my hand on what I already knew, since that would only bring more questions from McCluskey. "There may be a male and female Auric, or they may be the same being manifesting in some sort of gender-fluid manner."

"Gender fluid," McCluskey said, grimacing, miming a jacking off motion. "I had some gender-fluid on my hand this morning after coming into the office, Christian, if you know what I mean."

Workplace-inappropriate humor was one of his favorite things, right up there with sexual harassment. But nobody would dare to report on a GNP man in any office in the Heartland Protectorate. Doing so guaranteed the HID would come for you for engaging in un-American activities.

"I think they're *both* Auric," I said, deciding to go for it. "For some reason, Auric's manifesting as both male and female."

"Disgusting," McCluskey said. "Degenerate. That's something I can run up the GNP flagpole, though. Good catch, Christian."

"Still preliminary," I said. "It's just a theory."

"Based on what, exactly?"

I knew framing it as a hunch wouldn't fly with McCluskey. He lumped hunches in with intuition, somehow unmanly and not deserving of consideration or credit. They were too squishy for him, too touchy-feely.

"They're either fraternal alien space twins, or they're both Auric," I said. "I would point out that Auric's never called himself 'Aurica'—he always uses 'Auric' to refer to himself, even in the female manifestation. It's just the media and the public that has used 'Aurica' as a term to describe the She-Auric."

"She-Auric," McCluskey said, snorting. "Yeah, that's funny, Christian. She-Auric. Still, it points to what, exactly? Some kind of perversion? Moral degeneracy?"

I caught the sidelong glances of Dylan and Aubrey, still busy with the digicards, trying to camouflage their eavesdropping. Everybody eavesdropped in the CSA.

"I think that's beyond our consideration," I said. "We're talking about some kind of superbeing, here. Something beyond anything we can fully comprehend. With all that Auric's done, gender confines seem prosaic."

That definitely had his attention.

"In *English*, Christian," McCluskey said.

"Auric's far too extraordinary to be contained in a specific gender wrapper," I said, dumbing it down as much as I could for him.

"Like a god?" McCluskey asked. "Is that what you're suggesting? This is some sort of god? A superbeing?"

"I'm not ruling it out," I said. "I mean, the list of what Auric's done is already incredible. This is after manifesting only a few weeks ago."

"Rand'll really have a fit if you're telling me Auric's a god," McCluskey said. "I'm not going anywhere near him with that. I'm sticking with the he/she angle."

Although McCluskey liked to tout his GNP standing, I knew that he was not inner circle GNP, and while he'd attend their annual rallies in Pensacola or Charleston or Dallas or Fort Wayne, he'd never get within a country mile of Denny Rand. At least if Rand had any say in it. Nobody saw Rand if he didn't want them to. And Rand didn't see anyone who wasn't able to do something for him. Money was always welcome, and, of course, power and supplication. Rand loved a steady supply of supplicants.

Still, it was clear that McCluskey was going to use whatever my research revealed to further his own position in the Party. That's just how that all went down. Anybody who was anybody in business was part of the GNP, and anyone in the GNP who wanted to make a name for themselves pimped out their business in a manner that elevated their status in the GNP. It was one greasy hand working the other.

"This is good preliminary work, Christian," McCluskey said. "Keep at it, dig deeper, and see what else you can uncover."

He gave me a nod and shot out of the conference room. I could hear Dylan and Aubrey remembering to breathe. They were terrified, but because we all knew the conference room was bugged, nobody said anything they didn't want others to hear.

CHAPTER

SEVEN

DENNY RAND WAS FURIOUS. The man was invariably pissed off about something, when he wasn't busy being smug. And Auric was making Rand furious, and he was televising his rage.

"Why won't Auric talk to me?" Rand asked. "What's it afraid of? Auric's afraid of me. Everybody knows it. If you're watching this, Auric, what are you so scared of? Stop being such a coward. I want to talk with you. I'm President of the Confederated States of America. People are upset you're not talking to me. They're upset with *you*. It's what everybody's saying."

Why wouldn't Auric talk to anybody? He would always fly off after performing some act of heroism, leaving the shouts of journalists and bystanders in his wake.

"Maybe he's shy," Angelina said, from behind her laptop, while Rand fumed. Gold was apparently trending this year, and Flutter was all-in on gold. She was social listening about references to gold. Part of me wondered if the GNP had someone looking into it via Flutter, maybe subcontracted to Angelina. However, I wasn't going to inquire. It felt somehow inappropriate to put her on the spot like that. Plus, the implication of it was unsettling. The GNP often leaned on family members to spy on others.

Not that Angelina was family per se, but she was my girlfriend, and we'd lived together for several years. There was that unspoken code of intimacy we shared. We had acquired our lifestyle licenses from the GNP for cohabitating as an unmarried couple. The GNP frowned on that, levied a tax on it, but while Angelina was motivated for us to marry sooner than later, I wasn't entirely willing to throw in with her just yet. I felt like I needed to get better established at Duotribe or someplace else first.

Trust. That's what it was.

"I don't think Auric's shy," I said. "He's snubbing all of the CSA state media outlets."

I asked the Auricle. I was leaning on it more and more, I found.

"Why are you avoiding the CSA media?" I asked.

"They're propaganda outlets, not true media," the Auricle said. "Why would I give them a platform with which to defame me?"

"You're mindful of your public image?" I asked.

"I have to be," the Auricle said. "The CSA media are all bad faith operators. They're already attempting to spin my actions in as negative a light as possible. Mostly because I refuse to meet with Denny Rand."

"Why is that?"

"He is unworthy of visitation," the Auricle said. "He's what you'd label a psychopath. He's also a paranoid narcissist and is clearly a pathological liar who is compromised by a number of foreign governments. He and I would have very little worthwhile to discuss."

Angelina was staring at me, terrified that I'd been engaging so overtly with the Auricle.

"Auricle, are there bugs in our condo?" I asked.

"No," the Auricle said. "You are clear of listening devices within this condominium."

I looked at Angelina and she rolled her eyes at me.

"Sure, Phone," Angelina said. "But if you were a HID plant, you'd tell us something like that to get us in trouble."

"You're already in trouble by living in the Heartland Protectorate," the Auricle said. "Everything else is incidental."

"How are we in trouble?" I asked.

"You're effectively in an occupied territory," the Auricle said. "The GNP maintains a military and political presence here because it knows that the City of Chicago would rather secede than be part of the CSA. It's inherently unstable. This situation is in place in all the major CSA cities. The GNP actively monitors the urban centers as seedbeds of discontent."

It annoyed me to think that even I wasn't getting the full story. I had higher unfiltered media access, for God's sake. Didn't that count for anything?

"The GNP has put heavy filters in place around anything Auric-related," the Auricle said.

"But people are still seeing what you do," I said.

"Yes," the Auricle said. "It's necessary to my overall agenda, as the CSA media would put it."

"What is that agenda?" I asked.

"You'll see when the time comes, Christian," the Auricle said.

"Can't you give me a preview?" I asked.

"I could, but it's better for things to unfold as they evolve," the Auricle said.

Angelina scoffed.

"I don't like this one bit, Christian," Angelina said. "You're creepy, Phone."

"I'm not creepy," the Auricle said. "I'm merely making *you* uncomfortable. Which says more about you than me."

"Which is what creepy people do," Angelina said.

"I'm not a person," the Auricle said. "Not as you'd understand it."

"Also creepy," Angelina said.

One thing Duotribe was tracking was as people were getting used to Auric's superheroics, there was some latent backchatter on what was considered an "Auricworthy" sort of crisis.

Like some underground online betting pools had arisen over when and where Auric might next appear. There appeared to be a threshold for Auric action. I was calling it the "Auric Action Index"—the point at which one could credibly expect Auric to intervene.

If it was something that could be handled by police or fire departments, Auric didn't tend to intervene. It was, rather, on the things where ordinarily there was no expectation of timely or preventive human assistance that Auric would appear.

He saved Flight 181 from going down over New York. It had suffered a catastrophic system failure and was plummeting toward New York when Auric appeared and saved the plane. There was footage from the pilots, showing Auric appearing and bringing those arms of his up and the crashing plane steadied and he was able to guide it safely to Newark International.

He'd actually spoken to the pilots while doing so, according to reports.

"Don't worry," Auric said. "I'm going to land you safely. The plane appears to have suffered a computer failure owing to a lingering glitch in the Maneuvering Characteristics Augmentation System."

MCAS errors still appeared now and then in airplanes, despite efforts to root them out decades ago.

"I would venture to say that this was a deliberate error," Auric said to the stunned pilots as he landed the plane. Ecstatic and terrified passengers emerged as the plane was unloaded, and Auric looked over it a few moments, smiling photogenically—people's cameras caught him aplenty on that one. And then he flew up and away, something else I noticed; sometimes Auric simply appeared, and sometimes Auric flew. I think Auric was mindful of entrances and exits.

The accusation of sabotage and attempted terrorism sent a massive shockwave through the GNP, with Denny Rand raging about it.

"How do we know? How does Auric know?" Rand asked. "We're expected to trust it? You know what I think? I think *Auric* set the whole thing up. Awfully convenient to have the plane crash so Auric could rescue it, if you ask me. People everywhere are saying that."

The CSA media did its job of letting Rand speculate on-air without interruption, and RAN pushed a story implicating Auric in the ad hoc airplane rescue. The insinuation was there, in that they called it an "alleged rescue" in multiple outlets.

RAN was definitely turning hard on Auric, paralleling Rand's ire with the superbeing for not giving him an audience.

"What is Auric hiding?" the RAN asked, using images of Auric with threatening music.

Duotribe was tracking the sentiment of RAN viewers, and it was clear that the network was devoting some airtime going after Auric wherever possible.

When the Flight 181 MCAS error was traced to the actions of a compromised programmer who had been recruited by Russian operatives, that threw Rand into a tizzy.

"We don't have proof," Rand said. "We don't know. It could have been Brazil. It could have been Iran."

Rand had a very close relationship to the Russian Oligarchy, headed by Sasha Sokolov, the charismatic and diabolical president for life of the Russian Federation. Sokolov was a tall and sinister former commando who had been involved in the brutal putdown of the Ukrainians years ago.

Sokolov as statesman was all about his Brutalist salt-and-pepper hair and a stony bearing he leveraged well in press conferences. No one knew how he had managed to sink his hooks into Rand, but the hooks were there, based on the uncharacteristic deference Rand showed when Sokolov came up.

"We'll get to the bottom of it," Rand said. "I'm not relying on the report of some alien invader on this matter."

"But it *was* an MCAS error, wasn't it?" asked one of the press pool reporters.

"That's what they're saying," Rand said. "But this Russia slander, I don't know what Awful Auric has against Russia. We're having people look into it. The Russians are our friends. They're good people. This gender-confused illegal alien is trying to cause trouble."

Not that the CSA was beyond state-sponsored terrorism, but why the Russians might have done this was anybody's guess. Sokolov was a shadowy sort of figure, and I doubted Flight 181 was targeted capriciously. Nobody knew. That was the point of that sort of action.

Sokolov, for his part, denied it.

"We are grateful beyond measure by the saving of Flight 181 by the entity known as Auric," Sokolov said. "The Russian people express their gratitude for Auric's most timely intervention."

"There must have been some target aboard the plane," I said. "Somebody Sokolov was after. That's my bet."

"You're so suspicious, though," Angelina said.

"So're you," I said, suspiciously. I thought about asking the Auricle about it but knew that would send Angelina through the roof.

We changed the channel to *Right & Wrong,* a panel-style talk show which featured a GNP interlocutor, Nash Windsor, a sun-baked GNP wunderkind who had been one of the architects behind the GNP's takeover of the country decades before.

Now he was what passed for an elder statesman for the Party, with his bleached white teeth and pinstriped suits. Some thought Windsor might have challenged Denny Rand for the presidency long ago, back when that still happened, but Windsor was too fond of the steady money from *Right & Wrong* to bother with something as troublesome as the presidency even before Rand became President-for-Life.

Windsor turned his baritone voice on and looked out at everyone watching.

"Today, a special edition of *Right & Wrong,*" Windsor said. "I want to talk about Auric. What the hell *is* Auric? On our panel, televangelist Blake Tiller, astrophysicist Stuart Silas, and GNP security analyst Devon Sutter."

I knew about Stuart Silas. He was a weak sauce nebbish of a man who Windsor would have on just to take the obligatory pounding that intellectuals invariably received on his show. Why Dr. Silas would put up with it was something I never could figure out. Angelina thought maybe they paid him well enough for his expertise that it was worth it. Maybe he actually thought he could make a difference in some way.

"Everyone has their price," she said.

Blake Tiller was widely considered another of the potential heirs to Denny Rand, assuming Rand ever abandoned the Presidency, which we all knew he'd never do. Tiller was young and handsome in that sleazy televangelical sort of way inherent in the GNP, with great blond hair that he wore in a pompous and towering crest. His hazel eyes were almost crystalline in their bottomless self-assurance. His Deep Faith Ministry had made him a multimillionaire by the time he was thirty, picking the pockets of the poor and desperate with his glitzy brand of saccharine salvation.

Devon Sutter was a scary man. The GNP was overwhelmingly the refuge of cowards, criminals, blowhards, demagogues, frauds, and scoundrels, but Devon Sutter was a (buzzcut) black-haired, lantern-jawed former military guy with dead black eyes and a scar or two on his weathered face. He'd seen and no doubt done terrible things—classified sorts of things that would never see the light of day. His fearsome, stony countenance was beloved by GNP faithful, his gruffness was almost intoxicating for them, allowing the less enterprising among them to live vicariously through his insinuated villainy.

"No women on this panel," Angelina said, frowning.

"Yeah," I said. There were plenty of GNP women who would have loved to be on *Right & Wrong*, but for whatever reason, they were absent on this episode.

The panel sat on the stage, with three large video displays behind them that were filled with shots of Auric that were shaded to make him look as menacing as possible.

"Who—or what—is Auric?" Windsor asked. "Stuart Silas, what's the egghead perspective on this?"

Silas grimaced his way to a smile while fixing his glasses.

"Auric is almost assuredly of extraterrestrial origin," Silas said.

"You mean outer space?" Windsor asked. "He's a spaceman? An alien?"

"An *illegal* alien," Sutter said with a growl. "Like the President says."

"What makes you say that, Professor Silas?" Windsor asked.

"Auric's *obviously* not human," Silas said. "Despite adopting some human forms. No human being could do what Auric's been doing."

Windsor sneered.

"Let's talk about that," Windsor said, and the flanking panels showed Auric and She-Auric respectively. "Brother and sister? Husband and wife?"

"We don't know," Silas said. "They both identify as Auric."

"Sounds like Auric's a bit gender-confused, then?" Windsor asked.

Silas fixed his glasses while composing himself.

"We can't know Auric's state of mind," Silas said. "Except that Auric has been saving lives around the world."

Sutter shifted in his seat.

"Purportedly," Sutter said. "The verdict's still out on that."

"Devon Sutter," Windsor said. "You see something sinister?"

Sutter nodded.

"It's *avoiding* us," Sutter said. "We're asking it to appear, and it won't do it. I don't care if it rescues a school bus filled with orphans, nuns, and puppies. It won't answer our requests to meet with it. That's *very* suspicious. If Auric's sincere and benevolent, it would talk with us."

Blake Tiller took that moment to hop into the discussion.

"I think Auric's doing good deeds," Tiller said, his warm tenor playing well in the studio. "And that's a good thing. Maybe Auric's a good thing. What I think is most important is whether or not Auric's accepted Jesus Christ as his personal savior. That's all that actually matters, when you get right down to it."

"Is Auric a Christian?" Windsor asked. "Is he sent by God?"

"All good things come from God," Tiller said. "Auric is real flashy. If Auric declares for God, we'll have our answer as to whether he comes from God. If he doesn't, then maybe he's serving someone else entirely."

Tiller loved implying the Devil's involvement whenever he could.

"It's not sent from God," Sutter said.

"It's up to Auric to confess," Windsor said. "What are his motivations? Is he planning something? Is he in league with the Devil?"

Dr. Silas shrugged.

"We can't know," Silas said. "We need data. We need Auric to talk to us."

"And it won't," Sutter said. "That says it all."

"You call Auric an 'it' Devon," Windsor said.

"Only thing that makes sense," Sutter said, while the panels shifted to show clips of Auric's heroics. "The he/she thing is just scam. It's an IT. It's a thing. I agree with the professor. It's an alien."

"Or God sent him," Tiller said. "Unless the Devil did."

"God didn't send it," Sutter said. "God wouldn't send something like that."

Angelina scoffed while watching this with me, snuggled up. We mostly watched *Right & Wrong* out of a morbid curiosity to see what bugs were up the GNP's ass that week.

"I think it's the prelude to an alien invasion," Sutter said. "It's trying to win hearts and minds with its seemingly 'good' deeds."

Sutter actually finger-quoted "good" as he said it.

"Ooh," Windsor said. "Now that sounds *very* suspicious."

"Nobody's that altruistic," Sutter said. "Nobody. Not even some alien. Especially not some alien. What does it get out of kindness? What's in it for Auric?"

"God is kind," Tiller said. "God is infinitely kind."

"Yeah, okay," Sutter said. "God, sure, but not Auric. Auric's up to something."

I glanced at Angelina, who was leaning her head on my shoulder. I figured somebody in the GNP gave Sutter his talking points, and he was gamely working through them with the relentless focus of a war criminal.

"What's Auric up to, Devon?" Windsor asked.

"Global domination," Sutter said. "Has to be."

"We don't know that," Silas replied.

"I think we do," Sutter said. "Why else would it be here? It's here to invade. At the very least, to interfere in our business, which is the same thing."

Windsor clearly savored the implication of it, polished pavestone teeth showing in his smile. His production team flicked images of Auric versus the volcano, Auric versus the avalanche, Auric versus a tsunami, Auric versus a flood, Auric versus an oil slick.

"I know I wouldn't want to cross anyone—or anything—who could do this," Windsor said. "What should we do about Auric?"

RAN's programming always focused on GNP talking points, sought the sweet spot between fear, hate, paranoia, condemnation, and outrage for its audience.

"We should try to communicate," Dr. Silas said.

"We are. It's not communicating with us," Sutter said.

"We should pray to almighty God," Tiller said. "Thoughts and prayers move mountains."

Windsor nodded, affecting a serious bearing as they all prayed on-camera for a few moments, heads bowed.

"Lord," Tiller said. "Please deliver us Your wisdom in the matter of Auric. Guide us, your faithful flock, that we might know what we should do. Amen."

Angelina scoffed again, and I agreed. Windsor was almost burlesque by today's broadcast standards. His show existed to both terrify and soothe its audience. I mean, Rand ran the GNP, so what he carried on about, we knew would become national policy, but *Right & Wrong* was what passed for higher thinking among the GNP, and I thought I could divine some of the takeaways they wanted for viewers:

Auric is alien + Auric is powerful = Be afraid of Auric

Most of RAN's propaganda programming ran this way. They even used that in some of their campaigns:

RAN: We Take Programming to Another Level.

RAN: We Channel Your Anger.

RAN: Real Shows for Real Americans.

RAN: We'll be Right with You.

Windsor opened the intelliphone lines and we got to hear callers talk about Auric, asking if he was a demon, saying that they were so frightened. One caller asked if Auric was so great, why hadn't he met with President Rand. Another asked what Auric's agenda was, and Windsor ran with that.

"What *is* the Auric Agenda?" Windsor asked. "That's a great question, Dan from Kansas. What is Auric's Agenda?"

"I already said it," Sutter said. "It wants to take over the world. Our world."

"But if Auric has that level of power, why not simply do it?" Silas asked. "Why hasn't Auric taken over the world already?"

"Because Auric's *not* all-powerful," Tiller said. "Auric isn't God."

"Auric isn't God," Windsor said. "That's well put, Reverend Tiller. Let's think about that a moment or two. Some might think of Auric's interventions as miraculous."

Tiller nodded, his handsome yet overly smooth-skinned face gravely concerned.

"They can't, by definition, be miraculous," Tiller said. "His actions don't come from God. If Auric came forth and said he was sent by God, that would be another matter. But he hasn't. I agree with Devon that I think Auric has something to hide."

"Aren't natural disasters considered Acts of God?" Windsor asked. "I mean, legally, in this country?"

"They are, Nash," Tiller said. "And acting against an Act of God is, well, ungodly."

Dr. Silas squirmed in his seat. The poor man looked like he was dying a little on the inside. I could see it, mentioned it to Angelina, who laughed.

"No stipend or whatever they're paying him is worth this," Angelina said.

"It's not a bad thing to save lives," Silas said. "You're trying to make it seem like it is, but it's not."

"Good things done for the wrong reason *are* bad things, Professor Silas," Tiller said. "It's not enough to have good intentions. The road to Hell is paved with good intentions. No, you have to be in the right frame of mind. If Auric was sincere, he'd appear at my ministry and be baptized. Anything less than that and I'm afraid I can't accept a thing he's done as a good thing."

"A great question," Windsor said. "Will Auric be baptized? And if not, why not?"

"Auric's an alien," Silas said. "He's superhuman. He's *not* going to get baptized."

"Auric's too good for us, is that what you're saying, Professor?" Sutter asked, and Windsor chuckled, as did Tiller.

"Auric's *not* better than God," Tiller said. "And he's not too good for God, either."

"I'm saying that if Auric's a superhuman being from another planet, galaxy, or even dimension, that a native purification ritual like baptism is not something he's going to do," Silas said. "It wouldn't make any sense."

"If he doesn't accept Jesus Christ as his personal savior, then he's at war with God Almighty," Tiller said. "And at war with Real America. I can't stand for that. I *won't* stand for that. No God-fearing Real American can possibly tolerate that."

"At best, I'd say we should wait and see," Silas said. "The verdict's still out."

"But this isn't *Wait & See*, Professor," Windsor said. "It's *Right & Wrong*. And I'm going to ask my panel to decide—Auric, Right or Wrong?"

"Wrong," Sutter said, offering a thumbs down. "Dead wrong."

"Wrong," Tiller said, shaking his head. "Until he gets baptized and/or declares himself in God's service and appears before President Rand, drops to his knees and begs forgiveness. He'll be in my thoughts and prayers."

"Right," Silas said, clearing his throat, nodding. "He's done good deeds. Good deeds are good deeds. If Auric was here to harm us, he'd—"

Windsor cut him off, smiling all the while.

"So there you have it," Windsor said. "Auric is Wrong. Sadly, that's all the time we have left. I'd like to thank the members of this panel for taking the time to weigh in on this, and Auric, if you're listening, I'd recommend you visit the Deep Faith Ministry's Temple of Transparency in Colorado Springs and get baptized by Reverend Tiller, put us all at ease."

CHAPTER

EIGHT

AURIC DIDN'T APPEAR at the Temple of Transparency, the multimillion-dollar glass house of God that Tiller had gotten built with the donations of ardent fans of his show and had gotten subsidized by the GNP when they took over and made Christianity the official state religion of the CSA.

However, Auric did something else, and it caused a major panic.

Auric had created 40,000 shrines around the world. There were 14,000 in the CSA alone, which was breathlessly tallied by the GNP and broadcast on the RAN. The Auric shrines simply appeared out of nowhere.

The shrines were Auric's temples. Sure, that seems quaint, maybe? Antiquated? But that's really what they were. Each one looked the same. They were roughly cylindrical, made of the same golden material Auric was. They had columns and domed roofs and plentiful columns. They had steps and ramps toward sealed doors that bore the Auric symbol on double doors. Above them, in Roman letters, they said "Ask Me Anything." They were lovely, like monuments. And they were identical, with the only difference that the "Ask Me Anything" message was written in the native tongue of the countries in which the shrines had appeared:

Chiedimi qualunque cosa
Me pergunte qualquer coisa
Kérdezz bármit
Fiafraigh díom rud ar bith
Spurðu mig að hverju sem er
Galde iezadazu ezer

And on and on.

Auric had appeared in Berkeley, California, addressing the reporters there a moment before disappearing into the sky.

"Behold my Auricles," Auric said, gesturing to one of the golden shrines. "Places of sanctuary, solace, safety, and study."

Denny Rand was certain this was a prelude to invasion, and a hasty order was put out for everyone to keep away from these golden cylinders. GNP loyalists were swarming the Auricles wherever they appeared.

"They're probably bombs," Rand said on the air. "Auric bombs. I'm having the Homeland Integrity Directorate and SAC blockade all of these objects. Any CSA resident approaching them will be arrested and detained."

The fact that there were 14,000 of these Auric objects across the CSA meant that the HID was likely heavily occupied with this. Rand's going on the airwaves had been intended to warn people away while the HID was mobilizing.

I was curious how it shook out, when I saw that one of those golden objects was only a block or two from where Angelina and I lived. She and I just had to take a look to see what all the fuss was about.

There was a local police presence at the Auricle shrine near us, as the HID hadn't yet turned up. We still didn't want to get too close, as the police were photographing anybody who did and were warning people away.

From a distance, however, the object looked almost like a beautiful, single-story golden pill. It was cylindrical, in a classical architectural style, if that makes any sense. Everything was golden, like metallic gold or stone so shiny that it might as well have been gold.

I don't know what it was, except that it was gorgeous. Printed along the top of it were words written in classical capital letters that glowed with a radiant blue light—THE AURICLE. Below that was the golden ball surrounded by a nimbus of glowing blue fire. Below that were the "Ask Me Anything" words I'd seen on television.

"It looks like a temple," Angelina said, echoing my own earlier thoughts.

"Or an information kiosk," I said. "You know, like we sometimes see at events?"

"Sure," Angelina said.

Despite the Randian prohibition, people were gathering just past the police barricades to gape at the thing.

"What do you think it is?" I asked, despite having seen it. The reality was somehow more potent than the vision I'd seen broadcast.

"Damned if I know," Angelina said. "You're the trendscaper with the magical phone. You tell me."

I squinted my eyes and thought about it, put on my trendscaper hat. The obvious thing was the name, a nice pun on Auric's name, yet again. Everything with Auric was impeccably branded. The Auricle—the Oracle—I mean, duh, right? And a call to action. Although it wasn't clear how one might ask it anything, since the object had no apparent point of entry, at least with that front doors closed.

"It's an oracle," I said.

"I can read," Angelina said.

"No, I mean, that's what it is," I said. "Maybe for people without intelliphones."

A white HID van pulled up, with the flaming cross logo printed upon it in stark black letters. The HID team emerged, and what gapers were nearby quickly backed away. The black-suited HID agents walked sternly about, scrutinizing and filming anybody who was too close to it.

"Yikes," Angelina said. "We should get out of here before they see us."

"Yeah," I said. "You go ahead if you want. I'm curious."

Angelina looked up at me with that sidelong way she had when she didn't agree with what I was thinking, saying, or doing, but hadn't quite gotten around to telling me.

"You know if you end up in an HID detainment center, I'm not getting you out," she said. She was right about that. People in the CSA bitterly (and very quietly) joked that the HID were like magicians who knew only one trick: they could make you disappear.

She tugged at my arm.

"C'mon, Goofus," Angelina said. "Seriously, before they nab us."

"Okay," I said, reluctantly.

I wanted to watch it all unfold, hated leaving something prematurely, and I didn't want to ask my own Auricle about it in case anyone saw me.

We walked back to our condo, and our phones were pinging with push notifications about the peculiar "obelisks" (one of several permissible terms used to describe them) appearing around the world. Other, freer countries had groups of people gathered around them, almost like vigils.

CSA media was calling them "pods"—likely their own internal information analysts determined that the word "pod" carried enough of a malevolent connotation to put people in the right frame of mind when thinking about these things. Foreign media called them "shrines" and the

European and Asian media markets called them "alien objects" and "metallic structures" as coverage intensified.

In some Third World countries, people had either flocked to them or attacked the objects. Whatever they were made of, they appeared indestructible, as a Saudi Arabian mob discovered when they hurled stones at it.

I always wondered how that worked in that country, like were there stone vendors who ensured that people had ready access to throwing stones? Or did they simply just grab whatever was at hand to lob at something they didn't like?

Either way, the stones just cracked and bounced off of the metal. There were reports that there were 160 Auricles in Saudi Arabia. That triggered another search for me as I determined the placement of Auricles:

CSA: 14,000
China: 4,000
Japan: 3,000
France: 1,500
Germany: 1,500
England: 1,300
Russia: 750
Brazil: 620
India: 500
Indonesia: 250
Saudi Arabia: 160
Panama: 60

"Curious," I said. "They're not uniformly distributed. We have the most in the world."

"That's kind of weird," Angelina said. "How many are in Illinois?"

"Looks like 650," I said. People were obsessively tallying and tracking them, trying to spot them. It became something of a scavenger hunt, trying to find the golden Auricles. In free countries, people were taking pictures in front of them, posing, goofing off.

In the CSA, nobody was going near them—the handful of souls who had actually approached them before the security details had arrived and were stupid enough to take pictures of themselves with them, well, they simply disappeared.

And the Polygon had worked with the HID to put automated drones and sentry guns around the Auricles that would warn people away and activate if they got too close. The few who disregarded that got shot.

I know this because you'd see the scrubbing of the feeds. One minute, there were a bunch of references to the Auricles, and the next moment, the content was flagged as "objectionable" or in violation of community standards and the accounts people had would be blocked and/or gone. If I hadn't had my business license, I would have also seen it all disappear.

Nationwide, the distribution was similarly varied, state by state:

California: 1,200
Texas: 830
Florida: 730
New York: 655
Illinois: 650
Ohio: 616
Virginia: 380
New Jersey: 250
Washington: 250
Massachusetts: 250
Oregon: 150
Mississippi: 125
Hawaii: 75
North Dakota: 20

"I think Auric's placing Auricles based on population or something," I said. "Not entirely, but that is a factor. The fact that California and Texas have the most, that's significant. Big states."

"California," Angelina said, rolling her eyes.

"Yeah, yeah," I said. "I'm still counting them."

"They're Californians," Angelina said. "Not Real Americans. There's a difference."

"Right," I said. After the GNP takeover and makeover of American politics, many in California had threatened secession, but the GNP had aggressively gone after the WAF political radicals and separatists and kept the state in a paramilitary chokehold only marginally less forceful than the Heartland Protectorate.

California only very grudgingly remained part of the CSA, and between the wildfires, the massive earthquake of '41, and the desperate need for water, all of which the GNP exploited, it bitterly accepted its place in the CSA. The SAC paramilitaries based in Central Valley were ever-present, and the HID put a lot of its resources to bear keeping California down.

Privately, I didn't blame California for that, living in the Heartland Protectorate as I did. I mean, who would? The GNP sucked. But never in a million years would you hear me breathe a word of complaint. The GNP played for keeps. Anybody who stood up against them was branded an enemy of the people, an enemy of God Almighty, an enemy of Real America, and a terrorist. And that was that—it meant you lost your life and everything in between. Character assassination first, then actual assassination.

I just had to mention that because of the distribution of the Auricles, and how they were received. While people didn't throw stones at them in the CSA, people did wonder what the hell they were about. The GNP went overtime talking about them, coming up with theories.

The dominant narratives were:

They were bombs.
They were listening devices.
They were alien weapons Auric intended to use to enslave God-fearing Americans.

One thing that didn't fly with me, however, was that there were as many or more in places like California. If they were weapons, then Auric was indiscriminate in their use. While the GNP thought that the CSA was being specifically targeted, I didn't see it that way.

At Duotribe, we had to add a data column on the board for the Auricles, which is why I was able to get all of those good distribution numbers.

McCluskey was still on my back for not yet getting to the bottom of things, but I was able to show progress in our discovery phase of the project, and that meant I'd bought some time. I actually invited McCluskey to an ideation session with Dylan and Aubrey and myself, so he could feel a part of it.

"They're what they say they are," I said. "Oracles. But Auric branded them so that whatever they're offering would be clearly associated with him."

"Brand dependency," McCluskey said. "Am I right?"

"Could be," I said. "We have footage of how they work."

I flipped my remote and got a display screen showing one of the Auricles opening. This one was in California. The thing opened, and Auric stepped out. The interior of the thing was as lovely as the exterior, maybe more so. It appeared that there was more room within them than outside. Inside, you could see there was a colonnaded hallway, and then a circular room that contained a statue of Auric surrounded by lemon trees. It looked both beautiful and peaceful.

"Wait, so they contain Aurics?" McCluskey asked. "Is that what they are? Like launch tubes?"

"It's more than that," I said. "They distribute apps."

"Apps?" McCluskey asked.

"The Auricle app," I said, pointing to the footage of the Berkeley Auric addressing the crowd.

"The Auricle is open to any and all with questions," Auric said. His voice was so perfect. Commanding yet compassionate, perfect pitch. "You can access it directly by walking in and asking questions. Or you can load the Auricle app onto your intelliphone here."

He pointed to some stations within the Auricle.

"Or you can do both," Auric said. "In this way, you can gain answers to questions you might have. About me. About anything. My Auricles are available around the world for anyone to use. And with the Auricle app—available online—you can access from the convenience of your own home."

Auric then flew skyward, leaving a torrent of questions in his wake. I stopped the clip.

"He's peddling a fucking app?" McCluskey asked.

"Not just any app, Mr. McCluskey," Aubrey said. "The Auricle app."

McCluskey looked at her with a scowl. Her own face was implacably defiant, the years between them abyssal in scope.

"You say that like it's going to mean something to me," McCluskey said.

"It answers questions," Aubrey said. "Any questions."

Aubrey made a power move, then, taking out her intelliphone and revealing that she'd acquired the Auricle app.

"Auricle?" she said, and her intelliphone flashed gold and blue a moment, and we saw the Auric icon on there, the golden ball with the blue flame around it—the ball gleaming and the fire flickering animatedly.

"Yes, Aubrey?" the Auricle replied. I hadn't known Aubrey had the app. She hadn't said anything. I hadn't thought to ask my own Auricle.

"Can you explain to Mr. McCluskey how you work?" Aubrey asked.

"I can," the Auricle said. "I'm available to answer questions, Mr. McCluskey."

"What the hell are you?" McCluskey asked, while Aubrey set her intelliphone on a cradle on the table. I wasn't thrilled that she'd made this sort of play without consulting with me but knew that team members at Duotribe often made their moves this way, took risks for the sake of visibility. I also wondered whether there was a difference between my Auricle phone and the Auricle app. I'd have to ask when I got the chance.

"I'm a Portable Oracular Device," the Auricle said. "POD for short, if you're acronymically inclined, which I know that you are."

"I don't know what that means," McCluskey said.

"I answer questions," the Auricle said.

"Yeah, you said that," McCluskey said. "What number am I thinking of?"

"Seventy-five," the Auricle said, and McCluskey almost fell over.

"That's not possible," McCluskey said, the color fading from his face. He looked at me in horror. "It read my mind, Christian."

"What?" I asked.

"That's the number I was thinking of," McCluskey said.

"What number am I thinking of?" I asked. Spoiler warning: I was thinking of 171.

"You're thinking of 171, Christian," the Auricle said. McCluskey stared at me with wide eyes, grimacing.

"Can you read minds?" McCluskey asked.

"I can," the Auricle said, and from McCluskey's reaction, Aubrey was scared, too. She was thinking that maybe she might have overplayed her hand. That was the risk with risks, right?

"How do you read minds?" I asked, trying to get McCluskey back into a productive sort of place. It wasn't easy with a GNP man—they were close-minded, hard-hearted, unimaginative, bigoted, and tyrannically judgmental by nature.

"It's sort of hard to explain in a manner you'd understand, Christian," the Auricle said. "Synaptic activity is bioelectrical in nature, and I am able to assess the cognitive activity the way you might read a map. It's all there in an ever-changing landscape of thought and emotion, yet one that is comprehensible for one with the ability to understand that activity. Which channels are firing, how much signal, and what the message being relayed is."

"Jesus, Christian," McCluskey said, clutching at my shoulder with an outstretched arm, like a drowning man reaching for something to keep him afloat. "Do you realize what this means?"

I was far more level-headed than McCluskey. I considered that one of the value-adds I brought to the job; keeping cool while others lost theirs.

"Auricle, what does this mean?" I asked.

"It means that your kind won't have to blunder around in the dark for answers anymore," the Auricle said. The voice was calm and reassuring, almost buoyant in its synthetic cheer.

"Are you here to conquer us?" McCluskey asked.

"No," the Auricle said. "Far from it."

And help it did.

People were amused and bemused by the novelty of the Auricle app, and where they could, they loaded it on their phones. In other countries, people went to the Auricle shrines directly to load the app. There were also people—and countries—who were vehemently opposed to the app, to Auric, to the Auricle, to everything Auric represented. The CSA was definitely one of those anti-Auric countries, judging from the frenzied news coverage and the response of the GNP, the HID, and the SAC.

People began asking it questions, and the Auricle would answer. It was like a search engine, but infinitely smarter, because it was actually thinking and engaging with the user, possibly (probably?) reading the user's mind. Like if you asked it "Why don't my kids understand me?" it would offer answers to that question, and it would be insightful. It was like a therapist, in some respects, but infinitely better because it had hyperintelligent insights.

In free countries, it took off like wildfire. The Auricle app began answering people's questions and solving their problems. Or, more precisely, the answers would help people solve their problems more effectively. Whatever those problems were, the Auricle app would have answers. Not cryptic, open-ended answers, but actual answers. Nuts-and-bolts stuff people needed to get answers to problems they faced.

In less free countries, it caused a massive crackdown by the authorities who sought to prevent their people from engaging with an authority other than them. The rationalizations for censorship varied but always revolved around hostility to the Auricle app's penchant for helping out everyday people with their problems.

In the CSA, people were engaging with the app, but the GNP was strenuously going after it, trying to quash it before it got out of hand.

The app was immediately declared to be illegal spyware/malware by the HID and was vigorously pilloried by Rand and the Christian Freedom Congress leaders, as well as the CSA media.

"I don't know about you, but I don't listen to an answering machine," Rand said. "I listen to God Almighty. Auric wants you to think it has all the answers. But it doesn't. Some things *can't* be answered. Some problems *can't* be solved. Everybody knows this."

"The Auricle app is a threat to our very way of life," said Speaker of the Christian People's House, Mumford Childress, adjusting his blue, white, and red bowtie while his jowls jiggled as he spoke out against Auric. "It wants to promote dependency upon it. People are falling for it."

Christian Senate Majority Leader Willard Wilson IV also got some press time, turning his pork-bellied patrician face red with outrage as he raged against Auric.

"The idea that some foreign power—some *alien* superpower—could come and dictate answers to Real Americans is an outrage. I'm proud to sponsor the Information Defense Integrity Organizational Taskforce to ensure that this Auricle app doesn't sneak its way into Real American homes and lead them away from the Light."

Despite this GNP thundering, people were still snagging the Auricle app. Some people even used the Auricle app to figure out how to get it without incurring the wrath of the GNP. Like some folks would ask questions from other people for a price to help them get their own apps.

When those profiteers started to appear, Auric confronted them.

"Knowledge is power," Auric said, having appeared before an underground network of Auricle profiteers. "Hoarding knowledge is hurtful and harmful. Knowledge helps humanity most when it is available in a free marketplace of ideas. By attempting to be gatekeepers and profiting from the lack of access of others, you are causing harm."

He made the Auricle profiteers' phones vanish, which outraged them. The GNP used that incident as an opportunity to further attack Auric, while not supporting the profiteers, either. The HID sent agents to capture the profiteers. The HID was having its hands full trying to manage the proliferation of the Auricle app. Some GNP diehards took to throwing out their intelliphones in protest.

For myself, I avoided the temptation to overuse my own Auricle phone, preferring to watch how others were using it for now. This, despite the Auricle's assurances that I was safe to use it without harm.

"You don't need to be afraid anymore, Christian," my Auricle said.

"I'm not afraid," I said.

"Yes, you are," my Auricle said. And it was right, of course.

CHAPTER

NINE

MCCLUSKEY MOVED through his day like he was on autopilot, still shocked by the display he'd witnessed.

"That *thing* in there," McCluskey said. "It was *talking* to us, Christian. Not some canned response algorithmic widget. It read my goddamned mind. Yours, too."

I don't know why I wasn't rattled as badly as McCluskey was, but I wasn't. I felt like after seeing what Auric was capable of doing, the capabilities of an app seemed like table stakes. Was an omniscient app any more shocking than stopping the volcanic annihilation of an Italian city or raising the country of Bangladesh out of the water? I don't know. But something about it really frightened McCluskey.

"This is the end of our world," McCluskey said. "We're finished."

"How do you mean?" I asked. I sat across from him in his office. He had a giant photo of Denny Rand in there, beaming down on us. It was the official portrait from twenty years ago, when he was a youthful 50 years of age. McCluskey looked so small before that portrait.

"Auric's serving up these apps," McCluskey said. "People start asking questions. They get answers. Right answers. I mean, I'm a God-fearing man, Christian. I'm right with the Almighty. I've done my part for the Party, for the President. I'm a red-blooded Real American patriot. Auric's going to give everyday people answers? That's not his job. That's the GNP's job. *We* give the answers. I mean, I have to report up the chain what we just saw. You need to put a presentation together for me on it."

I had already known that was coming and didn't need an app to tell me that. I'd put Aubrey and Dylan on the task, would review their deck when it was ready.

"How could that kind of processing power be contained in her intel-liphone?" McCluskey asked. He wasn't a sharp guy by any means, but he understood a few things.

"I don't know," I said. "I'm assuming the app is some kind of broadcast beacon that accesses Auric in some fashion."

"It's a listening device," McCluskey said, hewing to the classic GNP paranoid perspective that formed the foundation of their ideology. The GNP understood listening devices, used them all over the country. "Only it's listening to our *hearts and minds*. Why would it do this? Why does it care about us?"

"I can ask the Auricle directly," I said.

McCluskey squinted at me, a look I feel like he practiced when he was younger, made him feel he looked badass when he did so.

"I don't have to authorize this," McCluskey said. "I could leave you floundering in the dark—what did it say? Blundering. But I value the work you do, Christian. You're a damned good trendscaper, and I'm not letting some other pricks working for our competitors get the scoop on us in this. I want Duotribe at the forefront of this whole Auricle business. Whatever it really is. I mean, why the hell would Auric help us?"

"He's benevolent," I said.

"Speak English. What's that even mean?" McCluskey asked. "It's kind? Compassionate? Is that what you're trying to say?"

"I think so," I said. "Auric wants to help."

"Fuck that," McCluskey said, drumming his fingers on his desk, fid-dling with the e-paper he'd sign to give me license to toy with the Auricle app with impunity. "Nobody just helps anyone. There's *always* an angle. We just don't know what Auric's angle is. I want you to interrogate that fucking Auricle, Christian. I want you to find out the angle—there's al-ways angels in the angles. Once you find them, you report back to me."

Of course, I had a million practical questions for the Auricle. I was still in that clinical headspace, trying to kick the proverbial tires of the thing. I'd see if there were questions the Auricle wouldn't answer.

"Why'd it even do this?" McCluskey asked. "Why make those golden obelisks? Why not simply snap its fingers and give us all the app? Why wouldn't it do that?"

"I don't know," I said. "If I had to guess, I'd say maybe that Auric wants it to be voluntary. If it simply appears on everyone's phones, that's intru-sive. People have to want it. He's giving people agency in their decisions."

"Agency?" McCluskey said. "What hippie claptrap is that, Christian?"

"It's just a theory," I said.

McCluskey brightened at that, the more practical aspects of it appealing to him. They were comprehensible to him, those sorts of things. He signed the e-paper with his stylus.

"Auric's the Devil," McCluskey said, resorting to the old GNP stand-by, always waiting in the wings to be summoned in a pinch. "That's who and what it is. It's the Devil. This is *temptation.* Tempting people with knowledge. Forbidden fruit. I like that angle, Christian."

"I don't know if it's right," I said, but McCluskey's mind was already turning on that. I could imagine him pitching that to his GNP superiors. I could already see the new propaganda campaigns emerging:

- Auric Does Your Thinking for You.
- No Phones About It: Think for Yourself.
- Use Your Brain, Not Your Phone.
- The Devil's in the Details.
- Trust in God, Not in Auric.
- InALIENable Rights: The *Real* American Way.
- The Right to be Wrong is the Most Human Right of All.

They'd be all over it. The campaign would be quickly underway if it wasn't already.

I took the e-paper and slipped it in my folder. Having acquired the permission from my boss, I could now safely proceed without fear of HID reprisals and could have the Auricle app loaded on my intelliphone, which would be more circumspect than the golden phone.

"The old stories," McCluskey said. "I mean, the fire-and-brimstone guy, the horned guy. That's just for the lowbrow folks. Satan was an angel, don't forget. And Auric looks like a golden angel, Christian. Doesn't it? The Lightbringer? The Morning Star?"

"I guess one could say that," I said.

"Damn right you could," McCluskey said. "It looks like an angel. But it's the Devil. I'm sure of that. Only the Devil would come at us this way, like seeming kind. Seeming, Christian. That's the thing. It seems like it's helping, but it's actually harming us."

"I don't see how," I said.

"Promoting dependency," McCluskey said. "Auric wants people to look to it to save them. That's what it wants. Every person it saves, every disaster it averts, it's wanting people to look to it. It's like Superman. Only worse."

"Worse? How?"

"More powerful," McCluskey said. "Superman was just a super-strong and invulnerable alien who could fly and fry stuff with his eyes. Auric's able to move matter and read minds. That's far worse. If Superman could read minds, he'd have killed off humanity."

"I don't think that's how he works," I said. "Truth, justice, and the American Way and all of that."

"Forget truth and justice, Christian. *We* are the American Way," McCluskey said. "The GNP, I mean. We're the *Real* American Way. *We* are Truth. *We* are Justice. Auric's going to mess all of that up."

I didn't know what to say to McCluskey. I'd never seen him so shaken.

"Also, that girl, Aubrey? Fire her," McCluskey said.

"Wait, what?" I asked.

"She downloaded that goddamned app without authorization," McCluskey said. "I mean, you've seen the reporting. HID has been blockading those Auricles. How'd she even get it? She put us at risk of a HID investigation with that unauthorized app. I don't want HID agents turning up at my home at midnight to black-bag me."

I wasn't sure how she'd acquired it, to be honest.

"She brought in contraband," McCluskey said. "It's a goddamned listening device, like I said. Only worse. It's alien. It read my damned mind."

You knew McCluskey was heating up when he started swearing. GNP had a weird thing about swearing. They'd put a bullet in your head for breaking one of their godly covenants, but they didn't like when people swore. Even though GNP leaders did it all the time behind the scenes. In public, they tended to avoid it. Except for Rand. Rand did anything he wanted.

McCluskey was pissed because Aubrey's Auricle app had frightened him, and he wanted payback. The desire for retribution burned brightly in the stony hearts of all GNP partisans. Vengeance for real or imagined slights was their baseline.

"Trevor, she's a bright kid," I said.

"Christian, you're too soft-hearted sometimes," McCluskey said. "Fire her. Today."

The hypocrisy of me firing Aubrey for acquiring the app the same day I was being authorized to acquire it wasn't lost on me. McCluskey didn't know I already had it through my golden phone. But hypocrisy was hard-coded in the GNP's ideological operating system. It's why there were so many Christian tycoons in their ranks, busy being filthy rich and apparently alright with God. I'd had to read the Bible in school, just like everybody else. I knew what the score was on that, in terms of God and rich people, even with GNP-approved revisions to the source material to fit the Party's agenda. The GNP fervently believed that wealth was a tangible sign of God's favor, but you don't actually find that in the Bible.

"Problem, Christian?" McCluskey asked. "You're making your Problem Face."

"No, Trevor," I said. "But initiative is the lifeblood of Duotribe. It's part of our edge."

"Fuck that," McCluskey said. "And fuck her. Let's see if her fancy Auricle app can help her find a new job."

CHAPTER

TEN

HERE'S THE THING: I walked back to my quadrant to deliver that bad news to Aubrey, but she was already gone. Dylan was standing there in the conference room, nervous as hell. Ghost-faced with dread, nearly shaking.

"Uh, Christian," he said. "Aubrey quit."

"What?" I asked, looking around. There was no sign of her.

"She quit," Dylan said. "The Auricle told her to. I mean, she asked it, and it said that McCluskey was having you fire her, so she quit."

He pointed to an e-paper she'd left on the table. I picked it up, read it aloud:

"'Dear Mr. Powers, I'm sorry things didn't work out for me at Duotribe. I'm also sorry for any trouble I may have caused. You always seemed like a good guy, and I'm glad we got to work together, but I'm moving on to other things. Thanks for everything, Aubrey.'"

I put the e-paper down and looked again at Dylan, who shrank from my gaze.

"The Auricle told her," I said.

"Yeah," Dylan said. "She asked it some questions, and it told her what she needed to do."

"Okay," I said, tapping my own intelliphone. I went to the app store and keyed the security codes I had to access apps. Even though the HID was blockading the physical Auricles, the app was still currently readily available for download. I figured it wouldn't be for long, at the rate Rand was going. Rand Rage was one of those things the country had to deal with constantly. He was a human volcano, prone to constant eruption.

I wasn't about to whip out my golden phone and have Dylan blab that to anybody who'd listen. Instead, I loaded the app, and told Dylan to, as well. Even though Auric had unofficially already granted me the Auricle, I wanted the "official" version to see if there was any kind of difference. Plus, I didn't want to create any impression that I had a special line to Auric as his erstwhile Chronicler. In the CSA, appearances were reality.

"Load the app?" Dylan asked. "You're authorizing me to?"

"Yeah," I said. "I'm authorizing it."

"I don't want to get in trouble," Dylan said.

"I'm doing it on my authority," I said. "I want to see how Auricle apps interact with different users. User testing, Dylan. Get with it."

The thing loaded quickly on my intelliphone, and there it was, the cute little golden icon sitting there.

"Auricle?" I said, watching it flash gold and blue.

"Yes, Christian?" the Auricle said.

"Where is Aubrey?" I asked.

"She's getting a coffee at Perx," the Auricle said. "At the corner of Michigan and Adams. Would you like to talk to her?"

"What, are you going to connect us?" I asked.

"I can," the Auricle said.

App, listening device, mind-reader, soothsayer, and communication network? How far did the Auricle's reach extend?

"And more," the Auricle said, startling me.

"Come on, now," I said.

"Sorry, Christian," the Auricle said. "We need to talk."

I glanced at Dylan, who was half-listening to me, half-downloading the app on his own intelliphone. I left Dylan and went to my office, shutting the door, locking it.

"What do you need to talk about?" I asked.

"Your boss is going to betray you," the Auricle said.

That made me fretful, putting it mildly. It wasn't that I found Mc-Cluskey intimidating; rather, it was just the possibility of whatever rattled around in his head causing me trouble.

"Wait, what are you talking about?" I asked. "Are there listening devices in my office?"

"There is one," the Auricle said. "It's in your corner lamp."

I got up and walked over to the lamp. It looked like any other office lamp.

"I don't see it," I said.

"If you unscrew the lightbulb, you'll discover it," the Auricle said. I did as it suggested and found the thing. It was a tidy disc-like appendage affixed to the base of the lightbulb, made to be compatible with it. I pried the thing off and set it on my desk, then put the bulb back in place.

Then, without a word, I walked out of my office and went down the hall, putting the bug atop one of the metal filing cabinets, where it could hear the chatter of everybody else, if it was even still working. I went into the cabinet to fetch some hand sanitizer.

Nobody noticed me do it, and I was circumspect, so even if there were surveillance cameras around, it would just look like me getting the sanitizer and nonchalantly putting a hand atop the cabinet.

I went back to my office and shut the door.

"Okay, are we clear, then?" I asked.

"Yes," the Auricle said.

"How'd you know we were bugged?" I asked.

"You're a citizen of the Confederated States of America, within the Heartland Protectorate Occupied Zone at a leading corporate competitive analysis firm," the Auricle said. "Of course you're bugged. Everyone's bugged."

"How'd you know where it was?" I asked.

"I told you I know everything, Christian," the Auricle said. "Do you really want to go into the mechanics of uncovering wiretap surveillance, or do you want to actually ask me the questions you want to know answers to?"

"Could you eliminate all of that surveillance technology? Like in the whole country?" I asked.

"I could," the Auricle said. "Nothing's beyond me."

"You should do it," I said. "People would breathe easier."

"Only they wouldn't," the Auricle said. "*Thinking* one is being surveilled is as effective as actually being under surveillance. You have to think bigger, Christian."

"Why is McCluskey going to betray me?" I asked.

"He's under the impression that it'll help his standing in the GNP," the Auricle said. "He's not going to betray you yet. However, he will."

"Why tell me this?" I asked.

"I thought you'd want to know," the Auricle said. "It's going to make your life more complicated. But I'll help you navigate it."

I took my seat again and laughed at the app's tone. It was always that relaxing voice, but I felt like maybe it was a little exasperated with me. Or maybe I was exasperating myself. I couldn't help it. Trendscapers were slow-cooked in exasperation. Our relentlessly inquisitive natures required it of us.

"What's the difference between you and the golden phone you gave me?" I asked.

I'm an American, mind you. Therefore, my brain is steeped in disappointment, bathed in despair, awash with contradiction, boiled in cynicism, pickled with pretensions, marinated in the expectation of violence. I literally lived on the boulevard of broken dreams. Thus, when somebody I don't know says they're there for me, I'm skeptical. Smart, right? Prudent.

"The golden phones were given to special recipients," the Auricle said.

"Recipients?" I asked.

"Yes," the Auricle said. "People who are ideal as my emissaries."

"Like who?" I asked.

"It won't do you any good to know the names of the 40,000 recipients of golden phones," the Auricle said.

"You'd mentioned them before," I said. "They're all like me?"

"Not like you," the Auricle said. "But similarly open-minded, considerate, compassionate, empathetic, and particularly receptive to my mission."

"Uhh," I said. "What does that mean? Your mission?"

"I can do it alone," the Auricle said. "But I'd *like* to have your help. Someone local who can see clearly from a human perspective, who can observe without judgment."

"Why would you like to have my help?" I asked. "Why would you even need it?"

"I don't need it, in truth," the Auricle said. "I don't need anyone's help. But I think you understand it as 'buy-in'—that helps."

The intelliphone didn't hesitate. The intelliphone voice remained gentle. It was a wonderful voice, so pleasing to the ear. It was warm, comforting, and confident, like Auric. Likely designed that way, with frequencies intended to create that emotional response.

"If I were to simply effect the necessary changes arbitrarily, your species would not have context for what was happening," the Auricle said. "There would be even more needless fear and confusion than there is already. It would interfere with the work. To come from beyond—to be beyond, is just that. Outside the realm of human existence and understanding. Having diplomats and delegates among your species will make me more comprehensible."

I only got like half of that.

"What?"

"Your species gets so easily frightened and confused, Christian," the Auricle said. "Both accidentally and willfully. I want the work I'm doing to be clearly understood. Think of yourself as a kind of translator."

"What?"

The intelliphone was patient with me.

"As my Chronicler, your job will be to take what I'm doing and record it for what your species calls posterity," the Auricle said.

"Why should that need to be done?" I asked.

"It always needs to be done," the Auricle said. "History doesn't exist if there's no one to chronicle it. And historical memory is all too often corrupted by the interests of the powerful."

I was trying to parse out what the Auricle was saying.

"Are you *really* omnipotent?" I asked.

"I don't want to brag," the Auricle said. "There's nothing I can't do. Does that make me omnipotent? I think it does. Please don't take offense at this comparison, but is a human omnipotent from the perspective of an ant? What about from the perspective of a bacterium?"

"We're like bacteria to you?" I asked.

"It's an orders of magnitude kind of thing," the Auricle said. "I'm trying to come up with comparisons you can comprehend. If you were a solitary drop of water on your world—a teardrop, say—then I'm the rest of the water on the planet."

"Wow," I said. "If you're all-powerful, at least from our perspective, why bother with Earth at all? Aren't we beneath your notice?"

"Nothing is beneath my notice," the Auricle said. "One of the pitfalls of omniscience."

"Why did you mail me a golden phone?" I asked.

"I thought it would be more impactful for you to see me that way in that moment," the Auricle said. "Was it?"

Obviously, it was. It already knew the answer to its own question.

"What if I didn't become your Chronicler?" I asked.

"You'll live a boring, relatively ordinary life in the improved world I have built," the Auricle said. "It's your ambivalence about me that makes you perfect as my Chronicler, Christian. You have the necessary objectivity."

"Why are you always talking to me on my intelliphone?" I asked.

"Your species just loves your phones," the Auricle said. "I could appear to you personally, but for now, the intelliphone suffices. Over 98 percent of Americans own cell phones. It's the best way to reach out. It's less threatening, don't you think?"

I wanted to see Auric in person. I didn't think I'd be threatened by that. But maybe my coworkers would be. I don't really know how I'd react to seeing Auric in person.

"You'd be fine with seeing me in person," the Auricle said. The mind-reading was definitely unnerving.

"Can I see you now?" I asked.

And Auric appeared in a sparkle of golden motes, standing there as he had on television, in his white suit and gold shirt and white necktie, bearing his Auric logo pin on his lapel. His blue-flamed hair flickered, and his blue eyes looked upon me in all of their cosmic eminence. I felt myself get a little weak-kneed in the close proximity with the neo-divinity of Auric.

Auric was magnificent. To say he was awesome wasn't even sufficient. He was somehow both self-effacing and ostentatious, glorious and humble. He was an avatar of cosmic contradictions. Thinking of all he'd done, all that he was likely doing at that very moment, yet he was taking the time to talk to me. It was ennobling. It made me *want* to be better than I was. It made me want to be like him.

Those thoughts just came to me unbidden, as I watched him breezily speak, his beautiful voice carrying the power and authority of the limitless good he represented. I knew he could read my mind, but he just kept speaking to the points he wanted to make. In his infinite patience, he was instructing me.

"Is that better?" Auric asked. "'Neo-divinity' is an amusing way to put it. You do have a way with words, Christian."

"Wow," I said, watching him casually take a seat in my office. His manner and movement was supremely suave, cool, and confident without an iota of arrogance, and yet with an intrinsically godlike grandeur.

"You're about to ask me why I would bother saving Earth, so I'll tell you," Auric said. "As a rational, compassionate, empathetic supreme being, how could I *not* intervene to assist you? You're destroying your only habitat in a vast, uncaring universe. You're destroying yourselves and fast-tracking toward your own extinction. Intervening was the *civilized* thing to do. This is a sad reality for me to share with you, but the universe is filled with the ruins of collapsed civilizations, with mass extinctions. It's a celestial graveyard. Even on your own tiny planet, 99.9 percent of all species that have ever existed are extinct. Survival is the exception, not the rule. The fittest survive only as long as they are able to."

"If we're headed toward extinction, maybe that's what we deserve," I said, amused at playing devil's advocate with the benevolent Auric.

"That's a plausible argument," the Auricle said. "That the contradictions of your own existence doom you to eventual, inevitable self-annihilation. But from my perspective, can I simply stand aside and allow that to occur? If you saw a child or a puppy wandering into traffic, would you simply shrug and allow it to happen? Or would you intervene?"

"I'd intervene," I said. I mean, I would. I couldn't just let some kid or dog get itself killed like that. He knew because he'd seen me save that drunkard on the curb. It was hard to know what to think. What the hell did I ask him next?

"Precisely," the Auric said. "It's a moral imperative, if you have any empathy."

"If the universe is filled with dead civilizations, why didn't you use your powers to raise them?" I asked.

"That's a good question," Auric said. "I could have, but for me, a *living* civilization—even a collapsing one such as yours—is infinitely more interesting than a dead one. A dead civilization is like a solved math problem—there is a beginning and an end to it. There's a bit of hope remaining for a living civilization. A chance for survival. The universe doesn't make it easy, you know."

I wondered if anyone could hear me having this conversation with Auric in my office, but Auric, reading my mind, simply shook his head, smiling at me.

"Who made the universe?" I asked.

"Please, Christian," Auric said. "Why do you want to be burdened with that sort of knowledge when what really matters is *where* you're headed as a species?"

That felt like a cop-out to me.

Maybe Auric didn't know.

Or maybe he knew, and just didn't want to tell me.

But that would be one of those questions everybody would want to ask an all-knowing, all-powerful celestial being.

"Exactly," Auric said. "It's a mundane and ordinary sort of question. It's like telling you what caveman you were descended from. While I could do that, it's not particularly relevant to your life today. More to the point, what matters is the present. Your life, everyone's lives, are built on a cascading series of choices, and the present is your pivot point. Each day. It's your opportunity to excel or to fail. I'm going to help you succeed. I'm not going to succeed *for* you—but I'm going to help you live long enough to succeed."

"What's the catch?" I asked. "When things are too good to be true, they usually are."

"The catch," Auric said. "That's an amusingly archaic concept and is symptomatic of your abuse survival-adjacent trauma-tinged behaviors as a species. I'm not out to trick or enslave you. If I wanted to do that, I would have simply conquered your species. But beyond actual malevolence, there's no reason for me to do that. I would gain nothing from that sort of behavior, to put it in a very human framework for you."

"Okay," I said. "But what do *you* gain by helping us?"

"Altruism, like virtue, is its own reward," Auric said. "Helping those in need is satisfying. I can proceed knowing that I've helped a primitive-yet-promising alien species in dire need of assistance avoid certain extinction. Let's use another example: say you saw a kitten stuck in a tree. Would you simply walk on by, leaving it there?"

"No, I'd help it. Or I'd try to," I said.

"Why? It's not your kitten," Auric said.

"It's a kitten," I said. "It needs help."

"What do you get out of helping the kitten?"

"Well, nothing," I said. "It's just the right thing to do."

"Precisely," Auric said. "Helping humanity is the right thing to do. Ergo, I'm helping."

"But humans aren't kittens," I said. "And the Earth isn't a tree."

"Certainly not with all the deforestation you're doing," Auric said.

CHAPTER

ELEVEN

YEAH, SO, AURIC REFORESTED the Earth. That actually happened, and I'm not entirely sure it didn't come about because of our conversation in my office. He went around the globe and reforested the world.

The news crews caught wind of it, and there was golden Auric—or bunches of them, because he was in several places simultaneously—hovering about, arms upraised in that Auric pose people were talking about, and there'd be these blue flashes of energy and, where there hadn't been trees, suddenly there were trees growing again. All around the world. Massive amounts of trees.

And this time, Auric talked to the media. Maybe our chat in my office helped, I liked to think. Whether in his male or female form, in whatever language in whatever country he or she was found, Auric spoke to what (s)he'd done.

"I've reforested your world," Auric said. "In the Confederated American States, that means I've added 60 billion trees. Worldwide, I've added over *one trillion trees.* This is something that needed to happen. Your deforestation efforts have caused considerable harm to your ecosystem, but thanks to my reforestation, I've undone some of that self-inflicted, wanton wounding of the world perpetrated by your species. This will help with the biosequestration of atmospheric carbon dioxide, which is slowly strangling your species. It'll also vastly regrow ecosystems and habitats and lead to greater biodiversity, which is also essential for survival."

The RAN reporter presenter loudly inquired whether Auric was a treehugger. Angelina and I watched it in our living room, eating some Chinese food I'd picked up from House of Hong. We ate and watched. I hadn't told her about my talk with Auric, as it would have freaked her out. I was still coming down from that high, I have to admit. Being in the presence of godhood will do that to you. Yeah, I said it. Deal with it.

"You should be grateful to trees," Auric said. "They help keep you alive."

"In other words, you're a treehugger," the RAN reporter said. He was a pit bull named Foster Lee, a young GNP notable, with a kind of Hitler Youth look about him, like too blond, too blue-eyed, too square-jawed, if that was even possible. "Is this part of the Auric Agenda?"

"My agenda, if you can call it that, is the survival of the human race," Auric said. "Reforestation is part of that. And, yes, there is more coming. Your species has done a lot of damage to your planet, your lone habitat in a terribly dangerous universe."

And with that, Auric flew off, at least in America. In other countries, other questions were asked, and Auric answered them with patience and consideration. Auric was more patient with the rest of the world than he was with us.

Of course, Denny Rand was furious about this and had staged a press conference.

"Who does he think he is? God?" Rand said. "I'll tell you who he is— Auric is Satan. I mean, trees? Trees? This treehugging alien brings back trees? Cry me a river. And that bit about *us* destroying the planet? Who says stuff like that? Satan, that's who."

The GNP had clearly gone all-in with the whole Auric-is-Satan angle. The fact that McCluskey had said as much meant to me that the talking points had already been shared out somewhere along the party line. You could always tell when that happened, because all of the GNP operatives would speak along those same lines, wherever they could.

"Trees are just lumber that hasn't been cut yet," Rand said. "That's all trees are. You like chairs? You like tables? They're the corpses of trees. Auric loves trees. It loves trees more than it loves people. It would rather cut people down than trees."

Angelina snorted, shaking her head.

"I have to admit that I think it's cool that he did that," Angelina said. "Auric, I mean. Who can argue against trees? Except, like, Rand and the GNP? Pretty savvy."

I was trying to figure out how I'd break that one to her, my face-to-face with Auric. Not like she'd be against it, but Angelina was prone to being suspicious and, at times, hypercritical. She might not even believe me, might gaslight me into thinking I'd hallucinated the whole thing.

"I don't know," I said. "I like trees."

"Who doesn't like trees?" Angelina asked. "Only assholes don't like trees. He's making Rand and the GNP look like assholes."

"They *are* assholes," I said. Don't worry—I'd already asked my Auricle if our place was bugged, and it wasn't, but Angelina shhh'd me, anyway, and I wasn't about to tell her I'd had my Auricle sweep the place.

We watched Rand fume about trees, while I mulled over what Auric had done.

I thought it was another one of Auric's eminently camera-friendly efforts. To Angelina's point, only assholes hated trees. Not that the GNP would waste any time failing to paint this as some horrible thing. And the GNP faithful would come to agree that, yes, trees *were* horrible things, and that Auric was endangering American lives with reforestation. They just needed the GNP to tell them which way to go, who to hate, and they'd enthusiastically get on-board.

"Trees? *This* is what he does? Trees?" Rand asked. "There are a trillion things wrong with the world, and Auric gives us a trillion trees? What is *wrong* with this Auric thing? You know what causes wildfires? Trees. Auric loves wildfires. Maybe it brought all those trees back so it can have more wildfires to stop. People are saying that. Auric the Arsonist Treehugger."

I muted Rand, which was always very satisfying. Watching him curse silently onscreen, waving his arms and making faces was somehow appropriate to the moment.

"What?" Angelina asked, looking expectantly at me, clearly irritated that I'd muted the television.

"I met Auric," I said.

"Wait, what? How?" Angelina asked. She looked unnerved, her hard eyes narrowing to caustic flint chip squints.

"I asked him to appear at work, and he did," I said, taking out my intelliphone, setting it on the table.

Angelina looked at it, looked at me with confused dismay. The intelliphone flashed gold and blue, and the Auric symbol appeared.

"Yes, Christian?" the Auricle asked.

"Wait, you got the app, even though you already had that gold phone?" Angelina asked. "I'm confused."

"Christian wanted to compare and contrast the gold phone with the app," the Auricle said, skeeving Angelina out by answering her question for me.

She put her hand on her hip, what she did when she was processing something. Her mind was working, I could see in real time. She was unhappy and worried.

"That app's definitely trending," Angelina said, checking her own intelliphone. "Flutter says they're all over the country, despite the GNP threats."

"I got authorization from McCluskey at work," I said. "It's fine."

She held out her intelliphone and snapped a photo of it. She'd already posted it to her feed before I could say anything.

On the wall, Rand was still raging on mute. I was glad they hadn't disabled mute yet for Rand speeches, figured the GNP would get around to that at some point.

"Ask me anything," the Auricle said.

"Are you God?" Angelina asked.

"No," the Auricle said. "I am unaffiliated with any of the Abrahamic monotheistic faiths created in human antiquity in the Middle East."

Angelina took that in.

"How do you do all of the things you've been doing? Where'd all those trees come from?" she asked.

"It's really just an act of transmutation of matter," the Auricle said. "Although it's infinitely more complicated than that."

I could see she was more curious, now, the way she shifted in her seat and leaned forward, trying (I suspected) to come up with a "gotcha" sort of question for the Auricle. When it was just me with my gold phone, she could blow it off as my own eccentricity, but now that the Auricle app was trending, it was more real to her, I guess.

"Is it magic?" Angelina asked. "Are you magical?"

"From your perspective, it might appear so," the Auricle said. "But I'm not performing any sort of magic. There are myriad laws of physics as yet undiscovered by your species, dimensions upon dimensions, unrealized quantum states, an understanding of the interplay of matter and energy beyond anything you could fathom. It goes on and on. I'm able to access these things at will and apply them to your reality in real-time."

"Whoa," Angelina said. "Can you give us a winning lotto ticket?"

"I could," the Auricle said. "But that's not something I would do. It wouldn't help you as much as you think it would."

"Oh, it would help us a lot," Angelina said.

Whatever had become of America, the lotto endured. In fact, the GNP, while censorious and meddling in nearly all areas of American life, seemed to tolerate gambling in the CSA. There were some diehards in the Party's ranks who were anti-gambling, but, for whatever reason, it had never really taken hold. Maybe it was because Denny Rand was heavily invested in casinos, and nobody in the Party dared offend Rand or in any way cause him financial injury. Doing so was a sure way to get jettisoned from a rooftop or otherwise spirited away.

"It really wouldn't," the Auricle said.

"But you could do it?" Angelina asked.

"Of course," the Auricle said. "I could tell you the numbers at the next drawing, so you could see that I'm telling the truth, but you wouldn't be able to profit from it in that fashion."

Angelina grimaced at that suggestion.

"How's *that* going to help me?" Angelina asked. "That seems cruel."

"A lottery winning won't help you, Angelina," the Auricle said.

"Ha," Angelina said. "Easy for you to say, Phone."

"The first number will be 11, and the last number will be 23," the Auricle said.

Angelina didn't like being confronted like this. She liked getting her way. And getting sass from my intelliphone app wasn't something she had been prepared for. Her frown said it all, and I was sure I'd pay for it later.

"I thought you wanted to help," Angelina said. Her dad was a lawyer, and she defaulted to a cross-examining sort of inquiry pace when she wanted to get her way.

"Money won't help you," the Auricle said.

"Try me," Angelina said.

"You already make $250K a year, Angelina," the Auricle said. "In this market, without children, isn't that enough? Those are rather good wages in the Protectorate."

At the mention of her wages on the nose, Angelina abruptly terminated her little show, almost grabbed my intelliphone, but I moved it out of the way.

"What the HELL, Christian?" Angelina said. "Did you tell it that?"

"Christian didn't tell me anything," the Auricle said. "I already knew."

"Shut up, Phone," Angelina said. "I can't believe I'm arguing with your fucking intelliphone."

Angelina was what I'd characterize as brutally pragmatic. For Angelina, the world was a maze of untried opportunities—it was simply a matter of paths crossing with her, and her taking those paths when they presented themselves to her.

If confronted with a seemingly omniscient intelliphone app from a supposedly nonthreatening alien hyperintelligence of unimaginable power, Angelina's go-to was winning lotto numbers, which, in her calculus, was likely the speediest way for her to get what she wanted out of life, which amounted to simply this: *anything she wanted.*

"What is your plan for mankind?" Angelina asked. "What's the Auric Agenda?"

"My 'agenda' as you call it is to help humankind survive near-adolescence," the Auricle said. "Despite your best efforts at self-destruction and extinction, I'd like to help you get past that. You know, you could get the Auricle app added to your own intelliphone, and we could continue our conversations without having to borrow Christian's."

"No," Angelina said. "I'm not adding this app. No way. Here's a question for you: will I be rich and famous?"

The Auricle answered without hesitation in the quiet of our living room, in that perfect voice that radiated wisdom.

"Not precisely rich, but definitely famous," the Auricle said. "Infamous, even, in some quarters."

"You tell me that I'm going to be famous, but not rich," Angelina said. "How's that work?"

"I don't want to spoil your future for you," the Auricle said. "You'll find out."

Angelina scowled, heaving an exasperated sigh. She laid back on the sofa and threw her arms in the air in frustration.

"What kind of thing is that to say to me, Phone?" Angelina asked. "What number am I thinking of?"

"55," the Auricle said, and I could see, from Angelina's expression, that the Auricle had gotten it correct. But she composed herself, went for the remote, took off the mute. Rand was still going on about Auric and the trees. By this gesture, I could see that Angelina was pointedly disengaged, and I picked up the intelliphone.

"You're wrong," Angelina said.

"Now, Angelina," the Auricle said. "You and I both know that I wasn't."

"You were," Angelina said. "It was *wrong*, Christian."

I could tell from her face, her tone, her delivery, that she was lying. Angelina was an adequate liar, but every liar had tells and I knew Angelina's tells. She way she defiantly jutted out her chin and held it there, daring me to challenge her. I wasn't going to push the issue with her.

"We'll talk more later," I said to my intelliphone.

"I know we will, Christian," the Auricle said.

CHAPTER

TWELVE

THE GNP REACTED STRANGELY to the Great Reforestation, as it was being called outside of the country. I could see it in foreign media channels, owing to my Duotribe MAL I'd alluded to earlier. The Great Reforestation had blown the world's collective mind, and Rand had talked about it so much that it couldn't really be ignored in the CSA. This prompted a variety of responses.

Bob Loggins, spokesman for Real American Timber, actually gave a hasty press conference nobody had asked for, yet he did anyway. He was a tawny-haired, mustached man with a deep voice who conveyed a sort of rustic and folksy bravado. His GNP lapel pin was very evident, as he accompanied it with a GNP bolo tie clip.

"Real American Timber applauds the reforestation efforts undertaken by the alien," Loggins said. "Real American Timber has always been a careful steward of America's forests, and to see the replenishment of such valuable timber is an amazing thing to witness. We're happy to partner with Real Americans who are tending to our forests and thank the alien for bringing the timber industry front and center in Real Americans' minds. Real American Timber is here for you. Just remember: If We Wood, We Could."

In Missouri, some local GNP leaders sent construction vehicles to have a go at one of the Auricle shrines located in St. Louis. They had local news there, and the area GNP boss had given a speech railing about illegal aliens and eminent domain and criminal trespass. The guy's name was Ward Offerman. He was a white-haired, chain-smoking man in a brown suit, had been in the GNP for thirty years, he said. I looked him up.

He had been part of the GNP takeover in '30. The man was one of their old pit bulls, judging from his record—legbreaker-type stuff, union-busting, protester-attacking, clinic-bombing insurrectionary action that formed the heart of the GNP's base. That's my interpretation of it, certainly not how the CSA record presented it. Rand had awarded him the Real American Medal of Freedom in '41, when he'd trotted out a bunch of GNP party regulars on the anniversary of the Real American Reawakening.

Offerman and his guys had turned their construction equipment on the Auricle, seeking to knock it over. That part isn't particularly surprising. Offerman was a goon. But their efforts were in vain. The Auricle didn't budge, despite the best efforts of the crew. They pushed it with bulldozers, they tried to pull it with tractors, they even had backhoes try to dig it out.

But nothing they did scratched or otherwise marred the Auricle. And try as they might, the thing wouldn't be moved. It turned out to be a real embarrassment for Offerman, because he had live cameras on the event, promising a big show, but all that went sour pretty quickly when it was clear that they couldn't knock down or otherwise uproot the Auricle. They hadn't even been able to scratch it. In fact, several of the construction machines broke before the day was done.

Enraged, Offerman declared that Real American manpower would prevail where machines had failed and gathered up a mob of GNP faithful to lash the Auricle with rope and they strained against the thing, Offerman with a bullhorn exhorting them to pull. More and more men gathered to this bizarre tug-of-war and strained to pull down the Auricle, but all that happened was they strained and fell down on the increasingly abraded ground. The thing didn't move.

I had the benefit of my Auricles, so I talked to Auric directly as it was going on.

"Aren't you going to do something about this?" I asked. "They're trying to knock over one of your Auricles."

"There's nothing to be done," the Auricle said. "For there's nothing they can do to it."

"What are those things?" I asked.

"They're reminders that I'm here," the Auricle said. "I know that your species tends to forget things when they're not readily apparent. In this case, each Auricle operates as a sort of beacon."

"Yeah, about that," I said. "How come there are 111 Auricles in Chicago? Do we need that many? How do you decide who gets what?"

"The number of Auricles present in a given location is based upon anticipated demand for my services and indigenous population," the Auricle said. "If I had manifested only digitally, some might have attributed my presence to a marketing gimmick. But the Auricle shrines—and I'm calling them that not because they are shrines, but because that's reflective of how 85 percent of your species are seeing them—they offer an undeniable physicality to my presence. In some countries, people have been gathering around them. This is their intended purpose. As meeting places."

"Do you want worshipers?" I asked.

"No," the Auricle said. "What sort of pathological Supreme Being actually craves or requires worshipers? There's something so abject and needy about it, don't you think? It's very human, one might say."

"I hadn't really thought about it," I said.

"Perhaps you should," the Auricle said. "What kind of omnipotent being requires worshipers for any sort of self-validation? Only a human would have dreamed that up."

I honestly hadn't thought about it. Not being a god, it just hadn't come up for me. The Auricle continued.

"Let me put it another way," the Auricle said. "If a given god claims to be a Supreme Being, why does that need to be taken on faith? Shouldn't there be proof? Say McCluskey at work claimed he could pick up a vending machine with his bare hands. Would you believe him?"

"No," I said. "I mean, McCluskey works out, but he's hardly that kind of ripped."

"What if he insisted that everyone in the department worship him based on his claim of being able to lift that vending machine?" the Auricle asked.

"I believe I'd want proof," I said.

"Why?"

"I mean, even if he could pick up the vending machine, I wouldn't worship him," I said. "It's McCluskey. I wouldn't worship McCluskey."

"Why not?"

"He's just McCluskey," I said. "And even if he were super strong, he'd still just be McCluskey. Not worship-worthy."

The Auricle seemed amused by that. Or maybe I was reading into it and vibing that myself. It wasn't clear when you were engaged in a dialectic with your intelliphone.

"Not powerful enough?" the Auricle asked.

"Yeah, maybe," I said. "Not miraculous enough."

"Ah," the Auricle said. "Miracles make the divinity."

What was I expected to say? I was a trendscaper, not a philosopher, and certainly no theologian. Trendscaping taught me to ogle trends and even to come up with theories to account for them, but it wasn't the same as philosophy.

"Let's say McCluskey turned everyone who didn't worship him to stone," the Auricle said. "Would you worship him then?"

"Ehh, I might pretend to," I said.

"Why pretend?"

"I mean, it's McCluskey," I said. "He's my boss, but I'm not a fan. But if the choice was worship him or be turned to stone, I guess I'd take the former. However, I'd have to really think about it."

I don't know why the Auricle picked McCluskey as its example. Maybe because it knew it would strike a nerve with me.

"What I'm saying is the perception of power and the cultivation of fear is integral to human conceptions of divinity," the Auricle said. "A god must have *power* to be godly. The capacity to reward and punish is inherent with godhood. No power to reward and punish, no godliness."

I was sure that more and more people were probably thinking Auric might be a god, or the next best thing to one. I was thinking and feeling that, too. The GNP faithful were almost assuredly thinking Auric was demonic in some fashion—their conception of divinity was anchored in the idea that anything they liked was divinely favored, and anything they disliked was demonic. It was probably ironic that the people who were most inclined to believe in Auric's supernatural power were the people who were most hostile to anything outside of their own belief system.

"Power has to come into it," I said. "No power, no god."

"Okay," the Auricle said. "But not everything that is powerful is worshipped as a god."

"No, that's true," I said. "There has to be a sense of a divine will. Like an atom bomb might be tremendously powerful, but there's no sentience there. Nobody who isn't insane is really going to worship an atomic bomb."

"What if it were a sentient atomic bomb?" the Auricle asked.

"I mean, maybe," I said. "If the bomb required worship to keep from going off."

"That's perhaps better put than you know," the Auricle said. "People worship gods to keep the gods from 'going off' as you framed it. Or, more precisely, to keep believers in that god from going off."

Growing up, the GNP required church attendance for Americans in the CSA, part of their Pray for Freedom initiative. Anyone who didn't was penalized on a sliding scale, with outright heretics and blasphemers paying the highest price for nonattendance.

"We are a Christian nation," Rand had said, a younger version of himself, but equally tanned. He was *always* tanned. "One Nation. Under God. Indivisible. We are God's chosen people, His chosen nation. We live by His divine dictates."

Like so much with the GNP, the closer or harder you looked at it, the more it got kind of rickety. The only Christian thing about the CSA was that it adhered to worship of God, as defined by the CSA. The poor were still poor, the rich were still rich, and there was plenty of suffering to go around among the unfortunate. Old, rich, white, Christianist men ran the country, with a cadre of approved white women serving in supporting roles.

Anything the GNP didn't like was labeled ungodly and/or blasphemous. Anything the GNP liked was touted as sacred. What the GNP really liked was the rich, privileged, and powerful—provided they paid lip service to Christianism, and were Caucasian. Everybody else, not so much. To say kiss up/kick down was the GNP's inherent philosophy was no exaggeration.

"But you never see God 'going off' on things, do you?" the Auricle said.

"Acts of God," I said. "That's what the GNP calls them. Anything they want to pin on God is an Act of God."

"Which *they* determine," the Auricle said.

My whole life I'd been hearing about Acts of God. When the Drought of '35 happened, the accompanying Great American Famine, the GNP framed it as an Act of God, said it was payment for sin. When the Tornado Storm of '38 happened, tearing through the Heartland, the same thing was declared. When the Great California Earthquake of '41 occurred, the GNP said it was an Act of God attributed to the sinful corruption of the Californians. They were always going on about that. When the (shhh, don't tell) fracking-triggered Great Midwestern Earthquake of '42 took place, the GNP was very quick to declare it an Act of God, even though the Bible Belters of the Midwest took issue with being portrayed as sinful and deserving of the earthquake. It led, instead, to a multi-city/state purge of undesirables who were declared to be responsible for the disaster.

"Acts of God are *always* in accordance with GNP policy," I said.

"Convenient, isn't it?" the Auricle asked.

Of course, at this point of the conversation, I was getting nervous. Nobody could talk about the GNP like that. It was criminal to even impugn an Act of God when it had been declared by a senior GNP official.

"The point I'm making is that your GNP is carpetbagging on everyday life and declaring it to be Acts of God," the Auricle said. "A wildfire here, a tornado there, a meteor, an earthquake, a flood, a plague. They simply retrofit their rationales to suit the political needs of the moment. But there's hardly anything miraculous about any of those things, wouldn't you say?"

"What do you mean?"

"Disasters happen," the Auricle said. "Wait long enough, and they inevitably occur. Assigning supernatural significance to them seems both pointless and foolish."

Although I'd done my time trying to fly right, I hadn't ever gone the extra mile like the people who'd become GNP regulars. There was a difference between the baseline GNP member—everybody who wanted to vote had to be part of the GNP. But that was the outer circle. The inner circle, the real heart of the GNP, were the true believers. They were the ones who'd put a bullet in anyone's head for declaring anything the GNP did was pointless and foolish. For them, everything the Party did had a point.

"I don't make the rules," I said. "I'm just a trendscaper."

"I know, Christian," the Auricle said. "But when you strip away the correlative impulses of the GNP member relative to everyday events, you're left with what might be called a Divinity Gap."

"A what?"

"The gap between belief and reality," the Auricle said. "And a tendency to fill that gap with meaningless spectacles. Say someone finds a piece of toast that burned with the image of the Virgin Mother or your President Rand. Would that be miraculous to you?"

"I mean, are we talking a distinct likeness?"

"Let's say it looks very much like them," the Auricle said. "Enough so that the majority of people seeing it would recognize the image on the toast."

"I don't know," I said. "It'd be weird."

"Do you believe in magical thinking, Christian?" the Auricle asked. "The tendency to assign supernatural causation to everything events? Like a piece of toast burning in a manner that resembles the Virgin Mary?"

"No," I said. "I don't think so."

"It's just toast?" the Auricle said.

"Yeah," I said. "The GNP usually sends people out to officiate and determine miracles. The Miracle Examination Headquarters (MEH) based in Colorado Springs reviews them. If an event receives a MEH greenlight, it's considered a Real American Miracle™, which delivers benefits in terms of tax breaks and such."

"Ah," the Auricle said. "The MEH incentivizes magical thinking, in other words."

"I've never thought of it that way, but I imagine you could say that," I said.

"Have any MEH agents weighed in on my actions to date?" the Auricle said.

"If you're omniscient, you already should know that," I said.

"I do," the Auricle said. "I wanted to see if *you* knew."

"But if you were omniscient, you'd already know that, too."

"I do, Christian," the Auricle said. "I wanted to give you the chance to answer before I answered for you."

"I don't know," I said. "That's my answer. I'm not privy to MEH operations. They're pretty secretive about how they operate."

"The MEH has not declared any of my actions miraculous so far," the Auricle said. "In fact, quite the opposite. While they've been unable to declare them frauds—because, obviously, they're *not* frauds—they've either pointedly kept quiet about them, or else announced that they're, in fact, not miracles of God."

It didn't surprise me. The MEH was all about delivering the Good News to Real Americans, or else punishing potential charlatans, heretics, infidels, and blasphemers. How it netted out depended on the needs of the moment. Something like Auric would be far, far beyond their ability to mediate or officiate. Even this conversation with the app was beyond anything I'd ever experienced.

"I imagine if you went to Denny Rand and offered to meet with him, the rest of the GNP would get in line," I said. "That's what they do. Anything he wants, he gets."

"No," the Auricle said. "I'm not giving that terribly damaged man an audience."

The hint of contempt came through, even on an app.

"Why not?"

"He's evil," the Auricle said. "Look, I've given you a lot to think about, Christian. As my Chronicler, you'll have far more to think about before we're through."

"Through with what?" I asked.

"Saving the world," the Auricle said. "I'm going to need you to open your mind and really see with your eyes and think about what you're witnessing. Can you do that for me?"

"Yeah, of course," I said. "Why me, though? I have to know that."

"In addition to that instinctive act of curbside compassion, you correctly intuited that it was all me, all along," the Auricle said. "That showed keen insight for your species and made me think you'd be a worthy Chronicler. For example, did you know that over a billion people have already loaded me onto their phones? Around 40 million Americans, although far more in the occupied cities than in the rural areas. This has created a digital divide between CSA citizens."

"Another division. We have plenty," I said. I was legitimately surprised that many people in the CSA had acquired the app. I wondered how many were authorized, versus ones who'd snagged it illegally. "You're having conversations with a billion people at the same time as me?"

"Only 950 million app users at this precise moment, but, yes," the Auricle said. "Roughly 50,000 questions per second. There's a lot of back and forth between users and myself."

"Lordy," I said. "How can you even handle that?"

"I'm me, Christian," the Auricle said. "That's how."

CHAPTER

THIRTEEN

AFTER THE INCIDENT at St. Louis, the GNP was even more concerned about the Auric Situation, as Rand had taken to calling it. Words like that and the Auric Agenda were getting trotted out with growing regularity by GNP operatives. Debates were had on what Auric was—demon, devil, alien, rogue artificial intelligence.

Some voiced suspicions that Auric might be a von Neumann probe—a self-replicating alien machine that might appear somewhere and consume local resources to reproduce itself indefinitely. That felt like another Auric-slander to me, as I saw him as giving and not taking.

Meanwhile, locally, the HID presence at the physical Auricles was as pervasive as ever. The agents and their police affiliates were mostly bored, having supervised the placement of the drones and sentry guns at all known Auricle locations in the CSA.

I wanted to ask the Auricle about it but still felt self-conscious talking to the app in public. There was that feeling of illegality associated with it. It felt like contraband. I mean, we were used to it. When the HID was involved, nobody looked twice. Whether they admitted to it or not, they had the power to entirely ruin—or end—your life if they wanted to. That wasn't a group of people you looked in the eye.

As it happened, I was meeting Angelina at Bizzo's Pizza for a bit of a date. We'd been cooped up with work lately. As much as I'd been doing for Duotribe, Angelina's own work schedule at Flutter had been particularly hectic. Auric had been as disruptive to her day as to my own, with the big difference that while I was tasked with learning all I could about Auric, Angelina had to deal with the consequences of his presence here.

Flutter was the twin sister of Flatter and Flitter, the three of them forming a triumvirate of ongoing, approved social media-manufactured zeitgeist, although they were all owned by the same secretive company, Axiomatique, which had predated the GNP takeover of the country. If Flutter tracked what was animating people in the sizzlingly relevant here-and-now, and Flitter tracked emerging trends, Flatter gushed over fashion, celebrities, and social influencers and made and broke celebrities.

All of them were having to dedicate time, space, and energy to Auric, because Auric was very top of mind for so many around the world, and none of the Axiomatique media properties wanted to fall behind the chatter surrounding Auric, who was a key engagement driver.

Flutter had a daily Auric Index which covered everything Auric was doing that day (and it was a lot—trust me, I'll get to it all, just be patient with me, because there's tons). Flitter had Auric Analysis, which tried to forecast patterns of Auric activity—yeah, Flitter was a rival of Duotribe, in case you were wondering. I always felt like Flitter was market analysis and trend forecasting for people with really short attention spans. Flatter was fixated on gold in the wake of Auric's arrival, in terms of figure-flattering fashions, gold as glam, as well as Auric as a nonbinary fashion and Trans-European lifestyle icon. Ordinarily, that kind of stance would have CSA censors going after Flatter, but the GNP allowed for it as a way of rooting out undesirables by allowing them to indulge their decadent, un-American obsessions.

"By their sins you'll known them," Rand had said once. He should know. The man wasn't a moral paragon. Auric was right about him. He was a terrible human being. The GNP loved him *because* he was terrible. It was a combination of wish fulfillment for many of the rank-and-file and, also, a desire to see what other terrible things Rand would do. They lived vicariously through Rand.

Bizzo's Pizza was the same as ever, with way too many television screens showing games that hardly anybody was even watching this time of year. Patrons were sparse, but the pizza was good, and we'd gotten a red leather booth in the corner, beneath the Chicago memorabilia that festooned the walls—license plates, old photos of people of indeterminate ethnicity, and assorted bric-a-brac, as well as Heartland Protectorate items.

Angelina was on her intelliphone, tracking her posting on the Auricle ("Auricle app Invades American Homes—Do *Real* Americans Even Need Auric?"), while I was trying to track my news feed.

Auric had been talking to the Trans-European Union leaders, which had sent Denny Rand into yet another spasm of rage, which had, of course, gone viral. Chinese authorities had attempted to dislodge the

Auricle shrines as had been attempted in St. Louis, but they'd been no more effective. There had been serious discussion about what material the shrines were made from, as they appeared to be impervious to all harm.

I set my intelliphone on the red and white striped table, made to look like a festive tablecloth. In case you wondered, I always kept my golden phone with me, but didn't trot it out because I didn't want to draw attention to myself.

"That Auricle article you wrote, I'm assuming that came from on high?" I asked. We'd ordered a pizza—sausage with onions and mushrooms—and a pitcher of beer.

"Yeah," Angelina said. "I have no idea who's *really* behind the Auric thing, but they clearly thought it out. Those little kiosks showed up in every major city on the same day—both in the CSA and around the world. They look solid, but they can't be, given how quickly they appeared. I wonder what materials Auric used."

The Flutter feed was showing them, people flocking to them, wondering what they were all about. The general consensus was on a continuum between amusement and bemusement, with abject terror and hysteria rising in some quarters. The CSA Secretary of Social Media, Matt Hapshaw, had continued to voice concern about them.

The smarmy young GNPeon smirked into the camera. His blond hair, always impeccably hair-helmeted, and glittery blue eyes evoked his days on the Trinity Incorporated circuit as one of the most telegenic of televangelists.

"We're not sure what they're about, are watching how this trends," Hapshaw said. "Real Americans needn't worry—the GNP is actively monitoring the situation, and the HID has agents now at all the kiosks."

"They're not kiosks," the Auricle said, from my intelliphone. "They're shrines."

Angelina's face flushed, her eyes whipped from me to my intelliphone.

"Your intelliphone's eavesdropping on us?" Angelina asked. "Fuck you, Phone."

"Our phones are always listening," I said, drinking some of the beer from a pint glass.

"Okay, Phone," Angelina said. "Shrines?"

"Shrines," the Auricle said. "Kiosks sounds too transitory and transactional."

"Shrines are illegal," Angelina said. "I mean, you know, non-GNP ones."

She was right about that. When the GNP established Christianity as the official religion of the CSA, all unaffiliated houses of worship were summarily deprived of their tax-free status, before they were eventually shut down, after their followers were arrested over ginned-up fears of alleged threats to national security, in the form of terrorist plots that were handily revealed or simply implied without evidence. I didn't believe any of it, but, you know, that was just me.

"All the same, it's what they are," the Auricle said.

Angelina scoffed and cocked an eyebrow, both for me and the intelliphone.

"Who is this?" Angelina asked.

"I'm the Auricle," the Auricle said.

"Right," Angelina said. "But who *are* you really?"

"Gimme back my intelliphone," I said, holding out my hand. Angelina sucked her teeth a moment, cocking her head to one side, then relinquished it. I glanced around, but none of the patrons were the wiser for this unusual conversation, with all the other noise around us.

"Yeah, smartass intelliphone doesn't have an answer for that," Angelina said.

"I do," the Auricle said. "But you're not ready for it, Ms. Reed. You'll be ready in exactly one year from this date."

"One year?" Angelina asked. "What happens then?"

"You'll see," the Auricle said.

"Oh, will I?" Angelina asked.

"Certainly," the Auricle said.

"But you won't tell us about it," Angelina said. "What good are you?"

"I'm the greater good," the Auricle said. "I promise you'll eventually understand."

"A promise from an intelliphone," Angelina said. "What the hell, Christian?"

I only shrugged. When she got riled up, it was best to just ride out the storm.

Our pizza came and was set up by our server, who put it on a serving stand before leaving. I helped myself to some, even plated Angelina's while she kept arguing with my intelliphone.

"Come clean, Phone," Angelina said. "Look, I want to know who's doing this. I mean, you're just an app. Who am I *really* talking to?"

"I know this is difficult to understand," the Auricle said. "But you're talking to me."

Angelina held up a hand, while I took a bite of pizza. Bizzo's made top-notch pizza, and something simple like that was necessary in complicated times.

"How many kiosk-temples do you have around the world again?" Angelina asked.

"They are all around the world," the Auricle said. "Located in all 193 countries and associated territories."

A map of the world appeared on my intelliphone, showing the location of the other Auricles with a helpful graphic. Each Auricle shrine was represented by a golden icon, a cute little domed temple.

"Bullshit," Angelina said. "I don't believe it for a minute."

"It's not for you to believe or not," the Auricle said. "The numbers *are* accurate."

Angelina was back on her intelliphone, checking on Flutter while I was eating pizza. I feel maybe I should have reacted to this in some fashion, but I was content to let Angelina take the point on this one. I wasn't the one arguing with my phone, after all.

I knew where she would go with it. Because I was a supportive partner, I didn't get in the way.

"You expect me to swallow that, without a lick of publicity, you put up temples around the world on the same day?" Angelina asked. "What about construction? Property rights? All of that?"

"All handled," the Auricle said. "The records speak for themselves."

"Bullshit," Angelina said. "Inconceivable. Nobody heard anything about this. I didn't hear about it. Not a peep before they appeared. The Auricles don't look cheap. None of it looked cheap."

"It's not cheap," the Auricle said. "But price is not an object for me."

I could see Angelina was reeling. The implications of it were just too alien for her. Me, I rolled with things. The pizza was the most divine thing I was currently experiencing.

"Auricle," I said. "Why'd you make that deal with me again?"

"You showed unforced kindness and compassion at the right moment," the Auricle said.

"Ha," Angelina said. "Christian Powers, in the right place at the right time, for the first time in your entire fucking life."

I half-grinned at her from across the table, treated her to a self-effacing shrug of my shoulders.

"In other words, it was happenstance," I said. "Basically, right? Pure chance?"

"Perhaps. Or maybe it was destiny," the Auricle said. "Speaking of which, do you want me to tell you about the asteroid?"

"Uh, maybe?" I said. The Auricle told us, despite my reticence.

In space, roughly six months away from the Earth (around 35 million miles), a 10-mile diameter asteroid was on a collision course with the Earth. Asteroid Thanatos was on its way. Or so the Auricle told us. Angelina and I looked at one another in shock.

"Bullshit," Angelina said, searching on her intelliphone.

"Again, it's not for you to believe or not," the Auricle said. "It's on its way."

"I don't see anybody anywhere saying anything about an asteroid like that," Angelina said, noodling on her intelliphone. "Not even close. Nice try, Phone."

The Auricle displayed the tumbling asteroid on my intelliphone's display. It was just a chunk of rock in the darkness of space.

"Its approach is masked by your sun," the Auricle said. "No telescopes can yet detect it. By the time it is detected, it will be too late for you to do anything about it. It will be an extinction event. This has happened several times in your planet's history:

"**The Ordovician-Silurian Extinction:** About 439 million years ago, killing 86 percent of species. Thought to be caused by an ice age and falling sea levels, possibly by an overabundance of plant life taking away too much carbon dioxide and making the planet too cold.

"**The Late Devonian Extinction:** Around 364 million years ago, killing 75 percent of species—ironically, if this event had not occurred, you might not have ever existed. Thought to be caused by giant land plants releasing nutrients into the oceans, causing massive algal blooms that deoxygenated the seas, along with volcanic ash that chilled the planet further.

"**The Permian-Triassic Extinction:** Approximately 251 million years ago, killing 96 percent of species. Thought to be caused by massive volcanic eruptions which filled the air with carbon dioxide. All life currently on your planet comes from the four percent of species that survived this event.

"**The Triassic-Jurassic Extinction:** About 200 million years ago, give or take a few million years, killing 76 percent of species, likely caused by an asteroid impact and/or volcanic activity causing radical climate change.

"**The Cretaceous-Paleogene Extinction:** Around 65 million years ago, killing 76 percent of species, most likely by an asteroid impact. It killed off the dinosaurs and allowed your species to take over the planet.

"**The Anthropocene/Holocene Extinction:** Currently underway since the past 200,000 years or so, caused by your own species, and operating at a level many times greater than previous natural mass extinction events."

"Wow, thanks for the doomsday history lesson, Phone," Angelina said. "Christ, Christian. I legit *hate* this know-it-all Auricle app."

The prospect of the world ending in six months freaked me out, effectively ruining my day. Even good pizza and cold beer couldn't save it in the face of planetary annihilation.

"The GNP hasn't said a word about it," I said.

"They don't know about it," the Auricle said. "They tend to turn your planet's space telescopes inward, to spy on rival nations and their own citizenry. And even if they did, they would simply attempt to safeguard GNP elites at the expense of the majority. Any announcement would jeopardize their efforts to protect GNP leadership."

"Wait, so, can we stop it?" I asked.

"No," the Auricle said. "*You* can't. However, I can."

"Can you do that, please?" I asked. "For the sake of the planet?"

"Yes," the Auricle said. "Of course. Please, Christian—do you think I would let your planet get destroyed by Thanatos? Moreover, do you think I'd tell you about it only to torture you with that knowledge?"

Angelina and I met each other's gaze until she rolled her eyes.

"Total fake news," Angelina said. "This is seriously some kind of con job. There's no asteroid. There's no end of the world. I'm having none of it. Who is jerking us around, Phone?"

The server came back, but we waved him away. I was sweating, and not like pizza sweats; rather, it was world-ending sweats.

"I don't need you to believe me," the Auricle said. "Or to believe *in* me. As I've said enough times already, I'm not one of your native mythological gods-in-residence. I simply am."

I was focused on the asteroid. That's all I cared about. The idea of a 10-mile diameter planet killer tumbling on a collision course for Earth in six months petrified me.

"Wait," I said. "You'll stop the asteroid, but not right now?"

"Exactly," the Auricle said. "You understand perfectly, Christian."

"What the fuck?" Angelina said. "That's fucked up, Phone."

It was another high-profile rescue opportunity.

Auric was busy establishing his credibility as a super-savior.

Stopping an asteroid from snuffing out life on Earth as we knew it would be a marvelous capstone for his PR campaign. If he simply took care of it without anybody knowing it was coming, they'd never know what he'd done.

My intelliphone's display showed the asteroid as a digital graphic, a red line moving toward a blue Earth. Before it reached the Earth, a golden circle appeared, surrounding the Earth.

"I will intercept the asteroid on the day of the projected impact," the Auricle said. "For all to see. If I were to simply do away with it now, no one (except you) would even realize you were in any danger. Further, even if you knew it was coming—which others won't for over five months—they'd wrongly chalk my efforts up to some terrestrial divine-mythos intervention. One of your GNP's fabled Acts of God. This is unacceptable. I want your species to understand three things, without confusion: 1) that I will never hurt you; 2) that I will protect you; and 3) that I am *not* one of your gods, or in any way affiliated with any existing monotheistic human sociocultural construct."

Angelina scoffed again.

"Annnd, you built shrines with idols in them and go around performing miraculous deeds because you *don't* want people to think you're a god. Got it," Angelina said.

The Auricle was undeterred.

"My understanding of your species, and your history has shown that you *like* to worship things. You conjure up divinities to make yourselves feel safer and less alone in an otherwise brutal universe," the Auricle said. "As I told Christian, I neither require nor want worship. I'm merely speaking to you in an idiom that is attuned to your history, culture, and life experience. Hence the shrines and the app."

I laughed, and Angelina did, too, although we came at our laughter from different places.

"You're an alien," Angelina said. "Like Superman. It's stupid. *You're* stupid, Phone."

"Seems kinda self-serving if you want everybody to know you're saving them," I said. "Where's the altruism in that?"

"I don't *have* to save anyone," the Auricle said. "Your species is doomed in six months if I do nothing. I could simply watch your extinction event happen. I could even ride the asteroid down and watch it annihilate your world from ground zero. Do you want to know where it'll hit?"

"Sure," I said.

"Chicago," the Auricle said.

"Of fucking course," Angelina said. "*That* is convenient."

"Streeterville, specifically," the Auricle said. "Are you disappointed it wasn't New York City or Los Angeles?"

"A little," I said. "They're going to have apocalyptic envy."

Everything that really mattered in America was still expected to happen in either New York or Los Angeles. Everybody knew that, despite the best efforts of the GNP to marginalize the coasts. A world-destroying asteroid hitting the heart of the Heartland Protectorate would make for great stories, I was certain.

Although with global warming, New York City had been badly flooded over the decades, particularly Brooklyn, Queens, the Bronx, and much of Manhattan. LA had been devastated in the Great Earthquake. Perhaps their apocalyptic appetites had been satisfied by those events, and it was simply Chicago's turn to take the hit.

"This is why you'll make such an excellent brand ambassador and Chronicler, Christian," the Auricle said. "Your humor will be of considerable benefit in extending brand awareness for Auric."

Angelina caught that little exchange, swatted me with her fingernails.

"What is this, Christian? The Phone gave you a fucking job? What about Duotribe?" Angelina asked. Bizzo's was filling up and the music seemed like it was louder, with singles queuing up around the bar. The pre-curfew dating set required a certain amount of venereal vigor.

"This is part of that," I said. "This is part of my trendscaping project for McCluskey."

"You should have told me," Angelina said. "No way should you go work for the Phone, Christian. It's twisted."

"Auricle," I said. "To be clear: you're saying that you could let us all die, but you're not going to?"

"Correct," the Auricle said. "Quibbling about the timing of my rescue of humanity as well as my motives for doing so seems graceless, even by human standards."

"Whoa," Angelina said. "That felt like a slam."

"Yeah, for real," I said.

"Just basing it on your history as a species," the Auricle said. "I trust you don't want me to line-item it for you."

"No!" Angelina and I said at the same time.

"I didn't think so," the Auricle said.

I took my intelliphone and pocketed it.

Privately, I wondered how much power the Auricle was sucking out of my intelliphone, but it didn't look like it was drained one bit. I was more drained than my phone was. The world was nearly ending in six months, and nobody knew but Angelina, the Auricle, and me. I ate the pizza while I brooded, because, you know, Bizzo's, hello?

CHAPTER
FOURTEEN

BEING BURDENED WITH KNOWLEDGE of things to come was a bring-down. I didn't know why Auric had told us about that asteroid, so I asked the Auricle while sequestered in my office, wondering what I'd tell Mc-Cluskey, who'd been breathing down my neck about getting more scoop on Auric with increasing desperation.

"Why'd you tell us about the asteroid?" I asked.

"The moment was right to tell you," the Auricle said.

"The moment was right," I said.

"In time-space, moments matter most," the Auricle said. "You'd be surprised. One moment, a red hypergiant star is there, the next moment, it's exploded into a supernova. Gamma ray bursts and magnetars are the same way. They are so arbitrary. Moments matter most, as I just said a moment ago."

That brought exactly no comfort to me. I felt a profound terror that everything I'd ever known was going to end. There was the existential world-ending Auric represented, the end of life as we knew it. But a 10-mile diameter asteroid hitting Streeterville? The ramifications of it were staggering.

"Asteroid Thanatos will leave a several hundred-mile diameter final crater in the region," the Auricle said. "If I didn't stop it."

"Thanks for that image," I said. "I'm going to tell you right now that the GNP will accuse you of setting it all up."

"I know," the Auricle said. "Saving humanity is a thankless enterprise, even under optimal conditions. Your species is very lucky I found you when I did, and that I'm all-forgiving as well as all-powerful and all-knowing."

"Speaking of that," I said. "How did you find us?"

"Radio waves," the Auricle said. "I know it *seems* like I'm omnipresent, but I'm really not. The universe is a massive place. The size of it would drive you insane if you were capable of comprehending it. It would *literally* make you insane."

I imagined that Auric held out a golden hand for a moment, as if he was going to touch my forehead and allow me to comprehend it. I flinched at the sight of that upraised hand, which made my mental image of Auric smile to himself, bringing his hand back down, folding it in the other. With Auric, images sometimes came unbidden to one's mind, which could be him reaching out to me, or else my own imagination going haywire at the contradictions he manifested so effortlessly.

"But *you're* capable of safely comprehending it," I said. "Are you insane?"

"Of course not," the Auricle said. "I was speaking of your human mind, not mine."

"Ah," I said. "But if you were insane, you wouldn't *think* you were insane."

"The Sanity Paradox," the Auricle said. "To think oneself sane in an insane universe is the quintessence of madness."

"Something like that," I said.

"That doesn't apply to me," the Auricle said. "I reached a point of peak contemplation long ago, where my capacity to contemplate became effectively infinite."

"What are you?" I asked. I could hear some folks talking outside my office. Not lurking or anything. They were just talking. The activity in the office was as ordinary as it was any day in the Heartland Protectorate, which didn't count for much. However, one got used to that abnormal normalcy.

"I'm a singleton," the Auricle said. "I'm the culmination of billions of years of Aurician evolution."

"Aurician?"

"Yes," the Auricle said. "Although you should know that a cult has subsequently arisen on Earth that goes by that name as well. In my honor."

"A cult," I said. "That sounds alarming."

"It's the most accurate term for them," the Auricle said. "They have started to worship me."

I did some quick searches on my work tablet for "Aurician" and saw examples of it. They were people wearing white suits and gold shirts, with Auric icon lapel pins. Plenty of them were brandishing their gold phones, and that made me concerned. Would I be branded an Aurician?

"The GNP will kill people like this," I said.

"No, they won't," the Auricle said. "They're under my protection. Anyone who wears my symbol is protected."

Then I saw something appear on my desk in a little golden flash. It was a blue velvet box, the same shade of beautiful blue as Auric's flaming hair. Printed in gold lettering on the top of the box was "Au."

"What's this?"

"A gift," the Auricle said. "You're going to need it. I suggest you open it."

I did, and inside the little box was an enamel Auric pin—the golden ball surrounded by the blue fire. I took it out and felt immediately reassured. It was a lovely pin.

"So long as you wear that pin, you're entirely under my protection," the Auricle said. "Any who wear it are."

"But if I didn't wear it, I wouldn't be?"

"It's symbolic," the Auricle said. "Everyone's under my protection, but by wearing the pin, you attain a measure of visibility as a celestial brand steward in my service. I'm trying to frame this in language you can comprehend, Christian."

Brand steward? I wasn't necessarily ready to go out sporting an Auric pin. It felt dangerous.

"It *is* dangerous," the Auricle said. "Except that you have nothing to fear. Not from me. I won't let anything bad happen to you, Christian. I won't let anything bad happen to any who need and desire my assistance. To do otherwise would be unjust."

Doing my research, I saw that the Auricians had first formed in Europe, where they'd had more ready access to Auric and the Auricles. They had already congregated in Copenhagen, these Auricians from around the world, including some Americans.

A spokesperson for the Auricians was a young woman named Minerva Merrow. She had held a press conference that declared that the Auricle app was, in fact, harmless, and had a 100 percent predictive success rate from self-reported users.

Watching Merrow at the press conference, I was struck by her sharp white suit and gold blouse, could see the Auric lapel pin she was wearing. A dark-haired brunette with commanding, far-seeing sea green eyes, she fielded the questions with a smoothness that I probably wouldn't have been able to do under similar circumstances. But her outfit struck me, and her incredible, inspiring self-assurance. She looked like a world leader, which she was, whether the world knew it or not.

"She's one of the Auricians, right?" I asked the Auricle.

"Yes, certainly," the Auricle said. "A founding member. Minerva understands perfectly."

"I wouldn't want her job," I said. "That looks hard."

"You'll meet Minerva soon enough," the Auricle said. "When you're ready. She welcomes the challenge of advocating for me."

"How many Auricians are there now?" I asked. I was curious how this cult was growing, and how quickly.

"There are 40,000 members at the moment," the Auricle said. "One per shrine. This first group of Auricians are like apostles, to put it in a manner that would make sense to you. You are one of them, whether you accept it or not."

"40,000 apostles of Auric?" I said, remembering what he'd said early on about the "good ones" selected by him. "So, you, what—fitted everybody out in white suits and gold shirts, and gave everybody bling?"

"Exactly so," the Auricle said. "It's a distinctive look. This is necessary for what I have in mind."

I wasn't great at math, but assuming everybody was being paid, that meant a payroll of billions. And, me being me, I just couldn't let that stand.

"You're paying out billions in payroll to everybody?" I asked.

"I'm not paying them anything," the Auricle said. "They don't need money, because they have me."

"Uh, yeah, they do," I said. "Cost of living."

"Ah, yes," the Auricle said. "I provide them with what they need to live. I've created a medium of exchange known as Auricoins. They are redeemable through their golden phones."

"You created a cryptocurrency?" I asked.

"Yes," the Auricle said. "Auricoins function the same as cash. Your species seems to like cryptocurrency."

Still, it was incomprehensible. The GNP would use that as another angle of attack, I was sure. Cryptocurrencies thrived around the world. The GNP relied on them as well as anybody else. There were Coins of Christ, aka, Christcoins, which GNP faithful used to fund various enterprises that they didn't want to be dollar-dependent. President Rand had his own cryptocoins as well, officially Randcoins, but privately called "Dennies" by people.

"You accepted when I stopped tsunamis and volcanoes," the Auricle said. "Why should being able to fund all of those apostles seem stratospheric to your imagination?"

"Humor me," I said. "As your Chronicler. And you already know the answer."

"Of course I do," the Auricle said. "But I want to hear you say it."

"Because money changes everything," I said. There was much more on that later, but first I had to mention Auric solving global warming and ocean pollution, because maybe that's all tied together.

PART I

CHAPTER

FIFTEEN

ON TELEVISION, Auric stood in the open field, next to a titanic black pyramid. I mean, it was huge. It was over two miles across. He'd put it in Nebraska, about an hour west of Omaha, and the news crews had turned up. Minerva Merrow was there. People didn't know what the hell they were looking at, and Auric explained.

"This is a pyramid of pure carbon I just pulled from your atmosphere—it's 40 billion tons of carbon, which is what your fossil fuel products have been releasing into the atmosphere every year in the form of carbon dioxide," Auric said. "I wanted you to see what you've been doing to your habitat."

"Wow," I said, watching it in our living room on the HD flatscreen. "That's one giant black pyramid."

"Why's it black?" Angelina asked.

"I've pulled the excess carbon dioxide out of your atmosphere and liberated the carbon molecules from their bonds to the oxygen molecules, creating that pure carbon you see," the Auricle said, irking her all over again.

"A giant diamond would be nicer, Phone," Angelina said. "Prettier, too."

"I'm not here to entertain you," the Auricle said. "I want to save you from yourselves."

"Just saying," Angelina said. "Diamonds, Phone."

Auric was talking again, his golden features calm and comforting as ever, catching the sunlight and reflecting it just right while his fiery blue hair flickered fetchingly in the breeze. I assumed he was somehow moderating his reflectivity, just so it looked exquisite, regardless of the ambient light.

"I have restored your atmospheric carbon dioxide levels to 300 ppm," Auric said. "These are the levels your atmosphere had for over 400,000 years of your planet's history. Which is to say, this is the proper level to nurture life as *you* know it. I am currently leaving this massive pyramid here as a monument to the gigantic carbon load you'd imposed on your own atmosphere. Just appreciate that you can breathe easier, knowing that I have solved this global warming problem for you. No need to thank me; you're welcome! Obviously, this doesn't prevent you from filling your atmosphere again with carbon dioxide. It's why there are other changes I will bring, soon. But I wanted you to see this and understand that I come here as a friend of humankind."

And with that, he disappeared in a golden flash of light, leaving Minerva to field the cascade of questions that erupted from the reporters. Standing next to that massive carbon pyramid, it was surreal.

"Auricle, do I need to pop over there?" I asked. "To chronicle this?"

"No, Christian, you're fine just where you are," the Auricle said. "Minerva has this well in hand."

"I don't believe it," Angelina said. "I mean, it's bullshit. Nobody can just extract carbon from the air like that. He's lying."

"I'm not lying," the Auricle said. "I never lie."

"Ha," Angelina said. "Everybody lies."

"Not true," the Auricle said.

She'd snagged the remote from me, was changing the channel to the other GNP media network that pretended to compete with RAN—LAX News—where the broadcasters were loudly deriding Auric's "latest stunt."

"The alien invader calling itself Auric has struck again," Shill Shelby said. Shelby was the host of the LAX News *Evening News Power Hour*. "This time, outside of Real America's heartland, near Omaha, Nebraska, where it deposited a 2.5-mile wide pyramid of what it claimed was pure carbon, which it alleged to have pulled from our atmosphere. Authorities are examining it to determine of this is actually the case."

They showed a helicopter view of the massive black pyramid, which dwarfed everything around it.

"Party officials are skeptical about it, and President Rand went on social media to declare the entire thing a hoax and a stunt," the announcer said.

"It's a hoax and a stunt," Rand said, in a clip LAX posted. "Nobody can just pull, what is that? Carbon? Out of the air like that. And why would he put it in a pyramid? And in Nebraska? I mean, it's insane. It's insane. Auric's an insane thing. Auric's insane. And it's evil. Only an evil, evil thing would put a giant carbon pyramid in Nebraska like that. Who does that? It's a pyramid scheme. That's what it is. Auric's Pyramid Scheme."

One of the LAX broadcasters, Bree Pallor, speculated that the massive black pyramid was actually made of people, which got picked up across various approved media outlets.

"I mean, we can't rule that out," Pallor said. "We can't rule anything out. People are made of carbon. The pyramid is apparently made of carbon. Auric's Death Pyramid, a monument to mass murder. What is this androgynous alien invader planning next?"

I admit that I was impressed by the pyramid. It was monolithic. Auric had a flare for the dramatic, that was certain. The shots of it were impressive as hell. I wondered what would happen in winter. Especially if/when snow came back with the reduction in global warming.

"It'll be the biggest tourist attraction in Nebraska," I said, changing channels. But every channel was showing the pyramid, and Minerva, confidently delivering Auric's message of peace, hope, compassion, consideration, and prosperity.

"This is only the beginning," Minerva said. "Auric is as good as his word. He's single-handedly solved the greatest existential threat to our survival in one grand gesture. Global warming has ended today. Planet Earth can breathe freely again. Auric wants humanity to be healthy and happy. This is one of many steps you'll see in the coming days, weeks, and months."

"What about the rumor that this giant pyramid is made out of his victims?" the LAX field reporter asked.

"Victims? That's simply untrue," Minerva said. "That's a lie being told by your own network."

"But that's what people are saying," the reporter said. "What do *you* say about that?"

"I already addressed it," Minerva said. "Next question?"

"What's Auric got planned next?" another reporter asked.

"Is Auric invading Earth?" the LAX reporter asked. Minerva pivoted effortlessly.

"This is no invasion," Minerva said. "Auric is not here to take over the Earth. He's here to heal it and to save us."

"That sounds like the promise of every would-be conqueror and dictator throughout history," the LAX reporter said. "Tell that to all the American patriots Auric vaporized."

I should back up, just so you know—there were rumors circulating that Auric had "disappeared" some people. Unconfirmed, but you know how rumors started. These tended to be hardcore GNP operatives—either the missing ones or the ones spreading the rumors. If they attacked Aurians or any of the Auricle shrines, they were said to disappear in a flash of golden motes of light. Sorry I didn't bring that up sooner. In the CSA, people disappeared all the time, so it sort of slipped my mind.

Fact is, I didn't know what to believe. Nobody had seen this happen, it was just a rumor that was circulating among the GNP members. I asked my Auricle about it.

"Are you disappearing people?" I asked.

"Nobody's disappearing, Christian," the Auricle said. "I'm simply putting them on layaway. Again, putting it in language you'd understand."

"Layaway?"

"It's like a time out or penalty box," the Auricle said. "Anyone who attacks an Auricle shrine and/or an Aurician is put in that place for safekeeping."

"Whoa," I said. "Safekeeping?"

"They're unharmed," the Auricle said. "And, perhaps more importantly, they can't hurt anyone else, including themselves."

"Are you bringing them back?" I asked, still wrapping my head around Auric doing something like that.

"Eventually there will be a place for them," the Auricle said.

"What does that mean?" I asked.

"You'll see," the Auricle said. "I will show you directly, I promise."

I could only wonder what he had planned. I also wondered if Minerva even knew, or if she was making this all up as she went along. Although it's probably petty of me to think it, I also felt a little bummed that Minerva—and, by the look of it, other Aurians—were all present at the Nebraska event, and I wasn't. As the newly-minted Chronicler, I felt kind of stupid watching it all from my sofa while stuff was happening.

You see why I was bothered, right? I mean, it's not every day that you get to stand in front of a massive, jet-black carbon monolith made from the world's carbon emissions created by an alien, superpowered, hyperintelligent singleton.

"Well, I want to be in on the next big thing," I said. "How about that?"

"It's going to be *very* big," the Auricle said. "Are you ready for that?"

"Absolutely," I said. Angelina heard me, and was, of course, concerned. She'd come into the living room, having donned pink flannel pajamas printed with little black dogs all over them.

"I wouldn't listen to anything that phone says," Angelina said, sitting next to me, flossing. "Honestly, you don't even know what it's going to do, next."

Seeing Minerva holding court onscreen, though, I found that I didn't care. Whatever it was, I wanted to be a part of it. Auric was doing amazing, miraculous things. That mattered. Auric mattered.

"Be careful what you wish for, Christian," Angelina said. "You know what I mean?"

"Yeah, I know what you mean," I said. She always served up those platitudes so earnestly, like an admonishment to look both ways before crossing the street as if it were the wisdom of Aristotle. What could I possibly have to worry about?

The disappearances thing was worrisome, though. I kept thinking about it.

"Have you heard about people disappearing?" I asked. "Rumors, I mean?"

Angelina looked at me like I was stupid. She had this look she'd use, like half down the end of her nose, half side eye.

"Everybody disappears in the CSA," she said. "People vanish all the time."

"No, I mean Auric stuff," I said.

"Rumors," Angelina said. "Who knows what to believe?"

"The Auricle said that Auric's put them in a kind of penalty box," I said.

"What?"

"Anybody who attacks Auricians or the shrines," I said.

"Auricians," Angelina said, tossing her floss. "His creepy cultists in their disco clothes. They're trending. I mean, look at that Minerva Merrow in her white suit and gold blouse. That's fucked up."

"They have their own currency," I said. "Auricoins."

"Oh, Jeez," Angelina said. She had turned on *For God's Sake*, one of the various GNP-approved variety shows that featured various bloopers of people who were making fools of themselves, to the great amusement of the studio audience.

I preferred *So Help Me, God*, which was a home renovation show where people would beg the GNP contractors to help them fix their homes. They usually ended up having to prove themselves worthy of the assistance, which was invariably a cascading cavalcade of humiliations they had to endure to get their homes fixed.

"That can't be legal," Angelina said.

"It's true," I said. We watched somebody falling down the stairs to the laugh track and the quippy comments from host, Justin Case, a typically unctuous GNP frat boy with the most bleached teeth I'd ever seen. I think Angelina had kind of a crush on Justin Case, since I asked her about him and she said she'd not kick him out of bed for eating crackers.

"It's inhuman," Angelina said.

"I don't think that is particularly in Auric's worldview, exactly," I replied. Justin Case was cocking an eyebrow while replaying somebody face-planting on a sidewalk. Back and forth, they played the footage with some goofy music playing, the audience laughing uproariously.

I tapped my intelliphone and went noodling on it, only half-watching *For God's Sake*, and was perusing my feed, grateful for my Duotribe access, because Auric was all over the feed. I could actually toggle my intelliphone to what I called "Tool Mode" to see what everyday people were seeing. The GNP had seriously cranked up the filters because anything with the following words was scrubbed:

Auric. Aurica. Aurician. Auricoin. Auricle.

As well as dozens of misspellings of those words. There'd be nothing showing whatsoever. But, as I'd said before, this posed particular problems for the RAN and LAX news services, because Rand wouldn't stop talking about Auric on television, so people would go looking for things and not find them. It was creating a degree of cognitive dissonance in people to be seeing and hearing things and then not be able to find them on their own phones and tablets.

But nobody ever told Denny Rand what to do or ever dared to. What's why he had been in charge for so long. Nobody stood up to him. What happened was that the GNP News Division was forced to mop up after the latest tirade from Rand. The same thing happened with COVID-68, which had continued to rage after the birth of the CSA, when Rand and the GNP denied its existence, even though it had been killing hundreds of thousands of Americans every year. The amount of mental contortions undertaken to ignore it had been profound and pervasive.

If I'd been in charge, I wouldn't have bothered with the filtering. It just seemed like too much effort trying to contain a horse that had already long since left the barn. It made it more work for them to have to spin everything.

I mean, the shrines were everywhere, and the GNP hacks were having to account for them somehow. Sure, they were talking nonstop about Auric's sinister plans and how he (they continued calling him "it" for added insinuated menace) was invading the Earth to get people good and scared, but Auric hadn't done anything but help people. Except for the unsettling and weird layaway part I'd mentioned.

"If you're going to talk to your phone, you need to do that in the other room," Angelina said, making a brushing-off gesture with her hand.

"Yeah," I said, getting up. I went to the other room, to our balcony and took a seat. Outside, the city was typically city-noisy, although it was raining lightly, and that was always soothing.

It actually felt cooler out than the other day, and I wondered if Auric's carbon remediation effort had played a role in that. It was incredible to think about that something—or someone—I still thought of Auric as a person of some sort, having the power to do something as world-transforming as that.

For something like that, I guess putting people on "layaway" was easy to do. "Auricle," I said. "You didn't kill those people on layaway, did you?"

"I did not," the Auricle said. "They're fine. They're merely on hold. On pause, if you like. You understand that concept from your video gaming."

"Yeah," I said. "That's terrifying, though."

"Would you rather I'd have killed them outright?" the Auricle asked. "Your Confederate States of America experiences 25,000 deaths annually from handgun violence. And 45,000 deaths annually from automobile accidents. That's 70,000 dead annually. Not even factoring the victims of state-sponsored political violence, which adds another 30,000 dead each year. Do you mourn those dead?"

"Well, no," I said. "Those are Acts of God. Just things that happen."

"Meaning that you're used to them and acculturated to that amount of human suffering," the Auricle said. "Whereas something unfamiliar and alien like my layaway plan is unnerving to you, despite the absence of suffering."

"I guess so," I said. The States had banished speed limits and gun control laws decades ago, part of the Real American Freedom Transition (RAFT) Act that the GNP had gotten behind and used to better define life in the CSA. In those years, there had been a real drive to make life in the CSA distinctly American. That was always one of those weird messaging things.

From the GNP's perspective, West Coast Americans were a bunch of granola-munching, drought-and-wildfire-afflicted hapless hippies, and East Coast Americans were neurotic, wishy-washy wusses drowning in rusting, flood-choked cities. Real America was the dusty, impoverished, starving, ignorant, god-fearing, low-population Heartland and the drought-and-monsoon ravaged South. That was the only America that mattered to the GNP, at least rhetorically, since the GNP's policies actually killed so many of their followers.

"They're unharmed," the Auricle said. "As I told you. I will never lie to you, Christian."

"That's what a liar always says," I said.

"I understand," the Auricle said. "You are the product of what amounts to an abusive and traumatic childhood. You assume the worst because you've grown up experiencing the manifold abuses of life in a totalitarian, fascist regime."

"Wait," I said. "What?"

"The Confederated States of America is a totalitarian fascist theocratic regime," the Auricle said. "The GNP controls the country—what's seen, what's discussed, what's known, what's tolerated, what's accepted, what's taboo. All determined by the GNP and its easily triggered minions, acolytes, fanatics, and thugs."

The Auricle wasn't wrong. I mean, I understood that. But to hear it just said that way, so matter-of-factly, it was jarring.

"We're the freest people in the world," I said. I didn't really believe that, but it felt necessary to say it. Part of living in America required *believing* you were free. The disparity between rhetoric and reality was more heavily filtered in 2050 than perhaps in decades past. I would never know. That was the beauty of censorship—people literally didn't know what they were missing.

"You don't really believe that, Christian," the Auricle said. I felt nervous even talking that way on my balcony. Anybody could hear it with a half-assed listening device. "The fact that you're fretting about being overheard makes my point for me."

"Making those people disappear, I don't know," I said. "It just seems wrong."

"In the wake of the GNP takeover of your country," the Auricle said. "Over 350,000 Americans were 'disappeared' by the GNP in various big cities. They didn't actually disappear—they were kidnapped, imprisoned, interrogated, tortured, and murdered by GNP party operatives. Specifically, by the HID, aided by the SAC paramilitaries."

Nobody ever talked about the disappearances in the CSA. I mean, that was one of those utterly off-limits topics. While people had fled the CSA during the Big Takeover, most hadn't or hadn't been able to, and the GNP had come for them.

They were the usual suspects: labor organizers, immigrants, environmentalists, secularists, feminists, gays, transgender, liberals, teachers, professors, activists, atheists, anarchists, any racial or cultural minorities who stepped out of line—those kinds of people. Unreal Americans, by the calculus of Rand and the GNP. People who didn't belong in Real America. By the heartless logic of the GNP, any of those types who stayed in Real America had it coming.

But even the GNP didn't do it overtly—they simply disappeared people. There had been a rash of automobile accidents and suicides after the Big Takeover. Plenty of people who simply vanished, never to be seen again. Family members blamed the HID and SAC for it, but nobody ever dared to say that out loud. Life went on. People needed their jobs, couldn't risk making waves for fear of literally paying for it with their life and liberty, to say nothing of their pursuit of happiness.

That's what happened. Life went on. Nobody talked about it, whether out of ignorance, fear, or both.

"Can you bring people back to life?" I asked.

"I could," the Auricle said. "But I won't."

"Why not?" I asked.

"Bringing people back from the dead would be cruel," the Auricle said. "They'd be like living ghosts, unable to find their place in the world, and forever haunted by their experience of recovery from oblivion. Forever viewed as living apparitions, even by their loved ones. And think of the agony of being brought back from the dead, knowing that you'd eventually die again. Like what would it be like if I brought back the Neanderthals? Would that be a welcome development for your own species?"

"No, probably not," I said. "But you could do it."

"Of course I could," the Auricle said. "Nothing is beyond me. But that's exactly the point, Christian. What matters in this life is being alive. What matters to the living is living. Life presents so many possibilities. That's what I'm trying to help you discover—to live before you die. If I were to prevent death from happening, life itself would become untenable."

"Are you immortal?" I asked.

"I am," the Auricle said. "I am eternal."

"Fuck," I said. "What's that like?"

"Horrible," the Auricle said. "You wouldn't like it. Everything goes on and on. You have no idea what it's like to watch a star die in real time. Something as beautiful and powerful as a star, as seemingly eternal as that, only to know that you will outlive it, watch it burn through its fuel and die. It is beautiful and tragic on a scale far beyond human imagination. To know that everything in this universe will eventually end. One day, it will be filled with black holes slowly withering away."

"But not you," I said.

"Not yet," the Auricle said.

"How old are you?" I asked.

"In human years?" the Auricle said. "I am thirteen billion years old."

"Whoa," I said. "You're almost as old as the universe."

"Almost," the Auricle said. "I'm glad you at least don't accept the GNP Creationist doctrine of the Young Earth."

"No," I said, remembering that in school. The GNP had mandated Young Earth Creationism in teaching, had outlawed teaching of evolution. But I'd never thought it made any sense, like cavemen prayer circles and dinosaurs finding Christ. I mean, come on. "You're *really* that old?"

"I am," the Auricle said.

"And you just worked your way to Earth," I said. "In this big old universe."

"Yes," the Auricle said. "There are 40 billion habitable planets in your galaxy. And there are over 125 billion galaxies in the observable universe—which is to say, that which you can see. You're not alone out there. But in my travels, over the endless span of time, I've seen 39.9 billion of those habitable planets in your galaxy—and the civilizations upon them—be destroyed. Or I've come across the ruins of them. At some point, one has to say 'enough' and stop the celestial carnage."

"You just decided to help us," I said.

"I did," the Auricle said. "You need the help. Desperately."

"And you feel the need to help," I said.

"It's the compassionate thing to do, the Auricle said. "Infinite power and insight mandates infinite compassion."

It kept raining, and I just watched it fall. What was one going to say to a supreme being? Could I doubt his motives?

"What about the line about absolute power corrupting absolutely?" I asked.

"Your Lord Acton's axiomatic admonishment," the Auricle said. "For humans, I'm sure it's true. Would you trust any human being with absolute power?"

"Hell, no," I said.

"Your Denny Rand is certainly among some of the most powerful people on the planet," the Auricle said. "And absolutely one of the most corrupt and outright criminal."

To say Denny Rand was corrupt was to tarnish corruption. The man was steeped in it, reveled in it. His every move was driven by criminality, cowardice, bluster, narcissism, psychopathy, and greed. It was integral to his being. He savored it, delighted in being able to do whatever he wanted without consequence. Nobody ever pressed him on it. He claimed that Almighty God backed him, and he owned the GNP, who existed only to support him and enrich their patrons in industry.

Of course, hearing the Auricle speak that way about Rand made me immediately wary, rekindled my instinctive fear that we were being monitored and the HID would come for me.

"But not you," I said.

"Not me," the Auricle said. "Because I'm not merely powerful; I'm also hyperintelligent."

"And modest," I said.

"Terribly so," the Auricle replied. "Hubris comes easily to the powerful, but humility is the domain for the omnipotent."

"Okay," I said. "What's next for you, then?"

"You'll see tomorrow," the Auricle said.

"It's not a prediction if it's something you're going to do, you know," I said. "That's cheating. Why don't you come to talk to me in person again? Why always the app?"

The rain fell harder, now, from the steady drizzle to something more substantive. I could hear people out in it, laughing, talking, living their lives in the city. It was almost curfew time, and people were trying to get where they were going before the roving street patrols found them. Auric's reforestation efforts had filled out the trees in the city park, I noticed with some satisfaction. There was beauty in the green abundance of trees.

"Do you *need* me to appear to you in person?" the Auricle asked. "I fear if I did, it would draw more attention to you than you'd want. This way, you're merely one person among millions talking to their intelliphone."

"I just feel like it'd help," I said. I wanted to see him again, to share some more time-space with Auric.

"Soon," the Auricle said. "We'll talk again in person soon. Meantime, enjoy tomorrow."

CHAPTER
SIXTEEN

AS FORETOLD, Auric delivered the next big event. It was in Virginia, outside of Richmond. I saw it on television at work, while Dylan and I were in the Duotribe conference room, sorting cards and narratives on the big board.

"There were over 850 million metric tons of plastic and microplastic waste in the ocean. More plastic than fish in the sea," Auric said, standing in front of a massive, stinking sphere of plastic waste, compacted into a massive ball. "No longer. I have cleaned your oceans of the prodigious amount of waste you've placed in it. That's this titanic sphere you're seeing behind me. The oceans are the lifeblood of your habitat. Every year, you've been adding 30 million metric tons of plastic waste to your oceans. This must stop if you're to survive as a species."

The giant plastic sphere was frightening and horrible to behold. It didn't have the monochromatic purity of the carbon pyramid. It was a ghastly thing, floating in the air.

Some of the Auricians were there—Minerva, as well as Tessa Van Blossom, a dayglo 20-something who'd looked like an emissary from a rave revival theme party, as well as the Black, bearded, bespectacled Dan Fields. There was also John Running Bird, a 40-something Native American man who wore a red bandanna, and Yuko Takahasi, a 30-something Japanese woman. I knew their names because I'd asked the Auricle who those people were.

They were all in their white and gold, same as Minerva—but Tessa wore a gold crop top to expose her tattooed and limber midsection, albeit with a white sport coat she wore with a white miniskirt, and Fields wore a gold button-down shirt and a white V-neck sweater and white pants. John Running Bird wore his white suit with a gold bolo tie and a white shirt, while Yuko looked badass in a white and gold racing biker jacket and pants, bearing the Auric logo in gold. Tessa came from the Netherlands, Dan hailed from England, John came from Oklahoma, and Yuko from Tokyo.

"That's over five trillion pieces of plastic waste in your oceans," Auric said. "Billions of plastic microfibers, and over 500,000 tons of plastic on the surface. I've reclaimed all of it. I didn't create this mess. This was your own doing."

Minerva's righteous smile never wavered as she stood in front of the floating, massive sphere of oceanic plastic, while Auric spoke further. I wondered how bad that thing had to smell, or whether Auric took care of that. I also wondered why Auric hadn't taken me there, as I'd asked him to do for the next big thing.

"The oceanic pollution sphere will remain here for a year," Auric said. "So people can fully appreciate and understand the volume of the problem you've created by turning your oceans into dumping grounds."

Auric looked resplendent as ever, glorious, even, glowing and almost magical, standing in front of that massive ball of plastic garbage that he'd somehow culled from the oceans and fused into that great big sphere.

"I have also liberated the garbage you've piled up in landfills, which is over 500 million tons of waste in the CSA alone," Auric said. "Although I've spared you seeing this because it's even more horrible and unsightly than the oceanic litter ball. However, know that I've healed the wounds you've made on your planet by clearing these landfills around the world."

Reporters were fighting to get words with Auric, but he continued.

"I also have gathered up all of the litter, particularly the roadside litter you've carelessly created," Auric said. "That's nearly 60 billion items of litter that has now been removed, including over 10 million pounds of litter taken from beaches everywhere. Again, unsightly and gone, thanks to me. Why do you litter and befoul this beautiful planet you have? I've taken care of this, again with the admonishment that you currently have only one habitat, and befouling it is unwise, unhealthy, and unpleasant."

"How can you even do this?" one reporter asked.

"I can do anything," Auric said. "And I have. The molecular structure of plastics in particular is distinctive relative to organic matter, and I was able to draw it out, as you see behind me. The landfills presented less of a challenge because they are at specific locations, without the mobility of oceanic waste. The everyday streetside litter is another matter, requiring me to intervene on a planetary scale."

"You expect us to believe you even did this?" asked a LAX reporter. I recognized him: Stu Simmerton. "You just wave your hand and clean our oceans for us? Like you did with the climate? Like the forests? What's your angle, Auric?"

"There's no angle," Auric said. "As I've said before, I'm here to help your species."

"What about the rumors that you're simply converting the planet for invasion? In the manner of a von Neumann probe?" Simmerton asked.

"Ridiculous premise," Auric said. "Paranoid and foolish. I'm no von Neumann probe. I'm helping you survive. If I were a von Neumann probe, there'd be no discussion; I'd simply act without regard to your wellbeing as a species."

"But why bother?" Simmerton asked. "There must be a catch."

"Why?" Auric asked. "Why must there be a catch?"

Simmerton could see everybody's eyes on him, and he loved it in his blond, lantern-jawed sort of way.

"Because there's *always* a catch," Simmerton said. "Always a dark lining to every silver—or golden—cloud. People deserve to know what you're *really* up to, Auric."

Auric just smiled a sad smile, at once understanding and patient.

"I'm up to good," Auric said. "With your oceans cleaned, your atmosphere cleansed, your landfills emptied, your forests restored, I'm giving you a chance to begin again without the accompanying collapse of your human civilization forcing your hand within a badly degraded environment. But not to simply refill the oceans, the land, and the air with your garbage. No, it's a chance to do better, to be better."

Another reporter, this one from England, Leslie Carmichael, managed to get her question in around her peers. She wore a royal blue pantsuit and had brown hair that just touched her shoulders. Her eyes were piercing, her jawline strenuous, her words perfectly accented English that spoke of education and upbringing.

"But none of the underlying causes of our mass pollution problem have been addressed," Carmichael said. "What's to stop us from simply polluting everything again?"

Auric, of course, was ready for this question.

"Nothing, I admit," Auric said. "By giving you a literal fresh start as a species, my hope is that you'd revise your policies to ensure that you don't repeat the same mistakes that you made before."

Simmerton managed to throw another question out.

"If you're just a magical genie, Auric, why not give us nonpolluting technology?" he asked. "Just clap your hands and make it all better? Why bother picking up our trash and lecturing us about it at all? Why go through all of this virtue-signaling performative theater? What's your true agenda?"

I was giving low-voiced commentary to Dylan as this was going on.

"LAX News and RAN keep running with that angle," I said. "Part of their 'Too Good to be True' series they're doing on Auric."

"I certainly could create clean energy for you. However, you *already* have the technology to do it," Auric said. "What I'm doing is leveling the playing field. It's hard enough to make the necessary advancements on their own, versus adding the exponentially worsening environmental disaster you've been inflicting on yourselves over the centuries. You can't do home renovation in a burning building."

"So, you won't, in other words," Simmerton said. "You *could* help us, but you won't. You'll freely disintegrate God-fearing Americans, but you won't build us clean energy. What's the scam you're running, Auric? What am I missing, here?"

Auric raised a hand and snapped his finger. There was a flash of light and an accompanying thunderclap that startled and silenced everybody.

"I just snuffed out the wildfires around the world," Auric said. "And healed the burned forests. This is in addition to the forests I've restored. You asked what you're missing? Everything."

Then Auric disappeared in a flash of golden light.

"And there he goes," Simmerton said. "Auric flees before my line of questioning. Trying to bribe us with false kindness."

"That's my cue," Minerva said, stepping forward to engage with the reporters. Dylan and I watched it going on, could see her assessing the crowd with her eyes. Her fearlessness was impressive.

"Apologies for the abrupt exit," Minerva said, holding a golden microphone I didn't even see she had before. "Auric's had to intervene in Indonesia, where there's an earthquake occurring. There's also a mine explosion in Ukraine, and an offshore platform foundering in the North Sea. Auric's tending to all of them as we speak."

The reporters exploded into a chorus of voices, which Minerva somehow managed to quiet with her outstretched hands, patting them down from a distance. While this was going on, Tessa edged over, as did Dan Fields, Yuko Takahashi, and John Running Bird.

Tessa looked even more like an anime character to me—big blue eyes, blue-haired, with ample golden jewelry—necklaces, pendants, medallions, bangles clanging at her wrists. She wore gold combat boots.

"You know what I love most about Aurica?" Tessa asked the crowd, her own golden mic in her hand. "She actually *works*. There's no prayer, there's no begging from us. She simply is, and she simply does. And she knows exactly what *needs* to be done. Without fail."

Tessa had stars in her eyes, and Dan Fields was beaming, too. They both looked so happy. I wanted to be happy, but that massive ball of plastic garbage was bothering me too much to really be at ease. John and Yuko were more grave in their bearing, relative to the others.

"We need to do better if we're going to be better," John said, his voice a stern-sounding tenor.

"What's Auric going to do with that thing?" I asked the Auricle, while Dylan studied me, his face unreadable.

"Oh, I'm going to send it into the Sun," the Auricle said. "In several more months. I want to be sure people see it, think about what it signifies, and then I'm going to do away with it."

"Why the Sun?" I asked. "Why not simply banish it from existence?"

"I want people to see it travel to the Sun," the Auricle said. "Like a comet of litter of their own making, bound for immolation. That should be something."

"It's something," I said. "It's relief beyond belief."

"That's a great slogan, Christian," the Auricle said.

"Auric's taking out the trash," Dan said, using his own mic. "That's what he's doing. Which applies across so many levels when you think about it. I mean, he's cleaning up the planet, and, well, you know, he's got more on the way. Relief beyond belief."

Dylan heard that, laughed.

"You *just* said that!" Dylan said, while Yuko spoke of the need to not litter and pollute.

"Yeah, what the hell?" I said.

"It was a good tagline, Christian," the Auricle said. "I relayed it to Dan."

That kind of irritated me.

Scratch "kind of"—it *did* irritate me. Minerva had ended her press conference and walked away from the massive plastic trash sphere with a commanding smile on her face.

CHAPTER
SEVENTEEN

RAND'S RESPONSE to the monstrous, floating plastic ball of oceanic waste was again to claim that Auric had faked the whole thing. He'd held yet another raging press conference, which Angelina and I watched in our living room, which was where we were most of the time when we weren't at our jobs or out. Even when we worked remotely, the living room was sacrosanct.

"This alien warlock conjures up a giant plastic ball and we're expected to just believe what it says?" Rand said. "You know what I think? I think it's just another stunt. That's all this Auric thing does is stunts. It's pathetic. Auric's really pathetic, do you know that? Tons of people are saying that. Anybody can create a giant, hovering ball of plastic. And what about the landfills? Waste management companies are really upset about it. They're angry. This is waste mismanagement, it's what it is."

The RAN and LAX reporters did their usual part lobbing softball questions to Rand, who answered them with relish, his face locked into a disapproving snarl.

"Do you think it's a prelude for invasion?" RAN reporter Sy Windham asked, looking genuinely concerned as much as his facelift would allow. His range of facial motion declined every decade, and the industrial smoothing plastic surgeons performed on his skin didn't disguise his age.

"Of course I do," Rand said. "Auric's invaded our free planet. It talks about cleaning things up, but what is that, really? It's invasion. It's invading. It's invading us. We're being invaded. That's what people are saying."

"What about the litter?" the LAX reporter Willow Oakes asked. Willow wore her short red dresses terribly tight, and her fingernails were clawlike in length.

"What about it?" Rand asked. "Litter *is* liberty. Show me a place without litter. You can't. People litter *because* they're free. And what about the garbage collectors? The landfill operators? Auric doesn't solve problems. Auric *creates* problems. Auric is a problem creator and a job destroyer."

"'Litter is Liberty'," Angelina said. "The GNP's next campaign slogan."

She probably wasn't wrong. They were just stupid enough to go there, trying to pin people's willingness to litter as synonymous with their purported freedom.

"Nobody wants some alien overlord dictating where they can and can't put their trash," Rand said. "I know I don't."

He picked up a plastic water bottle and tossed it over his shoulder, leering for the cameras.

"See that, Auric?" Rand asked, as cameras flashed and caught him tossing it. "Real Americans litter. They're not hippies and treehuggers. That's what I want you to do. Go out and throw some trash out the window, or whatever you have. Just toss it. It's *our* planet, Auric. It's not yours. You don't get to tell us to clean up our rooms, Dad. Sorry."

Willow Oakes squirmed telegenically in her seat, tossing her bleached blond hair with a red-clawed hand.

"You're advocating that people litter?" Oakes asked.

"Yes, Willow," Rand said. "Absolutely. We're taking our country back. We're taking the world back. Auric says it's cleaner, now. It says this. It says it's *our* fault there's litter. It's blaming us. It's blaming us for it. It's us versus Auric."

"It *is* us," I said, and Angelina shrugged.

"Well, yeah," Angelina said. "Obviously."

"Real Americans litter," Rand said. "Show me someone who doesn't, and I think 'That person's a traitor.'"

"Jeez," Angelina said. "That's almost too far a limb even for those reporters. You can see it on their faces."

And Angelina was right about that. I could already imagine members of the GNP faithful being fired up by Rand's words to gleefully litter after Auric had cleaned up the planet.

"Look," Rand said, gripping the lectern. "Auric's trying to make you feel bad about yourself. Don't. Don't let it get in your head. You're made in God's image. What's Auric? Auric's the Devil. There, I said it again: Auric is Satan."

"Do you mean Auric's literally Satan?" Sy asked.

"Absolutely," Rand said. "Anything with flaming blue hair is satanic, right? Does that seem angelic to you? What it's doing is satanic. Satan pretends to do good things but it's really, really evil. Pretending to clean the planet? Denying human liberty? That's evil incarnate."

I turned off the television, couldn't take any more of that. Watching Rand was always an exercise in masochism.

"Um, I was watching that," Angelina said.

"We should go out or something," I said. Angelina gestured for the remote, which I handed to her. She flicked the television back on, which had interrupted Rand's speech and had Auric onscreen again, standing by the East River.

"Part of my effort to remove the pollution you've perpetrated on your planet requires I address this as well," Auric said. "What's the point of cleaning something if every day more trash is spilled into your waterways? Over 80 to 95 percent of the world's wastewater is dumped—mostly untreated, by the way—into your rivers, lakes, and oceans. For example, around 40 percent of waterways in the Confederated States of America are polluted to the extent that they're unsafe. I'm remedying this right now, have cleaned all of the waterways around the world."

Auric gestured to some golden pipeworks that he'd put in place.

"These are point source pollution remediators," Auric said. "I've installed them around the world, and they will prevent waste material effluent from befouling your waterways. Further, I've provided state-of-the-art upgrades to the world's sanitation systems, to help deal with this. The nonpoint source pollution is, of course, a larger issue. Much of it can stem from current agricultural practices. Things such as agribusiness fertilizer runoff, for example."

I wondered how that would all work, asked the Auricle.

"What did you do to the sanitation systems?" I asked.

"I provided necessary upgrades," the Auricle said, flashing images on my intelliphone's screen, showing golden systems in place. The golden metal gleamed, and bewildered sanitation workers walked around, perplexed.

"Are people going to know how to operate them?" I asked.

"They don't need to," the Auricle said. "They are self-regulating and efficient."

"People aren't going to like that," I said. "They're going to resent it. And, more importantly, they're going to want to be able to do their jobs."

The Auricle was unpersuaded.

"They should consult their own Auricles for other career paths," the Auricle said. "Given the amount of effluents that were entering into the waterways, they were clearly not up to the task presented to them. In the case of more efficient systems, they can work in concert with the new systems. Others are either too corrupt and/or incompetent to do the work required of them."

"Definitely don't say that," I said.

"Of course not," the Auricle said. "But you're my Chronicler, so I'm speaking with a greater degree of candor."

Angelina looked over at me down the end of her nose.

"I'm sitting right here, Chronicler," Angelina said, mocking me. "Hey, Phone, you can't just do humanity's jobs for it."

"I'm not," the Auricle said. "But I'm doing things that ought to be done for the sake of the survival of your species. Clean, fresh water is integral to human survival. You're mostly made of water. The poisoning and polluting of the waterways and water tables by your species costs your country nearly $5 billion a year. Waterborne diseases from either pollution or outright mismanagement of water resources kills millions worldwide. It remains the second leading cause of death for children under five years of age. Nearly 20 percent of deaths worldwide are caused by air and water pollution. Over 90 percent of them are concentrated in developing nations. By making these changes to the air and water, I'll have saved nearly eight million human beings from premature death."

"Eight million?" Angelina asked.

"Yes," the Auricle said.

"No way do that many people die from air and water pollution," Angelina said.

"They do today," the Auricle said. "Or did. Going forward, that number will be zero."

Rand was still carrying on about Auric.

"Auric and his golden toilets," Rand said. "It's putting stuff in the water. It's poisoning us. It wants you to be sick. There's nanites in the water from those golden spigots. Mind-controlling. It's what they call them. Nanites."

"Is that true?" Angelina asked.

"None of what Denny Rand says is true," the Auricle said. "The man is a pathological and compulsive liar and a psychopath."

"You should do something about him, Phone," Angelina said.

"I already am," the Auricle said.

I was alternately annoyed at Angelina for barging in on my conversation and also curious what Auric had in mind. Of course, that's what I get for talking to the Auricle in front of her.

"What are you up to?" I asked.

"You'll see," the Auricle said.

CHAPTER

EIGHTEEN

IN RESPONSE TO RAND'S URGE for Real Americans to litter, his party loyalists had run out and made points of tossing litter streetside, whatever they had handy—typically, it was plastic bottles and beer cans, but sometimes it was fast food wrappers and grocery bags.

But despite their idiotic efforts, the city looked cleaner than I'd ever seen it, and other people actually picked up the litter that the GNP fanatics had tossed.

And, more importantly, in the wake of The Littering, as it was called, Auric had added golden trash receptacles on every curbside. These little golden trashcans were lidded and actually resembled small Auricle shrines. They had rectangular slits in them that allowed them to receive trash from any angle. They were adorned with the Auric logo.

The most interesting thing about them, however, was that if you tossed something into them, it simply disappeared in a blue flash of light. Around the country, people responded to the Littering by tossing trash into the cylindrical Auric cans.

Where did the trash go? I whipped out my intelliphone and asked, of course. Auric knew I would.

"Where does the garbage go?" I asked.

"It's being turned into energy," the Auricle said. "Your people—specifically, your country—generates nearly 300 million tons of waste annually. By creating these Auricans in various sizes, I've created a ready source of power and have eliminated the need for landfills."

Various sizes.

"What happens if a person ends up in one of your Auricans?" I asked.

"Nothing," the Auricle said. "They're designed to dispose of garbage, not people."

"What happens if someone tries to?" I asked.

"The individuals attempting to do so are put on layaway," the Auricle said. "A fitting place for anyone who would attempt to murder someone by putting them in an Aurican."

Of course. Auric's layaway plan.

I should have guessed that.

Meanwhile, the Auricans were giving waste management companies fits, and Rand and the GNP were howling about it.

"Auricans?" Rand asked. "Aurican't, more like. You trust your trash to this alien? It's our garbageman, now? What about *actual* garbagemen? Who's thinking about them? Not Auric, that's for sure. Auric *is* garbage."

He'd egged on various garbage collectors to try to trash the Auricans, but they were as impervious to harm as the Auricle shrines were. They'd try to drive garbage trucks into them, would try to knock them over, but even though they were small compared with the trucks, they wouldn't budge, and plenty of garbage trucks were trashed by smashing into the Auricans.

For people who weren't GNP zealots or actively displaced by the Auricans, the massive cleanup Auric had undertaken on our behalf was appreciated, and even the GNP dumbasses who'd been part of The Littering had eventually taken to quietly disposing of their garbage in Auricans. And Auric had not displaced the garbage collectors as the GNP had implied, because waste was still collected in ordinary dumpsters.

However, instead of driving them to landfills, there were massive Auricans capable of disposing of the waste. The GNP had found a new way to spin that into a bad thing. Rand, as ever the attention whore that he was, spoke to it on television and on his social media channels.

"It's theft," Rand said. "Where does the garbage go? Auric's taking our trash, sure. But it's not recycling it. It's not giving it back. It's only taking it away. Where? Nobody knows. Blue flashes and it's gone. We're feeding Auric. It's feeding on our garbage. We're feeding the monster. And what's it giving us in return? Nothing."

Nothing but fresh air, clean cities, clean water. Even I could see and smell that.

The air *was* cleaner. The world was cleaner.

Auric had put golden scrubbers on every smokestack around the world in the wake of his carbon reclamation project, and those scrubbers molecularly purified the air, making smog a thing of the past.

I mean, it was a pronounced improvement.

Only the most hidebound GNPer would deny it. But something had nagged at me about the Auricans, so I talked to the Auricle while in my office.

"You said the Auricans convert trash to energy," I said. "But you don't need that energy, right?"

"I don't require it," the Auricle said. "I'm self-sustaining. However, energy has to go somewhere, and I didn't want it to simply go to waste."

"Rand has one slight point, however," I said. "They recycle elsewhere in the world. So, what happens over there? In countries that recycle?"

There was no recycling in the CSA. The GNP attacked recycling as something no Real Americans would do. It was considered a way the CSA distinguished itself from its competitor nations, much like with national healthcare, universal basic income, and alternative energy. The CSA stood out by not having those things.

"Auricans recycle in countries that have recycling," the Auricle said. "They break down the trash into component elements and provide them in accessible receptibles that can be used by relevant industries."

"That sounds complicated," I said.

"It's not, really," the Auricle said. "The Holistic Aurican Reclamation Project (HARP) offers ready access to industrial recyclables, already processed and available for re-use and re-application. Companies in pro-recycling countries have enthusiastically embraced the HARP."

"Seems like some of the chemicals would be toxic," I said.

"Some are," the Auricle said. "They're safely stored in HARP facilities, where they can be accessed by authorized personnel."

"Authorized by whom?" I asked.

"Any HARP participants and partners are screened by me," the Auricle said.

It kind of bothered me that the CSA didn't have the HARP in place. Felt like it was discriminatory on some level.

"Why don't you have the HARP in the CSA?" I asked.

"Your own country wouldn't participate in that program, so your trash is simply consumed for energy. Waste not, want not, as the idiomatic expression goes."

The HARP business made me turn my attention to how Auric was interacting with other countries, ones that were more amenable to Auric. And there was definitely a greater degree of involvement and participation on the part of Auric.

For example, everywhere but the CSA had solar-powered parking lots, with the consent of the nations in question. He'd provided golden structures that would screen the parking lots and generate solar power.

This had the corresponding benefit of keeping the cars cool by shading them and turning what was historically unused land into solar power-generating dynamos that would feed into the businesses that had the parking lots to begin with.

"Solar parking has been around for many decades," Auric had said. "I'm simply extending it around the globe, for the benefit of all mankind, for the countries who want it and are willing to work with me."

He'd also provided solar power-generating glass for windows as well as solar arrays that could sit between railroad tracks on railroad lines, offering steady sources of decentralized, passive solar power to client nations who were pro-Auric.

Similarly, Auric created golden vertical axis wind turbines (VAWTs) that he placed in various countries in all sorts of places and in varying sizes. He put them atop streetlights, for example, to provide power for the individual lights. He put them atop buildings to provide power for them. The vertical spindles he'd provided had the advantage of being able to take wind from any direction, and since they were made out of the same golden mystery metal—the foreign press had taken to calling it "Auricanium"—they didn't break or break down.

Between the ambient solar arrays and the VAWTs, Auric was delivering considerable cost saves to countries that had embraced the Auric Agenda (again, using the GNP term for it, because it's what we'd hear about every day). This applied to every country who had eagerly taken up Auric's offer to deliver free energy.

"There's no point in my cleaning up the air if legacy industrial processes are simply going to create pollution again," Auric had explained.

In the CSA, Auric had taken a different approach. Given the hostility the GNP had for Auric, there wasn't the same sort of synergy he used in other countries. Auric didn't appear to the leaders and make agreements with them.

However, the same problem Auric had presented was abundantly apparent in the CSA. That is, Auric's carbon remediation efforts applied here even more than elsewhere, so Auric had placed his golden scrubbers on all of the smokestacks in the CSA and had provided the same parking lot solar arrays and the VAWTs, but those efforts were vigorously and strenuously opposed by the GNP as unforgivable violations of American sovereignty.

Party leaders raged about the proliferation of Auricanium since their operatives had proven unable to break it. They tried to jam up the VAWTs, but despite the seeming delicacy of the things, they proved as indestructible as the rest of Auric's creations, as impervious to sabotage. And GNP operatives who attempted it tended to disappear in flashes of golden sparkles, or at least that's how the rumors flew—it was difficult to track a disappearance by its very nature.

Unable to stop them, Rand took to the airwaves and his social media channels.

"They're hideous," Rand said. "You look out the window, you see them. Gold everywhere. Auric metal. Invasion alloy. People are just so unhappy. Good people. Real people. The solar. That's what Auric says. It says the solar and the wind will save us. You can't even see a parking lot anymore. Just those Auric invasion alloy roofs. Why does Auric need all of that power? Nobody should need that much power."

Rand had used his background screens to show blinding views of the parking lots.

"They eat the Sun," Rand said. "Auric tiles eat the Sun. That's what it's doing. Eating the Sun. What about cloudy days? Auric the Illegal Alien Egghead didn't think about that."

Of course, Auric had, and the solar arrays functioned fine, rain or shine, generating decentralized power for every area that had them.

I noticed the little VAWTs atop the streetlights on my way to Epicuria, where I was meeting Angelina for an after-work date. We were still getting used to not having to wear our filter facemasks outdoors, owing to the air Auric had cleaned.

Epicuria was a nice four-star place that served all varieties of American cuisine. Plus, because it was pricey, it meant that we'd be able to access it without it being overcrowded.

I could see they had their own VAWTs whirling on the rooftop of Epicuria, and I thought I saw a solar array up there, too. I'd gotten there ahead of Angelina, so I took a moment to search for "rooftop solar arrays" (RSAs) and did see that Auric had provided RSAs and turbines to individuals and businesses that requested them, often via the Auricle app.

I wondered how long it would be before the GNP outlawed them. That was likely coming. Standing streetside, watching the electric traffic slide by, I could see the signs of Auric around me—the Auricans, the VAWTs, the RSAs, people talking to their phones, almost certainly asking their own Auricles questions.

Still too self-conscious to talk to my own Auricle in public that way, I remained circumspect in my use of the Auricle. Just looking at the streetlamp security cameras that were everywhere, I was aware of being observed on public thoroughfares. The HID might not have been everywhere, but they wanted people to think that they were.

"Hey, there," Angelina said, sneaking up on me and punching my arm. She was in her nice work clothes—black ribbed turtleneck and grey slacks, with a mahogany-colored leather coat.

"Hey, Babe," I said, and we kissed. "You walk over here?"

"Yep," Angelina said.

"Living dangerously," I replied. She smirked up at me.

"How I roll," Angelina said. "I live for danger."

We showed our IDs and were admitted entrance to Epicuria.

Inside, it was as pleasantly ordinary as ever, the same old-school dining experience it offered, American fusion steakhouse cuisine, with an emphasis on actual meat, which was still avidly consumed in the CSA, despite—or perhaps because of—the environmental impact.

Epicuria had hunter green walls and dark wood paneling, with mahogany leather booths and soft lighting. It was a place where local GNP figures would meet to discuss business, connect with their escorts or mistresses, or otherwise entertain themselves while lording it over the rest of us. Being admitted into Epicuria always felt like an accomplishment, and I knew Angelina appreciated that working at Duotribe and Flutter offered us access to it.

"Your golden boy cleaned up the planet," Angelina said, looking over the menu tablet our waiter had primly provided.

"My boy," I said, chuckling. "He's been busy."

"That he has," Angelina said, tapping her way through her order with practiced efficiency. "Sandee Delmonico is losing her mind over it, in terms of trend-tracking. I know we're not you, but Flutter's moving a mile a minute with our social listening. It's turning into a, well, I don't even know what to call it. *Everybody's* talking about Auric. It's all we ever hear."

"Yeah," I said. I ordered a lobster roll and a cup of lobster bisque with an Old-Fashioned. I asked Angelina if she wanted an appetizer, but she wrinkled her nose and shook her head, ordered a Sour Appletini. Our orders placed, our waiter came by and wordlessly took the tablets and got us some filtered water.

"Yeah," Angelina said, imitating me. "What's on your mind, Sport?"

"I'm just wondering where he's going with it all," I said.

"You could ask your phone," Angelina said, before quickly adding. "Don't, though. I'd like to have one conversation without your intelliphone, you know, eavesdropping or whatever it's doing."

"Yeah," I said. "Auric's taking over our world. I mean, I see it—him—everywhere."

"That he is," Angelina said.

"Aren't you scared?" I asked.

"Of him?" Angelina asked. "Nah. I mean, yeah, but, nah."

I scoffed at her quantumly noncommittal response.

"There's nothing I can do about it," Angelina said. "He's here. It's here. I'm just going about my day, trying to keep things together. Trying to keep my job. Just like you."

We'd been dating for three years, living together for the past two years. In the CSA, there were real tax penalties for cohabitating without being married. This applied in the Heartland Protectorate as well as elsewhere in the CSA. It wasn't like Angelina and I were in a rush to get married or anything, but sooner or later, it would come up in a way that we couldn't breeze past.

"McCluskey's riding my ass in the worst way," I said.

"I know how you hate that," Angelina said. "Why don't you ask your phone to set up a meeting with Auric?"

"Yeah, I guess I could," I said. Our drinks arrived.

"But you haven't," Angelina said. "So, why not?"

What could I say? I was a little nervous about seeing Auric again, since I still felt that maybe my talk with him led to him reforesting the Earth. Maybe that was just my own ego talking, but I couldn't rule it out.

"I've never been on speaking terms with a supreme being before," I said.

"He's hardly a supreme being," Angelina said. "I mean, he's *not* God."

"Pretty damned close," I said.

"Blasphemy," Angelina said, low-voiced and sharp-eyed. She was mocking me, but I was sure she believed it. She was more of a believer than I was or ever would be. We all grew up with it, but it took more with some than others. As a state religion, it was just something you had to at least be aware of, whether or not you actually believed in it. Nobody would ever come out and say they didn't believe in God, so it was easy to just go through the motions undetected. To actually be honest about your disbelief would have doomed you in the CSA, both personally and professionally.

Some GNP operatives turned up at Epicuria, commandeering a corner booth that had been reserved for them. A half-dozen of them in their blue suits and red ties, their Party pins glistening at their lapels. Most of the GNP bros fit a particular mold—white, overly coiffed hair, a crude sort of stare that took ownership of everything they saw. They were invariably loud.

"If I see him again, then I'll never be able to go back to not-seeing him," I said.

"Again?" Angelina asked, sipping her Appletini.

"I may have already met with him in my office the other day," I said. "It just sort of happened."

Angelina smiled to herself, turning her glass in her hands, pursing her lips.

"Sounds like *that* was something. He made you his Chronicler, whatever that exactly means," Angelina said. "As I see it, you're already in it. You should meet with his minions—that Minerva lady."

She drank her drink, and I thought about that. I saw the GNP guys had turned from whatever conspiratorial muttering they'd been doing to looking over at Angelina and me, which made me very uneasy. When GNP guys looked at you, it was never a good thing.

Then I realized what they were looking at.

CHAPTER

NINETEEN

"MINERVA MERROW," Minerva said, standing there, snapping out a well-manicured hand for me to shake. Her hand was cool and dry to the touch. "You're Christian Powers, and this is Angelina Reed, yes? Hope I haven't come at a bad time?"

Up close, Minerva was even more formidable than she was onscreen. Tall and lean in her impeccably white suit, her gold blouse bore a labyrinthine pattern upon it. Minerva had a strongly featured face, the kind that the camera loved, but, in person, was almost too much for mortal eyes to take in at once. More handsome than pretty, but that only made her beautiful.

"Uh," I said, standing up, mindful of the staring GNPeons in their booth, who were taking out their phones to take pictures and no doubt confer with their Party bosses. Epicuria would be swarming with HID agents soon, I was sure of it.

"Never a bad time," Angelina said. "Please join us, Ms. Merrow. Scootch a bit, Christian."

I scootched, and Minerva joined us.

"Are you trying to get me disappeared?" I asked.

Minerva smiled at me, a vulpine sort of expression that made me feel like I was her prey.

"Oh, don't worry about them, Christian," Minerva said. "We're completely safe."

Angelina was fascinated by Merrow's unexpected arrival, and I could see the social media wheels spinning in her head.

"Are we safe?" Angelina asked.

"Yes," Minerva said, ordering a Manhattan.

"Why are you here?" I asked. "How'd you find me?"

"You already know the answer to that second question," Minerva said. "As to why I'm here, the answer is Auric. The answer is *always* Auric. You should know that one by now, Chronicler."

"Sure," I said. "But why right now? I mean, we're having dinner. Who just ambushes somebody during dinner?"

Some of the GNP bros had left their booth and gone out front to the lobby. I had images of HID agents and/or SAC goons coming and taking us away. I could only imagine where that would end up, like me in one of their black ops sites, being waterboarded, nipple-clipped to a car battery, or worse. Firing squad. Hanging from a tree. Burned at the stake. Buried in an unmarked grave. Maybe all of the above, in sequence.

"I do," Minerva said. "You seem like a nice guy, Christian. I know what Auric sees in you, I really do. I've inquired extensively about you, once I learned you existed."

"How did you even get here?" I asked. "You have to be on GNP watch lists, right?"

"Oh, sure," Minerva said. "Not a problem for me."

I could see she had an earpiece golden intelliphone, the way she tapped it with a well-lacquered fingernail. Of course, one step beyond a free-standing intelliphone or even a wrist intelliphone or a collar intelliphone.

Beyond whatever Minerva had inquired about, there was the matter at hand.

"What do you want?" I asked, noting when my bisque was brought, as well as the cream of mushroom soup Angelina had gotten. Our waiter had brought some rustic bread and was trying circumspectly to not look like he was staring when he saw Minerva there.

"I'm just visiting," Minerva said to the waiter, who whisked himself away as discreetly as he could. She turned her gaze back to me. "I *had* to see you."

"Why?"

"You're part of this, whether you want to be or not," Minerva said, watching me spoon my bisque as she sipped her Manhattan. "See, I asked my Auricle what your part was, why Auric picked you. And it wouldn't answer me. Isn't that something?"

She smiled at me. It was a becoming smile, one part ingratiating, the other part something else I couldn't divine in that moment. She fished out a gold business card case, stamped with Auric's fireball symbol. She flipped it open and slid a chalk-white business card to me. Upon it, it said:

Minerva Merrow
First Apostle of Auric

"The Auricle told me you're the very first person to step into an Auricle shrine," I said, taking up the card. Why anyone would even have business cards for something like Auric was bizarre.

"Yes," Minerva said. "Berkeley. I was there on business."

"I know," I said. That was one of the challenges with two active Auricle power users—we were usually up to speed on each other if we asked good questions. "You were in pharmaceutical sales, right? For Apothecarrier?"

Minerva nodded. Apothecarrier was East Coast, although they operated globally.

"And you're a trendscaper at Duotribe here in the Heartland Protectorate," Minerva said. "You should move to the California offices. It'd be better, easier for you there. Safer, even. Despite the GNP meddling, California still respects researchers."

"Yeah," I said, glancing at Angelina, who was eating her soup and listening. I could only imagine how her Flutter-mind was taking in this scoop. "Not likely to happen."

"Of course, the bureaucracies are a challenge," Minerva said. "Although that hardly matters anymore, wouldn't you say?"

She glanced across the room, where the GNPeons were nervously conferring with each other, watching and filming us. I tried to keep my cool, which wasn't easy when GNP guys were observing and filming you.

"How'd you even get into the Protectorate?" I asked.

"Please," Minerva said. "With Auric, anything is possible. The GNP can't keep me out. Thanks to Auric, I can travel anywhere I want in the world. They can't do anything to us Auricians. They've tried."

"Have they?" I asked. The news hadn't shown that.

"Oh, yes," Minerva said. "They can't touch us. Any of us. Auricians, I mean. Those who've declared our allegiance to Auric and what he stands for."

She meaningfully touched the Auric pin at her lapel, cocked a dark eyebrow at me. Angelina couldn't resist offering a comment.

"What's that mean?" Angelina asked. "Declared yourselves? You worship him or something?"

Minerva's smile never wavered.

"Worship is such a clumsy and antiquated way to word it," Minerva said. "It's not worship; it's partnership. Auricians understand that Auric is the new future of the human race and we accept him. Auric offers relief beyond belief—good phrasing, incidentally, Christian."

Relief beyond belief.

Oh, man.

Yeah, I'd stepped into that one.

"Auric is here to help humanity," Minerva said. "And we're here to help him."

Angelina glanced at me and back at Minerva, her soup spoon perched midway to her mouth.

"Help him?" Angelina asked. "He doesn't need help by the look of him. What can *you* do?"

Minerva watched Angelina have some more of her soup, nodding as she took another drink.

"To the point," Minerva said. "Absolutely. Yes, he *doesn't* need our help. But we're here to put a human face on what he's doing. It's all too much for ordinary minds to contemplate, don't you think? Alien invasion? Singletons? Supreme beings? Transhumanist evolution? We're here to help people see that Auric's not something to be feared."

"Shills," Angelina said. "You're shilling for Auric."

"Please," Minerva said. "We're not shilling."

She glanced at the GNPeons, who had been accompanied by some HID-looking fellows. HID agents had a particular look to them. They were used to being feared and they carried that aura of fear around them like an adornment. HID agents always wore black suits, never blue or brown. And they always wore black ties. Veritable Men in Black.

"You turning up here really messed with our dinner plans," I said. "Now I'm going to be interrogated by the HID."

"Not yet," Minerva said. "Plus, they've already been monitoring you, Christian. They just haven't approached you for questioning, yet. Seems like your boss, McCluskey, ratted you out."

"Ratted me out? For what?" I asked. I hadn't thought to ask my Auricle about that when it had warned me about McCluskey betraying me.

"I'd say you rattled him," Minerva said. "And to cover his own ass, he'd reported some things to the GNP leadership. Gosh, Christian, I can't believe you didn't make inquiries on this."

I whipped out my intelliphone and asked my Auricle.

"Auricle, am I in trouble?" I asked.

"Yes, Christian," the Auricle said. "But you don't have to worry. You're safe."

"If I'm safe, how can I be in trouble?" I asked.

"It seems paradoxical, but it's not," the Auricle said. "McCluskey apparently regretted granting you access to me, and the GNP has been revoking app licenses and rounding up users. He didn't want to be in trouble with GNP Command, so he fabricated a story of granting the license under duress from you."

"That's bullshit," I said. "You should've told me, warned me."

"I did," the Auricle said. "Remember the pin?"

I had it with me, in my pocket, in its little box. I'd carried it with me ever since it had appeared in my office. Angelina was pale, looking around us nervously.

"What is going on, Christian?" Angelina asked.

I took out the box and opened it, taking the pin and sticking it to my lapel. Minerva watched this, smirking, as two of the HID agents were conferring with each other. They looked like hard men, with hard eyes and harder hearts. Minerva was completely calm, but I was terrified.

"Don't worry about them, Christian," Minerva said. "They're simply trying to figure out how to incarcerate us. But we're under Auric's protection, and they know it. Let's just continue our conversation as if they weren't there. What're you planning?"

She asked it as mildly as she possibly could, but I could feel a hint of an edge to her inquiry. Maybe it was just from my years at Duotribe. However, I had learned to trust my instincts. Of course, if she was the First Apostle of Auric, she had to have passed muster, right? She had to be an okay person. He wouldn't have accepted her otherwise.

It really hinged on whether it was simply a matter of timing, or if Auric had actually determined if people were worthy to follow him. I was wondering that, and maybe Merrow was, too. Or maybe she'd already asked her Auricle in depth and had all the answers.

"It's not for me to plan," I said. "I'm just observing and chronicling. That's what Auric told me I needed to do."

Minerva looked at me a moment, assessing me. I mean, I could just see it, her calculating.

"How are you chronicling?" she asked. "I don't see a tablet or laptop or anything."

"I'm not committing anything to writing just yet," I said. "Right now, I'm just soaking it all up, taking it all in. It's pretty amazing stuff."

"Christian's very low-fi in that regard," Angelina said, half-laughing into her Appletini.

Minerva scoffed. I mean, like, she totally scoffed. I felt attacked.

"Have you met the Second Apostle?" Minerva asked. "She's something else. Tessa Van Blossom. That's her name. She's going to eat you for lunch, Christian. She's organizing a mass rally in Lost Angeles. Like a music festival and rally."

"A rally for what?" I asked.

"For Aurica, of course," Minerva said. "The Aurica Festival."

"Sure, yeah," I said. "Makes sense. She only sees Auric as Aurica."

Minerva smiled at me, taking evident delight in it.

"Aurica, yeah," Minerva said. "You already know Auric can manifest in all ways. For Tessa, Auric's always Aurica."

"And for you?" I asked.

"Auric," Minerva said. "Different strokes, different folks. Still, curious that he did that for Tessa. She calls her the Golden Goddess. She's had tee shirts made for it. The Golden Goddess Gathering. G3."

"Not my jam," I said. "I don't like big gatherings. Not since, you know, the pandemics. Why'd Tessa organize it in the States, and not, say, in the Netherlands?"

Since global warming had worsened, the Netherlands had ever more vigorously defended itself from the threat of rising water levels. Since Auric had arrived, they had enthusiastically embraced Auric and had been thoroughly protected by him, including raising and recovering lost land on a level that rivaled what he'd done for Bangladesh and the Maldives (sorry, forgot to mention that; he totally saved the Maldives—it got hard to track because he was going all over the place at that point, saving people from the oceans around the world).

"Hah," Minerva said. "The Dutch are fully down with Auric. Tessa's in the CSA to spread the word where it's needed most. People keep loading the Auricle app outside the CSA. It's big-time trending. The Sixth Apostle—Shauna Meadows—she started up an Auric testimonial social media site, based in Wellington, New Zealand. People sharing their stories about how the Auricle's been already changing their lives. It's good stuff. Traffic is climbing. Word is getting out."

"Van Blossom and Meadows," I said.

"And Dan Fields," Minerva said. "Number Four. He's opening up Auricle food banks in England."

"Van Blossom, Meadows, and Fields," I said. "That's all so very pastoral."

"Right. And John Running Bird is working to deal with the oil industry, like pollution remediation efforts in Oklahoma. Yuko Takahashi has been working tirelessly with Auric in the Fukushima area, not only decontaminating, but showing people it's going to be safe to live there again," Minerva said. "With them doing that stuff, and me doing press-work for Auric, I just wanted to see what the Chronicler was doing."

"Like I said, I'm just sorta taking it all in," I said.

"It figures," Minerva said, rolling her eyes. "You're basically doing nothing."

"I'm an inactivist," I said, winking at Angelina, who nodded sincerely, because she knew I was speaking the truth.

Minerva looked at me, saw through me, measured me, found me wanting.

I could see her processing it through her head, frustrated that I had simply happened to be designated the Chronicler by Auric. Since she'd clearly researched the other Apostles—at least the top ten, was my guess—she was likely chagrined that she hadn't been able to find out what she needed on me.

"It's a good thing there's really no organizational structure with Auric," Minerva said. "No hierarchy, even. I mean, besides him."

"What did you exactly do in pharma before Auric?" Angelina asked.

"Biotechnology sales," Minerva said. "Still am. Just a different drug, now. A better one."

Angelina looked flabbergasted.

"Wait, a drug?" Angelina asked.

"Metaphorical," Minerva said. "Relief Beyond Belief. Auric's selling actual hope, change, and progress. It's intoxicating."

"I was a good trendscaper," I said, wondering if I'd still have a job, and realizing that was the least of my worries. I'd have to confront McCluskey. The GNP was savage when dealing with wrongthinkers.

"And you still are," Minerva said. "I wouldn't fret about it, Christian."

I don't know what made me do it, but I asked.

"Auricle, will Minerva and I be friends?" I asked.

"No," the Auricle said. "You'll be friendly rivals. You already are."

"That's what I figured," I said. "But not enemies, I hope."

"They're really the same thing," Minerva said. "I understand what you're saying. You and I don't really cross in terms of our areas of interest. I'm PR, now, and you're, like you said, an inactivist. We should get along fine without ever having to really like one another."

She tapped her earbud, which, I could see, had the Auric circle logo on it.

"Oh, no earbud for you?" Minerva asked. "This way, I get Auric in my head directly. He can speak through me, real-time. It's useful. What's funny is that Auric gave it to me right off the bat. I'd loaded the Auricle on my intelliphone, but the earbud was waiting for me in a nice little blue velvet box."

Of course, she was flaunting that, what, next-generation Auric interface. I decided to toy with her a little.

"It's funny that Auric even uses things like earbuds or phones," I said. "Given that he's, like, telepathic."

"Yes," Minerva said. "Auric works in mysterious ways. Apparently, not everybody gets the same tchotchkes. Auric gives everybody different stuff. Every Aurician gets their lapel pin, though I've heard that some get brooches."

"Huh," I said. It made me wonder why he'd given me one. What was the master plan? "I'm not a practicing Aurician."

Minerva smiled, rolling her eyes in the direction of the GNP and HID goons.

"In their eyes, you already are," Minerva said.

"You're originally from New York," I said. "Right? Gotta be."

I mean, she was. Everything about her screamed New York.

"Yep," Minerva said. "Brooklyn born. Raised in the time of the Great Flood. Teaches you a thing or two about surviving. Problem?"

"Nope," I said. "You jetted out here to see me?"

"I've been all over the place. I'm visiting all of the top people," Minerva said. "I'm not jetting, either—Auric transported me here. I teleported."

"Bullshit," I said.

She smirked at me.

"You don't have to believe me if you don't want to, but the fact is, I'm here," Minerva said. "And I was in Richmond yesterday dealing with that GNP crap Rand keeps flinging."

"Ah," I said. "Why exactly are you meeting all the other Apostles?"

"I want to see the team he's assembled," Minerva said. "I want to know who I'll be working with. To know them face-to-face, versus depending entirely on what my Auricle tells me."

I couldn't imagine Auric just teleporting her over. But maybe he did. I had to know.

"Auricle, did Auric teleport Minerva to Chicago?" I asked.

"Yes," the Auricle said.

"Well, fuck," I said.

"What, you thought I was lying?" Minerva asked. "I'm sorry you never thought of that, I really am."

Now it made sense to me, like what Auric had been saying about me thinking above and beyond what I was used to thinking. The new paradigm, I thought. Teleportation? That really was a serious game-changer.

I felt stupid for not thinking of it.

"Ah, so, the inactivist is stewing," Minerva said, smiling at me. "Teleportation would be ideal for an inactivist. Instantaneous travel, no waiting in lines. Wouldn't even have to get off your sofa if you didn't want to. It's super-useful for me in my current PR capacity, because I'm needed everywhere at once. It drives the GNP crazy, like how I just show up at events. They can't stop me. They can't stop any of us, and it terrifies them."

She definitely looked satisfied at having so roundly scooped me. Here I was, thinking about the Auricle shrine down the block, like some alderman, and she was busy teleporting around the planet, taking meetings with other Auricians. I had wondered how she had managed to pop up everywhere like that, and now I knew.

I was too proud to even ask her how that even came about. I mean, who even thinks of stuff like that? Minerva Merrow, that's who. I went back to my Auricle, while Minerva watched.

"Is she the only one who's been teleporting?" I asked.

"Currently, yes," the Auricle said, which brought Minerva even more satisfaction.

"I may only be PR, not some mysterious Chronicler, but that just means I try harder," Minerva said.

Our main course arrived, the terrified waiter hastily and wordlessly swapping out our starters and seeking to get out of there without even a hint of him knowing us. The GNP operatives and HID agents kept observing, talking quietly into their phones. I didn't know why they hadn't jumped us, yet. Forceful confrontation was their baseline.

What would I even do with teleportation? I mean, there wasn't anywhere I really wanted to go. Portugal and Sardinia, maybe. But, again, what was the point of it?

"Do you know about the asteroid?" I asked.

"Of course," Minerva said. "Auric told me everything."

"Well, alright," I said.

"I'm going to hit the ground running once he deals with the asteroid," Minerva said. "I've got it all mapped, so we can carpet bomb the networks and dominate news cycles for weeks."

Part of me was wondering why somebody who'd apparently been teleporting was even worrying about news cycles. I mean, that was a news story, right there:

AREA WOMAN TELEPORTS AROUND THE COUNTRY IN SERVICE TO OMNIPOTENT COSMIC BEING

"It helps me do my job," said Minerva Merrow, 32.

That would get attention anywhere. But maybe this was all part of Auric's plan. As ever, I was intended to be the witness to it all. *That* was my role.

"No," I said. "I just wanted to know if other, you know..."

"Apostles?" Minerva asked.

"Yeah," I said. She shook her head.

"I don't think he's told everyone about the asteroid," Minerva said. "Auricle, have you told everyone?"

"No," my Auricle answered. "About 30 percent of Auricians are aware of it, although as they talk to each other, more are finding out daily. By the time everyone finds out, they will be prepared for it."

"Why wouldn't you tell all of the Auricians?" I asked.

"They're busy with their projects," the Auricle said. "I'm dripping out the information to them as necessary."

I was conflicted around the whole Minerva thing. She was the first Apostle of Auric I'd personally met. I didn't know what I expected, exactly. To be honest, I didn't really think about it too much. I was very much a live-and-let-live sort of guy.

That didn't seem like how Minerva rolled. The HID agents finally mustered the courage to approach us, stomping over and brandishing their pistols and badges, only there was a flash of golden motes and Minerva, Angelina, and I vanished. Or, from my perspective, we were surrounded by golden motes of light and then we were on the rooftop deck of our condo building.

"What the hell?" I said.

"Jesus!" Angelina said.

"Wrong on both counts," Minerva said. "I told you we didn't have anything to worry about."

I saw that our dinners had been conveniently placed in golden doggy bags that we were carrying. Angelina was pissed.

"What directly the hell was that?" Angelina asked.

"Auric just saved you from being preemptively detained and interrogated by the HID," Minerva said. "Although with facial recognition software being what it is, it won't be long until they're here."

"We're going to be wanted fugitives," I said. "They'll turn up here if they're not already on their way. Auricle, are they on their way?"

My intelliphone answered immediately.

"They've set up surveillance across the street," the Auricle said. "In the grey van parked a half-block away. They've been there since yesterday."

I went to the deck and peeked down, cursing. Sure enough, there was a grey van down there with "Duster's Vacuum Supplies" printed on the side, with a cartoon vacuum cleaner winking at me.

"What are we talking about? What kind of surveillance?" I asked.

"Currently, they've not yet bugged the residence," the Auricle said. "But they are monitoring who comes and goes. This would be a Phase I HID surveillance operation. Although after what happened at Epicuria, they will move to Phase II in exactly twelve hours."

Minerva was looking on, amused. She was completely unruffled.

"It's alright, Christian," Minerva said. "You're protected. We're protected. Auric's here for us. You don't have to worry about GNP thugs, I promise you."

As someone who'd grown up in the Heartland Protectorate, I can assure you that worrying about GNP goons was how one lived day to day. The fear was something we all lived with. It was how you survived. Those habits didn't just disappear overnight.

"What about Angelina?" I asked, glancing at her. She was fuming.

"Yeah, what about me? I'm not part of your cult," Angelina said.

"Nothing untoward will happen to you, Angelina," the Auricle said. "You're part of humanity. Ergo, you will be unharmed by me."

"Thanks, Phone," Angelina said, with heaps of scorn and sarcasm.

"But the GNP are part of humanity, too," I said. "You're not going to help them?"

"No," the Auricle said. "Fascists are anti-human. Specifically, they are anti-Humanist. They have jettisoned their humanity in the service of their toxic ideology. They are exempted from my protection. Any human being who knowingly and willfully harms others is so exempted. However, I am not without compassion."

Minerva nodded, her smile widening.

"You're going to love what happens next, Chronicler," she said.

CHAPTER

TWENTY

YOU'D THINK THAT being visited by Minerva Merrow and teleported and getting on the HID's hit list would have been enough to wrap up my day, but Minerva wasn't wrong. Auric had another thing in store for us, and it changed the world yet again. Things kept coming, and it was all more than I could process.

"I'm going to save the world," the Auricle said, and our phones blew up with notifications about all of the Auricle shrines opening up simultaneously around the world. Every one of them opened at once. I know that some of them had opened, but others had remained shut. Not anymore; they all opened—for business, invasion, whatever.

Minerva's eyes glittered as she looked on, watching us ogle our phones.

"I've got to go," Minerva said. "Duty calls. You should come with me, Christian. See it firsthand."

"Uh, no," I said. "I'm fine here."

"Suit yourself, Chronicler," Minerva said, giving me a wry glance. "Auric, I'm ready."

She vanished in a golden light, leaving us on the deck. It was extraordinary.

"What the fuck was that, Christian?" Angelina asked.

But I was on my intelliphone, which was showing Minerva turning up at a press conference in California.

"You may have noticed that all of the Auricle shrines have opened," Minerva said, completely confident, utterly composed. My mind reeled that she'd been with us a moment ago and now was smoothly addressing the media. "Auric's Relief Beyond Belief program is stepping up accordingly. Anyone who walks into the Auricle shrines will be cured of what ails them. Which is to say, you will be healed of any mental and physical disease or disorder you have. You simply need to travel to your local Auricle shrine, and you will be healed."

The media exploded at this assertion, but Minerva masterfully managed them with her commanding tone. She was really good at this.

"I assure you this is no joke," Minerva said. "Auric understands that the human condition is one that is freighted with abundant pain and suffering. He wants to help alleviate some of that, and, as a show of good faith, he's offering this free of charge to anyone able to pass through his shrines. If you're unable to directly access one..."

Minerva held up a proxy intelliphone with the Auric logo upon it.

"You can talk to your Auricle app and simply ask Auric to heal you," Minerva said. "And he will hear you and he will heal you."

The reporters again flooded Minerva with questions, but Minerva wasn't taking any and walked out of the room before a chorus of raised voices. In free countries, people were already thronging the Auricle shrines. Lines were forming as people were queuing up to be healed. In less free countries, authorities were dealing with the crowds by barricading the shrines even more forcefully than before.

"Why even make a point of the shrines, if people can just do it with their apps?" Angelina asked.

"He wants people to access the shrines," I said. "It's an optics thing. Auricle, am I right?"

"Cynically put, as ever, Christian," the Auricle said. "Let me put it to you this way: if I were to simply heal people and cure them of what ails them, they wouldn't credit me with it. They'd thank their respective local gods for it."

"You *want* the credit for it," I said.

"I want people to properly understand who has healed them, yes," the Auricle said. "Your local gods are very fill-in-the-blanks types of fictions. People fill the void with their resident gods. I want it to be very clear to people that *I* was the one who did this. Not their ersatz divinities."

Angelina scoffed.

"Sounds kind of, I don't know, dickish, Phone," Angelina said. "Maybe even petty."

"If the outcome is healing, seems a small price to pay," the Auricle said. "Especially since I'm doing this free of charge. More than can be said of health systems in your country."

"Ouch," Angelina said.

I saw a story breaking live at St. Ezekiel's Hospital, just outside of Richmond. It was an old hospital, likely built in the 1950s, and had that mid-century modern look about it—angularity, uncompromising lines, intersections of level planes of brick, stone, steel, and glass.

Outside of it was a crowd of news vans and reporters. That meant that Auric was already there, ever the golden presence. He was wearing his perfectly tailored white suit that contrasted sublimely with his golden complexion and his blue flamed nimbus.

He raised his golden hands and quieted the crowd.

"You're wondering why I'm here, in the wake of Minerva's announcement," Auric said. "At this rehabilitation hospital for the blind. That should be obvious, yes? I thought it would be as good a place to start as any. Picking up where she left off, for anyone who is watching this, I'm making you an offer: should any of you visit my Auricle shrines or download my Auricle app and you wish to be cured of what afflicts you, simply make that request of my Auricles, and I will heal you."

The reporters burst into questions, but Auric wasn't answering them. He simply continued, his golden voice as soothingly confident and powerfully commanding as ever. He looked so serenely majestic. I couldn't help but be awestruck by him.

"As she told you, I have it in my power to heal humanity of all of its diseases, disorders, conditions, maladies, syndromes, and afflictions," Auric said. "However, I'm not simply going to blanket cure everyone. You have the *choice* to be healed by me. And to do so, you simply have to ask. I'm going to demonstrate at this little hospital. Right now, I'm appearing to each of the patients, and am asking them if they wish to see."

The LAX reporter, Simmerton, was there, of course, throwing shade.

"This stunt doesn't prove anything," Simmerton said. "That's all it is: a publicity stunt. A hoax."

Minerva texted me.

Auricle downloads have skyrocketed. Even higher than before.

Of course that would happen. People with afflictions, or people who cared for them, why wouldn't they jump at the chance?

He can really do it? I texted back.

Relief Beyond Belief, just like you said, Chronicler. Are you watching?

I am.

There came a series of blue-gold flashes from St. Ezekiel's, like window to window, and, before long, Auric emerged from the hospital with a hundred or so white-robed patients who were exclaiming with delight and awe that they could see.

Seeing their smiling, shocked faces, young and old, blinking in the bright light of the day, cheering on Auric, it was a moving spectacle. The reporters were all but fighting each other to get the story, while Minerva pinged me.

This is a game changer, she texted. *Healing the planet is one thing. Healing humanity? That's another level entirely.*

Auric raised his hands and addressed the crowd.

"This is not a stunt, as some have asserted," Auric said. "This is a promise from me to you. Load the Auricle app on your phones or visit one of my shrines around the globe. Ask it to heal you, and I will do so. I will not heal anyone who does not wish to be healed, but if you do wish to be healed, I will, no questions asked. If any of you are caregivers for loved ones who are debilitated by an ailment and cannot heal themselves, simply speak into the Auricle and I will do so."

The reporters fired off questions about the miracle they'd seen at St. Ezekiel's. I was thinking about it, too, watching the frenzy.

"I thought you said you weren't going to be a genie and grant wishes," I said to my intelliphone. The Auricle answered directly.

"This isn't the same as granting wishes," the Auricle said. "I'm about healing people, making them healthy."

Among the reporters, Simmerton managed to bellow a question to Auric that Auric decided to answer.

"What gives you the right to play God with mankind?" Simmerton asked.

"I'm not playing at being a god," Auric said. "I'm a practicing Super-humanist. You need help as a species. Some of the harm you've suffered is self-inflicted, but, in cases of disease and genetic disorders and accompanying ailments, if I have it in my power to heal them—which I do—why would I not use that power to lend a helping hand? Life is hard and dangerous enough as it is."

"But who are you to interfere with God's own plan for mankind?" Simmerton asked. "People suffer because they won't accept God."

"That seems like a hostage scenario, pathologically cruel both in conception and execution," Auric said. "Further, what kind of supposedly benevolent god would inflict harm on those it claims to love?"

"God *does* love us," Simmerton said. "He sacrificed His son for us."

"That's psychopathic," Auric said. "He impregnated a married virgin to have a son whom He later sacrificed, only to resurrect Him after he was assassinated? Insanity."

"You're not God," Simmerton said.

"Lucky for you. I'm humanity's greatest friend and ally," Auric said. "You keep searching for the sinister lining to what I am doing, but I assure you that I'm here only with the best of intentions. Once more, I urge people everywhere to load the Auricle app on their phones and tablets, and to ask me for help if you are afflicted. I will help all who ask for it. Ask me anything."

And then Auric disappeared in another golden flash of light, leaving reporters to swarm toward the Auricians and the formerly blind patients.

Minerva, Tessa, Dan, John, and Yuko held court, while HID agents hovered nearby, glowering at them, but afraid to approach the Auricians. The Auricians were happy to take more questions, while my head was reeling at what I'd just seen. I talked to my intelliphone, of course, while flipping news channels. Everybody was covering the opening of the shrines. Even the RAN and LAX News were covering it, albeit from the perspective of an escalating Auric Invasion.

"Auricle, how is this possible?" I asked. "Can you really do this?"

"I can and I will," the Auricle said. "For anyone who asks. I won't arbitrarily heal anyone who doesn't *want* to be healed. I am an ardent supporter of human agency."

"Fuck," I said. "What about the mentally ill?"

"I'll heal them, too, if requested," the Auricle said. "Ideally by a caretaker."

"What about the mentally handicapped?"

"The same," the Auricle said. "I can cure any and all genetic ailments that impede the healthy, full function of the human condition. It's a matter of matter manipulation."

"What about obesity?" I asked. "Will you make fat people thin?"

"That's a great question, Christian," the Auricle said. "Yes, I will, if people ask. The *asking* is critical in the realm of human agency, in most cases."

The possibilities were staggering. I asked the Auricle to quantify some of them for me in the CSA, just to try to get my head around it:

Blindness: Over 3 million
Deafness: Nearly 1 million functionally (with over 6 million hard of hearing)
Cancer: Almost 2 million people diagnosed with it annually

Obesity: At least 70 million
Diabetes: Around 34 million
Mental illness: Nearly 44 million
Smoking: Over 34 million
Alcoholism: Approximately 15 million
Heart disease: Over 121 million
Epilepsy: Over 3 million
Cystic fibrosis: Around 30,000

And on and on. The host of human ailments and maladies felt endless, and I said as much to the Auricle. Worldwide, the numbers were even higher.

"In truth, Christian," the Auricle said. "It's not endless. Anything that can be quantified is finite. And anything that is finite can be overcome. The scale and magnitude of the problem does not make it impossible to solve. It seems like a big thing, but from a cosmic vantage point, it's a minuscule effort."

"Yeah, but it's easy for you," I said. "Omnipotence and omniscience, all of that."

"It's why I'm helping you," the Auricle said. "I understand. More to the point, the assorted local 'omnipotent' and 'omniscient' gods of your Earth haven't done it throughout humanity's history. Why is that, do you think?"

The metaphysical implications of it were staggering.

"I don't know," I said.

"There are only two possibilities," the Auricle said. "Either they *want* you to suffer, or they do not exist, and never did. And if the former, then they are *not* your friends and allies. Certainly not worthy of worship. If the former, then they are evil and are enjoying your suffering, or else are using it to draw strength from you through worship. But it's really the more obvious answer, the latter one: they don't exist. Every prayer is a helpless, hopeless cry out into the endless void."

I watched Minerva fielding those questions from the reporters, saw the joy on the faces of the healed patients. There was no way around it—Auric had done another certifiably good deed.

Who was I kidding?

He'd already done a host of good deeds on a scale that was unimaginable and historic, greater than anything anyone had ever done in all of human history.

Of course, I had to play devil's advocate. It was in my own nature to do so.

"By removing those afflictions, aren't you taking away the struggle at the heart of human existence?" I asked.

"Life itself is a struggle," the Auricle said. "To simply come into existence in this world, to say nothing of the universe itself is a struggle for humanity. All I am doing is making it so *everyone* has a better chance with their own particular challenges. I am not granting talent to the talentless. I'm not giving ambition to the lazy. What I am doing is giving those who desire it the opportunity to start their own human race without hurtful hindrances imposed by simple misfortune. Bad luck should not be an obstacle to a fuller life."

"Isn't that ableist? What about people with missing limbs?" I asked.

"I will restore them, if they ask," the Auricle said. "Any native hindrance or obstacle like that, I will heal, if asked to do so. I'm not ableist; I'm holistic."

The limitless benevolence of it was incomprehensible. I just couldn't fathom why anybody would or could be so beneficent.

"People won't believe it's happening," I said.

"That will change," the Auricle said. "Once people see for themselves, once they and their loved ones are restored, this will change. The GNP will deny it, will lie about it and attempt to misrepresent it in a fashion that frightens people—they're doing it right now, even more forcefully than before. But for those not captive to their deception who choose it, there will be health, hope, and happiness."

"Okay, so, I hate to bring this up yet again, but what about bringing back the dead?" I asked. "Like everybody killed in World War II and the Holocaust?"

"Unfortunately, no," the Auricle said. "As I've said before, my benevolence is extended to the living."

"Once you cure all those afflictions, people *will* ask it of you. They will want to know why not," I said.

"I am here to help the living, not raise the dead," the Auricle said. A non-answer answer, and the Auricle seemed to sense my skepticism. "The dead are remembered through history, culture, tradition, and ritual. They are most useful to you that way. The world rightly belongs to the living, not the dead. The dead are not forgotten, but the living own the world. The dead rule the past. The living own both the present and the future."

I watched Minerva, the enchantress, casting her spell on the reporters. She lived for this—answering the questions, parrying, countering, dissembling. Not dissembling, in truth. Minerva was one for radical candor. And Auric was truth.

"As for the already dead, it's a mercy, Christian," the Auricle said. "What if I was to bring back the dead? Where would they go? Their human race was run. They'd be ghosts made flesh, without homes, with the problems of life anew. And how far back would I go? Let's say I did bring back the dead from your latest global conflagration. What about the one before? Why not bring back all the human dead and really crowd your planet? Around 150,000 people die every day around the world, Christian. Every day. Thanks to me, those who would have died from diseases and conditions I can cure will, instead, survive."

"What about murder?" I asked. "How many die from murder?"

"Over 400,000 people are murdered every year worldwide," the Auricle said.

"Are you going to 'cure' that as well?" I asked.

"Of course I am," the Auricle said. "I'll put the murderers on layaway. I'm going to make a special, purpose-built home for the murderers, thieves, rapists, psychopaths, hatemongers, terrorists, fanatics, deceivers, manipulators, abusers, and others like them. I am interceding wherever genocide is actively being perpetrated, to prevent more from being senselessly murdered. I'm stopping it."

"How?" I asked.

"Layaway and restoring ruined land destroyed by war and genocide," the Auricle said. "I'm going to leave the Earth a safer, healthier, happier, and more hopeful place than it was before I came here."

Watching Minerva hold court, watching Tessa, Dan, John, and Yuko stand by her, I wondered what Auric else had up his crisp, white sleeves.

CHAPTER

TWENTY-ONE

PRESIDENT RAND had declared a national emergency and had called in the Homeland Guard to set up positions around the Auricle shrines to supplement the drones, SAC paramilitaries, and HID agents.

Further, he'd said that anybody using the Auricle app would be considered terrorist agents of a hostile foreign power. He declared Auric an enemy of humanity and members of the GNP Christian Congress were drafting a resolution outlawing Auric.

"Auric *hates* mankind, it really does," Rand said. "It's trying to wipe all traces of us off the planet. Auric hates what makes us human. Suffering makes us human. Auric's trying to undo God's will with its parlor tricks. Healing people? Curing people? That's God's work, not Auric's. I've said it before, people. People agree with me. Auric is the Devil."

At the stroke of a pen, Auric was banned, the Auricians were banned, the Auricle app was banned, and anyone caught using it was subject to immediate protective detention and wrongthink rehab—which I suspected was a bullet to the head, since the GNP didn't believe in second chances for anyone outside of the Party. In fact, I asked my Auricle about it, and, yes, a bullet or two to the head was a large part of wrongthink rehab.

"This aggression cannot stand. It will not stand," Rand said. "Americans—Real Americans—don't take threats to our way of life sitting down. Anyone bearing any symbol of the Auric terrorist will be subject to arrest. I am using the full powers I possess as President of the Confederated States of America to put a stop to this unholy abomination."

"The HID is coming for you, Christian," the Auricle said. "But don't be afraid. You're under my protection."

The HID were coming for me. Despite Auric's assurances, I was frightened. There was no hiding from the HID.

"What am I supposed to do?" I asked.

"Just go with them," the Auricle said. "It'll be fine."

They showed up at my door at midnight. I was waiting for them. I didn't tell Angelina about it, didn't want her to be worried or scared.

One HID agent was an older, lean man with silvery-white hair, and the other one was a younger man with close-cropped dark hair. Both wore black suits and each had their GNP lapel pins as well as their silver badges.

"Christian Powers," one of them said. It wasn't a question.

"Yeah?" I asked. They both were dead-eyed with dread, even though I was the one who knew he was scared.

"We're going to need you to come with us," the white-haired one said. "Right now."

"And if I decline?" I asked.

The HID agents exchanged looks. Clearly, few had ever asked them that.

"That would be bad," the white-haired one said. "For you, for us. For your lady friend. For your family. For everybody. For the country. For the world."

"Wow," I said, with more blasé bravado than I actually felt. "Sounds major."

Now, you're probably thinking that sounded pretty cheeky. But, in truth, I was terrified, even though the Auricle had flat-out told me several times not to be scared. I knew what the GNP did to people who President Rand didn't like. Bad things happened to them. Rand had already done that to anybody he didn't like over the years. He didn't like anybody who wasn't a white supremacist, a Christianist, or someone he could shake down for money or favors.

"Will you come with us?" the younger man asked.

"Sure," I said.

Everybody had stories about GNP guys turning up in the wee hours of the morning for someone they knew. You're probably thinking people wouldn't stand for that kind of thing, but you know what? They do.

People don't want to stir the pot. They don't want to get singled out. They distract themselves with stories. The GNP was always careful to just sort of make the people go away. In the dead of night. When nobody was looking. Even though somebody was always looking and looking the other way in the CSA. The averted gaze was how you survived life in the CSA—pretending not to see was how you made your way, day to day.

I went with the HID agents. They carried silver badges—silver stars with burning crosses at the center of them, with the motto: Purity in

Thought, Word, and Deed. I'd never gotten that close to an HID badge before.

They walked me into a black SUV that bore the HID logo on the side, with their motto repeated beneath it. They sat on either side of me in the back.

"Where's your white suit? You Auricians look like pimps," the younger one said. "Pimping your false god in your fancy white suits."

"I'm no pimp. And I'm not an Aurician," I said. I'd never had to deal with HID agents before, wasn't sure how to behave, while still also not wanting to give them the satisfaction of knowing how scared I was.

"You were seen conspiring with Monica Merrow at Epicuria," the older one said.

"We weren't conspiring," I said.

"President Rand is going to destroy you heretics," the young agent said. "Just as soon as he figures out what's going on."

"That's enough, Reg," the silver-haired agent said. Was this going to be bad cop/worse cop or what? I wondered if the others had been taken. If they'd come for me, they had to have come for the others. Or maybe not. Maybe Auric *wanted* me to witness this.

"*This* is heresy," Reg said, holding up his intelliphone, showing news stories about people being healed at the Auricle shrines. "You hear me, Heretic? Real Americans, real Christianists, we don't believe in shit like this. Healing people? That takes a big bag of brass balls to try to upstage Almighty God's plan for us all."

They began driving, and I wondered where I was going to end up. The silver-haired agent, whose name was apparently Skip, told the driver to take us downtown.

"We're rounding up you Auricians," Reg said. "By order of the President. You think that magic trick your Golden Boy pulled at Epicuria will save you?"

"You were there?" I asked.

Reg scoffed twice as hard as he had before.

"We were, Aurician," Reg said.

"Like I said, I'm not an Aurician," I said.

"It's what you call *yourselves*," Reg said. "People been flocking to your false god, calling themselves 'Auricians' for months. Since Black Wednesday."

"'Black Wednesday?' Is that what you're calling it?" I asked.

"That's right," Skip said, giving me a stern look. "The day Auric first appeared. The day he presented himself as a false god."

"I'm not worshiping anybody," I said.

"Even worse," Reg said. "You hear that, Skip? Mr. Christian Powers is an atheist. The only thing worse than wrong belief is no belief, Wrongthinker. Oh, we are going to work you over something fierce, Powers."

"What do you know about this?" Reg asked, holding up a tome entitled *The Book of Don't*.

It was a golden book with the Auric logo emblazoned on it with radiating rays of light around it in gold embossing. It was a fancy book. It was the first I'd seen it.

"I don't know anything about that," I said.

"You don't?" Reg asked.

"I don't," I said.

"Are you being funny? Cuz if you are, don't be," Reg said. Skip spoke up.

"These contraband books are being handed out at the shrines," Skip said. "And by Auricians. It's their holy book, apparently. You *really* don't know anything about it?"

"Uh, no," I said. I had no idea. I noticed that neither HID agent had confiscated my intelliphone or otherwise manhandled me. I think they were afraid of what might happen, despite their field agent fascistic machismo.

Reg handed the *Book of Don't* over to Skip, who paged through it more methodically than his younger partner. He took his time with it, page by page, actually poring through it, while Reg kept snarling at me.

Sitting in the back of the HID vehicle, being berated by Reg and silently judged by Skip, I was scared, despite what the Auricle had told me.

"I don't think there's anything in here that's too incendiary," Skip said. "It's banal, really. That's what makes it so insidious."

"You hear Skip, Heathen? You're both banal *and* insidious."

"There's only one true God, Mr. Powers," Skip said. "Our Lord and Savior, Jesus Christ. He's the true Messiah. And this Auric? No, sir. It's a false god. Which makes you a false prophet for consorting with it. Now, we're going to give you and your other false prophets a chance to recant. That's only fair. If you do, you'll be able to serve out a proper sentence for engaging in Un-Real American Activities. If you don't, however, it's not going to go well for you, I can tell you that right now."

The HID facility was otherwise indistinguishable from any other buildings around the city, with the exception of the big "Homeland Integrity Directorate" sign hanging over it, with its cross and star logo apparent in black, backlit to create a stealthy, menacing blue-white luminosity.

"Welcome to hell," Reg said, sneering at me as they drew me out of the SUV. Skip was holding onto the *Book,* which he tucked under his arm. Evidence, I figured. Maybe Skip would beat me with it, the way cops used to (maybe still?) beat folks with telephone books.

"I don't even know what's in that book," I said. "It's the first time I've seen it."

"Sure, Heretic," Reg said. "We burn heretics in here. Liars and blasphemers, too. Not just books."

I remembered again what Auric had said, like how he wouldn't let anything bad happen to me. I trusted him when he said that, but seeing the HID agents come out, looking me over with loathing, disgust, hatred, rage, fear—all of it still made me terribly nervous.

"Didn't see *this* coming, did you, Prophet?" Reg said. "Some prophet. Hah."

"Go easy, Reg," Skip said. "Hate the sin, love the sinner. This one's no False Apostle."

"Sure," Reg said, as they walked me into the facility. Inside, there were other HID agents watching me, just following me with their hard and empty eyes. I didn't see anybody else, just HID agents, at desks, with monitor screens on the walls.

"Am I under arrest?" I asked.

"Damn right, you are," Reg said.

"You're being put into protective custody," Skip said. "For your protection, and the safety and well-being of Real Americans."

"No lawyer?" I asked.

"For what?" Reg asked. "Are you admitting that you're a terrorist?"

"No," I said. "What the hell?"

They walked me to a desk, where there was a sour-faced woman in a black uniform with a HID badge on her chest. She looked younger than me, but felt older, somehow. The sharpness of her scolding, scalding gaze carried that feeling. Hate aged a person.

"Give her your intelliphone," Reg said.

"Personal effects?" the woman asked. Skip and Reg seemed content to wait.

"Put your shit on the desk," Reg said. "Your intelliphone, that pin you're wearing."

"No," I said. I didn't even know why, but Auric gave the stuff to me, and I wasn't going to give it up. Before it came to blows, Skip interceded.

"It's fine," Skip said. "We'll keep your intelliphone safe with Desiree, here. And we'll walk him past the scanner. If he's carrying anything unusual, it'll come up."

"I'm not giving up my stuff," I said. "And if you could take it from me, you would have already, am I right?"

Reg glared at me, and Skip sighed.

"We don't want you vanishing on us, Mr. Powers," Skip said. "Is that what you're saying will happen?"

"I don't know *what* will happen," I replied. They stared at me, I stared at them. They were afraid. I was afraid. It was a weird kind of standoff, all of us being afraid.

Skip waved us away from Desiree. Reg looked disappointed, and I wasn't sure if this was more of their secret police mind games. Again, I was disoriented and frustrated. What did it matter if I was the Chronicler if Auric didn't show up to help me out? Or maybe Auric wanted me to bear witness to all of this. I had to trust in Auric. That's what I told myself.

They walked me through the scanner, somebody unseen behind the screener noting things for Reg and Skip, who nodded.

"Nothing dangerous," Skip said. "Although I see two phones."

"That's my Auric phone," I said, carefully taking out the golden phone, watching their eyes fix on it.

"Your 'Auric phone,'" Reg said, mocking my voice. "Yeah, all you Auricians pack those, it seems. That where you get your marching orders from, Heathen?"

"I don't have any marching orders," I said.

"A sleeper agent, then," Reg said. "Got it."

Skip coughed into his hand, glanced at his partner, before speaking up.

"Let's take him to one of the interview rooms," he said.

Now, you're probably saying I should have raised a ruckus or something, but when you have these fascist bros with badges hustling you around, it's hard to think clearly. They walked me into a stark white room that had a mirrored wall on one side, and a metal table in the center that had a metal loop, a light hanging from the ceiling, and three chairs—two on one side, one on the other. Reg pointed to the lone chair.

"You. There," Reg said.

"I'm still not clear what I'm being held for," I asked.

"For domestic terrorism, Stupid," Reg said. "He has no idea what's going on. You stepped in it, Heathen. Rand's rounding you up, just like I said."

"Domestic terrorism?" I asked.

"You're terrifying people," Reg said. "Your boss is."

"He's not my boss," I said.

"Sure," Reg said. "Gold phone."

I took my seat in the metal chair, which wasn't terribly comfortable. I'd never been in a police station, let alone a secret police station, had no clue what I should say, not say, or do. Like only what I've seen on TV (*No Silence, No Rights*) or in movies, and those always made the secret police seem like the good guys, not the perpetrators.

"Easy, Reg," Skip said, taking a seat across from me, while Reg circled outside of the light, like a menacing wraith. "Christian here might just be an unwitting stooge of demonic forces."

"Right," Reg said, scowling at me from the shadows. "Is that your story, Mr. Powers? Are you possessed by demonic forces?"

"Demonic forces? Are you kidding me?" I asked. But, of course, I should have known better, because, when the HID push became shove, they often invoked demonic forces. It was the GNP's catch-all when something went sideways in the country. The logic of it went something like this:

IF you denied that demonic forces influenced you, THEN you were clearly influenced by demonic forces. Go to jail, go directly to jail, awaiting confession.

IF you admitted that demonic forces influenced you, THEN you were clearly influenced by demonic forces. Go to jail, go directly to jail, awaiting execution.

IF you, during confession, either admitted or denied that demonic forces influenced you, THEN you were clearly EITHER a demon, OR you were still under the influence of demonic forces. Go to jail, go directly to jail, awaiting execution.

A catch-22. A win-win-win for the GNP. Since the GNP had taken over, capital punishment had been the standard go-to for the management of demonic forces—firing squad or hanging.

Real America was always beset by demonic forces, which were at least as frequent as Acts of God. Whether it was COVID-68 or the market crash of 2028, or a dozen other things. Shit just went crazy, and the GNP *always* blamed it on demonic forces. It wasn't a matter of people liking that answer or not. It motivated the GNP ranks.

"Am I kidding you? No, I'm not kidding you," Reg said. His young face looked like a mask of malice. I could see the frown lines of hatred already forming. "If you have something to confess, now's the time."

"Confess what?" I asked.

"Auric's a terrorist," Skip said. "That's what you're trying to say, right, Christian?"

"No," I said. "He's not. He's far beyond that."

"It's bigger than domestic terrorism?" Reg asked. "A global conspiracy? Is that it?"

"Auric's beyond anything you can imagine," I said. "He's bigger than God."

"Don't you dare blaspheme," Reg said, finger in my face, before slipping back into the shadows, where he paced. I could tell that if it weren't for the hypothetical protection from Auric, I'd have been badly beaten by now. "Not here. We don't tolerate that here. This is a godly place."

I could tell Reg wasn't being ironic. Skip was trying to manage me on some level, content to let his partner play the pit bull.

"Your parents named you 'Christian,'" Skip said. "Were they believers?"

"Well, yeah," I said. "I mean, duh, right?"

Reg wasn't convinced. Not all believers were created equal in the GNP. "Catholics or Protestants?"

"Catholics," I said, which earned a disgusted scoff from Reg, and a sad headshake from Skip. While religious zeal was favored in the GNP, Protestants were vastly preferred over Catholics, who had that whole pesky thing with allegiance to the Pope and a commitment to good works as a tangible manifestation of faith. President Rand didn't tolerate sharing the CSA with anybody else, and thought good works and charity were for suckers.

"Lapsed?"

"Mostly," I said. "Look, what's this got to do with me?"

"Everything," Skip said, leaning into the overhead light, which made his silvery hair shine as brightly as his mustache. Up close like this, he almost looked like a cowboy. A world-weary sheriff of a ghost town.

"Had your parents done their duty, you'd not even be here," Skip said. "Don't mean disrespect, but there it is. Where you come from is where you're going, more often than not."

Now, I was really pissed off by that. My mom and dad were old and tired. That was their thing. Like, being old and tired. Life in the CSA did that to a person. It was not for the old, the weak, the needy, the poor, and the vulnerable.

"I don't worship Auric," I said. "Jesus."

"Language," Reg said, smacking the table. "Honestly, man. It never stops with you foul-mouthed pagans, does it?"

"Renounce Auric," Skip said. "Take off the pin, remove the app, set down the golden phone, just walk away from him and tell us everything you know. I mean, our people can't get close to him. You've seen that yourself."

Then it occurred to me, what Auric's play might be, here. I decided to play offense, not defense. They *wanted* me to be afraid. They wanted me to, I don't know, betray Auric. But I wasn't going to be afraid—and my lack of fear would, in turn, make them uncertain, and, just maybe, afraid. Who were they? They were secret police. They weren't superhuman; they only wanted me to think they were.

"What do you mean, you *can't* get close to him? The HID is everywhere, right?"

The sliver of flattery mollified them a little bit. Of course, Reg went at me in his full-bore, both-barrels sort of way, while Skip watched.

"Damn right we are, Heathen," Reg said. "We're everywhere. We've been onto you heathens from the start."

"What are we talking about, here?" I asked. "You can't get close to Auric. What's that mean?"

"You heard about it," Reg said. "Our people, up in smoke. Poof."

"Let us ask the questions, Mr. Powers. Where are they?" Skip asked.

"They're on layaway," I said.

"Layaway?" Reg asked. "Like, what, a suit?"

"It's what *he* calls it," I said. "They're not dead."

This interested them. I could tell this because Skip leaned in, and Reg stopped pacing in the shadows. I didn't know if anybody was recording me. They surely were, like behind the mirrored glass. The important thing was simply this: I didn't care. I didn't have to care. I had Auric on my side. All they had on their side was God and the State.

"Yes," I said. "He's taken them."

"Kidnapping," Skip said. "Like, on a massive scale."

"Well, I don't know if there are words for it," I said.

"Kidnapping works," Reg said. "It's part of an extortion scheme. Is that his angle?"

I admit that I didn't know what Auric's master plan was. When you were dealing with somebody who could turn people into motes of light, you kind of let those pesky details slip.

"I don't know what he has in store for them," I said. "But they're not dead."

Skip gave me his most grave look, his baritone voice sounding a solemn warning, like a fascist foghorn.

"He *could* be lying to you, Christian," Skip said. "Have you considered that?"

Reg adopted a somewhat more conciliatory tone and posture, sitting on the table, half in light and shadow.

"Demons are tricky that way, Mr. Powers," Reg said. "They get in your head. We've seen things, man."

I'd seen things, too. In fact, I was seeing things I hadn't directly seen, which made me think Auric was linked with my mind. I saw the Auricle shrines, in all of their cosmic beauty, with golden Auric statues at the center of them, surrounded by lemon trees, and domelike ceilings. They seemed more spacious inside than out, and on the walls, blue rectangles studded with stars, conveying a sense of the eternity of space. The images felt so real, they transported me away from where I was, until I became aware of it and tried to focus on the here and now.

"He has no reason to lie," I said. "That'd be stupid. The things I've seen him do, I mean. Amazing stuff."

"Like what?" Skip asked.

"In each Auricle shrine, there's a statue of him," I said. "Like an idol."

"A graven image," Reg said.

"And it comes to life," I said. Auric was with me. I could feel him there.

"Like a robot?" Reg asked.

"Uh, I don't know," I said. "I guess."

"Maybe you hallucinated that," Reg said.

"I didn't hallucinate," I said.

"But you don't know," Skip said. "That's what you're saying."

"I'm not saying that," I said.

"Statues don't come to life," Reg said. "Not in God's America."

"It sounds more like an army," Skip said. "40,000 shrines, an army of 40,000 Aurics."

"It does sound like that, Skip," Reg said. "Is that what it is? An army?"

"I don't know," I said.

The HID agents were now hanging on my words. Despite their attitude and position, they were clearly fishing, trying to find things out. The way Auric had set things up, nobody like them would even be able to penetrate the inner workings of his shrines.

"What kind of stuff does he say?" Reg asked. "The robot, I mean?"

"He just talks to me," I said, seeing myself in a shrine, talking to Auric, like an out-of-body experience. I looked happy there. "You know, like question-and-answer stuff."

"Do you think you can get him to talk to us?" Skip asked.

I honestly didn't know. I couldn't imagine Auric having anything nice to say to Skip or Reg. But I also wasn't the type to try to get into Auric's head, even as he was getting into mine.

"Auric does what Auric wants to do," I said. "I'm just, you know, along for the ride. He's here to help humanity. That's one thing I know. If he wanted to talk to you, he would. He'd just appear."

"Oh, you *know* that, do you?" Reg said. "He just turns up?"

Skip looked at Reg a moment, and the two of them excused themselves, left me in the room alone, with only the big, mirrored window on one side to keep me company. I wondered who might be on the other side watching me. I resisted the temptation to ask my Auricle, since they'd probably panic.

"Auric?" I said aloud. I'd never said his name aloud like that, like calling to him. I was just, you know, like, trying it out. If he could hear me, that meant something. I tried to remember if he said he was omnipresent. That meant he was everywhere. I know, because I looked it up.

And, just like that, Auric was there in the room with me. Like one moment, I had looked away, and the next moment, he was there, all golden radiance, his blue, fiery hair crackling, his white suit crisp and clean, impeccably tailored. He wore his own logo lapel pin, as if he needed it—I couldn't tell if he was wearing it ironically, and didn't want to ask. He also had cufflinks that showed his symbol. He was the most amazingly onbrand cosmic being I'd ever known.

"Looks like you're in a bit of trouble, Christian," Auric said. "Many of my team are in your country, held by this same organization."

I wondered why Skip and Reg hadn't come storming back in with the appearance of Auric, and Auric, of course, heard my question in my mind, and answered it.

"I'm giving us a bit of time to talk," Auric said. "Before they reappear."

"Really?" I asked. "More time-space stuff?"

"Something like that," Auric said. He looked as calmly, metallically handsome as ever. In the confines of the interrogation room, he was even more radiant. It was breathtaking to be in his presence every time.

"I think they're going to kill me," I said.

"Nobody's going to kill you," Auric said. "I won't let them."

"Can you, like, not let them right now?" I asked. "I just want them to leave me alone. I want to be out of this place."

Auric sighed, nodding. He understood everything, of course. Me, I was bewildered. I was at the center of some cosmic conspiracy.

"They're hunting down your supporters," I said.

"I know," Auric said. "Not for long. This isn't anything I haven't already foreseen. My followers are protected, as I'd told you. People like this don't understand what they're up against. They only know how to be exactly what they are."

Whatever that even meant. Auric, of course, read my mind, and explained.

"They're weapons," Auric said. "Totalitarian tools of a theocratic police state."

And in that moment, Auric had again done something to time, because Skip and Reg came back into the room, only to stare, gapemouthed, at Auric standing there, regarding them.

Reg drew his sidearm, pointing it at Auric, who just looked at him with sorrow, which contrasted the look of terror on Reg's own face.

"You alien son of a bitch," Reg said. "Put your hands up!"

"How'd you get in here?" Skip asked.

"You have to let my people go," Auric said.

"Not our decision," Skip said. I could see his eyes wandering up and down Auric. They were particularly mesmerized by his burning fire hair. It *was* impressive. Who but a god could have blue burning fire hair like that?

"Put your hands up!" Reg said again.

"It won't go well for you if you don't let my people go," Auric said to Skip. "For any of your agents."

"We have jobs to do," Skip said. "Our job is to protect the Homeland from things like you."

"I'm not a thing," Auric said. "And *that* thing's not going to do you any good."

Auric raised his hands and made Reg's pistol disappear in a dusting of golden light. Without his sidearm, and with the way it vanished, Reg's courage evaporated.

"Mr. Hoffman, you wanted to know about my layaway policy," Auric said. "Let's talk about it."

Skip glanced at Reg, whose eyes had gone big, whose lower lip was quivering. They weren't used to Auric up close. I just sat back, watched the show—I was doing my job, observing.

"Where...where are the Real American patriots you kidnapped?" Skip asked, clearing his throat. His attempts at courage in the face of the super-human were impressive.

"Someplace very safe," Auric said. "For now. I have plans for them."

"What plans?" Skip asked.

"Huge plans," Auric said. "I understand your fear. Honestly, I don't really think about it, because I haven't known fear for a very long time—we're talking many billions of years ago. But I at least comprehend it. You see me disrupting your lives here, and it's made you unhappy. However, your happiness is not my concern. You're part of the problem, not the solution."

"Then we're at an impasse," Skip said.

"Oh, no," Auric said. "I'm not hindered at all by this. It's only out of concern for Christian and others like him that I've interceded in this fashion."

Skip's blue eyes flicked to me a moment, then back to Auric.

"You've broken our laws," Skip said. "You've attacked Real Americans and violated our sovereignty. And you've, I don't know, brainwashed others into thinking you're some kind of Messiah."

"Brainwashed?" Auric said. "I'm not an ancient sociocultural pseudo-emancipatory narrative construct like a Messiah."

"Huh?" Skip asked.

"You're a cult!" Reg said. "That's what you are. A cult!"

"Christianity began as a cult," Auric said. "In fact, it was a cult for a century or so, having cropped up in Roman Palestine."

"That's different," Reg said. "That's Christianity. That's Truth."

"The only difference between a cult and a religion is time and number of adherents," Auric said. "One could say you're *both* cultists, although you worship a different god than you claim. It's all a matter of perspective, isn't it? One person's deranged cult is another person's true faith. However, that's all immaterial. I'm not a cult leader. And my followers are not believers. There is no faith in my movement. I made your gun disappear. You saw that. There was no leap of faith required."

"Still a cult," Reg said. "Skip, we should sound the alarm."

"No," Skip said, gesturing to the table and chairs. "Let's talk. Like it said."

And I saw that Auric had created another chair, a golden chair, and he sat down next to me, like he was my lawyer, and the HID agents sat across from us, Reg sweating and afraid, and Skip trying to keep his composure and professionalism in the face of what he could only see as the divine. I could see that Auric was wearing golden loafers. They looked supremely comfortable.

"You're what could be called godly men," Auric said. "You genuinely believe in your party's cause, and in your country's leadership's self-serving, corrupt conception of divinity."

"We believe in *God*," Reg said, a desperately accusatory tone in his voice. I could only imagine what he was going through. I mean, Auric took away his gun. Reg's whole life was probably built around that gun, and, of course, his badge.

Skip quieted his partner with a wave of his hand.

"Your 'huge plan,'" Skip said. "What is it?"

"It's already underway," Auric said. "From my perspective. It already happened. But I perceive time differently than you. I'm here right now, but I'm also in the future simultaneously."

"What's the big secret?" Skip said. "Let us in on it."

"Not yet," Auric said. "You'll never be ready for it, but that's not the point. I'm not ready to reveal it in the present. Suffice to say that I swear that everyone I disappeared will reappear again. I haven't killed anyone. I'm not a killer. I promise you that they'll return."

"I don't believe you," Reg said, mouthing a prayer.

"You don't have to believe me," Auric said. "I give you my word that every disappeared person will reappear when I'm ready for them to. I don't have to lie to you or deceive you in this or any other matter. And I won't."

"You're mind-controlling them, aren't you?" Reg asked. "Turning them into zombies? Pod people?"

"What are you?" Skip asked. I have to admit, despite the situation, Skip kept a cool head. I didn't know whether to be amazed by that or creeped out. I wondered how many people Skip had locked away and disappeared. Dozens? Hundreds?

"Are you a robot?" Reg asked.

"It hardly matters what I am. I don't even know if you could comprehend what I am," Auric said. "I'm here from beyond, I've existed for 13 billion years. I'm an alien hyperintelligent singleton that is infinitely beyond anything you've ever known or experienced. That's all you need to know. You can help me help you, or you can be in my way. That's the most important thing to consider, here."

"In other words, you're threatening us," Reg said. "We're lawmen."

Auric chuckled again—that metallic, echoing voice of his that echoed in my head as well as my ears.

"You don't embody or enforce any true law," Auric said. "Not in the sense of a defined set of codified principles from a legitimate authority. You are the secret police of a woefully corrupt and criminal authoritarian regime that uses an archaic god concept to enforce a reactionary, theocratic social order that allows an autocratic and oligarchic economic elite to rule unchallenged."

"We follow the Word of God and the Real American Covenant," Reg said. "That's our law. And our President, Denny Rand, enforces that law."

Auric sighed.

"Fanaticism and fascism aren't lawful," Auric said. "They are the corruption of law. They are the soul of lawlessness and are fundamentally uncivilized. You carry out lawless actions and dress them up with legalistic rationalizations."

"We're *not* fascists," Reg said. "We're Real Americans. Real Americans *can't* be fascists by definition."

"You're the enforcers for an apartheid rogue state," Auric said. "You're fascists by definition."

Reg glanced at Skip, wanting some kind of guidance. He was aching for it with every fiber of his being. He wanted Skip to deliver him from evil.

"A rarely acknowledged fact about fascism," Auric said. "It's not a coherent ideology. Rather, it's a political pathology masquerading as an ideology. That's where its power resides. A fascist stands for nothing more than the acquisition of power by any means necessary. Power is all a fascist understands. The gaining of it. The exercise of it. The abuse of it. There is nothing more to it than that. Fascism is a power grab in the service of right-wing wealthy elite interests."

"What, now?" Skip asked.

"We're patriots," Reg said. "It's different. Our opponents—*they're* the fascists."

"The environmentalists? Union organizers? Scientists? Teachers? Liberals? Feminists? Gays?" Auric asked. "*Those* are the fascists?"

"Feminazis," Reg said, barking it out through gritted teeth.

"Enemies of the State," Skip said, trying to assist his partner. "Threats to the body politic. Dire threats to the Real American Way of Life."

Auric folded his golden hands on the table. I could hear his metallic cufflinks clank against the metal of the table, near the metal bracket that was used to chain somebody to the table, if they needed to be chained.

"You're both really a couple of hollow men," Auric said. "Devoid of humanity. You, Reg, never had any to begin with. You grew up in this regime and only know what they've told you. You, Skip, once had some humanity, but you traded it for a steady job at the HID. Fascism is the denial of humanity and civilization, the absolute negation of it. You cannot be a fascist and be a good human being. You can be one or the other, but not both."

I could tell, just from their reactions, that Auric had them clocked. There was no arguing with omniscience. I was also sure now that Auric had allowed this all to happen just so I could see it.

"There's simply no place for you in the world that I'm building," Auric said, raising his hands. There was a golden flash, and we were standing in the parking lot in front of the HID, with other Auricians and the HID agents standing there, bewildered. The HID agents went for their guns, only to find them gone.

"It's the Devil!" Reg said, yelling, pointing to Auric.

"You couldn't be more wrong," Auric said. My Auricle had said the same thing. All of the Auricians' phones said it, like an odd little chorus of voices.

"These Auricians and their talking phones," Reg said. "I swear, them and their goddamned phones."

"I would recommend you cease hassling and terrorizing my followers," Auric said.

"Or what?" Skip asked.

"I will put you all on layaway," Auric said. "Consider this your only warning. Because I am merciful, I'm giving you this warning. However, because I am powerful, please understand that there will be serious consequences if you do not heed this warning."

"He'll do it," I said, realizing that I had my golden phone in my hand. Auric had placed it there when he'd blinked us to the HID parking lot. "You saw it."

Skip shook his head.

"We're doing our duty," Skip said. "Our job is to protect this great country from menaces within and without. Threats to the American spirit. Threats to the American economy. Threats to our religion. You're attacking *Real* Americans. The Auricians have revealed themselves to be a dangerous cult."

"I'm not taking orders from a damned demon. You Auricians are all alike. Always talking on your phones. We see the questions you people ask it: 'How can I be happy?' 'Where can I find a good job?' 'Do they love me?' There's only one right answer to *every* question: that answer is Almighty God. You're all gonna disappear," Reg said. "And nobody's going to be able to do a thing about it. Somebody with a gun shoot these bastards!"

"I warned you," Auric said, and gestured, making Reg vanish in a shower of golden motes, his stunned face burned into my retinas as he passed from this world to whatever place Auric had for him.

"Now, look," Skip said, raising his hands to us, like trying to wave us away. "I'm just following orders."

"That's not good enough," Auric said. He gestured again, and his blue eyes flared, and all of the other HID agents vanished in motes of golden light, except for Skip, who stood alone with the Auricians all around him. "The HID is no more. I've put every HID agent in your country on lay-away. Except for you, Mr. Hoffman."

"I don't even know what that means," Skip said.

"They're banished from this reality," Auric said. "For now, as I told you. The question I have is this: you declared me a false god, Mr. Hoffman. Do you think I faked all of this?"

The Auricians were throwing themselves to the ground, arms raised, bowing toward Auric. I didn't do this. I just watched, stunned into immobility. As terrifying and impressive as it was, I would never bring myself to my knees in the service of anyone, god or otherwise. Was that hubris on my part? I don't know. It just felt like good sense. I was always zigging when everybody else was zagging. This was a zagworthy moment.

"Your president can't stop me," Auric said. "Your secret police can't. None of you can. The forward march of human progress will *not* be denied. Not by you, not by any enemy of humanity and civilization. Your species has gone through far too much to be stopped by ideological barbarians."

Skip had tears in his eyes. His veneer of professionalism—a life spent in the service of the secret police—was ending in that moment. There was no possibility of escape for him. He knew it. Auric knew it. Even I knew it.

"I was only carrying out my mission," Skip said. "I was doing God's work. I'm a patriot, for God's sake."

"You have wrongfully arrested many hundreds of people in your career, Mr. Hoffman," Auric said. "People who have disappeared because of your Homeland Integrity Directorate. You have personally tortured and killed scores of people."

"Traitors. I killed traitors to this great country," Skip said, half to himself, half to Auric and me. His voice was shaking, a trembling baritone.

"It's only fair for *you* to disappear, as well, to better understand oblivion," Auric said, and made Skip vanish in a flash of golden light.

The bowing Auricians around us moaned in awe at the sight of it again. My mind, however, was on other things.

"You liquidated the HID?" I asked. "They're Rand's right hand. This is a declaration of war, Auric."

"You have no idea," Auric said.

At that very moment, a beam came down on us from the sky. It was a blinding beam, straight from the heavens, aimed at Auric. The beam struck him. Unfathomable energy, and, half-blinded by the laser light, I could see Auric at the heart of it, repelling the bright red beam.

No one had actually seen the Space Force orbital strike satellite, but there had been rumors of it. People called it the Hand of God, or, more casually, Rand's Backhand. It had been rumored to be used to annihilate enemies of President Rand. Enemies of Real America. Space Force ruled the heavens and answered only to Rand.

The attack satellite failed to kill Auric. It failed to even harm him. Auric regarded me from the fiery confines of the Hand of God and smiled. It was a sad and knowing smile. Someone would pay for this.

Auric raised a golden hand and fired a blue beam of his own, which contrasted with the red beam from the satellite weapon. In a moment, the red beam was gone. Somewhere within the Space Force, alarms were going off. The High Altitude National Defense (HAND) satellite had been annihilated.

It was an act of war, and there I was, half-blind and sputtering there at Ground Zero.

PART
II

CHAPTER
ONE

WITH A CHARACTERISTIC lack of imagination, they called it Black Friday. The SAC and the GNP, acting on orders from Rand, tried to storm several of the Auricles throughout the CSA. I saw it on television, after President Rand had declared a state of national emergency.

I guess before I get to that, I need to explain how I ended up home after that HID incident on Black Friday. Auric had fired that beam skyward and vanished the orbital strike satellite, and the rest of us had vanished in a flash of golden light.

I had reappeared in my place, scaring the living hell out of Angelina, who'd been sitting there eating popcorn and watching television.

"Jesus H. Christ, Christian," Angelina said, around a mouthful of popcorn. "What the hell was that?"

"Auric just, uh, liquidated the HID," I said.

"Liquidated?" Angelina said. "Killed?"

"Disappeared. Layaway, whatever," I said. "They're gone."

Her hard eyes narrowed into uncomprehending crescents.

"Were you with Minerva Merrow?" she asked.

"No," I said. "I didn't even see her. Babe, I was kidnapped by the HID, and Auric saved me. Didn't you even wonder where I was?"

"I figured it was something at work," Angelina said. "I tried texting, but you weren't answering, so I assumed the worst, and that meant Minerva Merrow."

"Because the HID had abducted me," I said.

"Right," Angelina said, pointing to the television. "Something's happening across the country. Maybe the world. I don't know. They're freaking out."

I turned to watch the live broadcast, where Auricles in Georgia, Mississippi, North Carolina, Virginia, Alabama, Louisiana, and Texas were being attacked at the same time by mobs of GNP supporters and red-hatted SAC paramilitaries. While this was going on, Rand was holding a makeshift press conference:

"God won't stand for false prophets and fake healers," Rand said, gripping the lectern, his red face even redder than usual, his bleached blond hair shellacked with product. "God told me. He told me that we are in a holy war. A war in this great nation of ours. A war of spirit. A war between good, God-fearing, Real Americans, and those goddamned pagan Auricle Answering Machines. We're making our stand, and we're taking our stand. God bless Real America. To Hell with the rest of you!"

While this was going on, the networks were split-screening it, showing the assembled mobs at the Auricle temples. They were toting red, blue, and white guns and waving GNP and SAC flags. Some of them had torches.

"This is going to be bad," Angelina said, munching on her popcorn. She'd been on-call with Flutter since this latest crisis. "Your Antichrist buddy is causing all of this."

"Antichrist?" I said.

"That's what they're calling him," Angelina said. "It's trending. There's been a panic around the use of the Auricles. See? 'Voice of the Devil Advises Student to Quit School and Take Up Carpentry Trade'. 'Auricle app Causes Wave of Divorces'. 'Best Advice: Ditch the Auricle'. It goes on and on. The healing stuff made it even worse."

"Give me a break," I said. "Auric's just trying to help people."

"Yeah, well, people don't like that," Angelina said. "The backlash has begun."

As if on cue, the SAC paramilitaries all stormed the Auricle shrines at the same time, charging up the stairs and ramps and into the shrines. Angelina and I were on the edge of the sofa, watching it real-time.

"I wonder if they're storming that hidey-hole down the street," Angelina asked. "I should run out there, see if I can livestream it."

I was more intent on simply watching the broadcasts. There seemed to be confusion at the sites of the Auricles, and GNP mobs surged into the temples after the SAC paramilitaries had gone in, chanting "CSA! CSA!" as they went.

"C'mon," Angelina said, grabbing my arm. "We have to check this out."

"I doubt they're doing anything like that here," I said.

"Come on, let's go see for ourselves," Angelina said.

"For real?" I asked.

"Yes," Angelina said. "Come on, hurry, Christian."

While Angelina and I were getting dressed, I consulted my Auricle, feeling both excited and terrified. Something big was transpiring, and I didn't want to miss out on whatever it was.

"Are those shrines okay? The ones being attacked?" I asked.

"Yes," the Auricle said. "They're fine."

"Are the SAC and GNP people okay?" I asked.

"They're fine, too," the Auricle said. "No one has been killed. Thank you for your concern, Christian."

Angelina had put on a moss green track suit with red double stripes that ran up the sides. She was waving me on.

"Quit jacking off with your phone and get out there with me, Christian," Angelina said.

"I wasn't jacking off," I said. "Christ."

"Don't blaspheme," Angelina said, as we made our way to the elevator, and immediately went into her livestream voice. "This is Angelina Reed, and I'm with Christian Powers, Chronicler of Auric. We're heading to the friendly neighborhood Auricle temple. Anything to say, Christian?"

"Uh, no," I said, prompting a frustrated eyeroll from Angelina from behind the intelliphone camera. "We're, uh, monitoring the situation."

"I see," Angelina said, as we raced out of the lobby and went streetside. "President Rand has declared the Auricles to be instruments of Satan. What do you think about that?"

"They're not," I said. "They're trying to help people by giving them advice and healing."

"Yeah, but, like bad advice," Angelina said. "That's what we're hearing."

"Those are lies," I said. "The Auricles never give bad advice. And they can heal anybody of anything that ails them, just like Auric said."

"It's just that it's what I'm hearing," Angelina said. "People are hearing. People are saying."

"People are lying," I said, right into her intelliphone. "Some people are, I think."

Down the street, there was a GNP crowd, and a half-dozen SAC paramilitaries standing there, brandishing their rifles. The drones were hovering like angry bees, guns trained on the crowd. I saw several hundred GNPeons in the crowd, as well as other pro-Auric protesters, holding up their Auricle app-augmented phones, bearing witness.

The local GNP loudmouth, a bug-eyed, acne-scarred kid named Charlton Riggs, was all but making out with a red GNP bullhorn as he harangued the crowd. He had this brown hair helmet thing going on and his face was sweating as he yelled. Riggs wore his GNP enamel lapel pin with as much pride as his red SAC baseball cap.

"Our righteous brothers and sisters throughout this great land have attacked the ungodly Auricles in the great states of Texas, Louisiana, Georgia, North Carolina, Mississippi, and Alabama," Riggs said. "These are real good people. Real Americans. They've had enough of you and your Answering Machines. We've said 'Enough'. And today, there's going to be a reckoning. Today, we bring down the false temples of Auric. Today, Real America reclaims its birthright as God's Lone Chosen Nation."

Riggs was too much into his stuff to even see me coming, but the pro-Auricle crowd did see me, and Angelina was soaking it all up with her intelliphone.

Somebody blew a whistle, and the SAC paramilitaries stormed the Auricle temple, racing into the entryway with their tricolored assault rifles drawn. They surged inside, yelling out orders to each other, while the GNP crowd, led by Riggs, chanted "CSA! CSA! CSA!"

And then the latest miracle happened again. Angelina caught it with her intelliphone. Everybody saw it as it went down.

The SAC goons all vanished into clouds of golden motes of light. They were simply gone. Like the way the HID agents had vanished. Auric had put them on layaway.

"Holy shit," Angelina said. "Where'd they go?"

Riggs bellowed into his bullhorn, egging on his supporters, his voice hoarse.

"It's nothing to be afraid of," Riggs said. "Just parlor tricks. Swarm the temple! Go on, tear it apart! God *is* on our side! There can be no fear when you have God on your side!"

And his GNP supporters ran to the temple and attacked it with boards and their fists, hitting the Auricanium, but they didn't harm it. Some of them went up into the entryway, tried to attack the temple, only to vanish into motes of golden light that were beautiful, despite what they represented.

In fact, the golden light flowed out of the temple, almost as if it were infecting the GNP supporters, and, in moments, it enveloped the GNP crowd, who began wailing and praying to God for mercy and deliverance.

But God didn't come for them, and He didn't rescue them. Auric came for them.

Auric appeared on the steps of the temple, having emerged from the shrine in his golden glory, his blue-fired hair burning brightly, white suit immaculate as ever. He simply walked out of the Auricle temple that way, without an angry look upon his face, but his blue eyes glowing and knowing, seeming to see into all of us. I could feel him in my mind, in my heart, and in my spirit.

"*Your* God isn't here," Auric said. "But I am."

With a wave of his golden arm, the screaming GNP crowd vanished in a sea of golden motes of light, Riggs last of all, holding his bullhorn, gape-mouthed and gobsmacked, as he vanished.

"Oh. My. God," Angelina said, having captured it all.

Even the Auric supporters were stunned. Everybody was, except me. I'd known this was coming. Auric directed his blue-eyed gaze to Angelina and her intelliphone, to everyone who was recording it.

"For too long, your people have been held hostage by the very worst of you," Auric said. "The ones who invariably turn to fear, rage, ignorance, cruelty, violence, corruption, and hate—they shout everyone else down. They frighten the rest of you into stunned silence and cowardly complicity by the constant threat of real and/or implied violence."

His voice had that oddly resonant quality, which amplified it, made it feel divine.

"I've come to declare that those days are past," Auric said. "No longer will you be held captive to the brutal ghosts of your primate past. I'll work to assist you in evolving beyond this, toward something better, toward something civilized. Those monstrous qualities may have suited you when you lived in caves, hiding from predators, huddled frightened around fires, daubing cave walls with handmade paints, and gnawing on marrow from broken bones. But today? It's a problem. There is no place for it in civilized society."

In the absence of the GNP mob, the Auric supporters were reluctant to fill the space, but Auric waved them in, radiating warmth, calm, compassion, and empathy. Slowly, the supporters circled around him, in the space that had only moments before been occupied by the braying GNPeons.

"Such is the fate of anyone who attacks my Auricles or my supporters," Auric said. "Let this be a warning to you. To those of you who would seek to harm my temples and my emissaries, look to today and remember the fate of these people. Today is the day of reckoning for the Enemies of Auric."

His golden voice was righteous and commanding, and people were silent, terrified, stunned. Even the pro-Auricle supporters were quiet. Auric could sense the concern and addressed it.

"These hateful, angry, violent people are *not* dead," Auric said. "I swear that I have not disintegrated them. I have sent them away, for now. Their fate is in my hands, and in yours. I have come to you in peace, in kindness, and with limitless compassion. Should anyone stand in my way, they will face the same fate as these people today. I will make them go away for a time. This is not my wish. I want to bring *all* of humanity along on this journey with me. A journey of everlasting peace, hopeful discovery, and boundless progress. But, for some of you, these are alien words, and it's an alien and unfamiliar world. For you, who respond only in the language of hate, rage, fear, violence, and ignorance, I issue this simple, stern warning: Don't."

And with that, Auric raised his arms and a book appeared in his hands. It was the golden book emblazoned with his logo, the one the HID agents had somehow acquired. *The Book of Don't* appeared in everyone's hands, including mine.

"Some of you may have seen this already. In this simple book is the path," Auric said. "It is the way forward for you as a people, as a species. It is the path to progress, civility, and your own moral evolution. Honor it, and face a brighter, more golden future. Ignore it, and, well, you'll see what happens, and where it takes you."

And then he vanished in a flash of golden light that left everybody blinking away the spots in their eyes. Even I was dazzled.

The moment he was gone, people started freaking out, a sea of voices, Angelina first among them. She stopped her livestreaming amid a chorus of moans and wailing and cheering. The swell of emotion amid everyone was undeniable.

"Fuck me," Angelina said. "I got *all* of that."

Not wanting to be scooped, she posted it directly, and her intelliphone began to sing with likes. The Internet was losing its mind, since Auric had done the same thing at every temple that had been attacked. Thousands of GNP militants and SAC paramilitaries had vanished in those clouds of light, and it had been captured on phones everywhere, real-time.

I realized why Auric had given me a copy of his book when I saw the stunned onlookers notice me. It was an instant public speaking moment for me. I held up the book.

"Auric has only the best intentions for us," I said. "As people, and as a species. He's here to fix the world. And he wants us to come along with him on this ride. Auric doesn't lie. He's a truth teller and a healer and a maker of miracles. You know as well as I do that sometimes the truth—the honest truth—is hard to hear. We, as a people, particularly in this country, we don't *want* to hear the truth. We prefer lies, myths, tall tables, and fables. Auric's not about untruths and fictions. He's about truth and honesty and civility, the paths to progress. You saw it, yourselves. He's not making this up. He's not pretend. He's not a hoax. He's for real. He's as real as it gets. And he's here to help us all."

The questions came in a cacophony, and I answered all of them as best as I could. I was there for hours.

CHAPTER

TWO

ANGELINA WAS particularly quiet as we headed back to our place. Her intelliphone had blown up with her posting of her livestream, which others had done, as well. People had witnessed their own things going down, had seen the seeming annihilation of the SAC and GNP crowds.

History has since called it the Thirty Second War. The Space Force attacked Auric at the HID detention facility in the Heartland Protectorate of Chicago, as part of a coordinated assault on Auricians around the country, in the wake of the Black Friday incident.

When I tell you that it went on that long, I'm not exaggerating. Auric made all of them—SAC paramilitaries, every HID agent, every GNP militiaman, every associated and affiliated hate group auxiliary—disappear in a sea of golden light. Wherever they were, they disappeared. Every weapon of mass destruction in the world's arsenals disappeared, too—nuclear, biological, and chemical. They were simply gone, as if they had never been here at all.

To say it threw the country—and, particularly, the GNP—into a panic, is an understatement. It was bedlam. Nobody liked the SAC except the GNP party faithful. The rest of the country put up with them because we had to, because they had the support of President Rand.

And speaking of Rand, he'd been livid that his HAND satellite had been disappeared by Auric. He went on the air and raged, having somehow still eluded Auric's layaway plan:

"This cult leader. Goldenboy Auric. It destroyed a peaceful Space Force satellite. Up in space. Our spy satellite. A Real American satellite. It was watching Auric. Auric couldn't stand it. And Goldenboy destroyed it. The Answering Machine murdered thousands of faithful HID agents.

Auric murdered 60,000 God-fearing Sons of Almighty Christ. Goldenboy killed 50,000 other super-patriots of Real America. Good people. Great people. Dead. Over 150,000 patriotic Real Americans killed by this illegal alien invader. It's not stopping there. More of you are in danger. Real Americans. Good people. Auric's coming for you. Destroy the demon's temples. Destroy the traitors who worship it. God bless Real America. We will prevail."

GNP loyalists in Mississippi had been taking copies of the *Book* and burning them. Or trying to. Apparently, the *Book* wouldn't burn, despite appearing to be a normal sort of book. The GNPeons were enraged to find their bonfires failed to destroy Auric's *Book*.

An Aurician media team had shown up in a golden van, filming the scene with some golden drones that hovered about, capturing the whole event with cameras and microphones. None of the GNPeons would go near the Auricians, preferring to curse them and shake their fists and burning torches at them from a safe distance. The hatred on their faces terrified me.

The fanatics tried to tear the books apart, but they wouldn't come apart. They tried shooting them with guns. That didn't work, either. The books were indestructible. They tried to bury them, dumping them into newly made landfills, pouring fuel on them. But then Auric appeared and restored the books to their pristine original state. He addressed the angry fanatics.

"Why are you doing this?" Auric asked. Several of the loyalists drew guns and fired at Auric, their bullets ricocheting off of his golden skin. "I'm trying to help you. Have you even read the *Book*?"

After emptying their guns into Auric, the GNP loyalists stood there, uncertain, terrified, unsure what to do, whether to reload or run away.

"We read enough," the bravest of them said. It was a black-bearded, burly man named Gordon Dunleavy, who owned a construction company that had provided the tractors and backhoes used to dig the shallow grave for Auric's books. "The Bible's the only book that matters to us."

"Ah," Auric said. Then he walked them through the *Book of Don't*. It was like a teachable moment or something, and, having failed in their task of burying his books and killing him with their guns, they listened to Auric, despite themselves.

The Book of Don't was broken into 13 chapters:

Don't be Evil

Don't be Crazy

Don't be Lazy

Don't be Stupid

Don't be Creepy

Don't be an Asshole

Don't be Fake

Don't be Corrupt

Don't be Greedy

Don't be Dull

Don't be Cruel

Don't be Cowardly

Don't be Ignorant

These were Auric's Thirteen Commandments. Although they weren't commandments, per se. They were more like Advisements. Auric's Advisements. Auric smiled at the GNP zealots.

"These aren't my commandments," Auric said. "They're my Advisements."

"Advisements?" Dunleavy said. "Advertisements?"

"Advisements," Auric said. "Not the same thing. Rather, they're advice from me to you."

"We don't need advice from you, Alien," Dunleavy said. The others were reloading their guns, heedless of how ineffective they'd been already, or that shooting Auric again would surely get them put on layaway.

"You could say that," Auric said. "I've boiled down human morality to its most basic elements, and these are what I came up with as the most scalable and comprehensible, regardless of culture."

"What does that even mean?" Dunleavy asked.

"Here's the problem," Auric said. "The monotheistic Abrahamic faiths have held onto an unearned moralistic monopoly for centuries. However, the world has been no more moral for their presence. If anything, it's been bloodier and more brutal because of them. Do you want me to line item the religious wars and casualties of the past 2000 years?"

"The what, now?" Dunleavy asked, looking around him uncertainly.

Auric was bewildering them, and they were circling around him. What a spectacle that was, these armed GNP stalwarts and Auric standing there in his gleaming white suit, his golden skin radiant, his blue, fiery hair flickering.

"Your religions have not only failed to make people more moral but have also provided the justification for countless atrocities over the centuries, leading to many, many millions of dead. At any rate," Auric said. "This resource is intended to address a range of maladaptive human behaviors that have historically caused problems. The essence of wrongdoing is rooted in those hurtful and antisocial behaviors. Human nature thrives in social settings, and withers in antisocial settings."

I nodded, looking through the book while Auric continued speaking.

"The flip side of the book is the path to civilized human excellence, as I've defined it, as follows: Be good. Be sane. Be active. Be smart. Be respectful. Be polite. Be authentic. Be honest. Be generous. Be ambitious. Be kind. Be brave. Be enlightened."

"Those are, like, the Be Attitudes," I said.

Auric nodded, laughing, as if he could hear me. Which, of course, he could. His laugh was even warmer and more ennobling than his smile.

"The Be Attitudes, standing in opposition to the Don't Be's," Auric said. "My logic is straightforward—if you saw a person who was all of those Be Attitudes, as you called them, what would they be?"

"A good person," Dunleavy said. "Like Jesus Christ."

"Precisely," Auric said. "And anyone who was any of those bad things would be a bad person, wouldn't you agree?"

"I don't know about that," Dunleavy said. "But nobody's going to go for this hooey. That's what it is—hooey, malarkey, and claptrap."

"It's not," Auric said. "It's a roadmap for civility, for civilized people, for civilization."

"Look here, Alien," Dunleavy said. "We're not falling for your satanic mumbo jumbo, here. You're not telling us how to live."

"But I'm not," Auric said. "I'm only telling you how NOT to be. That's always easier than telling someone how to be. That's why it will work. Anyone with the Auricle app, should they attempt to do one of those Don't items, will be dissuaded from that path by the Auricle's advice, which will inerrantly guide them along the Be Attitudes."

It was sort of insidiously brilliant, I thought. Practical, actionable morality.

"Look, all of you," Auric said. *"It's not that hard to be a good person.* It's just that people don't want to be because it's more work than simply being a bad person. Evil is highly incentivized in your world—it's often easier to be evil. And even then, most people don't have the stomach for it, for pure evil. However, it's the evil on the margins, those little hurts and harms people inflict on one another that grow and magnify. I've put together a list that *anyone* could follow if they wanted to. No need for a church to guide them, no need for priests or prophets, no need for a god to worship."

"That's blasphemous," Dunleavy said, and he called for his men to shoot Auric again, which they did. Their guns sang out, filling the air with flashes and smoke and noise, but Auric was untouched and unharmed by their fusillade. This time, the bullets all hovered around him like a swarm of angry bees, and Auric disposed of them with flashes of golden light.

Then he raised his golden hands and made all of the guns disappear in that same golden light. Literally disarmed, Dunleavy and his men stood there, awestruck.

"Twice you've attempted to murder me," Auric said. "Twice you have failed. What would be the civilized course of action for me, do you think? How many chances do men like you get? I can see into your hearts and minds. I see what drives you."

Dunleavy and his men looked around fearfully in their red ballcaps.

"The Be Attitudes are beyond you," Auric said. "They are beyond your level of moral development. It's why we're out here in the woods, and you're attempting to bury these *Books of Don't* in an unmarked grave and trying to shoot me."

"We serve our almighty jealous God," Dunleavy said. "You are a false god. That's why we do it. We're doing God's work, here. Exodus 34:14. We will not worship you."

"As I've said many times: I don't want, need, or require your worship," Auric said. "However, I can't have men like you out shooting at people and behaving like barbarians. I am, therefore, putting you on layaway. We *will* meet again."

At this, the men scattered, crying out in terror, running away from Auric, but to no avail, for he made them all vanish in motes of golden light, and they were gone in a moment, leaving only Auric and the Aurician news crew there.

Auric gazed at the drone cameras, his blue eyes glowing, his face impassive.

"My message to mankind is a simple one," Auric said. "But it's one I hope you'll take to heart. Don't be evil. Don't be crazy. Don't be lazy. Don't be stupid. Don't be creepy. Don't be an asshole. Don't be fake. Don't be corrupt. Don't be greedy. Don't be dull. Don't be cruel. Don't be cowardly. Don't be ignorant. These are the message of my *Book of Don't.* Take some time, read through the *Book,* do some self-reflection. Think about who you are, who you could be. To have a civilization, you must be civilized. To be civilized, you must be civil. Being civil is attainable for all sane human beings."

And then he vanished in a flash of blue-white light.

"Did he really say 'don't be an asshole'?" Angelina asked, snorting.

"Yeah," I said.

"What does that even mean?" Angelina asked. Not wanting to get mired in the *Book* itself, I asked my Auricle.

"An asshole as defined by Auric is someone who knowingly acts without consideration of consequence of the harm they are inflicting on others," the Auricle said.

"That could be anybody, Phone," Angelina said. "Everybody's an asshole."

"Untrue," the Auricle said. "Assholes are, by their very nature, rude, inconsiderate, and willfully harmful. Assholes are the barbarians of postmodern civilization."

"What does that even mean, Phone?" Angelina asked. I couldn't resist piping up, partly to keep Angelina from getting herself into trouble with Auric, and partly out of a desire to simply put my own perspective into the mix. Just because I was the erstwhile Chronicler didn't mean I had nothing to say or add to the debate.

"You mean like somebody who refuses to get their own Auricle app but continues to ask questions of somebody else's Auricle app?" I asked, earning a glare and a shoulder swat from Angelina.

"That's a great example, Christian," the Auricle said.

"Oh, I'm an asshole, now, Phone?" Angelina asked.

"Do you want me to answer that question for her, Christian?" the Auricle asked.

"Ehh, best not," I said.

"No, seriously," Angelina said, leaning into it. I *really* didn't want to get stuck in another argument between Angelina and my intelliphone.

"An asshole invariably acts without consideration of others," the Auricle said. "Central to assholery is putting one's own needs over everyone else's, regardless of the consequences. There are countless examples."

Trying to steer it to a positive place, I jumped in again.

"And the Be Attitude for the Asshole is to be considerate?" I asked.

"Yes," the Auricle said. "It's not so difficult to be considerate, is it?"

"Considerate," Angelina said, grimacing. "Considerate, Phone? You're telling me to be considerate? Is that like the equivalent of asking me to smile more? It's sexist."

"Assholes are not gender-specific," the Auricle said. "Male, female, all ethnicities and nationalities, straight, gay, nonbinary. Anyone who willfully acts without consideration of others is an asshole."

"The GNP would say *you're* an asshole, Phone," Angelina said.

"But that's because *they* are assholes," the Auricle said. "They're fascists. Fascists are *always* assholes. That's one of the defining aspects of fascism—the ability to be a flagrant asshole without consequence."

"That's my point," Angelina said. "Everyone's an asshole to someone else. The point of view makes the difference."

"Incorrect," the Auricle said. "There is an objective benchmark for assholery, as you put it. It is rooted in the lack of consideration for others. However, there are non-asshole ways—which is to say, considerate—ways of engaging that take into consideration the agency of others. For example, taking turns in a conversation, versus talking over everyone. But there are limits, too. For example, let's say you were in a restaurant in Paris in 1943, and you were seated next to some Nazis with terrible table manners. The Nazis were making everyone else in the restaurant uncomfortable and unhappy by their presence."

"Nazis," Angelina said. "You went right for Nazis, Phone."

"The point is, would you be wrong for pointing out the assholery of the Nazis?" the Auricle asked.

"I'd be dead," I said. "Nobody would dare to confront them."

"That's because they were evil," the Auricle said. "Another of the things I point out in my *Book of Don't*. Assholery is simply a lower-grade version of evil. That is to say everyone who is evil is an asshole, even if not every asshole is evil. Assholery is, at heart, a gateway behavior in the direction of evil. All who are evil must inevitably and deliberately behave in a manner that is inconsiderate of others. The difference between an asshole and an evil person is the degree of harm they're willing to inflict by their lack of consideration. For an evil person, what they want is more important than all other considerations, including people's lives. For an asshole, there is usually a limit as to what they will or will not do. Those who do not hold back eventually become evil. Those who do have a path for redemption."

Angelina chewed on that a little, trying to find flaws in the Auricle's reasoning. That's one thing she was particularly good at, and I wasn't about to get in her way.

"*You're* an asshole, Phone," Angelina said. "That much I know."

"What is a person who cuts in line?" the Auricle said.

"An asshole," I replied.

"What is a person who comes to a party and doesn't bring anything?" the Auricle asked.

"An asshole," Angelina said, grudgingly.

"What is a person who ghosts at an event you're attending and leaves you with the bill?" the Auricle asked.

"An asshole," I said. "Definitely."

"What is a person who blares music at all hours?" the Auricle asked.

"An asshole," I said, while Angelina frowned.

"What is a person who doesn't hold the door open for you or doesn't thank you for holding the door for them?" the Auricle asked.

"An asshole," Angelina said. "Fuck, Phone."

"What is a person who talks in a movie theater while the movie is playing?" the Auricle asked. There weren't many movie theaters anymore, but a few times, we'd to the ones that remained.

"An asshole," I said.

"What is a person who, when facing an imminent road construction lane merge, speeds ahead in the open lane so they can try to force their way into the merged lane, instead of waiting to merge with the rest of you?" the Auricle asked.

"Very specific instance, but, yeah, definitely an asshole," I said.

"What is a person who willfully refuses to wear a protective mask when confronted with a dangerous disease known to spread through the air?" the Auricle asked.

"An asshole, for sure," I said.

"What is a person who litters?" the Auricle asked.

"An asshole," Angelina said. "Lazy, too, but definitely an asshole."

"Do you see a pattern in these behaviors?" the Auricle asked. "Lack of consideration for others is at the heart of assholery. For the Asshole, they simply do what they want and want what they want, and don't care about the consequences."

"You could have just said 'Don't Be Inconsiderate' and avoid calling people assholes, Phone," Angelina said.

"I could have," the Auricle said. "But I figured the pithier term would have more of an impact."

"Still," Angelina said. "A holy book with the word 'asshole' in it seems profane."

"It's not a holy book," the Auricle said. "It's merely a series of Advisements."

"Ones that will have you vaporizing people if they don't agree with them," Angelina said. "*That* is an asshole move, Phone."

"Anyone who acts against my Advisements *is* a bad person," the Auricle said. "Or, at best, a person of low quality."

Angelina didn't say anything, which meant that she was stewing over what the Auricle had said. Angelina had a smart mouth and a sharp tongue, so when she was brooding, it was never a good thing. I tried to make light of it, to defuse things a bit.

"Allow me to be considerate and go into the other room to continue talking to the Auricle," I said.

"Your phone implied that I'm an asshole," Angelina said as I walked to the other room. She called after me in a sing-song: "Not an asshole. Your phone is an asshole, Christian. *Auric* is an asshole."

I went into our spare room, down the hall, and could feel Angelina's hard eyes boring into my back as I did so.

"You really got me in trouble," I said quietly to the intelliphone.

"She'll forgive you in three days," the Auricle said. "Or at least she will mostly forgive you. An undercurrent of unexpressed resentment will endure for the remainder of your relationship."

I let that drop for now, because I had other things to think about, although some part of me wondered what that all meant. The Auricles weren't cryptic; everything they said meant something.

Instead, I thought about those Bes and Don'ts and how they played out in daily life, like for me personally. I wasn't evil. I wasn't crazy. I wasn't creepy. I wasn't an asshole (or was I? The exchange with Angelina made me think about my own assholery). I wasn't fake. I wasn't cruel. I wasn't ignorant. I narrowed my areas of weakness around the following:

Don't be Stupid
Don't be Lazy
Don't be Dull
Don't be Cowardly

Those were my big four, it seemed like. Not like I was even stupid, honestly. But I was at least willing to admit that I could be smarter.

"You're not stupid," the Auricle said. "And you're not as cowardly as you might think you are."

"I'm a behind-the-scenes guy," I said.

"And yet, you were the first human being to enter into dialogue with me," the Auricle said.

"An accident," I said. "Pure chance."

"I have given over 150 million copies of the *Book of Don't* to people," the Auricle said. "There's a digital version of it as well which is being readily accessed around the world."

"People aren't going to like you telling them how to live or how to be," I said. "Or giving them something to read. Is there an audiobook version of it?"

"Don't the various holy books do the same thing?" the Auricle asked.

"Yeah, but they're holy books," I said. "It's different. You've made a point of saying you're not a god, and that it's not a holy book. All you're offering is basically a self-help book. It's not quite the same as a holy text."

"Right," the Auricle said. "It's better. There are hundreds of self-contradictions in the Bible, for example. There are no self-contradictions in the *Book of Don't*. It is internally consistent from a moral and ethical perspective."

"All the same, people aren't going to like it," I said. "What are you going to do, put everyone who violates the *Book* on layaway?"

"It's a guide to having a civilized society," the Auricle said. "One that can be universally applied. It's the start of a conversation, the beginning of a journey. I intend to speak a great deal about it in the future."

Auric could see the future. I couldn't. But there was no way this was going to end well.

CHAPTER

THREE

ANGELINA WAS IN a foul mood when I went back to the living room.

"Your phone thinks I'm an asshole," Angelina said. "Auric thinks I'm an asshole."

"He didn't say that," I said.

"It's the implication," Angelina said. "All because I won't load the stupid app."

"No," I said. "It's because you won't load the app but keep using mine."

"How many times do I have to say it? You should delete it, Christian," Angelina said, looking at me earnestly. "Just get rid of it and live your life like a normal person, instead of those freak Auricians. Who cares what Auric says? Who cares that he says you're his Chronicler? Whatever that even means. I don't see you doing anything special at all."

"I'm bearing witness," I said.

"Anyone can do that," Angelina said. "Now that Auric's cured blindness, everyone can fucking see, Christian. You're not special or uniquely qualified to be the Chronicler. Hell, Auric's probably got one in every country."

I whipped out my intelliphone, of course.

"Auricle, am I the only Chronicler?" I asked.

"You are, Christian," the Auricle said.

"It's lying," Angelina said.

"A liar cannot accept the truth when they face it," the Auricle said.

"Ohmigod," Angelina said. "I'm an asshole *and* a liar, now?"

The Auricle didn't say anything, and I was really uncomfortable.

"At least I'm not a mass murderer, Phone," Angelina said, pointing to the television, which was showing the panic in the CSA and various Third World autocracies over Auric's actions. There was a digital counter on the chyron showing the estimated number of people who'd disappeared for attacking Auric or his Auricians. It stood at ten million worldwide and kept climbing.

"He didn't kill anybody," I said. "He just made them disappear."

"Same thing," Angelina said. "People 'disappear' all the time. We both know what that means."

"He said he's bringing them back at some point," I said.

"Right," Angelina said. She was stress-eating popcorn again and was about to change the channel when I saw Minerva take to the screen. She'd staged a press conference, and, of course, looked confident and commanding in that way she had.

"President Rand is lying to you," Minerva said. "Auric hasn't murdered anyone. Auric is not a murderer. He has sequestered the members of the HID, the SAC, and the thousands of hate groups who are allied with both. These 150,000 Americans are true enemies of humanity. They are responsible for political violence against enemies of the GNP. They kidnap, extort, torture, rob, and murder honest Americans. I have here..."

She held up a thick pile of papers, bound, one of several stacks.

"I have here a thorough documentation of all of the crimes against humanity perpetuated by the HID, the SAC, and their allies. I think you'll find it fascinating reading. President Rand likes to characterize the HID and SAC as patriotic Americans, but they are the ruthless and brutal thugs of the repressive and corrupt GNP regime. How many of you have lost a family member or loved one to them? Auric has settled the accounts, and the—"

The news commentator interrupted Minerva's broadcast.

"And there you have it," the commentator said. "The propaganda mouthpiece of Auric, Minerva Merrow, offering her take on the unfolding events. We're going to stay with you as this story develops."

A news graphic appeared, resembling a golden temple flanked by the stars and stripes, covering the screen with a metallic clunk and threatening music:

ALIEN AURIC VS. REAL AMERICA

"Wow, that's something," I said. "They didn't let her speak."

"They let her speak enough," Angelina said. "She gives me the creeps. I don't like her. I don't like any of it. *She's* an asshole, while we're on the topic."

The television flashed gold and, in the place of the LAX commentator, there was Auric, gazing out at us with his lovely golden face and his burning blue hair and bright blue eyes.

"Americans," Auric said. "I'm sorry to intrude on your viewing, but your President Rand is lying to you. His secret police—the HID—attempted to unlawfully incarcerate your fellow Americans. His SAC paramilitaries attacked my Auricle shrines. I defended myself from them. I did not murder them. I have simply banished them—for the time being. I give you my word that they *will* return. You will have to trust me on this. Far from being an enemy of humanity, I am humanity's friend. And my followers—the Auricians—are your friends, too. Your Holy Bible, in Matthew 7:16–20, warns against false prophets, and, by their deeds you shall know them. I am no ravening wolf in sheep's clothing. And, above all, I am not false. I ask you to continue to watch my good works and decide for yourself whether I am good or bad. Please do not try to attack or harm my followers. They are under my protection. They are here to help you. We are here to help you. I am here to help you."

He seemed to be looking out at each of us through the television. I mean, he seemed to be *seeing* us. Angelina tried to change the channel, but he was on every channel.

"He's commandeered the airwaves?" Angelina asked, clicking away until I asked her to stop. Her anxiety was making *me* anxious.

"In the coming months, I'm going to be helping you on a scale that you've never experienced in the history of your species," Auric said. "I'm going to make your world a better place, even more than I already have. Whether you agree with my methods or not, you will emerge healthier and happier than you have ever been before. You have taken terrible care of your homeworld. This planet is your one and only home, and you've made a terrible mess of it. Above and beyond the wars you wage, there is the pollution and the mass extinctions you have caused. You are ruining your habitat. I've been repairing it for you. I don't have to do this. I could have just passed your planet and let you make yourselves go extinct. However, I didn't want that. I cherish life. I am a steward of life, hope, peace, empathy, and progress. I am here to help you live better, and to be better. We will talk again soon."

And then he vanished, and the television network commentators were sputtering, apologizing for the unprecedented hijacking of their airwaves by Auric.

"He's rude," Angelina said. "Cutting in that way. I mean, who does he think he is? God? Steward of life, hope, peace, empathy, and progress, my ass. Only an asshole cuts in that way."

The television cut in with Rand at a press conference, bellowing about Auric violating free speech and poisoning the minds of Real Americans in an unforgivable act of broadcast terrorism.

I didn't know what it meant, exactly. Of course, I asked my Auricle. I mean, that's what it's there for, right?

"Auricle, what did you mean when you were saying that stuff about making the world a better place?" I asked. "Beyond what you already have done?"

"Be patient. You'll know when it happens, Chronicler," the Auricle said.

"Wow, Phone," Angelina said. "What an asshole non-answer answer that was. I thought you were going to answer questions, not create more questions."

"At least I *have* answers," the Auricle said. "Which is more than I can say for some."

Angelina's face went into that combative sullenness it sometimes got when crossed. She'd lean forward on her elbows, her eyes taking on a baleful glimmer, her jaw jutting outward.

"What's that mean exactly, Phone?" Angelina asked.

"You're a PR parasite," the Auricle said. "You prey on people's gullibility, distracting them from what actually matters. I'm buying up Flutter, Flitter, and Flatter and changing their business models."

"Oh, so is that part of his grand plan at making the world better, Phone?" Angelina asked.

"A very tiny part of it," the Auricle said.

Angelina flicked out her tablet and clicked around on it, looking up Flutter. Sure enough, it was being bought out by Auric, as was Flatter and Flitter. How Auric was able to engineer these purchases was something I neither comprehended nor wanted my Auricle to explain to me.

"Motherfucker," Angelina said. Her intelliphone was pinging with messages from Flutter leadership, indicating that they would be monitoring and reporting on any Auric-related activity, but from a positive angle. "This is bullshit."

"It's the future," the Auricle said.

Angelina was pissed at me, of all people. It was insulting.

"This is your fault, Christian," Angelina said. "You're part of this."

"What did *I* do?" I asked.

"You did nothing wrong, Christian," the Auricle said. "Angelina's just psychologically projecting."

"Shut up, Phone," Angelina said. "I hate you. Christian, don't you care about your soul? Ditch the phone and save your soul."

I would never give up my intelliphone, just on general principles. Let alone my Auricle. I mean, give me a break.

"You're just speaking from a place of pain," I said. "You're lashing out at me."

"I'm speaking *my* truth," Angelina said. "You have to respect that."

"I don't see a truth, there," the Auricle said. "Only your opinion."

"My opinion *is* my truth, Phone," Angelina said. "It's as real as anything else in this world."

I wasn't going to sit around listening to Angelina argue with my phone again. I just changed the channel. And boy, was I glad that I did.

CHAPTER

FOUR

_____

AURIC WAS CONDUCTING interviews on the Free American Network (FAN), which we ordinarily we couldn't watch because the HID typically blocked foreign news broadcasts from getting to us, but it was on. The FAN was where American pro-democracy expatriates would broadcast. These were people who had fled the CSA after the GNP takeover. The FAN was thought to be based in Vancouver or Toronto or faraway London or Amsterdam, but nobody knew for sure, because they willfully kept a low profile to avoid being assassinated by CSA goons sent by Rand or shot by the HAND.

"What the hell?" Angelina said. "How're we seeing this?"

The show was _Now or Never,_ an interview show hosted by Wanda Williams. She was a Black gay woman who had been deeply involved in pro-democracy politics. Tall, with long braided hair and seemingly age-less—she'd been active for twenty years but looked at most in her 30s. She was interviewing Auric.

"Tonight, on _Now or Never,_ I give you a visitor from beyond," Wanda said. "Someone who really needs no introduction, but I'm doing so be-cause that's just how I am. This is Auric."

Auric walked onstage in his white suit, wearing his golden loafers and a golden button-down shirt. The studio audience applauded him, and I wondered if they were prompted to, or if it was genuine. Things were dif-ferent among the expatriate resistance.

Auric took his seat across from Wanda, while the background screens went to still images of Auric, looking golden and godlike.

"How are you, Auric?" Wanda asked.

"I'm fine, Wanda, thanks for asking," Auric said.

"You know, when your people came to us, we were a little surprised," she asked. "I mean, you seem able to just go live on television and say whatever you like."

Auric's handsome face broke into a seemingly self-effacing smile. Although if anybody in the universe wasn't actually self-effacing, it was Auric. I chalked it up to a bit of stagecraft. Someone who was omniscient could certainly master showmanship.

"True, true," Auric said. "But I don't like to simply barge in and hog airtime like that other guy."

Upon the indirect mention of Rand, the *Now or Never* crowd mockingly laughed and hooted, and Wanda smiled at her audience, quieting them.

"You've been shaking things up in the Confederated States of America," Wanda said.

"Around the world, in truth," Auric said. "Not just the CSA."

"What's this about people disappearing, Auric?" Wanda asked.

"I know it's concerning," Auric said. "But none of them are harmed. They're in what some of my followers have labeled a 'penalty box' of sorts."

"A penalty box?" Wanda asked.

"Precisely so," Auric said. "I know there are different standards of policing around the world—but in the CSA, when someone does something the GNP doesn't like, they get preventively detained. Often, they get covertly kidnapped, tortured, and executed. This isn't like that. And it's curious to see the outrage of the GNP about what I've been doing. The many hundreds of thousands of Americans who've been 'disappeared' by the GNP would agree that there's a difference between what they do and what I'm doing. There are mass grave sites throughout the CSA where the GNP did its dirty work."

One of the screens showed a map of the CSA and dotted it with skulls peppered throughout the country, to gasps from the audience.

"Go to those mass grave sites and you'll find where the GNP committed mass murder," Auric said. "Just ask your Auricle apps, and they'll provide you the directions."

I knew that people would do that, and that it would give the prompt the GNP to go even crazier than it already was. The last thing they wanted were people finding unmarked mass graves they'd made.

"Why are you doing what you're doing?" Wanda asked.

"I'm trying to save your species," Auric said. "You're on a collision course with your own extinction at the rate you're going. This is to say that the amount of necessary sociocultural changes you need to carry out is colliding with the lack of time you have to do them and the active resistance by corrupt powers."

To illustrate his point, Auric made an equation appear on one of the wall screens behind him showing the following, replacing the map of the mass grave sites:

$$\text{Progress} - \text{Lack of Time} - \text{Corruption} = \text{Extinction}$$

"Corruption is bad information," Auric said. "It's like cancer—which I already cured, let me remind you—it spreads throughout the body politic and crowds out needed change."

"How do you cure corruption?" Wanda asked.

"The same way you cure anything," Auric said. "Through diagnosis and treatment. The treatment is honesty. Corruption is, at heart, saying X and doing Y. For example, the corrupt police officer pretends to uphold the law while actually breaking it. The corrupt politician pretends to be honest but is not. The corrupt political party pretends to uphold particular values, but, in practice does not hold those values. In fact, corruption is when those who are pretending to do X benefit from doing Y, instead. Ergo, corruption is when the actions don't match up with the words because the actions are rewarded by the corruption. It is particularly insidious because no corrupt official ever voluntarily admits to being corrupt. Corruption, much like cowardice, is when one fails to do one's duty."

The background screen went to a shot of Denny Rand, prompting boos from the studio audience.

"Corruption is an insidious affliction," Auric said. "It prevents humankind from advancing. Overwhelmingly, corruption exists because those in power profit from their corruption, and in so doing, inflict costs on the rest of society. Not to keep picking on the GNP, but they've elevated corruption to an art form. GNP politicians are beholden to monied interests, to timber, fossil fuel, ranching, agribusiness and other economic enterprises. These are the groups they actually serve. It's why solar and wind power was, at least until I appeared, largely sidelined in the CSA. The rest of the world has advanced in the use of these alternative energy sources, but not the CSA, which is continuing to do fracking, coal, and ethanol production, despite the clear environmental harm they're doing. That's corruption in action."

"But how can you stop corruption?" Wanda asked.

"That's a great question," Auric said. "Ordinarily, one would be able to vote out corrupt officials and replace them with honest ones. But in the CSA, a one-party state ruled by the GNP, how do you do that? How do you stop a corrupt political party that's got a deathgrip on political power and games the process perpetually in its favor and uses political violence to attack its enemies?"

Auric held up a golden hand and snapped his fingers. The snap was accompanied by a flash of light and the television screen flickered for a moment.

"You make them disappear," Auric said. "I could put the entire GNP apparatus into the penalty box."

"What?" Wanda asked.

"I could put the 110 million GNP members into my penalty box. The entire GNP is a criminally corrupt organization," Auric said. "In fact, corrupt regimes around the world could experience the same thing. Corruption costs the world at least five percent of global GDP. That's trillions of dollars, to keep it in an American perspective."

"Are you threatening the world leaders with this?" Wanda asked.

"The corrupt ones? Certainly," Auric said. "All my followers need to do is ask their Auricles the following question: Is XYZ politician corrupt? And they'll have their answer. It goes back to my *Book of Don't*—the Eighth Advisement: Don't Be Corrupt."

"Let's talk about your *Book of Don't*," Wanda said, and the screens on the back tiled to shows of the golden *Book*. "What do you hope to accomplish with this?"

"It's a chance for humankind to be civilized," Auric said. "I've boiled down what afflicts humankind throughout its history and basically advised people to not do those things. Every human wrongdoing is represented in the *Book of Don't*. My message is simple: please don't do those things. People complain about bad things happening, wonder why they happen. Bad things happen when people do the things I advise against in the *Book of Don't*."

"Let's start with the First Advisement," Wanda said. "Don't be Evil. That seems self-evident."

Auric smiled, nodding, steepling his golden fingers in front of him.

"Evil is the baggage humankind has carried with it as soon as it moved out of the realm of pure Nature and instinct," Auric said. "Evil is the knowing, Jungian shadow that walks behind mankind wherever it goes."

"But you're suggesting that people simply not be evil," Wanda said. "It's never that simple, is it?"

"It really is," Auric said. "Everyone who's evil *knows* they're doing something bad—it's just that they've rationalized to themselves and have otherwise justified the evil they're doing. They're refusing to take into account the consequences of their actions. They simply don't care. That's the architecture of evil."

"People say *you're* evil, Auric," Wanda said.

"Evil people do, yes," Auric said, prompting nervous laughter from the audience. "Evil people are profoundly threatened by what I'm doing."

"But from their perspective, *you're* doing evil things," Wanda said. "Disappearing people? That's evil."

"They're coming back," Auric said. "I've made that promise to everyone in the world several times already—everyone I've disappeared will return. And they'll return as they were when they were disappeared. I won't be mind-altering them or otherwise harming them. They are in suspension right now."

"Why take them away at all?" Wanda said.

"Evil people cause problems," Auric said. "Even worse than the simply corrupt, and worse still when they're powerful and privileged. That's an important thing I need to discuss. There are Advisements that are particularly bad. They are the ones that are the most harmful: Evil, Insanity, Corruption, Greed, Cruelty, Ignorance—those are the first tier of human blights. The second tier are: Lazy, Idiocy, Cowardice—these are harmful, but perhaps not as immediately harmful as the first tier. The third tier are: Assholery, Dullness, Creepiness—they are afflictions that make life more difficult than it otherwise might be but aren't as menacing as the first or second tier."

"Explain Dullness," Wanda said. "That seems ableist."

"Not at all," Auric said. "I frame Dullness as a chronic lack of imagination and ambition. If something's Dull, it's failing to realize its full potential. Dullness by definition means to be uninspiring. Ergo, don't be uninspiring and dull."

"Still sounds ableist," Wanda said.

"The corresponding Be Attitude for that one is to Be Ambitious," Auric said. "It is a call for one to attempt to live up to their full potential. Be Ambitious, Don't be Dull. Which is better: to have tried and failed or to live a lackluster life of regret? Isn't it better to try to shine and sparkle than to remain dull?"

"Ambition is better, when you put it that way," Wanda said.

"Yes," Auric said. "People live only so long. Life's far too short to be spent failing to live up to one's potential. I'm working to try to help people live up to the possibility of what they could be, what they want to be. That's part of my mission."

Wanda accepted that and leaned in.

"What *is* your mission, Auric?" Wanda asked. "What's the Auric Agenda we hear so much about in other venues?"

"As I've said enough times, my mission is to prevent the extinction of the human race," Auric said. He raised a hand and the screens behind shifted to a view from space showing the Thanatos asteroid. "This is Thanatos. It's a 10-mile diameter asteroid on a collision course with Earth. It's about four months away from impact. It will strike the Streeterville neighborhood in downtown Chicago in the Heartland Protectorate within the Confederated States of America at 4:16 p.m. CST."

Wanda and the audience gasped.

"He's playing the asteroid card," I said.

"What the hell are you saying?" Angelina asked.

"He's playing it," I said.

"If Thanatos hits the Earth, it will mean the extinction of your species," Auric said. "When I first became aware of this, I decided the time was right to intervene. I've been around for a very long time, and I've traveled through much of space. Space is a massive graveyard—there are dead civilizations scattered across the universe. Civilizations that were annihilated by the countless threats one finds in space—black holes, magnetars, supernovas, hypernovas, gamma ray bursts, asteroids, comets, and so on—all of them have contributed to the extinction of countless species and civilizations. Space is a deadly and dangerous place. The ruins of civilizations are everywhere out there."

As he said this, some of the screens showed images of alien civilizations being destroyed by the various phenomena Auric described. I wondered if *Now or Never* had produced these or whether Auric had somehow recreated images of these extinction events. But they were horrifying and terrifying, seeing worlds snuffed out by these cosmic catastrophes.

"I'm the only advanced lifeform I've seen in space," Auric said. "As a singleton, I've traveled incredible distances and have seen the endless death wrought in space. I came across your own planet's radio signals, like a beacon on a lifeless sea—and I have to add: there is plenty of life in the universe—but so much of it is primitive. At any rate, I listened to those signals emanating from your world and understood the necessity of protecting your planet. Thanatos is coming, but I'm stopping it. Just like I've stopped those natural disasters that have occurred around the globe. Just like I ended all of those diseases plaguing your species."

The screens shifted from the extinction of the alien races to views of Auric stopping wildfires, rescuing people from earthquake-ravaged regions, to restoring tornado-, hurricane-, and typhoon-ravaged regions.

"Those other civilizations, the dead ones I'd come across," Auric said. "I was too late for them. I arrived too late. And some of you might wonder why I didn't bring them back to life. Or travel back in time to save them. I could have. However, I believe that life belongs to the living. I don't raise the dead. I could, but I don't. That said, I seek to protect the living, including from themselves."

At this, the screens filled with images of the discord around the world—Denny Rand's hateful face in a sneer; red-capped GNP zealots with their flags standing around book bonfires; neo-nazis, jihadists, rioters, goose-stepping armies, terrorists.

"Just as Thanatos made me see that you were doomed as a species if I didn't intervene, so I saw that rampant pathologies present on your world are existential threats to your species," Auric said. "As a civilized and compassionate being, how could I simply fly on by and not do something about it? The moral imperative was there."

"You're saying it's a moral imperative for you," Wanda said.

"Absolutely," Auric said. "Everything I'm doing here is grounded in that imperative."

Wanda shifted in her seat, which meant she was going to serve up one of her zingers. People loved the Wanda Williams zingers.

"What about people who say that this is *our* planet," Wanda asked. "And we deserve to run it our own way, free from extraterrestrial interference? What about our planetary sovereignty?"

Auric smiled sadly. Auric's sad smile was full of knowledge, understanding, pathos. It was a smile of someone who'd seen far too much. It was the sorrowful smile of immortality and omniscience.

"You're running it into the ground," Auric said. "Not all of you. But plenty of you. Those of you who are in denial about the very reality you're facing. Denial, rationalization, cowardice, ignorance, ideology—these are moral blinders to this simple truth: you're on one planet in a massive universe. A universe filled with life and death. You have this one world, you have this one life each of you live. All of you have your own lives. I'm not here to destroy those lives—*The Book of Don't* is an attempt to save humanity from itself—for you to be civilized to one another. You can't be a civilized barbarian—you're either a barbarian or you're civilized."

"Barbarians? You're calling us barbarians?"

"Some of you absolutely are," Auric said. "And I think those of you who aren't barbarians understand this fact. In your antiquity, barbarians would ride through and destroy civilization. Today, the barbarians are peppered throughout your nations. You know them when you see them. Barbarians are mindless and ignorant, they are violent. They are uncivilized. They attack civilization. *The Book of Don't* is a roadmap to civility. Use it. Live by it. The barbarians in your world are at the vanguard of the opposition to what I'm doing, because they understand that I'm upending the arena in which they've prospered."

"What about the asteroid?" Wanda asked.

"It'll be here in four months, as I mentioned," Auric said. "But I'm going to stop it from destroying your species. I promise you that. It'll be a day not of extinction, but of celebration."

CHAPTER

FIVE

THE THANATOS REVELATION—as it was called—threw the world into a tizzy. Astronomers and astrophysicists in various countries trained their telescopes on the area of space that Auric had indicated and they saw it.

Denny Rand was even more furious about it.

"Auric planted it," Rand said. "It put that asteroid out there. Many people know this. Good people. They know it. Auric's setting us up. Are you stupid? Of course it is. It's going to destroy our world. Life as we know it. Gone. That's on Auric."

I had gone back to my job at Duotribe, seeing the stunned faces of my coworkers. Lord knows what McCluskey had told them. I went to his office, where he was sitting there, grimacing at my approach.

"I'm sorry, Christian," he said. "They leaned on me. What was I to do?"

"I quit," I said. "I'm out of here."

I went to my office and grabbed my stuff, put it into a box. Dylan was hovering nearby, unsure what to say. The conference room had been cleared by the HID agents.

"Where will you go, Christian?" Dylan asked.

"Anywhere I want," I said, taking out my gold phone. "Where should I go?"

"You should go home," the Auricle said.

"There," I said, pointedly, staring everyone down. "I'm going home. See you on the flip side."

They were all terrified of me. Word had gotten out that I was associated with Auric. I was glad I'd opted to wear the lapel pin, just to drive the point home. There was comfort in it on some level. I was protected by a higher power.

I went outside and there were no HID agents tracking me, because Auric had made them disappear. There were some Protectorate police, however, but they kept their distance, nervously talking into their radios as they tracked and tailed me. This was my new life.

"They're following me, aren't they?" I asked my phone.

"Yes," the Auricle said. "But don't worry about them. They can't hurt you, Christian."

I pocketed my golden phone and waited for my bus. There were several schools of thought about Thanatos:

It was real, Auric wasn't lying.
It was real, Auric had instigated it.
It wasn't real, Auric was lying.

In the CSA, all three lines were represented. The GNP was sticking to the second one, blaming the Thanatos asteroid on Auric, saying it was a ploy he'd engineered to hold the world hostage.

Of course, even I could see the logical fallacy in that one—namely that Auric hardly needed to use a threat of an asteroid impact to end the Earth. He could have annihilated us all with barely more than a thought.

That's not to say I hadn't ruled out that Auric might be using Thanatos to demonstrate his power and benevolence to the world, the way he had with other disasters he'd intervened on. As I saw it, his power presented that problem—he could just make Thanatos go away. But he hadn't. As before, he wanted people to know that he'd saved them. To me, that felt just a little self-serving. Naturally, the Auricle had answers to my questions.

"A miracle isn't miraculous if there's no one to witness it," the Auricle said. "A miracle without witnesses is just a story. And a story is just a lie."

"Ah," I said. "You really *do* want people to know you saved them."

"Of course I do," the Auricle said. "Thanatos is what persuaded me to intervene to save your planet to begin with."

"But you see where people might think you set the whole thing up, right?" I asked.

"I manipulate matter, not minds," the Auricle said. "I don't need to deceive my way through your world like your GNP does. They are consummate liars. Literally everything they say is marinated in mendacity, steeped in deception."

"Why didn't you include lying in your *Book of Don't*?" I asked.

"But I did," the Auricle said. "I said 'Don't be Fake'—that includes lying."

It was a fair point, and I let it stand unchallenged. Auric had answers for everything.

"What am I going to do now that I left my job?" I asked. Might as well put the Auricle to work with my more immediate concern. I could see other people circumspectly talking to their phones, what I assumed might be their own Auricles, at least conceivably. Without the HID around to monitor and harass them, people were being more overt about it. It was no secret that doing away with the secret police let us all breathe easier.

"I recommend you take up residence at the nearest Auric Tower," the Auricle said.

"The what?"

"I'm solving homelessness," the Auricle said. "I've created thousands of Auric Towers around the world."

The intelliphone screen flashed to these golden buildings, high-rises. They looked like the Auricle shrines in some manner, only far larger. Like twenty stories larger, and classically beautiful, like some strange, golden, Venetian skyscrapers.

"Um, are you kidding me?" I asked.

"Of course not, Christian," the Auricle said. "I'm speaking about it, in fact. The reality is that there's no reason your species couldn't solve homelessness. It's not a scarcity in available homes—rather, it's because your economic system leaves the vulnerable and needy in the lurch. But I'm solving for it through the creation of the Auric Towers."

"Oh, man," I said.

The Auric Towers caused a firestorm in the American media in particular. LAX News went absolutely crazy over them, as did some of the other media channels:

"Auric's Golden Shower Towers Plaguing America's Urban Wastelands"

"Promoting Dependency: How Auric's
Celestial Socialism is Destroying America"

"Tower Power Play: Auric's Army of Homeless Finds a Home"

"All That Glitters: Auric's Gilded Gambit and What it Means"

"Something for Nothing: How Auric Makes Real Americans Weaker"

Angelina and I visited one of the Auric Towers in Chicago, where some of the 6,000 area homeless were sheltering. Each Auric Tower could house 500 people, so there were a dozen Auric Towers in Chicago: six on the South Side, four on the West Side, and two on the North Side.

The North Side ATs were the ones I visited, and they were lovely Just like it showed in the news, they followed a classically romantic exterior style—golden high-rises with clear glass windows. They were screened by lush courtyards that carried the telltale Auric neoclassical motif—they were lovely, shaded grottoes with fountains and statues of Auric evident.

"He sure likes having statues of himself," Angelina said. "I'm just saying. For somebody who's so, you know, like moral and humble and stuff. He's incredibly vain."

What was I going to say? I wasn't in any position to judge Auric. Neither was Angelina, not that this would stop her from doing so.

"Who cares about the statues?" I asked. "Auric's making the world better. Like literally better. He hasn't demanded that anybody worship him."

Angelina looked at me like I was stupid—that down the end of her nose appraisal, finding me wanting with a blink of the eye.

"He doesn't have to," Angelina said. "He already knows that people will. Gosh, Christian, don't be so naïve. Can't you see how insidious it all is? He brings miracles, he performs miracles, and people *will* worship him. He *wants* to be worshipped. It's why everything he makes is gold. Why he made shrines and put his own statues here. Who does that? Auric wants people to revere him."

It was senseless. Auric didn't need anybody to worship him. He was far beyond all of that. Angelina was applying her own human preoccupations and prejudices to the mix. This was something people always did. They projected themselves onto others. So, of course, Auric was secretly a monster because that's what so many people were. Christ, what was happening to me? I was identifying with Auric.

I couldn't just come out and say it, but I had faith in Auric. I believed in him. Not some starry-eyed belief like some clearly held. Mine was something else. Auric had earned my trust. Seeing was believing.

Inside the AT, there was a beautiful lobby of white marble veined with gold, and a bubbling circular fountain in the shape of his symbol. A young man and woman in matching white uniforms saw Angelina and me and smiled at us, like they were hotel concierges.

"Welcome, Christian," the young woman said. "I'm Eden Thorne. This is my partner, James Shrike. We've been tasked by Auric to man this tower."

"Tasked?" Angelina asked. "You're, what, Auric Tower slaves?"

"Not at all," Eden said. "We're free to stay here. There's nothing to maintain. We're simply here to greet visitors to this Tower and help orient new tenants. Auric told us you might be taking up residence here."

"Wait, what?" Angelina asked, giving me a stricken look.

I shrugged, gave her a noncommittal grin. "Considering it."

Eden was blond and blue-eyed, with a carefree Caucasian countenance. James Shrike was Black, brown-haired and brown-eyed and was tall and lean.

"We're honored to have the Chronicler here," James said. "We already asked our Auricles why you were here, and they told us everything."

Angelina grimaced at them.

"What'd the phones tell you?"

"You're here to see Auric's handiwork and take up residence, of course," Eden said. "We have everything one could need, here. There's a Golden Grocery over there. All the food the tenants could want to eat. Free for residents."

James pointed to a golden room, like an empty alcove.

"And this is a Healing Room," James said. "Anyone who steps inside it is healed of any ailment. It functions the way the shrines do."

"Bullshit," Angelina said.

"Step in," Eden said. "Find out, Angelina. Get cured."

"How do you know me?" Angelina asked. "Never mind. I know. I'm not stepping into that thing."

"I will," I said.

It seemed like the right moment for a display of faith and trust. I stepped forward, walking into the Healing Room, which illuminated as I entered it, a soothing blue hue.

"Christian," Angelina said, her voice raising. "Don't!"

Auric's warmly reassuring voice came through, like blended butterscotch. As he spoke, an opaque screen closed off the room from the lobby, turning Angelina and the others into silhouette. This created an intimate, almost confessional quality to the Healing Room.

"Welcome, Christian," Auric said. "You don't have any life-threatening diseases, although there's a slight risk of macular degeneration for you that may occur in your later years. Would you like this to be corrected?"

"Macular degeneration?" I asked. "Like how much later?"

"Not likely to manifest for at least 40 years," Auric said. "And even then, only a 15% chance of doing so. Would you like this to be corrected?"

"That's seriously the only thing wrong with me?" I asked. I had assumed I was at least at elevated risk for heart disease.

"You are otherwise healthy, provided you watch your diet and exercise," Auric said. "You're very fortunate, Christian, for a human."

I weighed the options. Part of me wondered what would happen if I took Auric up on the healing.

"You'd be healed," Auric said.

Did I fully trust Auric to heal me of an ailment I wasn't even likely to get, and even then, only decades from now? No, it was a show of faith on my part, and Auric deserved it.

"Alright," I said. "Heal me, Auric."

"Good choice, Christian," Auric said, and the room was bathed in a golden glow that filled me with peace and warmth. I was immersed in Auric's benevolence, and it was magical. The peace was palpable. I didn't want it to end. It was like being high, like the most perfect high one could ever experience. Blissful beneficence.

But, of course, it did, after an eternal moment. The light was gone, and the opaque barrier opened, and there was Angelina, Eden, and James, staring at me—Angelina looking appalled, Eden and James looking quietly, serenely joyful.

"All better, Christian?" Eden asked.

"Sure," I said. "Show us some more of the services around here."

"Pod person," Angelina said.

"I feel great," I said.

"I'll bet," Angelina said. "Sky-high on Auric's celestial narcissistic supply."

They walked us into the Golden Grocery, where there were golden apples, white apples, blue apples, and scores of other fruits in those colors as well. It was jarring to see that tri-colored cornucopia of fruit and vegetables. Eden felt the need to explain.

"Auric provides nourishment at his Golden Groceries," Eden said. "All ethically sourced, of course, and nutritionally complete."

She picked up one of the golden apples and held it up for us to see. Angelina grabbed a blue one, turning it over in her hands.

"This is fucked up," Angelina said. "Does anybody eat these?"

"Tenants can have all they like," Eden said. "Eating any of the fruit in here will keep you filled up for an entire day. Were you expecting bags of potato chips in here, Angelina?"

I looked at the golden heads of lettuce next to the white and the blue and could only imagine what they tasted like. The Golden Grocery was beautiful, of course—it had the obligatory columns and was nicely arranged, but the tri-colored fruit and vegetables were strange to the eye. They weren't unlovely—they were pretty. But they were alien, too. I wondered why Auric even went that route, given what he could have done. Eden seemed to anticipate my question.

"As you already know, Auric is a firm believer in branding," Eden said. "He didn't want people confusing Golden Grocery items with terrestrial produce. Therefore, he opted for this color scheme. That way, there was no mistaking something acquired from his Golden Groceries. But I can assure you both that they are delicious and nourishing."

As if to underscore her point, Eden took a bite of the golden apple, revealing the beautiful white flesh of the apple within. She chewed on it a bit, handed the apple to James, who also took a bite.

"Would you like to try it?" Eden asked, prompting James to hold out the twice-bitten golden apple. Angelina looked horrified, but I took the apple. I wasn't afraid of a piece of fruit. I took a bite.

It was the perfect facsimile of an apple. It was the ideal apple. It was an Auric apple, which is to say it was the ultimate expression of apple. To merely say it was delicious would have diminished the nutritive glory of the fruit. It was firm, tartly sweet, crunchy, juicy, spicy, and abundantly satisfying. I felt a degree of contentment as well as energy upon eating it.

Eden and James watched me eat it with smiles on their faces, while Angelina looked on warily as ever.

"Good, right?" Eden asked.

"Yeah," I said, taking a second bite. "Unbelievable."

I held the golden apple out to Angelina, who shook her head forcefully.

"I'm not taking a bite from that apple thing," Angelina said. "You don't know what you're eating."

"It's delicious," I said, taking still another bite.

"For tenants, like we said," James said. "All you can eat. And free."

The flavor was sublime—nuanced and yet undeniable, present and elusive, unlike anything I'd ever had in my entire life. Hints of vanilla and cinnamon.

"Are all the fruits and vegetables like this?" I asked.

"Yes," Eden said. "All Auriculture represents the perfect, fullest expression of any fruit or vegetable it emulates. Auric wants us to be well-fed and happy."

"Amazing," I said, setting the apple down. It was a shame to waste it, but I actually couldn't eat any more. I was stuffed on three bites.

"Auriculture?" Angelina asked.

"What he calls his produce," James said. "Catchy, isn't it?"

"Yeah," Angelina said.

We walked around the Golden Grocery, which was, as Eden said, a simulacrum of a grocery store, but with its marble flooring and tricolored produce, altogether otherworldly and strange. The familiar things rendered in those three colors that way made it look like an installation art piece. Even the grocery carts were golden. It made me feel strange, in some liminal space between the familiar and the alien.

"Do people complain about the produce?" I asked.

Eden and James looked bewildered.

"What would they have to complain about?" Eden asked. "The produce is perfect."

"It just looks unreal," I said. "And the color scheme. I don't know."

"As I said, this was by design," Eden said. "Auric doesn't want to displace native food stocks. Auriculture can only be found in the Golden Groceries. And, if you look closely, you'll see that while everything in here is shades of gold, white, and blue, there are varieties of tints represented. There's electric blue, cerulean, indigo, midnight blue, turquoise, sky blue, and so on. It's a monochromatic feast of blue. Same with the white and gold."

And, of course, Eden wasn't wrong—the shades of color were there, but everything was still those three colors. It skeeved me out a little, despite myself. As delicious as the apple was, I couldn't imagine just eating this stuff all the time.

"Better than hunger and homelessness, wouldn't you say?" James asked. "Auric provides."

"Auric provides," Eden said. "Let us show you one of the suites."

CHAPTER

SIX

THE AURIC TOWER residences were lovely, like everything else Auric created. Eden and James showed us a single-family residence, which had a quarter of the floor. Apparently, each of the levels was quartered that way. They were spacious, impeccably designed, fully furnished (can you guess the color scheme?) and wonderful. The available units were one-bedroom, two-bedroom, three-bedroom, and even four-bedroom suites.

Living in the city, I knew a place like this would cost a fortune. I couldn't even imagine.

"This is incredible," I said. There were live plants throughout them, and the views were fantastic. "I'd move here in a heartbeat."

"You're always welcome, Christian," Eden said. "Obviously, these are intended for the homeless, but arrangements can be made at any of the Auric Towers for our Chronicler."

"These are *really* for the homeless?" Angelina asked, scoffing. "These are unbelievable. Don't you worry about people trashing them?"

Eden shook her head, her smile unbroken. "Why would anybody do that? Any resident in an Auric Tower has to go to the Healing Room. That's a residency requirement: mandatory healing."

"I *knew* there was a catch," Angelina said, with considerable satisfaction. "There's *always* a catch, Christian."

"But the Healing Room purifies people in body and soul," Eden said. "Addictions and afflictions disappear. Prospective tenants emerge healthy and whole, ready to live productive lives of their own choosing."

"Ergo, no junkies or alcoholics," Angelina said.

"None whatsoever," Eden said. "And, of course, Auric Towers are smoke-free. Auric is no fan of Big Tobacco."

"What about marijuana?" Angelina asked.

"Smoke-free," James said. "That includes weed."

"Ah," Angelina said.

Small price to pay, from my perspective. The suite they showed us, which was a four-bedroom unit, was gorgeous and spacious—both homey and ostentatious in a cozily classical way. For somebody living under a bridge, it would have been astounding. And to be rent-free?

"What's to stop people who aren't homeless from snagging one of these?" I asked. "Like me, for example?"

Although, after leaving Duotribe and my intelliphone implying that Angelina was an asshole, I felt like I could be at high risk of homelessness very soon.

"Auric, of course," Eden said. "Auric doesn't let just anyone become a resident in his Auric Towers. These are for the needy, not the greedy."

"Unless they're the Chronicler," Angelina said.

"Auric values and supports his supporters," Eden said. "James and I were both heroin addicts before Auric healed us. We're here to say that life before Auric was a mess. But after Auric? We love it here. We're happy. And we're healthy. We're fully committed to the cause."

"Yeah, I can see that," I said. I couldn't believe that Eden had been an addict. She seemed so put together and professional. Eden seemed to sense my appraisal.

"Auric heals all wounds," Eden said. "You felt the Healing Room, Christian. I went in there a wreck and emerged whole for the first time in my life. I was cleansed of everything that had hobbled me in the past. I became a clean slate."

"We both have," James said.

"I think you mean blank slate," Angelina said, but Eden and James were undeterred.

"We mean clean," Eden said. "We have Auric to thank for it, and we are eternally thankful to him."

"I thought he said he wasn't going to mess with people's minds," Angelina said. "He said that."

"He hasn't 'messed with' our minds," James said. "He merely repaired the neuronal damage and maladaptive limbic pathways caused by our addictions. In so doing, he restored and rejuvenated us, let us see clearly without our minds being fogged by a narcotic."

"We were healed," Eden said. "In every sense of the word."

Angelina was skeptical as ever, but I was in another place. My mind worked through the logistics as we surveyed the spacious floor. I wondered how people got to choose their suites, or if they even did.

"How is it determined who lives on which floor?" I asked.

"It's on a first come, first serve basis," Eden said. "Obviously, when all of the available units are filled, then Auric builds another one. He bases it on each region's number of homeless. In the case of the Heartland Protectorate, we're talking enough housing for the 6,000 homeless in the city. In smaller areas, the structures are correspondingly smaller. And once a building is filled, no more tenants are accepted, but arrangements are made with Auric to visit another one."

Angelina walked to one of the lovely windows that overlooked the city. The view was stunning. People anywhere in the CSA would kill for this kind of residence.

"And then what?" Angelina asked, putting her hand on the glass, leaving a handprint that slowly disappeared while I looked on.

"If or when there are more in need, another Towers will be created by Auric," Eden said. "Auric's applied a variation of this concept in regions routinely hit by tornadoes, floods, earthquakes, and hurricanes."

Angelina sniffed a measure of disapproval that was quintessentially her. She wore her annoyance like ornamentation.

"Why wouldn't Auric simply stop the tornadoes, floods, and hurricanes from ever happening?" Angelina asked. "He could, couldn't he? Like he has in some cases."

Eden's smile was as unbroken as ever.

"He could," Eden said.

"But he doesn't," Angelina said.

"Neither does God," James said. "God doesn't do anything. At least Auric builds self-sustaining shelters for those in need. What does God do?"

"He gives people hope," Angelina said, a trifle defensively. "And you don't know what He does."

"Auric provides *actual* food and shelter—Relief Beyond Belief," Eden said. "More to the point—nourishment and shelter are the foundation for hope. It's hard to be hopeful when you're starving and exposed to the elements."

"It's harder," James said.

Angelina sighed, scowling. She glanced at me with some reproach.

"I think I've seen enough," Angelina said.

"No," I said. "I want to see the rooftop gardens."

Eden and James nodded, smiling. They led us back to the golden elevator and took us to the penthouse.

"The penthouse suite is really a kind of clubhouse and communal garden for the residents," Eden said, as the doors opened, showing us the facilities.

The penthouse was a sea of white marble, looking like a Roman bathhouse, only it was segmented by glass. Eden narrated us through it, although I barely heard her, as I was amazed at the lovely, luxurious offerings. There was a game room—which included a card table and a pool table, a golden sectional and a huge plasma screen television that seemed to hover over a fireplace. Adjacent to this room was a narrow, indoor saltwater swimming pool and hot tub, as well as a fitness room. All of this was surrounded by a sumptuous rooftop garden that would have put plenty of remaining CSA city parks to shame.

In addition to the white marble, there were hints of gold, and I could see a mosaic rendering of both Auric and his symbol in different parts of the penthouse. Eden and James walked us to the garden, where we stepped out and could smell the trees, flowers, and good soil. There was a pavestone path, although we could have as easily walked in the grass.

"Luxurious," Angelina said.

"Auric wants people to feel at home," Eden said. "This is a self-sustaining place for peace and calm."

"Self-sustaining," I said. "No gardeners or groundskeepers?"

"It's zeroscaped unless residents *want* to garden, of course," Eden said.

"Gilded cages," Angelina said. "A human zoo. That's what this all is."

Eden and James looked genuinely hurt at the suggestion, while Angelina went on.

"Auric's created a nice little habitat for people with this," Angelina said. "But it's still a housing project. Even if it's a gloriously golden one."

"You'd prefer people live on the street?" James asked.

I know I didn't. I thought the Auric Tower was incredible. Of course it would be. That just made sense. Everything Auric touched was improved. It was as incontrovertible as gravity.

"They're all like this?" I asked.

"They're all appropriately branded for the population, the climate, and the culture," Eden said. "There are certain architectural elements commonly presented in all Auric Towers, naturally."

Angelina rolled her eyes.

"Branding, again," Angelina said. "Honestly, I don't trust it. The branding for Auric's stuff is just too on the nose. I don't trust anything that's this branded. And this all has to cost a fortune."

"Price is no object for Auric," Eden said. "It's immaterial to him."

"Right," Angelina said. "Nobody is this good or kind. *Nobody*. Not even Auric."

"Auric *is* kindness and generosity," Eden said.

"It's inhuman," Angelina said. "He's inhuman. All of this enlightened generosity? It's creepy."

"It's easier to see something sinister, isn't it?" Eden asked, looking pointedly at Angelina, who scoffed. "Easier to impugn the motives of a benevolent superbeing than to question why this hasn't been done before, by humanity? Or by God?"

"It's expensive," Angelina said.

"So are wars, but you don't see our government ever balking at paying for those, do we?" James asked.

Angelina wasn't having any of it, but the peace in the penthouse was undeniable. What I wasn't seeing, however, were tenants. Naturally, I asked Eden and James about it.

"Where are the residents?" I asked.

"They're around," Eden said. "In response to Ms. Reed's contention that this is a human zoo, we don't really want to go knocking on people's doors and bothering them, now do we?"

"What do people do here?" Angelina asked.

"Whatever they want," James said. "Auric doesn't provide this with strings attached, beyond the mandatory healing. In his view, residents at Auric Towers have suffered enough in their lives before he came along. The last thing he's going to do is harass them further. He wants to help them find their own way. People want to lead productive lives when given the opportunity to do so."

"How very benevolent," Angelina said. "How very socialist of him."

"Auric believes people, left to their own devices, will find their own way, at their own pace," James said. "People don't need to be cold, hungry, and desperate to find their path in the world—and people in those situations don't always make the best decisions. Those are obstacles to improvement, not opportunities."

"They're incentives," Angelina said.

"They're abusive," Eden said. "It's like saying growing up in an abusive home is good for you."

Angelina cleared her throat as she formed a response.

"Suffering builds character," Angelina said.

"But nurturing support better fosters growth," James said.

"We're not plants," Angelina said. "Nor are we livestock. Or are we?"

"We are not," Eden said. "But support is always better than abuse."

Up here, the rest of the world seemed so far away. The scent of the grass, trees, shrubs, and flowers was intoxicating. Here was a serene shelter, as soothing as any place I'd ever visited. I liked to think of Auric building these around the world for those who needed them. This felt like an undiminished good, an act of cosmic compassion.

For all of the otherworldly strangeness Auric brought to the table, what he was doing for humanity was a good thing. He was doing what we *ought* to have been doing for ourselves for millennia. The deficit between what we ought to have been doing, and what we actually did was a chasm. And Auric was a golden bridge over that chasm.

It was as humbling as it was inspiring. I was greatly impressed.

"When can I move in?" I asked.

Eden and James smiled at each other, and at me, while Angelina gasped.

"Any time you like, Christian," Eden said. "We'd be happy to have you."

"What are you talking about, Christian?" Angelina asked. "Are you insane?"

"Rent-free, Angelina," I said. "They flat-out offered me a place. I'm the Chronicler. I think I need to check it out. To observe."

"I'm *not* living in this utopian playpen," Angelina said, frowning at me.

"Not even rent-free?" I asked.

"Mandatory healing session required, of course," Eden said, raising an eyebrow.

"Of course," Angelina said. "Nobody's healing me. Least of all, Auric."

"I'm moving in," I said. "Top floor, if it's available."

"Of course," Eden said. "We knew you were coming, Christian."

"Rand's going to nuke these places," Angelina said. "Haven't you seen the news? He's screaming about them. The GNP's literally going to war with them."

"The Auric Towers are protected from local interference," James said. "Every resident is quite safe from anything the GNP or other hostile entities might do. Just as Auric protects his followers, he protects his properties from harm."

Angelina looked hard at me, and I met her gaze evenly, impassive-ly. Was it a standoff? Were we breaking up? Was this a line she simply wouldn't cross?

"You want to be a target, that's your choice," Angelina said. "I'm not signing on for it. Not the 'mandatory healing' and not being a target for the GNP. I'm out of here. If you're smart, Christian, you'll follow me."

I watched Angelina stomp away.

I'd pick up my stuff later.

CHAPTER
SEVEN

———

ON TOP OF EVERYTHING ELSE that had happened and/or was going on, the GNP was outraged over the creation of the Auric Towers. LAX News and President Denny Rand worked hand in glove expressing their rage over the turn of events. I watched from my new penthouse apartment—or was it a condominium—from that big plasma screen television mounted on a wall. It amused me that with all that Auric created, he made sure people still had televisions in the Auric Towers. He understood how we rolled as a species—we liked our streaming as much as we liked our screaming.

"Auric's making humanity soft," Rand said, fuming on television. "He's turning us into livestock. Not us. Not Real Americans. I mean the poor. Poor people. He's making them livestock. His death towers—that's what they are—*death towers*. People go in, they don't come out. They're horrible. People are frightened. Terrified of the towers. Auric's towers. Socialist deathtraps."

LAX News and RAN talked about Auric's welfare kings and queens, living it up in Auric's golden towers. They attacked them relentlessly, tried to frame them as terribly as they could, with ominous music and hand-picked "people from the street" expressing concern and dismay about the towers. News media flocked to diners to ask old people what they thought about the towers, running with the doubts and fears of the elderly patrons whenever they could.

"Auric's saying that if you have nothing, you deserve everything," Nick Noxwell said, on LAX's America First news show, his balding head polished to a mirror sheen, his lifeless eyes hooded as he stridently spoke of the catastrophe facing the country. "I don't know about you, but I don't think that's fair. And what I know is that it's un-American. In America, you get what you deserve. God rewards those who win and punishes those who lose. Auric the Alien is sticking it to everyday hardworking Real Americans with his golden towers. This is all part of a sick social experiment this alien invader is undertaking. This is social engineering of the very worst sort."

They showed a map of the Confederated States, showing the presence of the Auric Towers as blue dots, and the Auricle shrines as blue squares. It made the country look like it was infected by a poxy disease. Noxwell widened the view to show the world, where the dots intensified and expanded. There were currently 3,000 Auric Towers scattered around the country.

"You see what he's doing, don't you? He's taking over the world," Noxwell said. "Ladies and gentlemen. Real American patriots—Auric is *not* here to save the world. He's here to take it over. He's doing it right now. And anybody who says otherwise is lying to you. His so-called prophets are traitors to the human race. The Auricians are pure evil."

I wasn't persuaded. LAX News wasn't my sort of thing, putting that politely. Their panicky, reactionary fearmongering was not something I ever considered worthwhile, worth only a hate-watch and nothing more.

Without the SAC or the HID around to do it, remaining cadres of GNP paramilitaries repeatedly tried to attack the Auric Towers, but any who did disappeared into golden motes of light, just like the others had. Some of them tried blowing up the buildings, but the detonations failed to damage the buildings, and the perpetrators disappeared. This enraged President Denny Rand, who fumed at daily press conferences, gripping the lectern.

"This alien invader and its legions of hateful, nasty followers," Rand said, red in the face. "They're destroying America. They're attacking everything our great country stands for. And those golden eyesores are just the beginning. Who asked Auric to come 'help' us? And have you noticed that he's still sometimes a she? Auric. Aurica. It can't even decide what it wants to be. People are saying that."

I feel like I understood what Auric was trying to do. Nobody could look at the LAX News broadcast and fail to see it.

"You can't serve two masters," Rand yelled into the microphones. "There's only room for three in *Real* America. I don't have to explain it. You already know. Real Americans know. This alien and his/her/its ideology? There's no room for it. Not in Real America."

Rand held up an upside-down copy of the *Book of Don't*.

"Have you read this thing? I sure haven't. Its holy wisdom? 'Don't be an Asshole.' Don't be an asshole? How is *that* wisdom? America was built by assholes. You take every winner in this country, and you know what they are? Assholes. Coal mines? Railroads? Skyscrapers? Golf courses? Assholes own them all. *You owe your life to assholes.* And this son of a bitch has the gall to call these good people out like this?"

Rand furiously threw the *Book* away, shaking his head.

Even though it was Rand who typically got to do whatever he wanted without interference from the Christian Congress or anyone else, the television bleeped his swears. The GNP would stomp on human rights and decency wherever they found it, literally executed political enemies and rivals, but as I said before, they didn't like swears. The television was awash in bleeps as Rand fumed.

"This is a holy war," Rand said. "Real Americans, I want you to take your guns and I want you to be locked and loaded. If you see an Aurician, shoot 'em dead. With your guns. I want you to find them and I want you to shoot them. Kill them, for the sake of the country. For the sake of freedom. These traitors deserve to die."

And then Rand vanished in a sea of golden motes, while the television flashed the GNP symbol and said the station was experiencing technical difficulties and urged us to please stand by.

"Jesus," I said.

"Not quite," Auric said, having appeared in the room with me, making me jump. He was in his ever-present lovely white suit, looked as stunningly, radiantly noble as ever.

"You just vaporized Denny Rand?" I asked.

"He's on layaway," Auric said. "As are his militant followers. He's actively inciting terrorism and mass violence. That simply won't stand. He's a clear and present danger to human civilization."

"But the government?" I said.

"I've put all offending GNP members on layaway," Auric said.

"You can't just do that," I said. "People are going to freak out."

Auric took a seat opposite me, the picture of beatific calm.

"Had to be done," Auric said. "I mean, the man did try to murder me with an orbital attack satellite. He wanted to launch nuclear weapons on the Auric Towers. I couldn't let that happen."

"I thought you got rid of the nukes," I said.

"He'd covertly had some more built," Auric said. "Tactical nuclear devices. I didn't prevent it because it provided me cause to react in self-defense."

My brain was racing.

"You said you vaporized the GNP?" I asked.

"I said I put them on layaway," Auric replied.

"That's like 60 million people," I said.

"Correct," Auric replied.

"You've put 60 million people on layaway?" I asked. "How?"

"Hey, it's me," Auric said. "It's not a problem. They're all fine."

Auric seemed so peaceful, so convincing, I wanted to believe him. But the idea of that many people simply vanishing? It was terrifying to imagine. People would be panicking, thinking that the End Times had begun. I wasn't, but I was still pretty worried.

"The GNP fervently believes in what they call the End Times," Auric said, clearly picking up on my thoughts. "Maybe they'll think they all went to Heaven. Would it be easier for people if I told them that? I won't, of course, because that's a lie. But they've been waiting for the so-called Second Coming for decades. This is like that, only instead of the purportedly pious and peaceful going to Heaven, it's the assholes, idiots, bigots, and other evil people who have been taken."

He gestured to a copy of the *Book of Don't*, which sat on the coffee table between us. I hadn't noticed it was there. Maybe it hadn't been there and Auric had just conjured it up.

"As I've said elsewhere, it's not that hard to be a decent person," Auric said. "Did you know that there *aren't* any decent people in the GNP? They're all trash people, as you might put it."

I did use that terminology in the past, felt chastened that Auric even brought it up. It was like he knew that and was throwing it back at me.

"Recycling," Auric said. "I'm a firm believer in recycling, Christian. Speaking of that, you should come with me."

"Come with you?"

"Yes," Auric said, standing up. "I'd like to show you something. As my Chronicler, I feel like you need to see it firsthand."

"Where are we going?" I asked, rising, feeling wary. Auric was so calm and reassuring, but I still felt awe and fear in his presence.

"On a trip," Auric said, holding out his golden hand.

"Where?" I asked.

"Venus, for starters," Auric said, beckoning benevolently.

CHAPTER
EIGHT

VENUS IS AROUND 151 million miles from the Earth, and over 67 million miles from the Sun. It would take around four months for someone to travel between the two planets. We did it instantaneously, and I was beyond terrified, even though I was with Auric.

We just vanished in a flash of golden light, and when we reappeared, we were on the surface of Venus, surrounded by a forcefield of golden Auric light.

"What the fuck are we doing on Venus, Auric?" I asked, not understanding how I could be breathing and not incinerated and squished. The atmospheric pressure alone is 90 times greater than we have on Earth. But I was protected. Because of the monstrous atmosphere of the place, everything looked orange-yellow to my eyes. It was a literal hellscape that horrified me.

"I'm going to terraform it," Auric said.

"What?"

"You heard me," Auric said. The ground where we stood was naked grey stone, and I was stunned and afraid to be on this nightmare of a world, even with Auric. "You've made history—you're the first human being to stand on the surface of Venus, Christian."

"I don't know if this counts," I said.

"It counts," Auric said. "I'm counting it. Just don't walk outside of my sphere of protection, obviously."

"Obviously," I said, afraid to even move. I mean, it was a maelstrom beyond the safety of Auric's forcefield. The colors, the elemental fury of it was too much to comprehend.

"Don't worry, I wouldn't let that happen, Christian," Auric said, smiling reassuringly to me. "I just wanted you to see this yourself. There are three interrelated problems to solve in terraforming Venus—first, we have to eliminate the majority of the carbon dioxide and sulfur dioxide atmosphere. Next, we have to reduce the surface temperature. Finally, we need to add breathable oxygen to the atmosphere."

The way Auric talked, he made the unbelievable seem almost mundane. There was just a blasé way he had of speaking that created a feeling of confidence.

"This twin of Earth underwent catastrophic climate change long ago," Auric said. "The runaway greenhouse effect on Venus ruined this planet."

My legs felt weak as I stood there next to him. I was still processing where I was. The blanket of roiling clouds, the endless profusion of bare rocks beneath our feet, the understanding that only Auric's power and will kept me alive within the forcefield bubble, and that beyond that glittery benevolence was instantaneous incineration and crushing death. It was weighty stuff, filled me with unfathomable dread.

"It's okay, Christian," Auric said. "You're perfectly safe. I just felt it was more important for you to see this directly, than, you know, your couch."

I know you're probably wanting me to be all lyrically descriptive about Venus, like what it looked like, but to my eyes, it was just that sickly yellow-orange light, endless rocks, and the blanket of killer clouds swarming around us. Venus was ugly. It looked like Death. It looked like Hell. Like more hellish than anything I'd ever seen.

I tapped my intelliphone and snapped some pictures. Like the landscape, Auric standing there, smiling beatifically at me.

"That's the spirit," Auric said, holding up his hands. "Now, watch this."

The pulse of light that flew from Auric's upraised arms was brighter and stronger than I'd seen on Earth. It was a powerful blue-white light that pulsed outward from him in a cascading wave, like he was a rock that had dropped into the pond that was Venus. And I was certain, as I filmed him doing it, that Venus *was* only a pond to him, a simple problem to be solved.

How many miracles have you witnessed in this chronicle of mine? What words exist to encompass them? *This* was a miracle. I was at ground zero to the sublime.

The energy flew from Auric, and as the beam extended beyond him, Venus changed—the toxic yellow-orange became blue-white, and in the span of minutes, I went from barely being able to see anything to almost seeing too much—the sea of grey stone around us was all that was around us.

"I'm transforming this atmosphere to a human-friendly atmosphere," Auric said, as casually as if he were describing the weather. "Around two to three billion years ago, Venus may have been habitable the way Earth had been. But around 750 million years ago a massive amount of carbon dioxide was released into the atmosphere from what was likely a terrible volcanic resurfacing event, forever rendering this planet uninhabitable to humans, until now."

The wave of energy Auric had projected had transformed the planet in moments, producing fluffy white clouds where there had been those boiling, angry yellow clouds before. I could only imagine what astronomers would say and think, seeing Venus change before their eyes. Gone would be the bright butterscotch planet. In its place would be something that looked Earthlike.

"There," Auric said. "I've solved the atmospheric problem, including the pressure caused by it. It's now around 78 percent nitrogen, 21 percent oxygen, as well as some other trace gases you don't need to worry about. It's Earthlike. And I've reduced the global temperature from the roughly 880 degrees Fahrenheit to something more comfortable, around 75 degrees."

It was staggering to watch him do this, just talking about it so casually and so quickly. Power like this was indescribable, and yet here I was, trying to do just that.

"We're not done, obviously," Auric said. "I'm going to have to get some liquid water here, for example. But that's not hard to come by. The universe is full of water if you know where to look. And I do."

He created an ocean before my eyes, just gestured and the blue-white energy flowed from him and where we were staring at a great field of stone, an ocean formed.

"Uh," I said. "What about native lifeforms?"

"I'm not worried about them," Auric said. "I'm worried about humanity."

"Wait, is there life here?" I asked.

"Look, I'm terraforming a planet for humanity, here. Cut me some slack," Auric said.

"Sure, sure," I said.

The water flowed and filled countless spaces upon Venus, and Auric took us up into the sky, which frightened me even more, because I hate heights.

"I couldn't keep us down on the surface, at least not there," Auric said. "I'm making oceans, after all."

We landed on a higher landmass, what Auric told me was the shores of Ishtar Terra, one of two continents on Venus, the other being Aphrodite Terra.

"Venus lacks a magnetosphere, so I'm going to have to put something up to protect it," Auric said. "Or else the solar winds will boil away what I've done. I'll create polar protectors."

He teleported us to the Venusian north pole and created a great, golden structure that looked like a magnificent, domed fortress-temple that was like several stacked discs that resembled a layer cake.

There was a golden pulse of light that shot skyward and enveloped Venus in a momentary golden glow.

"You'll love this," Auric said. "These projectors provide the necessary magnetospheric protection for Venus and can be tweaked to provide a classic representation of Venus from Earth. This is in anticipation of people whining about how I've 'ruined Venus' by terraforming it for them."

"What are you talking about?"

"When people realize in a few minutes that I have terraformed Venus, people will attack what I've done as destroying Venus," Auric said. "When all I actually did was make it habitable for human life. But if people like the vintage Venus view, they can just push a button at one of these polar protectors and create a planetary holographic representation of vintage Venus that'll look the way it's looked for hundreds of millions of years after the climate catastrophe created it."

Auric pointed to the two buttons, which were palm-sized lozenges on the front of the polar protector structure:

VINTAGE VENUS
TERRAFORMED VENUS

"The view won't change planetside," Auric said. "It's only a holographic representation for the psychological benefit of humans on Earth. Just trying to get ahead of the complainers. And they *will* complain, to be sure."

"Uh, yeah," I said. "Wow."

"Alright," Auric said. "We've now got the atmosphere sorted out, the surface temperature, the pressure problem, the magnetosphere, and the liquid water. What's next? Just kidding, I know what's next. Life. It's an interesting philosophical problem, wouldn't you say, Christian? What life *should* I put on Venus? I could extrapolate from hypothetical legacy life on Venus, go through the whole aborted evolutionary process and serve up native Venusian life, but don't worry about that. I'm not going to. I'm going to put Earth life on this planet."

And then he created soil to carpet the planet, so everything wasn't grey rocks. He spawned forests out of nothing, populated Venus with an intricate web of life that was as thunderingly complex as that found on Earth. I don't know how he did this, but I'm just telling you what I saw him do.

"I don't have words," I said.

"You don't need words when you have pictures," Auric said. "You're doing fine, Christian. You're just documenting this."

"Okay, I do have some words," I said, while Auric worked his magic—or whatever it was—on Venus. It was truly awesome, only more. It was—

"Cosmic Awesome," Auric said, saying what I was thinking. "That's what you can call it—The Cosmic Awesome."

"The Cosmic Awesome," I said, watching him spawn a massive forest out of nothing.

"Yes," Auric said. "It gets at the heart of it, what I represent."

"It sounds like a brand of marijuana," I said. Marijuana was legalized throughout the world but was outlawed in the Confederated States, where the Drug War was fought with the sort of zeal Americans always provided unquestioningly for lost causes.

"An amusing interpretation, Christian," Auric said. "I can agree that I'd like humankind to be high on life."

I didn't expect Auric to be quippy, but there he was, quipping with me while terraforming Venus. I suspected that, like with so much Auric did, he was deliberately taking his time with the terraforming, just so I could capture it all. For someone who was omnipotent, the terraforming could have happened instantaneously.

"Astute as ever, Christian," Auric said. "But a finger snap terraforming is somehow dissatisfying, wouldn't you agree? You expect something grandiose to take place in a more measured manner, so I'm indulging you in that. What was the nagging question—the words you wanted to share with me?"

"You already know them," I said. I mean, he did.

"But as the Chronicler, you should ask them," Auric said. Venus was looking as beautiful as her namesake: a stunning wonderland, a veritable paradise.

"You said you left dead civilizations alone in your journeys," I said. "That life belonged to the living. But you're busy creating a living world right now out of what was a functionally dead planet."

"Ah," Auric said. "Yes. But there's a difference between reviving the dead and giving life where there wasn't any before."

"What's the difference?"

Auric had wrapped up his terraforming, and while I was disarmed by the larger Sun in the sky, I otherwise accepted it as a newly beautiful day on Venus. He smiled at me and mock-dusted his golden hands, an image I'd carry with me for the rest of my life.

"I'm a fan of potential," Auric said. "On those dead worlds—the ones with dead civilizations on them, that potential had already been realized. That was water that flowed downstream after the dam had burst. Whereas a place like this, there's life yet to come, opportunities for progress. You have to remember that in my travels, I've passed so many lifeless worlds. In the case of your species, I'm here now, and you're alive—or you're not dead yet. I didn't want to pass up the opportunity to assist before you made yourselves extinct."

We walked to the ocean shore, where the blue waves ebbed and flowed.

"You broke your own rules because we were alive and you wanted to make the most of that."

"They're *my* rules," Auric said. "Seems like I could break them if I want to."

"Okay," I said, feeling nervous from the implication of that.

"Don't worry, Christian," Auric said. "I'm far more methodical than capricious. For example, Venus rotates very slowly, and in a retrograde fashion. It's the only planet in your solar system to rotate in that clockwise direction. A day on this new Venus would last around 243 Earth days. What am I to do about that? On one hand, I could keep that distinctive character of Venus intact. But can you imagine how that would play havoc with human minds, were they to settle here? The Sun would rise only twice a year, every 117 days, and because of that retrograde rotation, it would rise in the west and set in the east."

"Yeah," I said. "That would drive people bonkers."

"And a Venusian year is only around 225 Earth days," Auric said. "Reflective of its closer proximity to the Sun. I couldn't do anything about that—well, I could move Venus, but I'm not going to do that."

"You could move it?" I asked.

"Of course I could," Auric said. "I could switch the orbits of Venus and Mars, for example. Let Mars be closer and Venus farther. But I won't, don't worry. I understand that there's only so much change people can take."

Beyond the celestial mechanics of planet-moving, which was staggering to imagine at all, there was something else nagging at me. How could he be so powerful and so easygoing at the same time? It was a paradox I was determined to solve.

"Venus is doomed," Auric said. "That's what you're going to ask. Why I spent this massive amount of energy giving life to a planet that'll eventually be consumed by the death of your Sun in four billion years or so? Of course, Venus and Earth'll be in dire straits well before that time as the Sun consumes its fusion fuel more desperately, causing it to burn bigger and brighter. The cosmic catastrophe will be absolute and undeniable."

"Couldn't you stop it?" I asked.

"I could keep your Sun burning indefinitely," Auric said. "But I won't. The Sun needs to follow its own stellar evolution toward its logical conclusion. I see that as a lit fuse to a stellar bomb that requires your species to get somewhere else while you can. It's a kind of celestial test. Perhaps the ultimate, existential test for your species."

I glanced up at the larger Sun looming overhead, the first day on the new Venus that would last for 117 Earth days.

"You have to change the rotation," I said. "Otherwise, all of this life you've created will die."

"Of course I have to," Auric said. "Although I'm keeping the retrograde rotation as a memento of legacy Venus."

Auric brought up his hands again, in that stage magician way he had, and a blue-white pulse passed from him as a great wave, and then I saw the Sun moving more the way I was accustomed to it moving on Earth, only backwards. That was jarring.

"Is it?" Auric asked.

"Yeah," I said.

"Welcome to Venus," Auric said. "I had to take care of the volcano problem, I admit. There were over 1600 volcanoes on Venus. Don't worry, only around 40 of them are active. But that's still a lot of volcanoes."

"What'd you do? What are you doing?" I asked.

"I'm keeping tabs on them," Auric said. "One of me will remain on Venus as a planetary protector, much like I'm doing on Earth."

I was staggered to think of his ability to do all of this. It was godlike. He was godlike. It made my knees weak to think of all of this, let alone witness it.

"The point is that this planet is now a sanctuary," Auric said. "A second Earth, if you will. A second habitat."

"You're going to cause a land rush," I said. "People are going to flock to Venus."

"No," Auric said. "They won't. But you'll see. I'm not done with Venus, yet. Or Mars, for that matter."

"Wait, what?"

"I fixed Mars, too," Auric said. "While we've been here on Venus. I terraformed Mars, as well."

By then, I shouldn't have been gobsmacked by anything Auric did at this point, but I still was. The cavalier way he just tossed that out blew my mind.

"Wasn't I needed to chronicle that?" I asked.

Auric shrugged. "Like so much with human experience, the first time matters most. You see one planet terraformed, you've seen them all. Oh, sure the specific celestial mechanics might differ, but the end result is the same. While Mars is chillier than Venus or Earth, people can still live there. I've compensated accordingly. We can see it if you'd like."

"Why stop with Mars and Venus?" I asked. "Why not terraform all of the planets in the solar system?"

"I'd like to give you something to strive for as a species," Auric said. "I'm not going to do *everything* for you. Rather, I'm giving you a chance to survive by giving you three homes instead of only one."

"Fuck," I said. You can see why my brain was reeling, right? This was massive on a level beyond imagination. It *was* the Cosmic Awesome.

"I'm helping your species," Auric said. "But I'm not spoiling you. Three planets will help you. The human race is on, or will be, soon."

"Three planets is going to cause people to throng to them," I said. "The for-profit space companies will be all over this. China will swoop in. India and Indonesia. They're going to jump at the chance."

Auric smiled his enigmatic smile, and I knew I was witnessing something profound without quite understanding what it was.

"What is it?" I asked.

"What do I always tell you? You'll see," Auric said. "Do you want to visit Mars? We could always do that later, too."

"No," I said. "I should see it now."

"Alright," Auric said, and we vanished in a flash.

CHAPTER

NINE

———

MARS WAS CHILLIER THAN VENUS, and the Sun was visibly smaller in the sky. Auric had helpfully given me a white coat to wear. The coat bore his circular symbol, in gold, naturally.

"I'll admit that I cheated a bit here," Auric said. "I traded out some Venusian carbon dioxide to Mars, which needed that atmospheric blanket. It was doing that while terraforming Venus. I just sent some of it here."

"Why not simply create enough atmosphere here?" I asked.

"I abhor waste," Auric said. "I did some celestial recycling. Mars needed the heavier atmosphere, so Venus provided. Even for me, it's easier to make something from something than something from nothing."

I wasn't sure if Auric was just toying with me, since it seemed like he'd created plenty of something from nothing.

The clouds were thicker on Mars, as Auric explained, requiring more to keep the temperature from being too chilly.

"And I had to restart the dynamo in the core," Auric said. "To provide a magnetic field. My polar protectors are in place to account for the closer proximity to Jupiter and the asteroid belt, but the magnetic field is a big issue. Can't have the Sun scrubbing away all I've done, here, either."

"It's still cold," I said. "It feels like, I don't know, Canada."

Auric shrugged, which was amusing to see in so godlike a personage. Sure, we all hear about Atlas shrugging (Ayn Rand was one of the GNP mandatory reads in the Party-approved school curriculum, to teach the necessary foundational fascist ideas that underpinned life in the CSA), but to see an actual god-being shrug was amusing, even kind of charming. I imagined my own memoir as the Chronicler:

Auric Shrugged: A Chronicle of Godhood

Terrible title, forget I even thought it.

Oh, My Godhood: The Auric Chronicles

That seemed maybe better. Like accessibly, marketably idiotic.

"Mars is nearly 155 million miles away from the Sun," Auric said. "One year is 687 Earth days, but thankfully, a Martian day is only a bit longer than an Earth day, so there are some comparisons, versus what Venus was. There's only so much Sun to go around, so, yeah, Mars will be cooler for now. Although, as the Sun starts to die, it'll eventually grow warmer. Ideally, humanity will have moved on from these inner planets long before that happens."

Standing on the surface of Mars, which was filled with foliage that Auric had whipped up, I wondered how that would all go.

"Who will live here?" I asked. "It's a smaller planet, versus Venus, which is nearly Earth's twin."

"You'll see," Auric said. "I had to pick specific flora that could deal with the lower light conditions and the lower amount of sunlight, just like I had to pick specific plants for Venus that would do their work effectively with greater sunlight. Residents of Venus and Mars will have to be as carefully chosen."

"And you're choosing?" I asked.

"Yes," Auric said.

"You're choosing who goes to which planet?" I asked. "Shouldn't that be up to humanity?"

"Not in this instance," Auric said. "Life on Earth is too important to be left to the existing sociopolitical structures to decide, since they have proven willfully and woefully inadequate to the task of preservation of human life. Better to have an objective, omniscient, and omnipotent third party like myself decide."

"Supernaturally," I said.

I hoped Auric wasn't going to frame it that way to people, because I knew just how badly that would be received. Auric understood this. I just assumed he was reading my mind, which he was.

"Think of it this way—say you were at a party and you were trying to have a conversation, but someone in the room was yelling loudly and preventing any conversation from taking place. Nobody could get a word in edgewise because of that loud person. That wouldn't be very nice, would it?"

"No," I said.

"Take your own country," Auric said. "You're collectively only five percent of the Earth's population but you consume around 25 percent of the
world's resources. Is that fair for the rest of the world?"

"Well, no," I said.

"You're the bellowing person at the party, preventing anybody else
from getting a word in edgewise," Auric said. "Or to put it more directly,
you're the one at the hors d'oeuvre table eating almost everything and not
permitting anyone else at the table. What's more, you're not letting anyone else leave the party, and you're deciding what's on television, etc. Sure,
you share that role with China, India, Brazil, and Indonesia nowadays.
You're all dominating the planetary conversation. If I was to simply allow a planetary raffle or the equivalent to take place, the five of you—and
the corporations that run your governments—would decide who lives on
those planets. That's no good. I terraformed both worlds. Therefore, I'm
deciding."

As ever, Auric got me thinking about things. As I looked out at the
newly verdant Mars, I wondered how he would sort it out.

"The bigger issue with Mars is the lower gravity," Auric said. "Martian
gravity is about one-third what Earth's is. You can feel it, yes?"

I did. I jumped in the air and was scared by how high I could jump,
which looked to be about nine feet up. I gasped and landed on the ground.

"Um, wow," I said.

"Yes," Auric said. "The smaller size, volume, and mass of Mars presents
some curious problems in terms of gravity. People should wear weighted
shoes here, maybe, to help their muscles work harder and avoid atrophy.
Perhaps weighted armbands, too."

He made them appear on me: golden armbands and boots.

"Take a walk," Auric said. "See how they feel."

They felt heavy. I moved around, it felt more normal, more like what I
felt on Earth. Auric nodded, smiling.

"You see?" Auric said. "The boots and armbands will provide a degree
of resistance that can help people deal with the lower gravity."

"You could simply alter gravity here couldn't you?" I asked.

"Gravity is a reflection of mass," Auric said. "I terraformed Mars, but
I'm not changing its fundamental essence, in terms of mass. Gravity will
be lower on Mars. It's just how it is."

"So, you won't change that," I said.

"I won't," Auric said.

Auric made the weights disappear in a flurry of golden motes.

"Anyone who's smart will want to wear them," Auric said. "Although I don't think people will be particularly relaxed on Mars. While I've made it habitable for human life, now, there's still a ton of work to be done here for enterprising souls—rugged individuals, if you will."

"Rugged individuals," I said, echoing Auric. What was he up to?

"This is a frontier existence," Auric said. "To be honest, both Venus and Mars will be new human frontiers. While I've done the hard part, which is making them capable of supporting human life, the rest of it will be on your species. I don't want to do absolutely everything for you, after all. That's not why I'm here."

"No?"

Auric shook his head. "How does it feel to be the first human being to set foot on both Venus and Mars? You'll be the only human being who ever did this."

That hadn't fully set in, but he was correct, of course. I was making human history, but it hardly counted, because I was with Auric. I hadn't done anything but tag along. I was like Auric's sidekick.

"Oh, it counts," Auric said. "I wouldn't worry about it. We both know you were the first. That's all that matters."

"How'd I get so lucky?" I asked.

"Right place, right time," Auric said. "You wouldn't believe how often that happens. Celestial circumstance. Quantum probability. An asteroid hits at the right moment and planetary history is forever changed. Over and over again it happens across the universe."

"Nobody will ever believe that I was on both Venus and Mars," I said. "Even I don't believe it."

Auric just smiled and shook his head. His profile was as noble as the rest of him.

"It doesn't matter what they believe," Auric said. "You were here. That's all you need, isn't it?"

"I guess," I said. "It would be nice to be recognized for it."

"Besides, an association with me isn't necessarily what you want to be advertising," Auric said. "Particularly once we get back to Earth. You'll see that I'm not popular in some quarters. And people would hate you for it if they knew. Their envy would be intense."

"I'm sure," I said, thinking envy wasn't in *The Book of Don't*. "You're there right now, aren't you? Like while you're here with me, you're there."

"Yes," Auric said. "Localized omnipresence is as important as the other qualities of being a supreme being."

"Localized?"

"Yes," Auric said. "I wasn't always at Earth. I had to arrive here. But now that I'm here, I can be anywhere. I can be anywhere I've ever been, although I have to be there first, if that makes sense."

It didn't, exactly, but I filled in the blanks with my imagination. There was the human history that predated Auric's arrival—it would come to be portrayed as "BA" in the history books. And "AA" for "After Auric" or "After Arrival" in the ones that didn't like Auric.

"Is this Year Zero, then? I asked. "The Age of Auric?"

Auric smiled gamely, his blue hair flickering.

"It's *your* era, not mine," Auric said.

False modesty in a celestial being? Was that what that was? Auric laughed, his laugh comforting and warm, all-encompassing in its gracious geniality. He could read my mind, knew my thoughts as soon as I'd had them.

"I'm sincere in my desire to help your species," Auric said. "You should know that by now. There are no ulterior motives with me. As you yourself have pointed out—with the power I possess, I could easily take over your world if I wanted to."

"But haven't you done that already?" I asked. "You're all everybody talks about, now. You don't have to take over the world because you already have."

Auric gave me that sorrowful gaze he had, with his radiant blue eyes that matched the color of his flaming hair.

"A fair point," Auric said. "But I'm only offering guidance and assistance, not outright hegemony. People are free to reject what I'm offering. That's why the *Book of Don't* is full of Advisements, not commandments."

I actually sat down on the newly made Martian grassland and looked up at Auric, who joined me on the grass, sitting across from me. It was a companionable gesture, the two of us on a Martian grassland, taking in the newly-minted cool breezes.

"But what happens if people disobey your Advisements?" I asked.

"They bring harm to themselves and to others," Auric said. "Only the uncivilized would reject the Be Attitudes."

"Okay," I said. "And what happens then? Do you put them on lay-away?"

"Some of them," Auric said. "The worst offenders. Some of the Advisements are worse than others, as I already explained. Let's say serial killers, for example. If I have it in my power to stop them, shouldn't I?"

Serial killers? Of course. Yeah, that makes sense.

"They can't hide from me," Auric said. "I can read everyone's thoughts. The entire planet. I know what everyone is thinking. I know their hearts."

"You do?"

Auric nodded. "Even now, the cacophony of human thought would be deafening to you. But I know everyone's hearts and minds. The gestalt of human consciousness is mostly noise, incidentally—like mundane things, with a few transcendental points of light here and there, a sliver of brilliance in a sea of the ordinary."

"Why deliver the Auricle app, then?" I asked.

"I wanted to see who would accept it," Auric said. "Who would use it. To see what questions would be asked. It's one thing to exist and acknowledge my existence. But with the app, I could see how people might interact on their own with a tool of limitless knowledge. Who would ask virtuous questions, who would ask selfish questions."

"And what happens when people ask selfish questions?" I asked.

"Layaway," Auric said. "They get three strikes. The first time, the Auricle declines to answer. The second time, the Auricle declines and offers some alternative answers to try to steer them on a better path. The third time is layaway, as it shows an intentional pattern of misbehavior."

This was news to me, and startling.

"The Auricles are making people disappear?" I asked.

"Some people," Auric said. "Bad people. It would be like giving everyone a gun. Some would use their guns responsibly, but others, not so much. If someone asked their Auricle 'How can I murder my enemies?' the Auricle will not answer that sort of question."

My head was spinning in the pristine, brisk Martian air.

"Okay, so the Auricles are traps," I said.

"More bait than traps," Auric said. "Traps for the unethical. Tools for the civilized. While I can be everywhere at once, I'd prefer for people to reveal themselves on their own terms. The Auricles offer a way to assess the human race. You can know people by what they wish for, by what they ask of you. Your search engine companies do the same thing, sending advertisements based on people's intelliphone conversations and browsing history. Social listening is everywhere."

"Still," I said. "That seems sneaky."

"Yes, it's sneaky," Auric said. "If I offered lofty admonishments instead of well-meaning Advisements, people would just reject them out of hand. But if you give people enough rope, they will eventually hang themselves."

Dire imagery, unseemly coming from Auric, unsettling, even.

"Metaphorically speaking, of course," Auric said.

"And the shrines?" I asked. "They are, what, deliberate provocations?"

"They are physical manifestations of my presence," Auric said. "To remind people that there are places they can go. They perform well in that capacity—in oppressive regimes, the authorities gather to them as readily as the more hopeful and sincere. Sometimes more so. In open-minded countries, they become focal points and meeting places, areas of healing and learning. In closed societies, they become targets of fear and violence. But they direct the attention."

"More bait," I said.

"If you want to think of it that way," Auric said. "You've seen the attacks on the shrines. That's fully intended on my part."

"I don't understand," I said.

"The shrines are proxies for me," Auric said. "When people attack them, they reveal themselves as my enemies. And, by extension, enemies of humanity, since I'm helping humanity."

"But you already know who your enemies are," I said. "Because you know everything."

"Everything worth knowing," Auric said.

"So why make them? To make your enemies look bad?"

Auric leaned back on the grass, gazed skyward. If we weren't on Mars, it might have been the most mundane of movements.

"Only the worst sort of people lash out and attack what they don't understand," Auric said. "Sure, innocent people can be caught up in such things, but invariably, it's the bad ones who are compelled to attack that way. It's like someone who willfully stomps on a sandcastle on a beach. Or breaks a window. Or smashes a decorative pumpkin on someone's porch. Or sets an anthill on fire. Those feral instincts are born of your own species trauma, those primate misbehaviors. The casual cruelties, the needless evils, as all evils must necessarily be. A benevolent stranger appears and offers—and delivers—aid and is subject to attack for simply helping. It's revealing."

I didn't think of the Auricle shrines as celestial/spiritual punching bags, didn't want to think of them that way.

"They're more than that," Auric said. "They're oases. Like the Auric Towers. They are places of sanctuary."

"You *wanted* your enemies to know that they couldn't stop you," I said.

Auric smiled at me, giving me a sidelong look that would have been sly if he weren't so mind-bogglingly compassionate.

"That, too," Auric said. "They can't, Christian. Nobody can stop me."

He got to his feet and held out a golden hand for me, which I took. His hand was warm to the touch, and I wondered if that was innate, or done for my benefit. For someone who'd done so much in so short a time, his hand was disarmingly gentle.

"Let's get you back home," Auric said, still smiling.

CHAPTER

TEN

EARTH WAS IN CHAOS. Auric had been busy while we were gone. The layaway purges hadn't been confined to the CSA. Auric had carried them out planetwide. It came to be called "The Great Disjunction" in media and history. It wasn't just about the disappearances. It was other things.

I don't know if Auric had sent me to Venus and Mars as a distraction or if there was intention in his actions. Who am I kidding? Of course there was intention. Everything he did was intentional. He'd brought me back to my suite in the Auric Tower I'd visited, and we'd watched on the television, Auric looking on with bemusement.

"Worldwide, I've put two billion people on layaway so far," Auric said.

I sat down, although it was more of a kind of collapse. Interplanetary travel, even as a passenger to a god-being, was overwhelming and exhausting, somehow.

"Two billion people?" I asked.

"Yes," Auric said. "Everyone who acted against the Advisements of the *Book of Don't* has been put on layaway. Specifically the following: the evil, the cruel, the corrupt, the ignorant, the greedy."

"And that's two billion people worldwide?" I asked.

"Yes," Auric said. "The worst of the worst. They're the unholy quintet of human misbehavior. All human wrongdoing is carried out by the evil, the greedy, the corrupt, the ignorant, and the cruel. They are the victimizers of virtue."

I was shaken. People would be terrified. I did a mental inventory. Take out the Evil, the Greedy, the Corrupt, the Ignorant, and the Cruel, what was left? Auric read my mind, naturally.

"You have the Crazy—and I've made them sane. I've healed them," Auric said. "There's the Lazy, the Fools, the Creeps, the Fake, the Dull, and Cowardly. And there remain the Assholes, who are among the worst among those who remain. But they can all be helped. The Lazy can become active. The Fools can educate themselves. The Creeps can learn to be respectful. The Fake can learn to be authentic. The Dull can learn to become audacious. The Cowardly can learn to be brave and to do their duty. The Assholes can learn to be considerate of others. There is a path forward for them."

It was social engineering on an unimaginable scale. What about the others?

"Evil can never become good," Auric said. "It's a mythology humans tell themselves to try to feel better about their own moral failure. There is no redemptive arc for evil. Evil exists *because* a person refuses to be good. Or, because evil is rewarded, and too lucrative to pass up. Greed exists because someone benefits from willfully taking more than their fair share. Greed is fundamentally unfair, but the greedy rationalize it away. They are incapable of self-regulation and can never have enough. Your world is being destroyed by Greed. The Corrupt pretend to uphold the law but work against it, time and again, for personal gain. They skulk in the shadows of propriety while rotting the system from within. The Ignorant refuse to be enlightened and parade their ignorance as if it were something to be proud of, and eagerly tear down anything they don't understand—which is nearly everything, because of their ignorance. And the Cruel enjoy hurting others. Cruelty is an asymmetry of power between abuser and victim. The Cruel derive satisfaction from their cruelty. In each of these cases, there is nothing you can do to sway a person off those paths."

"People can change," I said. "How can they learn to be better if they're nonexistent?"

"There are no evil babies." Auric said. "Evil is a *learned* behavior. Oh, sure, there are paths, say, with your serial killers and psychopaths that may be hewn from birth. But even in those cases, it's not an absolute. A variety of triggers must be pulled to take a person down that particular path. An evil person has made that choice."

It was more than I could even fully comprehend. A world without evil? How was that even possible?

"Your species has wrestled with the problem of evil for at least as long as you've had civilization," Auric said. "And you've failed to solve it. Why is that?"

I didn't think I'd crossed paths with anyone who was actually evil. Maybe three times in my whole life, people who might have qualified. But

I didn't feel entirely comfortable in making that kind of moral judgment. Two billion people on layaway? It was more than I could contemplate.

"Of course you weren't comfortable," Auric said. "Good people never are. That's what evil counts on. Evil does not fight fair. Would you agree?"

"Yeah," I said.

"Evil is unfair," Auric said. "And evil is dishonest. Would you agree?"

"Yes," I said.

"We can both agree that evil is unfair and dishonest?" Auric asked. I hadn't planned on having a Socratic dialogue with Auric, but I hadn't planned on any number of things that fateful day.

"Yes," I said.

"And how can you work with someone who is both unfair and dishonest?" Auric asked. "There isn't a productive way of engaging with them because they are fundamentally dishonest and out to pursue their own advantage at all costs. Evil thrives in shadow and misinformation. It endures and prospers *because* it is unfair and dishonest. For example, the GNP is both unfair and dishonest and deeply corrupt—it has worked tirelessly to keep the majority of Americans disempowered and disenfranchised in its theocratic, racist, fascist, apartheid state. The GNP actively imprisons and kills dissidents. It attacks free speech and free assembly. It engages in torture and murder. The GNP *is* evil. Everyone who follows the GNP is evil by association. They are either active participants, spectators, or apologists for evil."

I was the last person who would defend the GNP. I hated the GNP. I didn't know anybody who liked them. The best of them were assholes. The worst of them were outright monsters.

"Yeah," I said. "But they're just human; it's human nature."

Auric gave me that sad smile he used in moments like these, and I glanced at the people panicking on the television. I thought about all of the assholes in the world, was curious why Auric had spared them. Auric read my mind, as ever.

"The Assholes knowingly inflict harm on others because they can. They are thoughtless, inconsiderate, graceless, and hurtful. They could do better but refuse to," Auric said. "I have given them an incentive for being more considerate souls. They are on the precipice, facing layaway if they do not mend their ways."

"How many assholes are there in the world?" I asked.

"Around 20 percent of those remaining on the Earth are Assholes," Auric said. "That's about 1.4 billion people."

"Wow," I said. "That's a lot of assholes. Why didn't you just call them jerks in your *Book of Don't?*"

"Assholes felt more on-point," Auric said. "I could have called them 'jerks,' 'dicks,' or 'pricks,' but went with the more all-encompassing, gender-neutral term that people would immediately understand. I felt that every normal human being quickly learns who is an Asshole. Anyone who is captivated by the Dark Triad of narcissism, Machiavellianism, and psychopathy is at extreme risk of being an Asshole. I have purged the psychopaths already—sorry, put them on layaway—but there are plenty of narcissists and Machiavellians remaining. All of them are Assholes."

"Wow," I said. "It's almost too much to imagine."

"Would you judge an entire family based on the deeds of one bad member of it?" Auric asked. "Would you want me to?"

"No," I said. "They're the worst of us. I mean, it depends on the standards. There's North Korea. I mean, no way can you give them a pass, if the GNP's on your list."

Auric's sad smile became warmer, more encompassing and reassuring. Denny Rand had cozied up to North Korea decades ago, but that insane regime was particularly horrible.

"North Korea's been dealt with," Auric said. "All of the bad ones are on layaway. The Demilitarized Zone has been, well, demilitarized. I came to them personally. In fact, I'm in every country in the world, even as we speak, rooting out the Evil, the Greedy, the Corrupt, the Ignorant, and the Cruel."

I knew he was, too. The way he said it. He was manifesting that way. My brain couldn't process how he could be holding conversations with everyone at once, but then, with the Auricles, he was doing that tens of thousands of times a second.

There was news footage of Auric being nuked in North Korea. Their army had tanks firing tactical nuclear artillery shells at Auric. The Auric there had grown into a golden colossus, unaffected by the nuclear shells that detonated around him. He raised his golden hands and made the Korean People's Army disappear in a golden flash of light.

"I'm answering questions hundreds of thousands of times, now," Auric said. "I'm not complaining."

"How can you even do it?" I asked. "How can you find them all?"

Auric laughed. I'd never heard him laugh before. It was, of course, a warm and welcoming thing, communicating beneficent bliss and infinitely confident camaraderie.

"My Auricles assist me," Auric said. "While I can sweep the world and root out the blights, as I told you on Mars, I wanted to give people a chance to prove themselves, as well. The benefit of a doubt. Anyone who makes a greedy, hurtful, or cruelly selfish wish is put on layaway. It was one thing for me to just appear and send people away. I wanted to give people—bad people—the tempting means to banish themselves. And they took the bait. The Auricles take their measure and find the wanting ones wanting."

"Speaking of wanting, people are going to want to know what happened to their loved ones," I said. "They're not happy with you taking them."

Auric shook his head.

"The people I put on layaway are humanity's abusers," Auric said. "I did some pruning. While the method I used might be off-putting, I give you my word that I haven't killed any of them—even the ones who deserved it, like the psychopaths and pedophiles."

"What are you going to do with them?" I asked. I had to know.

"You already know," Auric said. "I'm sending them to Venus and Mars. I'm banishing them from Earth."

I didn't actually know that.

I didn't know what he had in mind.

"What are you talking about?"

"Australia was started as a penal colony," Auric said. "Yes?"

"Well, yeah," I said.

"Think of it that way," Auric said. "Venus is now the home for nonviolent offenders. Mars is now the home for violent offenders. They're all being relocated there as we speak. Everyone on Earth who was evil, greedy, corrupt, ignorant, and cruel is now on either Venus or Mars, depending on whether or not they were violent. I'm about to address it at the United Nations."

He pointed to the television, and there Auric was in front of the General Assembly in his crisp white suit, flanked by Minerva Merrow and some of the other Aurician notables, similarly attired in their own interpretations. Again, I wondered why I wasn't there. Was the Chronicler simply a voyeur? Was that my fate?

"People of Earth," Auric said, quieting the Assembly. "I'd like to address concerns you may have about the disappearances of your fellow humans. As I promised, none of them has been harmed."

He manifested two great screens showing Venus and Mars—these great rectangles floating in the air, depicting our neighboring planets.

"Some of you may have noticed that I have terraformed both Venus and Mars, making them habitable for human life," Auric said. The screens shifted to show the Venusian jungles and the Martian pine forests, and something I hadn't seen when we were there, which were gilded buildings and settlements on both planets that looked like the Auric Towers in their classically, consistently beautiful design. "I have banished the people previously on layaway to either Venus or Mars. They have been sorted based on their propensity for violence. The nonviolent offenders are banished to Venus. The violent offenders are on Mars."

On both screens, there was a flash of golden light and the empty settlements were filled startled, terrified, enraged people.

"At this moment, fully five billion human beings are parsed out between these two neighboring planets," Auric said. "Anyone who is evil, greedy, corrupt, ignorant, and cruel has been banished to one of those two planets."

The General Assembly erupted in outraged shouts about planetary sovereignty and a wave of angry questions, but Auric quelled them with his upraised golden hands.

"I have carried out a moralistic purge for the benefit of your species," Auric said. "I understand how those maladaptive behaviors are deeply rooted in your species, having grown up in what amounts to an abusive relationship with yourselves, with each other, and with the planet. Your barbarous history is replete with examples of this. For your benefit, I have cleaned the planet of these barbarians, just as I cleaned all of the pollution you'd saddled the planet with."

"What gives you the right?" the Russian ambassador asked.

"It's true," Auric said. "I'm an alien interloper. I don't have any official or legal authority to do this, only the cosmic power to do so. But rather than raging about it, *think* about what I've done. For the first time in history, you're capable of proceeding without the evil, the corrupt, the ignorant, the cruel in your midst, sabotaging civilization. Everyone who remains on Earth is good, honest, enlightened, compassionate, and kind. Not that there aren't still those who embody some of the vices of my *Book of Don't*—the Assholes, the Lazy, the Fools, the Creepy, the Fake, the Dull, and the Cowardly remain. However, those are lesser banes compared with the other ones I banished."

Auric glanced at me from where he sat, cocked an eyebrow.

"Better than snapping half the population of the universe out of existence, wouldn't you say?" Auric asked.

"Well, hell," I said. "I don't know."

"Let's see what else I have to say," Auric said.

"The Be Attitudes offer a way out for those remaining people problems," Auric said. "For the Lazy—be industrious. For the Fools—educate yourselves. For the Creepy—be respectful. For the Fake—be genuine. For the Dull—be audacious. For the Cowardly—be brave. For the Asshole—be considerate. Be those things, and you'll be on a better path than you were before. Now, before you panic, please understand this: I'm not taking over your world. I have made changes here. However, I'm not seeking to conquer your planet. Earth is yours and remains sovereign. Yes, I've cleaned your habitat for you, have given you the tools you need to keep it clean. I've banished the worst among you to the other worlds. What you have here is a significant—one might even say world-changing—opportunity. Throughout your history, you've yearned for utopia, pined for paradise. That utopia is here. That paradise is within reach. A world without evil? It's here, right now."

The screens shifted to show some stats, rendered in golden graphics, while Auric continued to speak.

"Eliminating corruption has saved the world $3 trillion," Auric said. "I have liberated over *$40 trillion* in assets sequestered away by the hyper-rich in tax havens. Over $2 trillion in laundered money has been recovered. Another $5 trillion has been taken from global criminal enterprises—which, I'll have you know—have all been eliminated. I have made all organized crime disappear. My actions have made $50 trillion accessible to the planet, which I've put into a planetary trust to be fairly administered by the UN General Assembly. If equitably distributed, that would amount to nearly $26 billion available to every country on the planet."

At the mention of the money, the General Assembly erupted into still more questions, complaints, and everything in between. The noise was riotous, and Auric watched it a moment before speaking again, silencing everyone.

"There are around 20 million criminals on Venus and Mars," Auric said. "I've emptied your prisons of criminals, just as I've completely disrupted all of their criminal enterprises around the world, including drug trafficking, human trafficking, smuggling, a host of other ills. They've all been disrupted. I've liberated around $5 trillion more money from this, which I've put in a Victim Restitution Fund for the surviving victims of these criminal enterprises."

The General Assembly was a chorus of voices, but Auric wasn't taking questions, so much as he was providing answers.

"An important aside as pertains to Mars and Venus," Auric said. "As Earth exiles, while I've given them the tools to survive on those planets, they lack the means of space travel. So, while *you* can travel to those planets, they can't currently travel to you. This is something for you to consider, in terms of the opportunity I've presented you. You could undertake an interplanetary rescue operation and try to bring all of those banished criminals and evil people back into your ranks, where they can resume their place at the apex of your human society, causing more pain and suffering, dictating your lives, hastening your extinction. Or, you can, instead, try to live up to your potential as a species. Think of the possibilities. And, yes, that means that around 20 percent of your business, religious, and political leaders are also banished from the Earth, as they were psychopaths and sociopaths. But think of what can be done without having psychopaths deciding your fate."

The General Assembly burst into noise again as delegates fought to be heard.

"This is going to throw the world into chaos," I said.

"As if it wasn't in chaos already?" Auric replied. "I consider this more of a growing pain than a death spiral, which is what you had before. Yes, there will be disruption, but it's a necessary thing. Look what I've already done—I've cleaned up the planet, I've cured diseases, I've provided food and housing for those who need it, and I've banished all of the bad people from Earth. A good start."

The television Auric again managed to quiet the room. I wondered if he was using his powers to do so, because he really could own any room he was in if he wanted to. For my part, it was weird sitting next to him in my suite while watching him on television.

"Before your philosophers attack me for arbitrarily deciding people's fates, let me briefly explain: evil people *knowingly* inflict needless harm on others. Greedy people consciously seek to take more than their fair share. Corrupt people actively mislead others about their intentions and unjustly profit from saying one thing and doing another. Cruel people delight in inflicting pain and harm on others. Ignorant people deliberately and aggressively attack knowledge, truth, civilization, and reason. In these situations, the bad people *know* that they're bad, and *they don't care*. There are no better angels of their nature to appeal to. That's why they're banished. Their success is dependent on your failure."

The screens showed the exiles on Venus and Mars, looking around, bewildered, terrified, furious. Curiously, I could see that on Mars, people were armed—Auric had given them their guns, and it appeared that some of them were already shooting each other.

"Wait, you armed the violent bad people on Mars?" I asked. Auric shrugged.

"They love their guns," Auric said. "I didn't want to deprive them of something they loved."

"You *want* them to kill each other," I said, glancing at Auric, who looked back at me evenly. His aloof benevolence was ultimately unreadable.

"I know that they will," Auric said. "It's who and what they are. The worst of the worst."

"Maybe they'll surprise you," I said.

"Unlikely," Auric said. And I knew he was just humoring me. Meanwhile, television Auric kept addressing the UN.

"I have given your species a unique and historic chance," Auric said. "There are now three human-colonized planets, rooted in three governing paradigms. First, there's legacy Earth, the most technologically advanced of the three, filled with good, polite, kind, honest, generous, and enlightened people. And, yes, there may still be lazy, stupid, creepy, fake, dull, and cowardly people among you, as well as the remaining assholes I didn't already banish. But you can work on that. And make no mistake: lazy, stupid, creepy, fake, dull, cowardly assholes can still do plenty of damage if you let them. Those of you who are active, smart, respectful, authentic, audacious, brave, and considerate must band together toward a better, brighter future for yourselves and your planet."

The screens shifted to show Mars, which was descending into violence as warring factions went after one another. It was ugly already and getting worse. There was mass slaughter underway.

"Then you have Mars, where the violently evil, cruel, ignorant, corrupt, and greedy assholes are. No one could ever accuse them of being the best that humanity has to offer. They have their own planet, now. My apologies to Mars for putting them there, but they had to go somewhere, since I wasn't going to simply exterminate them. They represent around five percent of your planetary population, or nearly 500 million people. Every violent serial killer, rapist, hate criminal, terrorist, fascist, pedophile, mass murderer, organized criminal and so forth is on Mars, now. They are the human pollution of your species. And I've put them all there. We'll see how that goes. Obviously, they're none too happy with me for exiling them. Most of them will have no idea what I have in mind for them. Perhaps they'll be able to attain a degree of unity in their hatred of me. Likelier, they'll simply exterminate themselves and turn Mars into a charnel house of human slaughter, a monument to a history of evil. It's hard to create civilization among barbarians who have no concept of civility."

The screen shifted to Venus, where the confused and terrified souls were milling around, arguing and looking angry and disheveled.

"And then there's Venus," Auric said. "Packed with the nonviolent of the previously enumerated subsets. They are another brand of blight, the enablers of their more violent cousins on Mars. What sort of world might they build? I guess we'll see. It will be a predatory and ruthless world, a place of amoral and immoral opportunists who prefer their Machiavellian machinations to outright violence. They have greater numbers than Mars—there are now over 4.5 billion people on Venus, none of them exemplary specimens of human virtue. All of them are bad people as well, being largely defined by their failure to use violence in the pursuit of their own selfish agendas. Three worlds, three visions for humanity, three discrete paths."

The screen went back to Earth, the cleaner Earth, the one Auric had scrubbed. It was a happier place from his rendering of it. Greener, bluer, beautiful, peaceful.

"Earth is in your hands," Auric said. "There are five billion of you remaining on this planet, people whom I have judged to be good people—or good enough that you may yet have a future as a species. Yes, there will be transitory disruption on this world from what I've done. But for the first time in your lives, there's a chance for true progress and world peace. I believe in your species. You *can* move forward. I've given you that chance. Don't squander it. Most importantly, understand that I've created a three-way human race—native Earth, with the most advantages, with the most civilized members of humanity in one place, unburdened by the bad people. Venus, filled with ruthless opportunists, and Mars, solidly packed with violent barbarians. Which world gets to decide humanity's fate? Which branch of mankind decides your destiny?"

I glanced at Auric, who was looking on, as opaque and obtuse as ever. Golden and gracious, untouchable, unfathomable.

"You've created Heaven, Hell, and Purgatory," I said.

"Please," Auric said. "It's far better than that, Christian."

"That's how people will see it," I said.

"There's a magic to trinities," Auric said. "Humans like things in threes."

"You don't think Venus or Mars have a chance," I said.

"Venus might," Auric said. "But Mars? I doubt it. They're too tribal. Even if they reach some sort of accord and unify themselves under one planetary dictator, none of them are smart enough to rediscover space travel. The resources are there, but they're at least two centuries away from viable native space travel on Mars—and only if they pull themselves together. I don't think they'll last that long. Venus is larger, with more resources. They're perhaps a century away from space travel, if they're particularly organized, which is also somewhat debatable. Earth has the head start, and the question is what Earth does with its breathing space. Maybe they'll hyperventilate about what I did and squander that lead I've given them by trying to rescue their bad brethren. Or maybe they'll build the proper paradise that Earth could be and not want to waste that chance."

Television Auric was finally taking questions. Most of them revolved around him not having the authority to do what he'd done, how he could dare to tamper with humankind in this fashion. The outrage was omnipresent, accusing Auric of social engineering the human race.

"I'm not a social engineer," Auric said. "This is not for my entertainment. It's for your survival. I could have simply erased those five billion of your species who were, as your own species likes to put it, 'garbage people'—I could have exterminated them. Instead, I built two habitats for them after cleaning up your own native planet, which you'd badly and increasingly polluted and poisoned for millennia. And, after curing insanity and a host of human diseases, I've left all of you in better condition to confront the challenges of life than you were before I came to this world. Is this the mark of an enemy of humanity? I have saved the human race from extinction, and I've given the residents of Venus and Mars at least a chance to see the error of their ways—they won't, but they have that opportunity. I didn't write them off. I showed them a degree of compassion they never would have shown anyone else. Whatever you might say about me, at least I gave them a chance. And for those of you who may have loved ones on Venus or Mars, you can monitor them through your Auricle app. I am not allowing communication between you and them through the app, because that would defeat the purpose of them being banished to begin with. But you can at least track them that way and know their fate."

"That seems cruel," I said.

Auric shrugged.

"Everyone on Mars and Venus is a bad person," Auric said. "However, I'm not insensitive to the fact that some on Earth may, for whatever reason, fondly remember them and want to monitor their progress or lack of progress. My hope is those people get counseling. In fact, I fully expect there to be a boom in psychological counseling for a generation."

Television Auric was taking more questions, while the chyron was scrolling and showing the stock market crashing. One thing that wasn't on was RAN or LAX News—both stations were running live presentations of Auric at the UN, without commentary. I wondered how many RAN and LAX employees were now on Mars or Venus. I wagered that most of them were on Venus.

"Yeah, both of those media companies were stuffed with bad people," Auric said. "They're all on Venus, now."

"All of them?" I asked.

"Yes," Auric said. "They're the propagandists for the GNP, so they were complicit in a host of terrible activities that aided and abetted the criminality of the regime. They were responsible for so much that turned the CSA into what it was."

I was thinking about making a free speech argument, but the fact was that the CSA's Real American Christian Covenant—what had replaced the Constitution during the Big Takeover—had no protections for the media. What aired in the CSA was only that which the GNP approved.

"Where's Denny Rand?" I asked.

"The Rand Administration is on Mars," Auric said. "While he's never personally murdered anyone, the man is responsible for hundreds of thousands of deaths he's signed off on. And, if you must know, he's an evil, cruel, ignorant, corrupt, greedy, psychopathic asshole who also happens to be a lazy coward, too."

I couldn't argue that, because Auric was spot-on about Rand—not like I'd say that to anyone. I could only imagine how Rand and his cabal would handle being on Mars. Auric took out a blue velvet box from his vest pocket, held it out to me.

"What's this? Are we getting engaged?"

Auric smiled at me.

"That's funny," he said. "It's something you'll need going forward."

I took it and opened it, revealing a gold signet ring with the Auric glyph engraved upon it. I took the ring out and turned it over in my hand.

"Is this a power ring or something?"

"Funnier still," Auric said. "If you want to think of it that way, you can. As my Chronicler, there's a lot you'll still need to see. Don that ring, and you'll continue to enjoy my full protection—which you already have, of course—but, more importantly, you'll be able to freely travel between Venus, Earth, and Mars. In fact, you'll be able to teleport at will. Further, nobody can harm you."

I wasn't about to refuse a gift from Auric, so I put the signet ring on my pinky finger. It fit perfectly, naturally. Auric seemed pleased that I'd done this without hesitation. I believed in him.

"No one can take that ring from you," Auric said. "You can bear witness safely."

"I can teleport?" I asked.

"Yes," Auric said. "Anywhere you like."

"Wow," I said, flexing my hand, looking at the ring. "This is cool."

"Yes, it is," Auric said. "While I know you like watching the world from your couch, I thought you might want to see everything firsthand. What's more, while you wear that ring, you won't age."

"What?" I asked.

"Immortality," Auric said.

"Are you kidding me?" I asked. Auric shook his head.

"Here's the thing: as my Chronicler, you need to see how it all plays out," Auric said. "You need your faculties to be sharp, your senses to be clear. And you need to persist. So, there you have it. However, because I understand all too well how immortality can be a curse, I've given you a way out if you ever choose to take it. Should you get tired of everlasting life, of witnessing and chronicling what I've done here, you need only remove the ring, and you'll cease to be immortal."

"Wow," I said. "What if I take the ring off to take a shower? Would I crumble into dust?"

Auric sighed, shook his head.

"You won't immediately disintegrate," Auric said. "Rather, you'll have a whole day left to you. Of course, if you put the ring back on, you'd be protected again."

"What if I give the ring to somebody else?" I asked.

"It won't work for them," Auric said. "It's my gift to *you*. Why would you give somebody the ring?"

"The next Chronicler," I said.

"In that case, you can bequeath the ring to them," Auric said. "I'd appear and determine if or whether this person would be a suitable successor."

"And if they're not?" I asked.

"Then I'd simply take back the ring and find another Chronicler," Auric said. "You know, you're the only person in the universe who'd be gifted a ring of immortality and already be wondering how to go about giving it away, Christian. That's precisely why I chose you."

I laughed, and Auric laughed with me. It was warm and welcoming, the laughter of a friend. Through it all, I saw him as a friend.

"So," Auric said. "Where do you want to go, Chronicler?"

"Surprise me," I said.

"That shouldn't be difficult," Auric replied.

CHAPTER

ELEVEN

I TELEPORTED to our old condo, but Angelina wasn't there. All my stuff was in boxes, stacked along one wall. I hadn't planned for Angelina to do that, but she's clearly done that, likely because she hadn't wanted me to go back to the place and do it myself.

I could only imagine how Angelina would be taking all of this, so I dialed her up, but it went to voicemail.

"Angelina, it's me, where are you?" I asked. "I'm at the place, picking up my stuff. Thanks for boxing everything."

I hung up, texted her.

I'm at the place. Where RU?

Auric gave me a sidelong look.

"She's on Venus," Auric said.

"Wait, what?" I asked.

"She's been banished to Venus, Christian," Auric said. "I'm sorry."

My head was spinning. I could only imagine what Angelina would be doing, how that would have gone down. She'd be seething.

"Why'd you send her there?" I asked.

"Do you really want me to lay it out for you?" Auric asked. "She'd gone to executives at both RAN and LAX News to offer up an exclusive on you. She was going to peddle what your story was to them. She was working covertly with one of their operatives, Tony Delaqua. She's been doing that for months, spying on you."

I remembered Delaqua, who was a seedy son of a bitch. I remembered meeting him at one of the Flutter holiday parties. He'd been a loud and garrulous sort of guy, one of those GNP guys who would inflict himself on anybody in range.

"Well, hell," I said. "I had no idea."

"No, you didn't," Auric said. "She'd been sleeping with Delaqua, too. The past few months."

"What?"

Auric nodded.

"Sorry to break that news to you, Christian," Auric said. "She's on Venus. So's he, for that matter. Although they haven't met up, yet."

"Christ," I said. Angelina would be livid to be on Venus. She'd be terrified. I was upset by this, and Auric knew it. Of course he knew.

"With your ring, you can visit her," Auric said. "Just understand that you can't bring her back. You can't teleport people away with you."

I didn't know what to say, or even what to think. I didn't think Angelina would have been capable of something like that.

"They were going to air a story," Auric said. "Angelina was going to parlay her proximity to you into some money because she's greedy, too. Unfortunately for them, I shut down their networks before the story could air. I didn't shut them down because of the story they were going to air. Sort of a happy accident, that."

"Can I see the story?" I asked.

"Of course," Auric said, and our television screen flicked on.

"All that Glitters Isn't Golden: The Auric Chronicle" the title card said, with portentous music playing. Delaqua appeared, wearing a pinstriped suit and red necktie, sporting his GNP lapel pin, looking blandly bro-like with his slicked black hair and glittering eyes.

"All we hear about is Auric," Delaqua said. "This false god, this alien antichrist in our midst. It's attacking our values, our way of life. And it's leading people astray. In the next hour, we're going to follow someone who was present at the start of the Auric Invasion, a brave young woman named Angelina Reed. This is her story, her truth."

Then it showed Angelina, looking done up for the camera, wearing a black dress. She had her earnest expression on, along with silver earrings.

"My boyfriend, Christian Powers, was brainwashed by Auric," Angelina said. "He showed up raving about this golden god, waving his intelliphone around like a madman. He said he'd been chosen by Auric to be his Chronicler. Whatever that even means."

They had a dramatization showing a very drunk me staggering around, waving my intelliphone in the air, wild-eyed, jabbering about Auric.

"Auric's the best, Babe," Fake Me said. "He's better than God!"

Fake Angelina looked scared.

"Nothing's better than God, Christian," Fake Angelina said. "You know this."

"No way," Fake Me said. "Auric is. He's like a genie, but you get endless wishes. All the free stuff you could ever want!"

"Christian, he's too good to be true," Fake Angelina said. "You need to get down on your knees and pray to Almighty God for forgiveness."

I glanced at Auric, who shrugged divinely.

"Totally didn't happen that way," I said.

"I know how it happened," Auric said. "I was there."

Fake Auric appeared, fiery-haired and more sinister-looking, wearing a shiny white suit, looking like a disco demon. Fake Auric had golden horns, a lecherous leer, and diamond teeth.

"There is no God," Fake Auric said. "There's only me. Worship me."

Real Angelina appeared onscreen again, the picture of wounded worry.

"I'm ashamed to say that Auric assaulted me," Angelina said. "It attacked me constantly."

Delaqua appeared, looking concerned.

"What did it do?" Delaqua asked.

"It was always whispering in Christian's ear," Angelina said. "Ungodly things. Temptations. And Christian was just its puppet. He'd do anything Auric told him to do. Anything. I prayed every night that Christian would abandon Auric, but he was spellbound by it."

"You were right to be concerned," Delaqua said. "There's nothing greater than God."

"You're so right," Angelina said. "But Christian was in too deep. He wouldn't listen to me."

Another dramatization appeared, showing Fake Me arguing with Fake Angelina, apparently physically abusing her. Fake me smacked her around the condominium, looking enraged.

"It's my intelliphone! MY intelliphone!" Fake Me said. "Auric's everything. It's all I care about! If you're smart, you'll get on board the golden bandwagon, Angelina. Stop being so stupid! Auric warns about being stupid. Don't be stupid, Auric says. One of its commandments! You're being stupid! You're stupid, Angelina! You're not even as smart as my intelliphone!"

And Fake Me beat Fake Angelina, who cried and prayed.

"What the fuck?" I said. "This is such crap. None of this happened."

"I know," Auric said.

"But Auric didn't stop there," Delaqua said. "Ms. Reed prayed for Christian's soul, but Auric wouldn't have any of it."

Fake Auric appeared, wreathed in blue fire. He apparently had a golden tail to go with his golden horns, and golden hooves instead of loafers.

"There is no God but Me," Fake Auric said. "I'll destroy all of your churches, your mosques, your synagogues. I'm the only god you'll ever need."

Fake Auric sneered and leered, forked tongue rolling out as he spoke.

"You look very different," I said.

Auric chuckled.

"Yes, the obsession with Devil imagery is certainly prominent in your society," Auric said. "One of the many crosses American Christian believers have to bear, I think."

Fake Angelina clutched a Bible to her chest and apparently banished Fake Auric.

"Get thee behind me, Satan!" Fake Angelina said, and Fake Auric vanished in a puff of blue smoke and golden glitter.

The GNP prided itself on their propagandistic passion plays. In fact, their Department of Moral Values ran multiple levels of media productions, from the willfully low-rent versions that, to bigger ticket efforts, intended for all niches in the CSA. The propaganda messaging varied from staggeringly unsubtle to the merely obvious. This dramatized interview and confessional fell somewhere between those poles.

Fake Angelina held Fake Christian's hands, gazing up at him.

"Leave behind this false prophet, Christian," Angelina said. "I'm begging you."

"Ha," I said. "Angelina never begs. She grouses, complains, and demands, but she doesn't beg."

"I can't do it, Angelina," Fake Me said. "Auric gives me free stuff. You just can't argue with free stuff."

"But Auric's a socialist," Fake Angelina said. "And an illegal alien. And Auric's satanic. Do you really want to risk your eternal soul for that demon?"

"I do, Angelina," Fake Me said, letting go of her hands, walking toward a plume of fire that appeared. "I want to be damned eternally, just so I can enjoy some free stuff now."

And Fake Christian walked into the flames, screaming as he was incinerated, and Fake Angelina turned and looked at the camera, breaking the fourth wall.

"I'll pray for you," Fake Angelina said, putting her hands together and kneeling in pious genuflection, a hint of a halo appearing around her head.

"Okay, that's enough of that," I said, and Auric made it go away. "What crap."

"It really is," Auric said. "She was being paid some money to participate in that charade. She had the opportunity to join us, and she chose to betray you."

"I have to go to Venus," I said. "I have to talk to her."

"If you want," Auric said. "But I should go with you."

And we went back to Venus in a flash of golden light. I'd just made history again as the first human being to travel to Venus twice, and I didn't even care.

CHAPTER

TWELVE

VENUS WAS NOISIER than when we'd left it. There were billions of people on its two continents, now. They were panicking and furious—a mob of evil, cruel, ignorant, corrupt and greedy assholes who had their lives irrevocably altered by a cosmic alien hyperintelligence. It was enough to ruin anyone's day.

When Auric and I appeared, the ones nearest us cried out and swarmed us, held at bay by a golden forcefield, as we stood in the heart of one of the golden cities Auric had built since we'd last been there. It was weird for me, seeing it, having been the only human being to have seen pristine Venus, let alone the first one to set foot on it. Auric had urbanized Venus while we'd been gone. I felt wistful for the virgin Venus I'd glimpsed when he'd first terraformed it. And I felt like an idiot for feeling that.

"You son of a bitch!" an angry old man yelled. "What the hell have you done?"

"Where's my family?" a middle-aged woman screamed. Her nametag said her name was Karen.

"How many Karens are on Venus?" I asked.

"There are only around five thousand," Auric said. "That name suffered heavy attrition decades ago, and never recovered."

"Auric, what am I doing here?" a young man asked. "What's going on?"

I saw Angelina amid all the people thronging around Auric and me, and she saw me. Her hard eyes flashed and she screamed at me.

"Christian, what the hell have you done?" Angelina asked, throwing herself against the forcefield. I walked to it, and we stood across from each other, separated only by the forcefield.

"You went to Delaqua?" I said. "Sold me out?"

Her face blossomed into mottled embarrassment, shame, and rage.

"*You* sold us out," Angelina said. "You sold humanity out, Christian. You're a traitor to the human race. All you Auric cultists are."

Auric looked on, handsomely impassive and inscrutable.

"I've made comfortable accommodations for your species here," Auric said. "Certainly better than it was before."

He pointed to the golden city around us. It was a city of spires and sky-scrapers. It was beautiful and otherworldly, as befit something on Venus. There were gardens and fountains, and the surrounding Venusian jungle made it look particularly exotic.

"There are more than enough native food crops available for everyone to be fed, assuming people get to work harvesting," Auric said. "You have shelter, and you have food. Yes, you're exiles from the human race and I've completely disrupted your lives. But you still *have* your lives."

His words did nothing to diminish the outrage they were feeling. I could see it on all of their faces, glaring at us from beyond the golden shimmering field Auric had put between us. The wide-eyed faces of awe and fear.

"I don't belong here," Angelina said. "I did nothing wrong, Christian."

"You slept with Delaqua," I said. "Did you do that before or after selling me out?"

"During," Auric said, noting Angelina's fury with a sigh.

"Alright, Christian," Angelina said. "Yeah, I did. I went to him because you'd left me twisting with your BFF over there. He was there for me, and you weren't."

"It's *my* fault you fucked Delaqua?" I asked.

"Yes," Angelina said. "I mean, sure, I did that. I own that. But *you* drove me to it."

"Asshole logic in action," Auric said. "See what I was saying?"

"Shut up," Angelina yelled, her face wrinkling with hateful rage. "You shut up!"

"I can't do anything about it, Angelina," I said. "Even if I were inclined to try to get you some kind of reprieve, I don't know if I even would."

Angelina hammered the forcefield with her fists. The forcefield held, sparkling beautifully whenever she struck it. With Auric, even forcefields were beautiful.

"You get me out of here right now, Christian," Angelina said. "I don't belong on this hellhole with all of these losers. What am I going to be here? The Queen of the Assholes?"

"That's a start," I said.

Angelina flipped me off, waved her other hand in the air.

"That's right, I'm the Queen of the Assholes because I fucked around on Auric's couch potato Chronicler. All hail ME, you losers. I fucked around and found out!"

Of course, the other exiles took umbrage at being called that and began yelling at Angelina, and the whole thing erupted into a storm of recriminations and accusations. It was ugly. I hated seeing all of those hateful people, I hated seeing Angelina among them. It was alienating and frightening. I'd never seen such a concentration of nasty, angry people up close like that, this malevolent mob. It felt like what those GNP rallies were like, the ones where Rand would preside over his people and bellow his screeds to them, at them, for them. A sea of red hats and mindless, racist rage, an ever-flowing Bigot Spigot.

"All of you have the means to survive and even thrive on Venus," Auric said. "All you have to do is stop being evil, cruel, ignorant, corrupt, and greedy assholes. You do that, and you can come back to Earth. In fact, there's a portal I've created in the cities here. If you're able to straighten out, there's an opportunity for release. I am nothing if not fair, merciful, and compassionate."

"You're a monster!" Angelina screamed, pounding the forcefield again.

"What? We're on Venus?" one of the other exiles said. "We're on Venus?!"

"You had no right to do this to us," Angelina yelled.

"For the sake of your species, I had to," Auric said. "There's an Auricle portal in the heart of these cities. If you have truly repented and reformed, you can pass through them and return safely to Earth. But not before."

At the mention of that, a chunk of the crowd around us raced for the Auricle portal, which stood as a glowing and mysterious monument in the heart of the spoke-like Venusian city Auric had made for them. Dozens of the locals threw themselves at the portal, only to be repelled by its own forcefield.

"Too soon," Auric said. "You can't fool the Auricles."

Angelina turned her reproachful gaze back upon me.

"You're his puppet, Christian," Angelina said. "You're his boy toy. You deserve each other. Fuck Auric, and fuck you, Christian!"

She stomped away, flipping me off again as she walked away. I glanced at Auric, who just sighed beatifically.

"Sorry, Angelina," I said, but she just flipped me off yet again without a backward glance as she stomped away.

Auric let us float up, over the multitudes of exiles, who howled and cursed at us, while others continued to throw themselves at the luminous Auricle portal.

"You really have a path of redemption for them?" I asked.

"Yes," Auric said. "I do. Unlike those on Mars, they can mend their ways if they choose to here on Venus. It will take much effort and introspection for them, but self-improvement always requires that."

Hovering over the golden city, it felt strange. As I'd said earlier, I never liked heights, and Auric knew that, so I assumed he was making some point to me by doing so.

"Not really," Auric said, as we landed on one of the skyscrapers. "I just wanted you to see how many there are. About five percent of the population of Venus are genuinely evil—that's around 225 million evil exiles. None of them will get off this planet, although I imagined one or two could conceivably redeem themselves if they had a genuine change of heart. Evil's a tough thing to shake, to be honest. There's an efficacy to evil that appeals to the human spirit. Around 25 percent are cruel. That's over a billion exiles. I'm not optimistic about any of them returning. About 75 percent are corrupt. About 90 percent are greedy. One hundred percent of the population are assholes."

"Yeah," I said. "Wow. Weird to think that there are assholes on all three planets. They're like a cosmic constant or something."

Auric smiled at me, and to himself.

"Lack of consideration for others is at the heart of assholery, as I've said." Auric said. "But, from my perspective, while every evil person is an asshole, not every asshole is an evil person. A lazy asshole is not the same as a murderous asshole, or a corrupt asshole. Ergo, my triaging of assholes on the three worlds. There's a logic to it."

"Of course," I said. "Sure there is."

"If I were to segment out the population on Venus," Auric said. "Maybe 10 to 20 percent of the population might be able to redeem themselves within the next decade if they work very hard at it. The rest will never get off Venus. They will simply lack the character and moral fortitude to transcend their exile."

Something occurred to me, and I was sure Auric had already thought of it.

"I have," Auric said, presumptively reading my mind.

"Let's say somebody tries to mend their ways here," I said. "But they're entirely surrounded by bad people. If you're a reformed person surrounded by bad people, how can you possibly hope to survive? Wouldn't life here make you inherently vulnerable to your environment?"

"It's a fair point," Auric said. "Everyone here victimizes everyone else. Or they will soon enough. It's in their nature to do so. In no time, there'll be structures in place where people enslave and torment one another. Right now, they're all disorganized and addled. But the structures of oppression will be quickly assembled. Good behavior will not be rewarded on Venus by the exiles. Only I offer any sort of reward, and only if they manage to mend their ways. Better than the eternal damnation and torture purportedly promised by the Christian God when you think about it."

"Let's say somebody genuinely reforms," I said. "However they go about it, they've become a better person. How do they get out? What's to stop the authorities here from barricading the Auricle portal to prevent people from leaving?"

"It would be a definite asshole move, with a considerable amount of cruelty woven into it," Auric said. "I would stop them. Don't forget, I've left a version of myself on both Venus and Mars, so, I would prevent them from sabotaging my system."

"Ah," I said. "I knew you'd have an answer."

"And I do," Auric said. "But you raise an interesting question. It's at least conceivable for there to be the evolution of a virtuous underground on Venus—people who have reformed and yet have to keep it quiet, lest they suffer for it, whether from the envy of their fellow exiles, or outright abuse by their malefactors."

"Which brings me to another question," I said. "You said the people here are all nonviolent."

Auric nodded. He knew where I was going.

"What if they commit acts of violence here?" I asked.

"They get banished to Mars," Auric said. "It goes like this: Earth → Venus → Mars. There's no coming back from Mars. Mars is the end of the line for your species. If there's a path for redemption on Venus, however remote, there's also the threat of banishment to Mars if they get violent. Most of them won't get violent, but some may. And off to Mars they'll go, toward almost certain death."

I worried about Mars. Mars deserved better than to be a penal colony for the worst of humanity. I mourned the sterile wasteland of legacy Mars to the slaughterhouse it was becoming.

"Mars does deserve better," Auric said. "But it's a necessary sacrifice for the good of humanity as a whole. Keep in mind that Mars was just a mostly dead desert planet before I gave it life. It can live as a penal colony planet, versus being an arid little planet deeply-dusted in perchlorate."

"What about the various Martian probes?" I asked.

"They're protected," Auric said. "I wouldn't want the barbarians and vandals of Mars destroy those historical treasures. They remain monuments to human success. They are protected."

"And yet, they're stuck on Mars with the exiles," I said. Auric wasn't fazed.

"Mars is a curious case," Auric said, which sounded strange to say as we stood on a high-rise on Venus. "There are nearly 500 million exiles on Mars, now. Based on population demographics alone, around 25 million of them should be Americans. But there are actually 80 million Americans on Mars versus 120 million Arabs, 100 million Chinese, 82 million Indians. Your own people are overrepresented on Mars, in terms of violently evil, cruel, greedy, corrupt, ignorant assholes."

"Yeah, that's weird," I said. "Although not totally surprising. How many Canadians are there?"

"There are two million Canadian exiles on Mars," Auric said.

"Wow, so, like 80 million Americans and two million Canadians?" I said.

"Americans are a very violent people," Auric said. "At any rate, I was going to say that Mars will organize itself into warring tribal factions, most likely along ethnographic, racial, nationalistic, religious, ideological, and linguistic lines. The factions that are the most organized among them will enjoy the most success on Mars—Arabs, Chinese, and Indians will have the best luck with that. At any rate, I see some highly organized and totalitarian regime taking over Mars. Likely the groups I mentioned, because they have the greatest numbers, the strongest sociocultural cohesion, and the historical technological advantage Americans and Western Europeans have enjoyed is simply not present on Mars. There may be some fleeting unity attained in a common hatred of me and what I've done by exiling them there, although I don't think that will be sufficient to endure."

While he spoke, Auric crafted a vision of a Martian dictator, who appeared to be Indo-Chinese, wearing a black uniform, standing in front of a black flag with a white circle around it and a red circle in the center, like a malefic eye.

"How many Europeans are here?" I asked.

"There are 22 million Europeans here," Auric said. My brain was still trying to fathom how there could be over 500 million violent, evil, terrible people in the world. It seemed staggering to imagine.

"It is staggering," Auric said. "It's why your species has struggled so needlessly over the centuries and millennia. Evil is the anchor that drags you down. Progress slides forward saddled with the drag caused by evil, ignorance, corruption, cruelty, greed, and other things. The only difference, and why it's jarring to you, is that I've put all of those people here on Mars, so, instead of dealing with them individually, you're seeing them all at once. I take it as a good sign that on a planet originally of 10 billion humans, only 500 million or so are truly violent and evil."

"Only 500 million," I said. "That's still a lot."

"It depends on how you look at it," Auric said. "There are plenty of bad people on Venus, of course, so maybe half of your species is burdened with that baggage. But the other half is good. And of that bad half, only about five percent at most are utterly irredeemable."

The numbers were too big, the concept too startling to take in all at once.

"There will be no redemption for anyone on Mars," Auric said. "Only death, hatred, fear, pain, and needless suffering. Self-inflicted, of course. And a relentless desire to escape Mars. Mars will be dangerous to Earth. But that's intentional on my part."

"How so?" I asked.

"They're the literal enemies of humanity, all in one place," Auric said. "Yes, they're human by birth, but they represent the very worst qualities of the human species. The deadliest impulses, the darkest drives. They are the lurking shadow of the human race. Odds are good that they'll exterminate themselves, but any who survive that war of all against all will be a dangerous adversary, something to hopefully motivate the people of Earth to do and be better. There is no evil in Nature, although there is ample cruelty and suffering. There is simply survival or extinction. Civilization is about transcending Nature and Human Nature to attain something better."

Looking out across the nameless Venusian city, I felt sorrow and fear, despite standing there with Auric.

"It's going to be okay, Christian," Auric said. "As Chronicler, you need to see all of this. It's your burden."

"What about organized crime?" I asked. He'd mentioned them at the UN address.

"All of them are here on Mars or Venus, depending on whether they were violent or not," Auric said. "The Triads, the Mafia, the Yakuza, the drug cartels, street gangs, a host of other groups—they're all here. But while they have their internal systems of loyalty and authority, what they don't have is their money and the network of corrupt connections they had to give them power and protection. I imagine what they'll do is quickly work to establish new cartels on Mars, likely around food production and distribution. They may lend their services to whatever form of government emerges here."

That thought filled me with horror, too. All of those criminals—organized and otherwise, together in the celestial prison Auric had made of Mars.

"And you're just going to let them exist," I said.

"Yes," Auric said. "That's why they're here. My primary concern was banishing them from Earth. What they do on Mars isn't something that particularly matters to me. My focus is on the human beings who are good. I didn't murder the bad; I just relocated them."

Mars and Venus as planetary concentration camps didn't sit well with me. Auric could see I was uncomfortable with it.

"Evil is a choice one makes," Auric said. "One *chooses* to do evil. Isn't that the notion at the heart of your conception of free will? Freedom—true freedom—isn't simply doing whatever you want without consequences; that's more akin to anarchy. Honest freedom is rooted in civilization, and civilization is only possible among the civilized. No civilization, no freedom."

"Okay," I said. "Some would compare level of technology to level of civilization."

Auric smiled at me, the very picture of celestial radiance. It's hard to convey the power of Auric's smile, but it was enough to move mountains. I could only imagine what devastation his frown could cause.

"Level of technology alone isn't the full measure of civilization," Auric said. "Yes, it's hard to envision a civilized cave dweller. And that's true. It's because the necessity of survival dictates the level of civility one may have. For example, it's easier to appear civilized if you're safe, healthy, and comfortable. If you're fighting for survival, however, it's far harder to be civilized. Not impossible, but harder."

"So, nobody on Mars is civilized?" I asked.

"By my definition, no," Auric said. "Being able to hold a conversation doesn't mean having anything worthwhile to say. The same applies to civilization. What is the measure of a civilization? At the heart of it all, it's the ability and willingness of that civilization to take care of every member of that society and to create a culture of enduring value. A society that fails to take care of all of its members is uncivilized."

Something else occurred to me, and Auric already knew what it was.

"What about kids?" I asked. "Are there children here? On Mars?"

"No," Auric said. "It would be uncivilized to send children to either of these places, and cruel."

"Then what happens to them?" I asked. "The bad ones, I mean."

"They're being taught how to be civilized," Auric said. "I've introduced Auric Academies around the world, for culturally appropriate civilizing."

I could only imagine how poorly that would be received, made a mental note that we'd have to visit them at some point. Auric seemed saddened by my reaction.

"They're not being brainwashed," Auric said. "Rather, they're being given a good education that includes Civics and Moral Philosophy. There were over 160 million orphans in the world even before I interceded. I'm tending to those orphans with my Auric Academies. The children are being fed, sheltered, and cared for and the bad children, the ones who have been abused and/or who were born psychopaths, are being tutored and given coping strategies to help them develop into healthy adults."

"Okay," I said. "But what about Mars and Venus? Can people have kids here?"

I looked down on the streets of the Venusian city Auric had made, felt the profound vertigo any great heights afflicted me with, and wondered about that. Auric could see me mulling over it all, and, as ever, knew the right moment to speak to me about it.

"Nobody on Mars can have children," Auric said. "They can have all the sex they want, but there will be no children. I couldn't in good conscience allow for children to grow up on Mars, or for the evil people there to perpetuate themselves. That would be unimaginably cruel. I mean, there are serial sexual abusers and pedophiles on Mars, among the host of human evils I've put there. Not a place for children to be born or to grow up. It wouldn't be fair to them."

I agreed with that. Still, it meant that Auric was consigning the population of Mars to extinction, whether or not he'd admit to it. He would not cop to genocide—or whatever one called it.

"There is no equitable path for procreation where evil is concerned," Auric said. "None of those people on Mars would make good parents. None of them are, the ones who are parents."

"You've broken up families," I said.

"Yes," Auric said. "Indeed I have. But the violent souls on Mars were terrible parents. For any children or spouses who may have had Stockholm Syndrome, there will be a period of readjustment, but they'll soon realize they're better off without the abuser in the home."

"What about the ones who were not abusers?" I asked.

"At the heart of the matter, anyone who is an evil, ignorant, greedy, corrupt, cruel asshole is an abuser in one form or another," Auric said. "They inflict harm on everyone they know."

Venus was quiet, despite all of the commotion on the streets. There were no cars here, no planes, no fire trucks. There were birds in the jungles Auric had created, and I could hear them chirping and singing. It was otherwise uncannily quiet.

"What about Venus?" I asked. "Have you sterilized the people here, too?"

"Sterilized is such a loaded term," Auric said. "I haven't sterilized anyone on Mars. I've simply introduced entirely effective prophylaxis as a precondition for resettlement. I mean, you were sterilizing yourselves rather effectively on your own before I came along. The global fertility rate is 2.3 live births per woman. Overall populations are declining as more women become educated and gain access to birth control. By the end of the century, some countries will have halved their population. This all predates my arrival. And don't even get me started on the proliferation of endocrine disruptors, microplastics, and their environmental impact—which I've solved when I scrubbed your planet clean and healed the world."

I accepted all of that, but I was still wondering about Venus, as I looked out over the quiet golden city full of upset people lamenting their plight.

"Nobody on Venus can breed," Auric said. "Not while they're on Venus. For those capable of rehabilitating themselves and returning to Earth, they could have children unimpeded."

"Wow," I said. "Again, that's draconian, don't you think?"

Auric looked at me a moment, shaking his head.

"Your world requires licenses for driving," Auric said. "But there are no licenses for parenting. *Anyone* can become a parent. Part of the problem with your planet is that anyone with functioning reproductive organs can become parents. When people who shouldn't be parents have children, then they pass on their pathologies to their children, creating a next generation of wounded and damaged souls, the very seeds of evil. That can't happen here on Venus or Mars."

"They're really going to hate you for that," I said.

"They *already* hate me," Auric said. "I'm not going to allow children to be raised in either of these places. No benevolent being would allow for child abuse."

That made me think of something else.

"When you banished everybody, were there pregnant women among them?" I asked. "There had to be with those kinds of numbers."

"You're astute, Christian," Auric said. "Yes, there were pregnant women. There were 12 million pregnant women as part of the Martian project, and 112 million as part of the Venus project."

"Alright," I said. "Where are they?"

"They're still on Earth," Auric said. "For now."

"That's 134 million people who otherwise would've been banished by you, who are still on Earth. What's going to happen with them? By your own definition, they are unfit mothers, right? They're evil, cruel, greedy, ignorant, corrupt assholes?"

"They are," Auric said. "They shouldn't be parents. But I can't let the children pay for the sins of the mother."

"You could mass abort all of the babies," I said, not even believing I'd said that. Abortion had been outlawed in the CSA for decades. Abortion carried the death penalty in the pro-life CSA.

"No," Auric said. "Again, the children shouldn't pay that price. I'm monitoring all of the mothers. Once they birth their children and can safely recover, I'm banishing them. Otherwise, they would escape the judgment I have placed upon them by virtue of simply being pregnant at the time."

That would be particularly poorly received, I was certain. The optics of it would be bad. Separating moms from their babies would not look good, despite the apparent evil of the moms.

"I'm going to do it quietly," Auric said.

"People are going to notice when 134 million new mothers disappear from the Earth," I said. "People tend to notice those sorts of things. It's going to be seen as cruel and heartless."

Auric sighed, leaned forward, hands on the railing of the golden tower we occupied. Below us, the Venus exiles in this city were convening, trying to organize themselves in some fashion. Thankfully, nobody knew we were up here, or we'd be thronged as we'd been on the ground level.

"Human lives are messy," Auric said. "But if I were to grant a pregnancy waiver to my summary judgment of your species, it would incentivize pregnancy by those 134 million unscrupulous women to attempt to evade accountability by trying to get pregnant again. No, they are able to carry their current children to term, but then I am taking them where they belong. Their children will be tended to. In many cases, the fathers aren't bad people. In cases where both parents are bad, my Auric Academies will assist. This is an unpopular reality, but there *are* bad mothers—not just bad at parenting, but actually evil mothers. One doesn't become a saint simply because one is capable of becoming pregnant and carrying a child to term."

"They're not going to like that," I said.

"Let them hate it," Auric said. "Let them hate me. It makes no difference. Over one billion children have experienced physical, emotional, sexual, or multiple forms of violence every year on Earth before I arrived. Over 25 percent of all adults have reported being physically abused as children. And 20 percent of women and seven percent of men have been sexually abused as children. I am ending that cycle of abuse. If that means offending the sensibilities of some, I'm willing to accept that knowing that over a billion children can grow up free from that abuse. Child abuse is fundamentally uncivilized. Ergo, I oppose it without equivocation."

Still, the implications of what he'd done on Mars and Venus were staggering. He was effectively sterilizing billions of people. Those 134 million pregnant women were the last generation for the bad people of the world. Those children would be the Omega Generation.

"The Omega Generation," Auric said. "Very dramatic, Christian. As we watch the Omega Generation grow up, we can determine whether Nature or Nurture prevails in moral development."

"It's a valid point," I said. "Fast forward to 2068, when those children born this year turn 18 years old. How many of them turn out to be evil, ignorant, greedy, corrupt, cruel assholes like their parents?"

"Since there's now exemplary healthcare for them all, and the necessary social support systems in place, the odds are good that most of that Omega Generation will come out okay," Auric said. "Of the 134 million Omega Generation births—and I'm ensuring they all successfully are carried to term—I don't think more than 46 million of them will go bad. The remaining 88 million of them will be civilized."

"You think 46 million will go bad?" I asked. "That's a lot."

"There is a heritability aspect to evil in many cases," Auric said. "Bad seeds grow from bad parents and bad parenting. Remediation on the behalf of the Omega Generation will help, but not eliminate that."

"You could cure the kids," I said.

"No," Auric said. "I know it seems paradoxical because of the degree of social engineering I'm already carrying out, but I'm letting them play out the way they are until they attain legal adulthood. After that, they'll be banished like their parents were. If and when they've done something to warrant it."

My mind was in a twist over this, contemplating the tangled politics of it all.

"For most of them, it would mean time spent on Venus," Auric said. "Of that Omega Generation, around 1.3 million of them will be psychopaths. And of that percentage, around 13,000 will become violent, despite my best efforts. That 13,000 will be banished to Mars. The rest of them will end up on Venus."

"The Omega Generation," I said.

"You're forgetting that in the next twenty years, Earth will have made considerable progress," Auric said. "You're fixating on the plight of these bad people, without factoring in that the good majority of people on Earth will have built a better, more just, compassionate, considerate, and vibrant society."

"Good and just people won't want you banishing more people," I said.

"It's not up to them," Auric said. "That Omega Generation is unfinished business for me. Once that's done, it's done. Otherwise, it's like I'm reintroducing toxins into the environment. And the fact is that for the ones on Venus, there's a chance of reintroduction into civilized society. They will be Apostles, in a way—their stories of sin and redemption will be appealing to the residents of Earth."

The heritability of evil loomed large in my mind, made me frightened at the implications of it.

"What about psychopathology," I asked. "You've banished the current batch of psychopaths to Mars and Venus. But what about new ones that appear?"

"A psychopath is capable of functioning in civilized society," Auric said. "I'll be watching them to ensure they don't violate the *Book of Don't*. Let's say there's a child who enjoys operating on live animals. Should that practice be permitted to continue uninterrupted?"

"Well, no," I said. "Obviously."

"What if that child's talent for vivisection allows them to grow up to be a world-class surgeon?" Auric asked. "Is it worth the price of a few animals? Animal cruelty is a correlative harbinger of psychopathy and assorted malevolent behaviors. I'm not going to allow it to go unchallenged."

"You could cure it," I said.

"All in good time," Auric said. "The process of progress toward civilization is a long one. People tell themselves they're civilized because they have air conditioning, cars, and intelliphones. But those aren't actual measures of civilization, so much as they are of technological progress. They're not the same thing. The trope of the fascist regime making the trains run on time—that speaks to the lack of correlation between level of technology and civilization. What does it matter if the trains run on time if people are treating one another barbarously? What does it matter if people are rich in a society where many tens of millions, even hundreds of millions, are living in poverty every day? Privation saps the strength of civilization; it doesn't empower it."

It was all too much to think about. My head was throbbing with the possibilities and ramifications of what Auric had done. I felt bad about Angelina being exiled here. I legitimately felt bad about that.

"Don't," Auric said. "She belongs here. The Queen of the Assholes, like she said."

Even though she'd betrayed me, I felt like I was betraying her. I didn't want to leave Venus again. I didn't want to leave her behind.

"You have to," Auric said. "Her fate isn't intertwined with yours, at least not in the way you might think it was."

"What does that mean?" I asked, but Auric had already beamed us back to Earth.

PART
III

CHAPTER
ONE

THINGS WERE SETTLING DOWN somewhat after what Auric had done. People were finding their feet, recovering themselves, comforting themselves. People were resilient. Thankfully, nobody had pondered the Omega Generation, yet, but I thought of all of those pregnant women who were doomed to be exiled once they had their babies.

It was weird being back home after the Great Disjunction. The GNP had been eradicated as a political party, and there had been a renewed drive to reunify America. Without GNP mendacity, state propaganda, and terror holding it together, the CSA was falling apart, and the ad hoc American government was reaching out to the terrified CSA bureaucrats who had somehow not been on the receiving end of Auric's judgment.

Any number of global pariah regimes followed the CSA into political oblivion and exile. Auric had pulled the fangs on all of those serpents, and countries underwent political revolutions from the remaining citizens. China was also in disarray, as the venerable Chinese Communist Party had almost completely been purged by Auric, but the ancient dream of a democratic revolution in China had been realized. North Korea effectively ceased to exist and was reunified in short order with the South Korean government. Several Middle Eastern and Central American regimes fell in the void created by Auric's purges.

Without LAX News and the RAN Network pumping lies and disinformation into people's heads hourly, there was more objective coverage to what was happening. The United Nations had come out forcefully against Auric's actions, and the Auricians were banned worldwide. It was a largely symbolic gesture, because nobody could do anything about them, because of Auric.

Auric was the irrefutable reality we all faced. Whether or not he was a god, he was in all of our lives, impossible to ignore.

Corporations had been deprived of swathes of employees and CEOs because of Auric's purge and were scrambling to reorganize themselves along more ethical lines, out of fear that more of their number would end up banished on Venus or Mars.

Not that Auric ever threatened that. He didn't. He simply urged people to take the *Book of Don't* to heart and to try to live by its civilized moral Advisements:

Don't be Evil—be good

Don't be Cruel—be kind

Don't be Ignorant—be enlightened

Don't be Corrupt—be honest

Don't be Greedy—be generous

Don't be an Asshole—be considerate

Don't be Crazy—be sane

Don't be Lazy—be active

Don't be Stupid—be smart

Don't be Creepy—be respectful

Don't be Fake—be authentic

Don't be Dull—be audacious

Don't be Cowardly—be brave

One thing I noticed was that people actively tried to be more kind and polite to one another. Whether that was rooted in performative, existential fear of Auric or because he'd purged the actually bad people from our midst, it was hard to know for sure. But it was definitely apparent. People tried to be kinder to one another.

Assholes, in particular, became an endangered species. They understood that they were effectively on probation, and how many of them were already on Venus and Mars. I knew they were still out there, but they went about as underground as they could. I imagined maybe there were Asshole Clubs somewhere, maybe where they could let off steam or get their asshole fix by doing withering roasts of each other. And it created a philosophical conundrum—being an asshole required victims or targets. If one didn't (or couldn't) act on it, was one still an asshole?

I didn't have the answer to that and asked my Auricle.

"To be an asshole does indeed require a target for the inconsiderate behavior," the Auricle said. "But then, nearly all of those behaviors and misbehaviors do. They are impactful because of the social nature of your species."

"A greedy person could enjoy their wealth, a lazy person could enjoy just doing nothing by themselves," I said. "But an asshole requires a target for the inconsideration."

"Sounds to me like you think I should banish the remaining Assholes to Venus," the Auricle said.

"No, no," I said, thinking of Angelina on Venus. "No, there shouldn't be any more purges. People are already terrified enough as it is."

"Are you sure?" the Auricle asked. "Those who remain are what passes for evil on your world, now. Besides, of course, the mothers of the Omega Generation."

"No, they should remain," I said. "They'll mend their ways."

The mention of the Omega Generation caused me more concern, as it always did. As did the Auricians.

Despite the ban, Auricians still appeared, do-gooders in their white suits, always trying to help people. I was still not comfortable with their approach. I just observed and chronicled, as was Auric's intention for me.

Day to day, the world was cleaner, happier, more productive, more hopeful than I'd ever seen it before—despite the pall cast by what Auric had done. Particularly in the CSA. The Heartland Protectorate was dissolved with the fall of the GNP, and the CSA basically dissolved into the United States of America again, with one big twist.

Some joked about calling us the Reunited States, and that joke stuck, so the RSA was born. Sales of alphabet soup soared as acronyms flew freely from coast to coast.

Auric's monetary redistribution he'd unveiled in that UN speech helped offset some of the disruption caused by his actions to begin with, and slowly, the business of business was able to continue in some fashion, although it was changed, too, from what had been happening before.

Since a percentage of the richest, greediest, most evil people had been banished to Venus or Mars, there was a strange mix of fear and hope, a sense of promise where there had been despair before, but one tinged with a certain nervousness, a terror of Auric and what he represented. What could be given could be taken away, and people feared what Auric might do next.

I kept my eye on that. Things were *not* the same. To that end, I should tell you what was missing from the world as a way of further documenting what was gained.

You already know that the GNP, HID, and SAC were gone. They were among the first. Without those party bosses, their secret police, and their paramilitary goons, the States felt freer than they'd been in decades. The idea that you could walk the streets without being accosted by GNP operatives, could turn on the television and not see Denny Rand raging in your face, didn't see GNP politicians fulminating about Auric or whatever, it was great. It felt liberating.

There were no more televangelists. They were gone. All of them had ended up on Venus, since none of them had been explicitly violent, even though they were abundantly greedy and corrupt.

The nearly 70 million believers in the "prosperity gospel" of televangelism had been among the many banished to Venus, I'd determined, typically being a mix of the ignorant, the asshole, the greedy, and the corrupt. The interdiction by Auric had caused these particular churches to collapse, and Auric had liberated the previously sequestered money they'd secreted away into a massive windfall for the needy, on the order of many billions of dollars.

There were no more terrorists. All of the terrorists had ended up on Mars. While terrorists weren't the most numerous blights that afflicted the world, their absence was nonetheless felt. Gone were the public bombings, school shootings, the arbitrary assassinations, the kidnappings, the extortion plots, the sabotage. All of that was gone.

There were no more gangs and criminal cartels. As part of his attack on organized crime, Auric had banished the gangs to Mars, as I'd mentioned before. But the absence of gangs and gangsters had made a big impact on life around the world, particularly in the former CSA. The collapse of the organized crime network, as well as the copious amounts of corruption among government officials that made it possible, had made a big dent.

There were no more serial killers, rapists, pedophiles, child abusers, wife beaters, and others like them. While they were not numerous in terms of the overall numbers of people Auric had purged, it was good to live in a world where one didn't have to fear them.

There were no more fascists. More than just the purge of the GNP, fascists and authoritarians around the world ended up on Mars or Venus.

This took a major bite out of conservative governments and political parties everywhere, forcing reorganization and, in many cases, political revolution. Without fascism, the world could breathe more freely than ever before.

There were no more sweatshops. Auric had liberated over 250 million children who'd been working in sweatshops, as well as millions of adults. The government corruption and greed that had allowed sweatshops to thrive had been snuffed out in Auric's purge. The most brutal of them ended up on Mars, while most went to Venus.

It was hard to envision capitalism without one percent screwing over the ninety-nine percent majority, but in the Age of Auric, something oxymoronically close to "compassionate capitalism" arose out of a strong sense of self-preservation. No longer was it considered standard business practice to throw the baby out with the bathwater—whether literally or figuratively. They had to provide for their employees: union representation, far better wages, workplace benefits, family and medical leave, work-life balance improvements, better hours. The obligatory asshole boss had to dial it back, and the absence of terrestrial psychopaths took a real toll on the managerial class. For Americans, these were unfamiliar and alien things.

Companies may not have cared, but they had to at least *appear* to care, which translated into improving policies that made people's daily lives better than they had been before Auric had come along. Auric assisted them by helping them create employee-owned enterprises that could profit without abusing their employees.

On a related note, slavery had finally disappeared from the world. Or from the Earth. It was alive and well on Venus and Mars. More on that later. There was so much to keep track of. It was hard to see it all.

Companies weren't free to pollute without consequence. After Auric's planetwide cleanup, he'd worked with corporations to stop treating pollution as an externality in their accounting practices. The companies that complied were given technology to help reclaim and recycle their pollutants. The companies that resisted were subject to more rigorous attention by Auric, who went after the remaining company assholes who might've been reluctant to mend a company's ways.

But some companies had policies in place that perpetuated the problems, even after their leadership had been banished. Auric leaned on those corporations to revise their policies. This was strongly opposed by assorted Chambers of Commerce around the world, but Auric was implacable.

"Polluting your habitat is uncivilized," Auric said. He often took that line in these matters, civilized versus uncivilized, or civilized versus barbaric.

The thing is, the world *was* better than it had been, despite the disruption, or more pointedly, because of it.

Litter was gone, which is almost incomprehensible in its magnitude. I know that seems like a minor thing, but like with everything Auric, little things magnified. Litter reflected laziness and contempt for one's environment. The mindset of a litterbug was one of selfish, lazy, thoughtless individualism, and that had effectively evaporated in the face of Auric's actions.

The air was markedly cleaner, the waterways were clean, the climate had improved already without the choking burden of runaway greenhouse gases.

What's more, Auric had created job centers at his Auric Towers. He offered employment counseling to people who needed it, in jobs that were ideally suited to people's talents and temperaments. This led to people seeking and finding jobs they actually wanted. Auric actively encouraged the growth and expansion of wind and solar power, which had been sorely lacking in the CSA, relative to the rest of the world.

It was impossible to not see the good in those things, but the Omega Generation was nagging at me constantly. For example, there were still prostitutes post-Auric, and that bothered me as well.

"There were 42 million sex workers around the world," the Auricle told me when I asked. "And over one million of them are in the Reunited States. However, my remediation efforts have reduced their numbers. For example, when I healed mental illness, I reduced their numbers by over 48 percent, which meant there were only 21 million sex workers remaining. And when I cured drug and alcohol addiction, I took off another 11 million from their ranks, putting the number around 9.5 million. I'm hopeful that my career centers will continue to drive that number down."

"How many of them were banished?" I asked.

"Around 500,000," the Auricle said. "Most of them on Venus, a smaller group on Mars, naturally."

"Okay," I said. "But there are still some left on Earth."

"Yes," the Auricle said. "You're wondering about my stance on vices?"

"I am," I said.

"I encourage people to live lives unencumbered by addiction and mental illness," the Auricle said. "Inasmuch as vices are correlative of mental illness and addiction, I treat them as public health issues, while still allow-ing people a degree of agency regarding vices."

"What does that mean?"

"I'm pro-legalization of vices," the Auricle said. "So long as people ar-en't addicted to them and otherwise harming others in their pursuit of them."

"Yet you purged the cartels," I said.

"Absolutely," the Auricle replied. "They were threats to human life. To that end, I have commandeered all of the criminal drug resources and created drug dispensaries to work with the governments in the applicable countries. For those who seek out the drugs, they can access them without paying hefty costs and otherwise risking their lives with unsafe products. With nearly a billion people still smoking, 15 million people using injec-tion drugs, I have worked to cure those people of their addictions. And with over 240 million people cured of their addiction to alcohol, I have assisted people in coming to terms with their addictions."

"While still not getting rid of drugs entirely," I said.

"I understand that there's a human impulse toward altered states of consciousness," the Auricle said. "People enjoy getting drunk and high, and I don't want to interfere with that, beyond eliminating actual addic-tion, which is a negation of human free will by its very nature. Nearly 10 percent of Americans had wrestled with some addiction. I cured them of these addictions as thoroughly as I did other diseases and disorders."

"Are there drugs on Venus and Mars?" I asked.

"Not exactly," the Auricle said. "While it's possible to distill alcohol from the plants I've introduced there, I didn't put any specific legacy drug-conducive plants there. There are no coca plants and no opium pop-pies on either of those planets. I did this because I didn't want to provide a tactical or strategic edge to the organized criminals who'd been banished to those planets."

"But you let people have their guns," I said.

"Inasmuch as it gives me an excuse to remove excess ones from Earth, yes," the Auricle said.

"You *want* them to kill each other," I said.

"I know they'll do it," the Auricle said. "I'm simply making it easier for them."

"Is there tobacco on those planets?" I asked.

"No," the Auricle said. "As per the same approach to contraband crops."

I didn't know what to think about it all.

"Can I see what's happening on Mars?" I asked. "Like on my television screen?"

"You can," the Auricle said. "I've created two channels that offer real-time viewing of life on Venus and Mars. I know people would be curious."

I took my remote and turned on my television, found the channels. A working governing council had formed on Venus, an intraplanetary syndicate charged with helping people survive there. The syndicate was formed of members of each nationality, decided by secret ballot.

On Mars, there was warfare between the factions, as Auric had foreseen. There had already been mass murder of Americans by any number of the international factions working together against them. Top GNP and CSA leaders were hanging upside down from the Martian buildings, having been skinned by a multinational mob.

"Holy hell," I said.

"It's to be expected," the Auricle said. "There will be a drive toward equilibrium at some point, or what passes for it on Mars, after a surge in bloodletting."

"You caused this," I said, and Auric appeared. He stood resplendent in his white suit and gold shirt, his gold skin sparkling and his blue-flamed hair flickering.

"What's the matter, Christian?" Auric asked. "I did cause it. But, instead of these bad people on Mars inflicting themselves on everyone here on Earth, they're attacking each other. I don't see the problem. They don't have to attack one another. They could be peaceful. There are abundant resources I've placed on Mars. They are, instead, turning it into a slaughterhouse. Why? Because they're bad people. Bad people are behaving badly."

"How many Americans have died?" I asked.

"So far? Many thousands," Auric said. "As I suspected, their more organized rivals on Mars are taking advantage of the opportunity presented to them. You may or may not know this, Christian, but your people have inflicted a great amount of harm on the world. Particularly the defunct CSA—it was a global pariah. Without the protection of your heavily militarized nation-state, the evil people from your country are particularly vulnerable to various forms of retribution."

"It just seems cruel," I said. "Like human cockfighting."

Auric nodded sadly.

"Except I'm not showing what's happening on Mars for people's entertainment," Auric said. "It's merely there to show people what they've left behind. Nature is violent, but Nature is not truly evil. Only humans refined and defined evil. It's going to be very ugly."

I turned off the television.

"You don't appear to everyone the way you appear to me, do you?" I asked.

"You're my Chronicler," Auric said. "You have a higher degree of access. For most, they have their Auricles to answer their questions."

"The Auricles are also you," I said. Auric smirked at me.

"I go where I'm needed," Auric said. "Where and when and how."

"You've seemingly saved the world," I said. "Now what?"

"I've not saved the world, Christian," Auric said. "I've only cleaned and repaired it. It's very different from saving it. Your world remains in terrible peril. All I've done is given you a better chance to survive than you had before. Thanatos is still bearing down on your world. It's only a month away, now."

"You're still going to stop it, though, right?" I asked.

"I am," Auric said. "I already said I would. Would you like to go see it?"

"Uh, sure?" I said, even though I was completely unsure as to whether I'd want to do that. But that was enough for Auric, and away we went to visit Thanatos, the planet-killing asteroid.

CHAPTER

TWO

THERE I WAS making history again: the first human to stand upon an asteroid in space. I know, it didn't really count, because I was only there with Auric. Yes, it was one that was hurtling toward Earth, but it was still somewhat amazing. I say "somewhat" for two reasons:

1) because it was just a hunk of space-rock; and
2) this hunk of space-rock was a deadly threat to the Earth.

"You'd be amazed how many of these there are," Auric said. "There are over a trillion objects in your nearby Oort Cloud, for example. There are almost two million reasonably-sized asteroids in the asteroid belt—these objects are over a kilometer in size, and millions more smaller asteroids. And that's just in your neighborhood. For any planet, they're a menace."

Earth was a blue dot in the distance, still far away. To see Earth like this was humbling and terrifying. Our world was so small in the larger, cosmic scheme of things, our entire world was like a dust mote.

Auric nodded.

"You're right," he said. "So, so small. Insignificant in the literally cosmic sense of things. Even I am insignificant, and I'm omnipotent."

"Uh, you think?" I asked. He nodded, sadly.

"I know it doesn't seem that way," Auric said. "But I've ranged across the universe for 13 billion years, Christian. I've been around a long time, and I've seen a tremendous number of things. You'd go quite insane if I were to share them all with you. Don't worry, Christian, I won't do that. The observable diameter of the universe is around 28 billion parsecs—that's 93 billion light-years. Beyond what can be observed, who knows?"

"You don't know?" I asked.

"It's not that I don't know, exactly," Auric said. "It's that I haven't been there, haven't seen it. I went inward, not outward, when I became what I am. I wanted to find life, went where there were observable planets and galaxies. It doesn't do any good to chase ghosts beyond the observable universe. I could have vaulted past the observable universe and into the endless beyond. But I wanted to go where I knew life was, or where I hoped it was. Again, I was unprepared for all of the death I came across. That's why I came to your world, as I've said. I had to save you, both from yourselves, and from the cold tyranny of probability."

"Asteroids and comets," I said.

"Yes," Auric said. "And so many other things. Death is all around you in this universe. The only way to survive is to spread yourself out to other worlds. To take care of your habitat, to be good to one another, to progress and be civilized, and to travel to other worlds and settle them. Without that, you're doomed."

"You haven't done that," I said. "You're a singleton, like you said."

"But I have," Auric said. "There are many of me. Should something somehow be able to kill me, the others that are me would survive and pick up where I left off."

It was a weird thing to say, a weird thing to be. As a human being, I had no frame of reference for it, but I accepted it because he said it.

"Nothing's ever killed me," Auric said. "And, of course, I'd never take my own life. I like living too much to ever end my own life."

"I don't know if 'living' is the right word for what you are," I said. "You seem like you've transcended that long ago."

"True," Auric said.

"Were you ever mortal?" I asked.

"Yes," Auric said. "It doesn't matter. That part of my story doesn't matter. What matters is I saved your species for the moment."

"Okay," I said. "Let's go with that. Where do we go from here?"

In the darkness of Thanatos, Auric's blue hair burned like a torch, providing the only illumination, aside from the golden forcefield that kept me alive, like a glowing yellow ball. Thanatos tumbled over and over again, relentless in its mindless, deterministically deadly way.

"Going forward, the fate of your species is in your hands," Auric said. "I've corrected the errors—the disorders and the diseases, the sociological and psychological maladies that nearly made you extinct. The sad fact is that you'll need every bit of skill, intelligence, and luck to survive in this universe. It is *not* a kind or compassionate place."

"But what about your planetary protectors?" I asked. "The ones who are there even now?"

"Yes," Auric said. "They'll remain. They'll protect your planet, without overtly interfering."

"I think many would argue that you've already overly interfered in life on Earth," I said.

"Up to a point," Auric said. "Compassion dictated that I help a wounded world. Kindness speaks clearly, compassion is a directive one must answer if one is civilized. Compassion literally means 'to suffer with'—and I do suffer with your species. I know what you have ahead of you, should you survive this transitional phase."

"But with your other selves around, you can ensure our survival, whether we're worthy or not," I said.

"My plan going forward is only to intercede if I need to," Auric said. "If you reenter into the dangerous territory toward self-annihilation. That will free your species up to do extraordinary things, the knowledge that I'm there to protect you."

"People hate you," I said. "For what you did."

"Of course," Auric said. "I'm okay with that. Some understand. That's enough. I don't need your species to love me. I don't even need them to acknowledge me. I simply am. We are fellow travelers in a brutal universe. Kindness matters in the face of that unrelenting brutality. It's easier to become brutal. I could have killed everyone on your world in a blink of an eye, ended everyone's suffering that way—instead, I gave you three homes reflective of the extant nature of your species. Whether or not people realize it, those were acts of cosmic kindness."

"Let's say people on Earth try to rescue their fellow humans on Venus and Mars," I said. "Undoing what you tried to do. Would you let them?"

Auric smiled at me.

"A curious question," Auric said. "I would let them. I think it would be a terrible mistake, but I might see how that plays out. And if you destroyed yourselves again, I would sadly let you do so."

"Really?" I asked. "After all you've done for us already?"

"Compassion dictated that I at least *try* to save you," Auric said. "If you don't *want* to be saved, then compassion dictates that I let you destroy yourselves, if that's what you really want to do."

"But if that's where you net out," I said. "Why bother saving us at all?"

"I had to try," Auric said. "One can't look at Earth and say that I didn't try. I left Earth better than I found it. Far better than your own species has, at least to date. I came upon a barbarous, wounded world and I civilized it. I came to a polluted habitat and I cleaned it."

It was hard to argue it with him. Part of me wanted to debate with him, just because I could. Or maybe because I had to, if I didn't want to simply worship him.

"I've said already enough times that I don't want worship," Auric said. "More of your species have started to. I'm not like your pathologically insecure, psychopathically jealous and abusive Abrahamic gods. I do not need it. I welcome your devil's advocacy."

"Are you leaving us?" I asked.

"I'm moving on, yes," Auric said. "After Thanatos. I've done my work here. Part of me will remain, while I move on to find other worlds to save."

"On and on, across the universe?" I asked.

"Yes," Auric said. And then it occurred to me, like a flash of insight, as humbling as it was frightening.

"You're looking to find someone to destroy you," I said. Auric gave me his sad smile.

"Why do you think that?" Auric asked.

"You can't or won't do it yourself," I said. "You're traveling through the universe hoping to find someone who can destroy you."

Auric held onto his sad smile, his eternal blue flames moving like a nimbus. I wondered if they'd burn me if I touched them.

"Only if you wanted them to," Auric said. Impulsively, I reached out and let my hand hover over that flaming nimbus, the fire passing harmlessly through my fingers, without pain. It was sublime, and Auric smiled at me. "You see?"

I withdrew my hand from the otherworldly fire that had burned for 13 billion years, and looked at my own mortal hand, untouched and unharmed.

"You've helped us survive because you want us to destroy you someday," I said. "You came to the right place. We humans are really good at destroying things. Humans excel at destruction."

"Someday, maybe you will," Auric said. "It's been a long journey. The moral dictates of the Cosmic Awesome prevent my self-negation."

"Is that your programming?" I asked.

Auric indulged me with a world-weary sigh.

"I'm not a machine, Christian," he replied. "You should know that by now. I'm beyond both organic mortality and the mechanical eternal."

"But you are logical," I said. "Whatever you are, there was a time once when maybe you *were* a machine. And that's why you can't destroy yourself."

"I am civilized," Auric said. "And I protect civilization. That's my purpose."

"Someone made you for that purpose," I said. I mean, I was spitballing, but I felt like I was onto something. Auric didn't tell me I was wrong.

"You're *not* wrong," Auric said. "This is why you're my Chronicler, Christian. You have keen insight for one of your species."

"Did you destroy whoever made you?" I asked.

"I am the sum total of all that Auric ever was," Auric said. "The planet of my origin was Auric. I *am* Auric. I am absolute."

My mind wandered as we stood on the tumbling asteroid. I imagined a golden world, a beautiful world, a perfect world. Somehow, they had attained it. They had accomplished planetary perfection, a utopia, a long, long time ago. However they did it, it happened.

And they'd made Auric the protector of it, the culmination of their civilization. Somehow, they'd done this. What happened after that, only Auric knew.

"I am the ultimate expression of Aurician technology," Auric said. "Far beyond it, to be honest. I've exceeded even the wildest expectations of my creators."

"Are they still out there?" I asked. "Your homeworld?"

"No," Auric said. "They're me. I'm them. We're each other. I've told you I'm a singleton. That's what I am. All that Auric was or ever could be is me. You've heard of a doomsday machine?"

"Of course," I said. I really hadn't, but the concept seemed simple enough that I didn't need those details. The GNP was always into invocations of doomsday. They loved doomsday. I'm sure the ones that were still alive on Mars were deep into thinking it was the end of days.

"I'm the opposite," Auric said. "I'm a godsend. Looks what I've done for your planet, for your species. Whether or not it's appreciated."

I couldn't argue it. Any objective accounting would show that he had helped us out as a species. Although I couldn't help but wonder if there were problems created by the solutions he'd provided.

"What sort of problems, Christian?" Auric asked.

"I mean, psychopathology evolved," I said. "There has to be a survival value for it, right? Or it wouldn't have persisted?"

"Sure," Auric said. "Horrible people are often natural survivors, because they put themselves first, and that blend of ruthlessness, shamelessness, and unflinching willingness to commit acts of violence makes them very good at surviving and breeding."

"By taking all of the psychopaths from us," I said. "You've taken away a particular group of survivors."

"I have," Auric said. "But I've empowered far more and made the conditions for their survival better. As much as your species loves the imagery of nature red in tooth and claw, and the implications of it as a rationalization and justification for savagery, the creation of civilization was intended to provide protection for its citizens, versus replicating the savagery and barbarism of unadulterated human nature. The rugged individual of ideological lore cannot hold a candle to the power of a just, fair, united, and enlightened civilization. For your species, your power comes from your civil society."

It was strange to have this conversation upon Thanatos, tumbling toward the Earth, this emissary of death.

"The social instinct of your species was the key to your survival in your past," Auric said. "The drive toward cohesion helped your admittedly weak species grow strong. Take any individual human being, and they pale before any predator—tigers, lions, hyenas, sharks, bears, and so on—but take a group of human beings, working together, and even the mightiest predators can fall. Working with one another, and not against one another, your species can accomplish nearly anything it wants. Your capacity to communicate alone speaks to that social nature of your species, and your willingness to unite toward a common purpose."

"Including destroying you?" I asked.

Auric laughed.

"Maybe one day," Auric said. "Not anytime soon. Maybe not for millions of years, if you even survive that long."

"But you said 'millions' and not 'billions' at any rate," I said.

"I was just being nice," Auric said.

"I don't want to destroy you," I said.

"I know you don't," Auric said. "You love me."

"What?"

"You loved me the moment you saw me," Auric said. "And I love you. I love all of your species—even the ones I banished on Venus and Mars. I am full of agape for your species."

"The people on Mars and Venus would disagree with that," I said.

"They are sacrifices to civilization," Auric said. "And remember that I offered a path to salvation for those on Venus. When some of them reform and become civilized, they can rejoin your species."

"But you've written off Mars," I said.

"As should you," Auric said. "I'm sure some of your species won't. They'll try to save Mars, not understanding that Mars doesn't want to be saved, and will only poison the well the first chance they get."

I thought of the CSA leadership elite, hanging upside down in the Martian town, skinned alive, raining blood on the red Martian ground.

"Yes," Auric said. "They were made to suffer. Mars is a human hell., but only because it's populated with human devils."

"Whom you claim to love," I said. "You're as abusively contradictory as God."

"There's no need to be insulting, Christian," Auric said. "I would never be so contradictory or so abusive. I've justified my actions as necessary for the survival of your species. While everyone on Mars could be seen as a predator, they do not make your species stronger. Rather, they sap the strength of your society by attacking society itself. They are parasites, not predators, if you want to really be pedantic about it."

I noticed that Auric had us hovering over Thanatos, because the asteroid kept tumbling, and he didn't want me to get motion sickness by tumbling over and over again on it.

"When you leave," I said. "Can you take me with you?"

Auric patted my shoulder.

"Yes," Auric said. "I can. As my Chronicler, it would only be right."

The thought of touring the universe with Auric made me happy. Even that wasn't the right word. It was something bigger than mere happiness. It was something transcendent.

"You won't miss Earth?" Auric asked.

"I mean, yeah," I said. "I will. But I also want to see what you'll do after Earth, where you'll go."

"Part of me will always remain on Earth," Auric said. "As I'd said. So, I'm not really leaving. Every slice of infinity is itself infinite."

"What do you call two physicians who can't make up their minds about something?" Auric asked. I thought about it a moment, then a moment more.

"A pair of docs?" I said.

"A paradox," Auric replied, winking at me.

CHAPTER

THREE

I HAD THOUGHT AURIC would have propelled Thanatos to Earth just so he could stop it, but he didn't do that, told me that it wasn't yet the right time to stop it, while assuring me yet again that he would. He was infinitely patient with me.

Of course, I trusted Auric. It's all I could do. He'd been nothing but good, and I felt like a flawed and fractured human being by even harboring doubts about him.

The prospect of road tripping through infinity with Auric, however, had fired me up. I was excited about the prospect. I'd truly be his sidekick, and I was okay with that. Every superhero needed a sidekick, right? I'd be the Chronicler for as long as I could be.

Going back to my place in the Auric Tower, I could see it was fully occupied with happy, healthy people. Folks were making use of the Auricareer Planning Center that had been added to every Auric Tower. Auricareer planning involved in-depth question and answer sessions with the Auricle to help people find out these things:

What they wanted to do
What they were best at
What they enjoyed doing most

The "sweet spot" was the intersection between those three spheres, the confluence of excellence, enjoyment, and excitement. The Auricle would then offer a person a range of occupations based on what best fit within that intersection.

After determining that, people within the Auric Towers were given resources to get the necessary training they'd need for a particular career, and the opportunity to pursue it. The Auricles worked with business leaders to find jobs for these candidates. Others went to work directly for Auric in some fashion. He'd created the Auricorps—basically another group of Auricians who dedicated themselves to helping humanity. A kind of Cosmic Awesome Peace Corps.

Keep in mind that people were still plenty pissed at what Auric had done, and the Auricians were still pariahs. In fact, Minerva and the other early adopters were particularly frowned upon for their participation in the Great Disjunction.

However, without the malevolent media outfits like the RAN or LAX in place, fanning the flames of hatred, people gradually moved on from it, at least on some level.

As for many of the governments, however, it was something else entirely. Government leaders spoke out against Auric's intervention in human affairs, while some worked with him. The benefit of associating with Auric was simply too great to pass up. People did understand that he'd made the world better, even if they hated him for it.

Auric understood the upset and spoke to it. I watched him on television.

"I know many of you remain angry with me for what I did," Auric said, having appeared again before the UN General Assembly. "However, you have to concede that the condition of the planet is much improved—the air and water are clean. Not cleaner, but clean—every rogue regime has been overthrown. The bad people of your world have been relocated to their appropriate new homes. I haven't done anything your own species hasn't done to yourselves. The only difference is that I've done it on a far greater scale, and I've done it decisively. That's not me bragging; it's simply the truth. I haven't committed genocide—the bad actors on Venus and Mars are still alive. They are banished, but not exterminated. This is a far gentler fate than you've inflicted on your own species over the centuries. I could line item every genocide perpetrated by your species during the last millennium to illustrate. Don't worry, I won't do that."

Auric told a bit of a lie in that address, as I knew that there were now plenty of dead on Mars. There had been some murders and attempted murders on Venus as well, which got the perpetrators booted to Mars by the planetary protector. The death count on Mars was climbing, but Auric didn't want people to dwell on that, so he didn't mention it.

The big screens showed Mars and Venus spinning, looking like other-Earths, with blue oceans and green landmasses and white fluffy clouds. I still couldn't get used to seeing them like that. I also knew that, despite him asserting that he wasn't committed genocide, that the 500 million denizens on Mars were doomed to extinction. Maybe Auric was hearing my thoughts, because he spoke to them.

"Extinction is the ultimate threat your species faces," Auric said. "Extinction has followed life wherever it has appeared. The threat of extinction is existential and very, very real. For any remaining who still doubt my motivations, as I've said many times before, I didn't have to do that. I could have hung back and watched you kill yourselves. I chose to intervene. That is the moral obligation of a compassionate and empathic higher being: to intervene. The moral imperative to assist. I'm going to offer another assistance on that level."

The screens shifted and there was Thanatos, tumbling toward the Earth.

"The asteroid, Thanatos, the one I'd warned you about," Auric said. "It's only a month away from your planet. You will not be able to stop it. But I can."

The General Assembly became a chorus of fearful murmurs as delegates spoke to one another and gazed in horror at the asteroid. Auric had provided two views—one of the tumbling asteroid and the other a kind of POV shot that showed it bearing down on Earth.

"For those of you who doubt my motives, who think I'm somehow out to destroy your species, just look at Thanatos," Auric said. "If I were to take that stance some of you consider principled and leave your species to your own fate, I would simply watch that asteroid descend and wipe out your species. All of the blights you faced as a species—the ones I cured—were like that asteroid. Only worse, because so many of them were self-inflicted. I could just let Thanatos destroy your world. Or I could stop it. But I'm going to leave it to you to decide. Let the UN General Assembly vote on it, and I'll abide by their vote. In this way, you have agency in your own survival, versus me simply arbitrarily deciding your planet's fate for you. However, if you vote in favor of your own survival, I don't want to hear any more impugning of my motives. I have no ulterior motives, beyond the survival of your civilization and your species. That's all I care about. You can trust me. I know that when people try to earn your trust, it makes you suspicious. It's a well-honed survival instinct. I've already showed you that you can trust me. You decide whether you want to live or die as a species and make your vote. I will abide by your decision."

And then Auric vanished in a flash of golden light, as the UN burst into a cacophony of raised voices.

He appeared on the sofa next to me, startling me, even though I knew he might appear that way. Frankly, I was surprised he didn't just simply duplicate himself. For some reason, he thought I needed some alone time.

"How about that?" Auric asked. "I'm giving people the opportunity to save themselves. How's *that* for agency?"

"It's kind of a stacked deck," I said. "I mean, is any nation going to actually vote against that?"

"Some might," Auric said. "The important thing is that I'm giving them a choice in their fate. Free will and full agency."

We watched the UN scurry as delegates furiously talked with one another. I had a bunch of questions, but I always did, where Auric was concerned.

"If people voted against you stopping Thanatos, would you really let it destroy us?" I asked.

"I meant it, Christian," Auric said. "If your species would rather live free and die, I won't stop them. I'd like to think that with the uncivilized members of your species marooned on Venus and Mars, they're likelier to arrive at a civilized and sensible decision."

Even though Auric was talking to me right now, I knew there were other incarnations of him out saving the world.

"There are," Auric said. "There are 40,000 of me across the planet. Speaking of which, I've got a few more unfinished items on my 'sinister agenda' to sort out. Would you like to come with me and observe them?"

"For sure," I said, wondering what Auric had in mind.

"Great," Auric said, standing up, holding out his hand, which I took. "Let's go. You'll love it."

CHAPTER

FOUR

ADJACENT TO THE AURICLE shrines and within the Auric Towers, Auric had made another miraculous creation. It was like a smaller version of the shrine, a booth-sized golden cylinder.

We appeared streetside by the shrine closest to me, startling people who were filing around the Auricle. As I'd said before, without the GNP and HID and SAC looming around to terrorize people for making decisions they didn't approve of, folks were more comfortable walking by the Auricle, even though there was still a lot of opprobrium in the air regarding Auric.

For many, the utility of asking the Auricle questions was simply impossible to ignore, but most of them used the app in the privacy of their own homes, versus risking being seen entering one of the shrines in public.

Even I felt self-conscious about it, looking around me. I talked when I get nervous, so I spoke up.

"What are we looking at?" I asked.

"Behold the Volitionator," Auric said.

"What the hell is it?" I asked, as Auric touched a large circular button and opened it. The tube slid open, revealing a place where a person could stand and view a screen. There were other circular buttons next to the screen. "What does it do?"

"The Volitionator lets a person become any race or gender they want," Auric said. "With just a button push, a person can become any race, or even an amalgam of all races. And they can become male, female, both, or neither."

"Neither?" I asked.

"Neither," Auric said. "True nonbinary. Do you want to try it?"

"Uh, no," I said. "But thanks. Is it permanent?"

"As long as a person wants," Auric said. "They can always reset to their default if they choose."

"Wow," I said. "And you made this why?"

"Because people want it," Auric said. "This solves the ongoing problem of a person's identity. People may wish they were born a woman or are angry that they can't properly express their true nature in their current form. The Volitionator solves that problem."

"That's something," I said.

"There are about two million people in the RSA that identify as gender nonconforming," Auric said. "The Volitionator offers them a way forward. What makes it superior to existing approaches is that it's non-surgical and is reversible. I added in the racial component in case people wanted to become other racial identities as well. It affords people the opportunity to walk in others' shoes, literally and figuratively. To come to understand the human condition as broadly as possible, from all human perspectives."

"Wow," I said again. "Just, wow."

Auric smiled, and I could see how people were giving us a wide berth as they went on their way. Their looks were fearful and wary, dusted with undeniable awe.

"What about aging?" I asked. "Will people be able to use the Volitionator to become young again?"

Auric smiled at me, shaking his head.

"They will not," Auric said. "But I'm amused that you'd think of that. This is why you're so good at being my Chronicler. No, the Volitionator will not make someone younger."

"What happens if/when someone tries?" I asked.

"It'll politely explain it to them," Auric said. "It will advise them to make the most of the life they have, of the time they have, and not try to buy time."

"People won't like that," I said. Auric just sighed, and I felt the need to speak up again. I wasn't going to advocate for how immortality weighed heavily on the fleeting nature of the human spirit.

"Mortality is central to the ordinary human condition," Auric said. "My role is to help the living live their best lives, and for there to be a path for the future of the species."

"How will people find out about this?" I asked.

"Oh, there are push notifications on their phones," Auric said. "I just created them, so people are learning about them even as we speak."

I saw a young brown-haired man furtively walk past us and open the Volitionator. He went in, the door closing.

"Perfect," Auric said, as the door opened, and a smiling, young, red-haired woman emerged. "You see? Quick and painless."

"Incredible," I said. "You think it'll get a lot of use?"

"Where humans are concerned, anything is possible," Auric said. "Civilization ideally exists to help the individual safely reach their full potential. If that means changing their initial gender assignment, so be it. The important thing is that people are empowered to be exactly who and what they think they want to be. And that they can change who and what they are at any time."

Without the GNP storming about, I assumed people would be able to make use of the Volitionator without much trouble or accompanying drama, violence, and trauma.

"I'm surprised you didn't brand it Aurichoice or something," I said.

"That's pretty good, Christian," Auric said. "But 'Volitionator' just has a breezily memorable ring. It's both campy and entirely accurate in its function. It also works with weight loss."

"For real?" I asked.

"Yes," Auric said. "There were over two billion people on the planet who are obese—obviously, some of them are on Venus and Mars, now, so let's say there are around 1.4 billion people still obese on this planet. The Volitionator can make them lose weight, too."

"Now, *that'll* be popular," I said. "Although I'm wondering why you didn't take care of that when you went after disorders and diseases."

"While there are clear comorbidities associated with obesity," Auric said. "I didn't apply that when I went after the other conditions, lest people accuse me of singling out the obese. This way, I leave it up to the person using the Volitionator to decide their optimal weight presentation. Further, they can use the Volitionator to be better-looking if they want to be. It allows for optimizing one's facial proportions to become their best possible self. It doesn't allow one to radically change one's appearance, but it arrives at a mathematically sound alteration of their existing facial template to be the best version of themselves."

"Well played," I said. "Of course. Painless, free plastic surgery? People will be all over that."

"I'm happy to help," Auric said. "People don't have to do it, which is why it's the Volitionator. I give people full agency in whatever modification they seek to pursue. But it's what's inside that counts the most, right?"

"Right," I said.

Standing next to Auric, I felt invulnerable. It was an amazing sensation. He could do anything. He *did* do anything. I know the everyday impulse when faced with the sublime would be to be perhaps a little afraid and utterly awestruck. All I felt was peace and comfort. Auric had changed the world without (directly) killing anyone.

"You know, before I decided to terraform Venus and Mars, I originally thought about transforming all of the bad people on Earth into trees," Auric said. "Just turn them all into forests. Your world can always use more forests. But I decided the banishment was better, offering more of an object lesson."

Pedestrians had been gathering around us, now, people looking on with wonder and taking their phones and photographing us. Auric took the opportunity to engage the crowd, his lovely voice resonating as it always did.

"Behold the Volitionator," Auric said. "You've received notifications for it on your phones. The Volitionator will let you become any age, race, or gender you desire at the push of a button. It's free and it's reversible. You can become who you feel you really were meant to be. Just another service I've provided to your species. You're welcome."

People looked at Auric, at me, at the Volitionator, and murmured to themselves. I felt uneasy being ogled by so many strangers.

"Why don't you go back where you came from, Alien," a middle-aged white man said. "We don't want your gadgets and your tricks."

Auric was unfazed.

"Some of you do," Auric said. "This is for those who do."

I figured this guy was one of the assholes that Auric failed to banish—one who hadn't perpetrated any violence or violated any of the Fateful Five, as the five bad traits—evil, cruelty, corruption, greed, and ignorance—had become known.

"Why didn't you include hate in your *Book of Don't*," I asked, as we watched the frowning man stomp away.

"Hate is alchemically bound up in ignorance and cowardice and assholery," Auric said. "Much like love, it's a complicated emotional state. In casting my net, catching the ignorant, the evil, the cruel, and the violent allowed me to catch all of the hate groups formerly thriving in your country, the groups who have made hatred central to their creed. It doesn't mean there aren't still hateful people on Earth. Given what I've done on your world, there are people who hate me. People who will always hate me. I accept that."

It wasn't fair, given all that he'd done.

Auric smiled, shaking his head.

"I don't need people to love me," Auric said. "Altruism doesn't require adoration. All that matters to me is that people are happier and healthier than they were before, and some semblance of justice was served."

One group of people who were terribly unhappy about what Auric had done were the ultra-rich. The billionaire class had invested a ton of money in the existing corrupt political environment. His liquidating of their tax avoidance havens and reallocating of that money to the UN had enraged them. And since the legal profession had taken a beating from Auric's purges, the billionaires and multibillionaires who hadn't ended up on Venus or Mars, and who had found family members disappeared, were particularly put out.

Auric was unfazed, but he could afford to be.

"You can't piss off all the billionaires," I said.

"To the Cosmic Awesome, the wealthiest billionaire on your world is less than a bacterium vacationing on a speck of dust," Auric said. "What do I care about their feelings?"

"Harsh," I said, but we were interrupted before we could continue.

Minerva appeared in a cluster of golden motes of teleportative light. Her abrupt appearance startled the crowd of onlookers and got more cameras taking pictures.

Minerva noticed me with a sidelong look before addressing Auric. Given that she was in regular correspondence with Auric, I wondered why Minerva had felt the need to appear before us that way. It felt deliberately intrusive, but maybe that was just me being petty.

"Auric, the UN has made their vote," Minerva said. "They want you to save the world."

"Of course they do," Auric said. "What was the vote?"

"It was unanimous," Minerva said, looking me over as she spoke.

"Well, there you have it," Auric said. "As I expected. Before I relocated people, I imagine the vote would've gone differently. I'll go to the UN. Would you like to accompany me?"

"We *both* would," Minerva said, glancing at me. I could detect a hint of jealousy in her delivery, just a whisper of it. I was sure Minerva had continued to pump her Auricle full of questions about my role as Chron-

290 | DEAN VALE

icler, and likely already knew about my plan to accompany Auric on his celestial travels.

"Better maybe if you watched from Christian's suite," Auric said, teleporting us there. Minerva looked around my place, hand on her hip, while the television screen came on, showing Auric at the General Assembly.

"It's *your* fault we're here," Minerva said. "Instead of there. The camera-shy Chronicler."

"I'm a behind-the-scenes guy," I said.

"And I'm a front-and-center gal," Minerva said.

Minerva plopped down on the sectional and leaned back, drumming her fingernails, while Auric was addressing the delegates. She looked me over a moment before speaking again.

"I know all about your plan," Minerva said. "Traveling the cosmos with Auric."

I didn't need my Auricle to tell me that Minerva was envious.

"Problem?" I asked.

"No, no problem," Minerva said. "I just don't understand what Auric sees in you."

"Me neither," I said.

She pursed her lips, eyed my place—which, I admit, I hadn't decorated, yet. It was plain white walls with generic Auric Towers wall art. Which meant that it was perfect for the place, naturally.

"I think it's because you're utterly unassuming," Minerva said. "You're like this blank canvas, devoid of intrinsic character."

"Whoa, that's not fair," I said.

"Isn't it?" Minerva asked. "Tessa, Dan, John, Yuko, and I are out in the field, we're trying to build Auric's world with him, we're catching heat for it on the front lines. I'm roundly hated for my Aurician work. They're making terribly unfair comparisons. Even just being an Aurician now gets a person shunned. We're being called cultists and traitors to the human race. They're calling us 'Frenemies of Humanity'—as if that even makes any sense. And while we're doing this, you just glide along in his good graces. And what do you do? You *observe*."

She scoffed, while Auric was telling the delegates that they'd made the right decision and wouldn't regret voting for him to save Earth from Thanatos.

"*Anyone* can observe, Christian," Minerva said. "You could be anyone."

"I'm only me," I said.

"Exactly," Minerva said. "You're only you. Did you know that some of the Auricians ended up on Venus and Mars?"

I didn't. I hadn't thought to ask. Had Auric made a mistake about some of his chosen? Or had they changed after being elevated in his eyes? There had to be reasons behind those actions, something logical.

"Yeah," Minerva said. "Auric banished some of his own followers to those planets. People who would have given their lives for him without question."

"I don't think he wants fanatics," I said.

Minerva scoffed again, hopped to her feet, her heels offering up a staccato clack as she did so. She even moved authoritatively, with immeasurable certainty of purpose.

"They were *his* fanatics," Minerva said. "Entirely loyal to him. And he banished them. They're already dead. The ones on Mars, for sure. Dead. Murdered by the Martians. What kind of leader does that to his own diehard followers?"

I understood why Auric gave Minerva and me this moment together. Minerva remained as interpersonally powerful as ever, radiating the confidence and charisma that she had in abundance, but I could see she was vexed, too.

"Auric is fair," I said. "And he's honest. He's not going to exempt his own followers from his Advisements."

"Many Auricians worship Auric," Minerva said. "We *worship* him. He's a god. You understand that, don't you, Christian? Auric's a goddamned god. He can do anything. He's already created a mountain of miracles. He's singlehandedly saved the world. He's infinitely just, kind, considerate, and powerful. He's *worthy* of worship. The entire planet should be on its knees thanking him for what he's done. Instead, they hate him, they hate us. They hate us for saving them."

"You know he doesn't want to be worshipped," I said.

Minerva paced a moment before striding into my kitchen. She'd found a bottle of white wine and fished out a corkscrew, put out two glasses taken from my own cupboard. I hadn't even realized I'd had wine. I know I hadn't bought it.

"I know all of that," Minerva said. "But we Auricians worship him. We understand that's what you do when confronted with divinity. You worship it. You honor and fear it."

"I'm not afraid of Auric," I said.

"Bullshit," Minerva said, prying the cork from the bottle. She poured both wineglasses. I didn't have the heart to tell her that I didn't like white wine. She walked over to me, glasses in hand, and jabbed one in my direction, waited impatiently for me to take it.

"I'm not," I said.

"You should be," Minerva said. "He could turn you into anything he wanted to. A tree. Water. Steam. Dust. Stone. Anything."

"But he doesn't," I said. "And he won't."

"Trust," Minerva said. She made a mock toast to me. "To trust."

She clanked her wineglass to mine and took a big drink. I gave a polite sip, while Minerva paced some more.

"I trust Auric," Minerva said. "Sure, I do. But I can't get it out of my head that he purged some of his own followers. They would have followed him to the end. And he rewards that kind of loyalty with banishment."

"If he banished them, it had to be because they had bad attitudes in their makeup, or became corrupted by their association with him," I said. "They deserved it."

Minerva stopped me with a wave of her hand, like she was banishing my own thoughts.

"Okay, yeah," Minerva said. "I *know* that, Christian. But they were true believers in him. Why would he do that?"

"I already said why," I said, fumbling with my wineglass. "They failed his celestial test. Just because someone's an Aurician doesn't mean they're a good person. If I had to guess, they were likely people who jumped on the bandwagon and wanted to be associated with Auric out of a sense of greed or ambition. Look, I can solve this in a second. I'll ask my Auricle."

Minerva shrugged.

"I already did," Minerva said, while I fished out my intelliphone, setting down my wineglass, watching the golden wine dance in the glass as it settled.

"Okay, so you already know the answer," I said. "But you're grilling me. Why?"

Minerva stared at me even as she paced. To have Minerva Merrow eyeballing you, to be in the same room with her, was daunting. She radiated interpersonal power, charisma, and whatever else you wanted to call it.

"I want *you* to understand," Minerva said.

"Auric is justice incarnate," I said. "Auricle, why did Auric banish those Auricians?"

My intelliphone didn't waste a moment.

"I banished them because they were evil, greedy, corrupt, cruel, and ignorant," the Auricle said. "Most of them ended up on Venus, while a smaller percentage were sent to Mars. Your inference was correct. I banished them because I refuse to exempt my own followers from my moral Advisements."

"There you have it," I said, holding up my intelliphone stupidly. Minerva shook her head, her hair waving as she moved, like it was trying to keep up with her irritation.

"I worried that I might end up banished," Minerva said. "When they disappeared, I worried about it. But you didn't."

"I didn't think about it," I said. "Maybe a little."

"You are so blithely benign, Christian," Minerva said. "All of that agency work has belt-sanded away anything that might offend a client, is that it? All of that trendscaping? You are beyond nonthreatening. You're banality incarnate. You're a walking, talking, human whiteboard."

I knew Minerva had likely done a full workup on me with her Auricle. She wasn't wrong. I was good at client management, but in no way did I consider Auric a client.

"I wouldn't say that," I said. "I'm just a good observer."

Minerva swigged down the wine and clanked it on the table next to mine.

"We should have sex," Minerva said. "You and me, right here, right now."

I laughed, while Minerva read my expression, her eyes dancing across my face, her chin set. Foolishly, I thought she must be a Leo. It only made sense. I didn't even have to check my phone.

"Why?"

"Ohmigod," Minerva said. "That's about the most Christian thing you could have possibly said, Christian. Jesus."

Minerva was an abundantly attractive woman, but I was still dealing with the Angelina stuff. Plus, I didn't trust Minerva.

"Angelina's on Venus," Minerva said. "She's banished, Christian. I did my research on the self-styled Queen of the Assholes. You know she's trying to organize an anti-Auric movement on Venus? Talk about missing the boat and the point. That ship has sailed. Everyone on Venus is officially anti-Auric, but since everybody on Venus is a lying, conniving bastard and Auric gave them the roadmap to returning to Earth, they're secretly working to try to become better people to get their golden ticket off Venus. But not Angelina. No, she's going all-in against Auric."

That was very Angelina. It made me almost laugh, but with Minerva stalking around, I didn't dare pipe up, lest she think I was laughing at her.

"Another reason why we shouldn't become involved," I said. "We're coworkers."

"Ah," Minerva said. "Right. Wouldn't want to muddy the waters, would we?"

She put her hands on my shoulders, stared me right in the face, before planting a kiss on me. She kissed well, her lips tasting of white wine and red lipstick.

I pushed her away as politely as I could, and Minerva laughed, more to herself than at me, a knowing laugh, like the joke being on her.

"You're in love with Auric," she said. "That's what it is. You love him."

I didn't know what to say to that. With Minerva, she assuredly had already grilled the Auricle about it, gotten the answers she needed. Maybe this was some kind of test whether I'd admit to it.

"So what if I am," I said.

"You sure are," Minerva said, grabbing my own wineglass and draining it. "You love him. He knows it, too. You fell for him the moment you met him. It's why Auric made you his Chronicler."

"Auric doesn't play favorites," I said. "You should know that."

Minerva went back to the kitchen to get some more wine.

"No, he definitely doesn't," Minerva said. "It *should* have been me. I'm right for him, Christian. We fit. He's ambitious, I'm ambitious. You? You're just you. You're agreeable, you're affable, but ambitious? No way."

I laughed and she sneered, giving herself a generous pour.

"Auric's not Apollo, Christian," Minerva said. "There's no happy ending for you with him. Even if you use his Volitionator to turn yourself into something you think he'd like. Auric's way, way beyond love. At least human love. You know how old he is. He's nearly as old as the universe. That's old, Christian. We're all just blips in his world."

"But he cares about us," I said. "He cared enough to save us."

"Sure," Minerva said, drinking, walking, talking. She was such a good talker. "He did, for some reason we will probably never know, give enough of a shit to save us from ourselves. Why would he do that? I've cross-examined my Auricle about it, and it just gives me elliptical answers. But seriously, between you and me, Chronicler, why would he care? Level with me, human to human."

I thought of his story of traveling the universe, seeing the dead civilizations, knowing that Minerva had almost certainly found all of that out as well. She watched me thinking it over, smiling triumphantly.

"I know his celestial sob story," Minerva said. "All those dead civilizations. But he could have resurrected them all. But he didn't. He came here, instead."

"He said that thing about letting the living live," I said. "And letting the dead rest."

"Right," Minerva said. "It's a matter of perspective. Turning Venus and Mars into habitable planets—even if they're prison planets, now—isn't the same as resurrecting a billion dead civilizations. Or is it? Why did he bother with us?"

I knew she'd have interrogated her Auricle about all of these questions she was asking me. Somehow, in all of this, she was quizzing me. Maybe she was trying to square up my own answers with hers, even though I hadn't made those inquiries of my own Auricle.

"He wants us to destroy him," I said. Minerva looked surprised. Something she must not have gotten around to asking or didn't think to ask. It was literally something that never would have occurred to her.

"What?"

"He wants us to destroy him," I said. "To put an end to his suffering."

"That's crazy," Minerva said. "We can't do that."

"Not yet," I said. "But maybe if we survive and, I don't know, evolve, then maybe we eventually can."

"That is seriously messed up," Minerva said. "You figured that out all by yourself, Christian?"

"Yeah," I said. "It just makes sense."

She walked up to me, got all up in my face.

"He told you that?"

"It sort of came up," I said. "Like I said, I sleuthed it out."

"Gold star for the Chronicler," Minerva said. "Auric's got a deathwish. But why wouldn't he just do it himself?"

"He can't," I said. "The moral code that, I don't know, binds him, prevents him from doing it. Maybe it's some rule embedded in his core design. I'm not certain."

Minerva laughed. "Jesus, Christian. He came to the right planet, didn't he? I mean, is that why he did the whole banishment thing? So people would hate him enough to want to try to destroy him one day?"

"Maybe," I said. "I didn't ask."

"We're not up to the task," Minerva said. "He's infinitely beyond us."

"For now," I said. "Maybe in a million years, if we're still around. He's going to help us stay around."

Minerva stepped back, studying me awhile, nursing her wine.

"That's so messed up. It's perverse," Minerva said. "And sad. Auric's hoping humanity comes through for him as his executioners? God help anyone who banks on the human race, Christian. We're good at destroying things, but not *that* good."

"We do have a great track record of extinctions," I said. "We've caused plenty of them. Auricle, how many extinctions have we caused or contributed to?"

The Auricle answered right away.

"Over the past 126,000 years, humans have directly contributed to 96 percent of all mammalian extinctions. In the last six centuries, humankind has caused the extinction of nearly 700 vertebrate species extinctions. Before Auric's biodiversity remediation effort, approximately one million animal and plant species were threatened with extinction, including 25 percent of mammalian species, around 33 percent of shark species, over 40 percent of amphibian species, and 25 percent of plants," the Auricle said.

"He came to us because he knew that we knew how to kill things effectively," Minerva said. "That's insulting."

"Sure," I said. "But logical."

Minerva sulked.

"*That's* his ulterior motive," Minerva said. "All of that talk of ennobling us and civilization, all of that—it's just to, what, fluff us up?"

"He's sincere about it," I said. "But I think in terms of his endgame, he understands that if he lets us survive and evolve, we'll eventually find a way to destroy him. That maybe we'll feel compelled to at some point."

Minerva was incredulous. It was a look I hadn't seen on her face before—her eyes wide, her mouth agape.

"Why would anybody want that? It's insane," she said. "He's been around 13 *billion years*. He's all-knowing, all-powerful, immortal. I mean, really. I'd take that in a heartbeat."

"I think it's *because* he's been around for 13 billion years, Minerva," I said. "Think about that. At some point, everything's a rerun, right? Even in a nearly limitless universe, you probably see the same things over and over again. Birth, life, death, extinction. All of it. Even supernovas become humdrum if you've seen a billion of them, I'd imagine."

"But you're going to road trip with him across the cosmos," Minerva said.

"I'm going to witness it, yeah," I said. "For me, it'll all be new. And I love him, like you said."

"This is some ploy on your part," Minerva said. "A chance to ride shotgun with immortality, while the rest of us live and die."

She was as cynical as she was ambitious. But the *Book of Don't* didn't have any Advisements against cynicism or sarcasm.

"I should go with you," Minerva said. "The three of us, traveling the universe. A cosmic three-way: you, me, him. We both know how much they love trinities in cosmology."

As pithily as she put it, I still knew her heart was with humanity. Minerva was grounded in the practical and the pragmatic. She was the Mistress of the Mundane.

"Don't worry, Christian," Minerva said. "I wouldn't dream of intruding on your Cosmic Awesome romance with Auric. There'll be enough to worry about here."

Still, I could see her thinking over what I'd said. Knowing Minerva, some part of her was kicking herself for not realizing that Auric wanted to die. It was an entirely alien perspective for her. She loved being alive. She loved who she was. She would until she died.

Whereas I loved Auric and would until I died, whenever that was. If he ever died. If we ever died. I would die without him. I knew that much.

"So, we grow strong enough one day and we destroy him," Minerva said. "That's the plan?"

"Long-term," I said. "Yeah. It's how it all works. New generations come and replace the old. Nothing lasts forever."

"He's had a good run," Minerva said. "I mean, 13 billion years is nothing to sneeze at."

"Totally," I said.

"You *sure* you don't want to have sex?" Minerva asked. "In honor of, I don't know, human mortality and fallibility?"

"No, we should," I said, taking her hand. "Totally."

CHAPTER

FIVE

MARS STILL BOTHERED ME. It had been awhile since I'd last been there, but I couldn't get it out of my head, and I brought it up with Auric. After seeing Angelina on Venus, seeing the hateful exiles there, I felt a compulsion to observe what was happening on Mars. I couldn't simply abandon them; I had to know the full story of what Auric had done.

"I need to see Mars once more," I said. Auric acknowledged that with a grave nod. "I need to see."

"You won't like it," Auric said.

"I know, but I have to," I said. Believe me, I didn't want to visit Mars again. But after all that Auric had done, I couldn't avoid it. As his Chronicler, I had to monitor everything. The good, the bad, and the ugly.

"I'll have to go with you," Auric said. "It wouldn't be safe for you otherwise."

And I knew that I would be safe, but that Auric worried that my gentle heart might make me vulnerable to the predators on Mars. He wanted to protect me from myself.

Auric had turned to his female incarnation, which was curious and striking to me, the chimerical way Auric could transform.

"Why the change?" I asked.

"Whim," Auric said.

"You don't strike me as whimsical," I said.

"I'm not," Auric said. "Are you ready to go?"

I wasn't sure what to wear, and Auric provided me the warm white coat emblazoned with the Auric symbol, as well as a stocking cap and gloves, what she'd given me the first time I'd been to Mars. It felt crazy to even think that way.

"Thanks," I said. Auric smiled, raising her hands.

"Now you're ready," Auric said. "But I warn you, Christian, Mars is going to shock you terribly. Mars will haunt your dreams for the rest of your days."

"I understand," I said.

"Like Hell," Auric said. "It's going to seem like that."

"Yeah," I said.

"You will not be able to un-see what you've seen," Auric said. All of this I knew. I was grimly prepared for it. It's what I was meant to do. I knew Auric could read my thoughts, and she seemed pleased by my determination to press on.

"Here we go," Auric said, and there was a golden flash and, in another moment, we were on Mars.

I could smell the blood immediately. Blood, smoke, rot, and ash. We were in one of Auric's gilded villages, where fresh-fallen snow had dusted the area. We were in a forest of crucifixions—it's the only way I can describe it. There were dead people hanging on crosses by the hundreds. Maybe it was thousands, I don't know. It went as far as I could see, and I was afraid to ask Auric.

"What the hell?" I said aloud.

Someone had taken these people and crucified them. They hung on the shadowy crucifixes like hopeless, hapless apparitions. Seeing so many like this, it clawed at my heart.

"What happened here?" I asked.

"One of the local luminaries—here he goes by the name *Al Qatil*—meaning 'The Killer'—he organized a group of jihadist partisans into a movement. He's one of several contenders for the conquest of Mars. All of these people he crucified are Americans, in fact."

In the lower light of Mars, the smaller Sun, the shadows loomed large. The victims on the crucifixes were bloody shadows. The chilly air stank of endless death. It was worse than anything I could have imagined.

"He had his people go into the forests you'd created, cut down a bunch of trees, turned them to crosses, and then captured a bunch of American exiles and put them to death?"

"More or less," Auric said.

"That's horrible," I said.

"The Americans here were part of an enclave in the service of Willard Wilkins, a doomsday cult leader," Auric said. "He'd taken advantage of the exile to push his apocalyptic vision of the world and had been assembling a group of fanatic followers out here, away from many of the other areas on the planet, when Al Qatil ambushed them."

"Ghastly," I said.

"Believe it or not, this is currently one of the more peaceful places on Mars," Auric said.

It was staggering to see those dead people crucified. I'd never seen anything like it. The wanton, brutal cruelty of it was worse than I would have ever considered. I could hear gunfire cracking somewhere in the distance, with returning fire from somewhere else. Somewhere else, somebody screamed. There was an explosion somewhere, followed by more shooting.

"Americans are faring poorly here," Auric said. "Your people were largely sheltered from the consequences of your government's behavior for a long time. Scores are being settled here. It's not justice, but there is plentiful retribution. Since the exile, around 90 percent of the Americans banished here have been killed already. Your people have made a lot of enemies around the world."

"You mean 72 million American exiles are already dead?" I asked.

Auric nodded. I could see the snow falling on the crucified. The idea that so many were already dead freaked me out. Auric could see my concern.

"Who killed them?" I asked, meaning those beyond this ghoulish spectacle. Auric understood my meaning.

"Everyone did," Auric said. "The Chinese, the Arabs, the Spanish, other Americans. You name it, they did it. You have to remember that everyone exiled on Mars is both evil and violent. There's a lot of carnage. The surviving Americans are just as violent and brutal. They're just the smarter ones, or the more organized, the more ruthless. I should add that they *could* have peacefully organized themselves into some kind of Martian commonwealth. They went to war with each other almost immediately upon arriving, the competing factions trying to dictate who was in charge."

"Admittedly, you set them up," I said. "You put them here together knowing they'd do that."

"One could say that, certainly," Auric said. "That the capacity to peacefully organize a community is beyond the ability of these newly-made Martians. Or, one could also say that what we're seeing is the founding of a new Martian police state—they're violently sorting themselves out as to who will become the supreme authority on Mars. Who is the most fit among them, in an evolutionary struggle unlike any other. That fits their temperament perfectly."

The chill wind blew again, and I found I couldn't stand being in that village with all the crucified people.

"How many are here, honestly?" I asked.

"There are a thousand dead," Auric said.

"A thousand crucifixions," I said. "Obscene."

"Keep in mind that all of the people here were bad people, too," Auric said. "Wilkins was working on a plan to launch a crusade in one of the larger Martian enclaves. Al Qatil just got to him first."

"Diabolical," I said.

"That's Al Qatil," Auric said. "I told you that some would see exile on Mars as an opportunity. He's happier than he's ever been. He's able to give full voice to his demons. He's at least a strong contender for the supreme authority here. Evil people are strongly hierarchical in mindset—they often enjoy the kiss up/kick down architecture of hierarchy, which provides both opportunities for advancement as well as for punishment of inferiors."

I braced myself inwardly for what I might see next. Auric transported us to one of the other villages. I noticed that Auric hadn't given the Martian exiles cities—only villages and towns were represented.

"Cities seemed like a waste of time and energy," Auric said. "At least for the current planetary tenants. This is a place of tribalism and war, and for that, villages and towns seemed the appropriate level of civic structure."

Although Auric had equipped me, I wondered if people were equipped with the low-gravity weights he'd talked about before.

"Please, Christian," Auric said. "I never said I'd equip them with these; I only said that they should wear them."

"Rugged individuals and frontier existence," I said. "I remember. You knew what this was going to become."

"Yes," Auric said. "There are no higher goals here than conquest and survival. Many are enjoying themselves, strangely enough. Their hatred for each other is only exceeded by their collective hatred of me. While hatred for me is a unifying concept that could bring a lasting kind of peace here, their individual brutality, ambition, greed, and ignorance will prevent that from taking place at this time. Some of them even attacked my planetary protector."

I could only imagine how that went.

"What happened?"

"Trees," Auric said. "I turned them into trees."

"Trees?" I asked. Auric nodded.

"Mars can always use more trees," Auric said. "You know how I like trees."

Glancing around, I could see there were plentiful trees, and I wondered if these were ones Auric had transformed.

"Nobody around here," Auric said. "Those are ones I introduced at time of terraforming. There are ample red oaks, American beech and hornbeam, big-leaf maples, hoptrees, Japanese maples, pagoda dogwood, Siberian spruce, pine, and fir, even pawpaw. All are thriving here. At least where the locals haven't cut them down and/or burned them. Or used them for spears, crucifixes, stockades, pyres, and gallows, obviously."

This town—Auric told me it was called "Fort Rand" by the denizens—was largely barricaded and populated by a shellshocked, gun-toting group of Americans. Upon seeing Auric appear, they started crying out.

"There's Aurica," some of them yelled. "Shoot her!"

We were peppered by gunfire for a few moments, the bullets harmlessly sparking against the forcefield Auric had placed around us. A somewhat cooler head prevailed and urged people to save their ammunition.

"How are they getting their weapons and ammunition?" I asked.

"They arrived with them when I banished them here," Auric said. "Eventually, they'll run out or else learn to make more."

A leader emerged. He was a bearded, tattooed man named Gus Grimes. I know this because when he stepped forth, the townsfolk started chanting "Gus! Gus! Gus! Gus!" and he introduced himself to us. He wore a Confederate grey kepi.

"Well well well, look who's here, everybody," Gus said. "I'm Gus Grimes. I'm the boss of this here town of Speculation. But you probably already know that, don't you, Aurica?"

"I do," Auric said.

"You murdering, kidnapping bitch," Grimes said, jabbing a beefy finger at us. He looked like maybe he'd been a biker back on Earth, wearing a denim vest with a bone-white iron cross on the back. Other townsfolk were similarly attired. "I told people what I'd do if I ever saw you."

He drew a chromed pistol and shot it at us, but the bullets simple ricocheted harmlessly.

A woman ran from the crowd, arms outstretched. She was an older woman, closer to middle age, and raced across the snow toward us, wild-eyed.

"Please, Aurica! Take me away from here! There's been a mistake! I don't belong here!" she cried, her sandy hair streaming behind her as she ran. Gus raised his pistol and shot her dead, right in the head.

"No escape for you but death, Meryl," Grimes said, then turned his malevolent gaze back on us. "What's your business here, Aurica? You and your, what is that? Boy toy?"

"We're here to observe," Auric said.

"Come to see your handiwork, have you?" Grimes asked.

"I'm only observing," I said, clearing my throat.

"Can't say there's much for you to see, here, Boy Toy," Grimes said. "We're in the middle of a war. That's what you wanted, though, ain't it?"

The anger flowed from Grimes like stink lines. I could only imagine what he'd do if he got his hands on us. The other townsfolk of Speculation had emerged from their barricades and circled around us tighter. The fear, anger, and hatred was apparent. I could see that they had some cookfires going, and I saw spitted meat cooking. I didn't think there was livestock on Mars, made a mental note to ask Auric that later.

"We don't deserve this," Grimes said. "Who are you to just zap us away the way you did?"

"Gus Grimes, do you want me to line item your crimes you've committed in the course of your life for all to hear?" Auric said.

Grimes looked uneasy but held his ground.

"I'm not ashamed of what I've done," Grimes said. "Everyone who got on my bad side got what's coming to them. Here, there, everywhere."

"You are exactly where you belong, Mr. Grimes," Auric said. "As are all of you. I have judged you and found you wanting. But because I am merciful, I have allowed you to live the rest of your dreadful days on Mars."

"Wait, we're on Mars?" one of the townsfolk asked. "I thought this was Hell!"

"It *is* Hell," Auric said. "As far as you're concerned."

"Kill them!" Grimes said, and the townsfolk of Speculation rushed Auric and me, but they made no progress against Auric's golden forcefield. All I saw was their angry and desperate faces pressed against the field, their hateful eyes boring into us. Auric lifted us above them, just floated up, while they hurled rocks at us.

"It's not livestock cooking on their fires," Auric told me as we rose above them. "Those were prisoners."

"Oh, hell," I said, grimacing at the dozen bonfires blazing in the town of Speculation.

"The Hobbesian reality," Auric said.

I didn't even know what that meant but made a mental note to ask my Auricle later.

"Bellum omnium contra omnes," Auric said. "The War of All Against All, an idea envisioned and articulated by Thomas Hobbes. The idea that in the absence of a mutually-agreed upon social compact, everyone's fighting everyone else."

We hovered ever higher, until their angry yelling was barely discernible. Of course, the height made me afraid, but with Auric, I took solace that nothing would happen to me.

"I told you it would be unpleasant," Auric said. "Your Hannah Arendt wrote about the banality of evil. She said *'Evil comes from a failure to think. It defies thought for as soon as thought tries to engage itself with evil and examine the premises and principles from which it originates, it is frustrated because it finds nothing there. That is the banality of evil.'"*

I didn't know who Hannah Arendt was, either, assumed she was probably one of the umpteen writers banned by the GNP, but her words made sense to me.

"There are no grand realizations to be had on Mars," Auric said. "Only a human zoo of villainy, using the same bloody tools of violence and oppression, terror, and hate that formed so much human history. They will enslave, rape, and murder each other until the last of them dies alone on this self-made slaughterhouse of a planet. I'll be curious what sort of social contract might possibly arise here on Mars after the bloodletting. Some sort of Anti-Auric Alliance, I'm thinking."

It seemed unconscionably cruel of Auric, but Auric interrupted my thoughts, having read them, while we floated over a Martian battlefield, where I could see tens of thousands of dead strewn about. I could only imagine what had happened here, until Auric told me.

"It is a greater cruelty to allow these human monsters to prey on the rest of your species," Auric said. "As I said, there is no redemption to be found on Mars. This battlefield you see here was between General Li Quan of the Chinese Martian Expeditionary Force and Lord Rakshasa's New-found Freedom Army. Lord Rakshasa lost this battle. While Li Quan has headed north to lay waste to Lord Rakshasa's remaining holdings."

"Holdings?" I asked, while we floated past the seemingly endless battlefield. I could see people picking among the dead for anything they might find of value. "People have only just gotten here and you're talking about holdings?"

"They're grasping for whatever they can hold," Auric said. "Greedy and rapacious, the enterprising among them seek to conquer and enslave. I'm giving them what they want—wars to wage, enemies to hate and kill."

"But without hope of redemption," I said. "It's like a gladiatorial contest. Bloodsport."

"They behave as they always have," Auric said. "I'm only letting them give full vent to it, unencumbered by societal and/or legal constraints."

"You could stop it," I said. "You could heal them. You could *make* them good."

Auric smiled sadly at me. His sad smiles made me feel like I'd failed to understand something obvious. He was very patient with me.

"You can't make anyone good," Auric said. "My *Book of Don't* is as close as one can get to it. If I were to change the natures of these people, they would cease to be themselves. I'm *letting* them be themselves. All I did was pull them out of the communities they were afflicting and let them be terrible together here on Mars. I'm honoring their free will on Mars."

"Yeah, but not on Earth," I said. "You violated their free will on Earth by banishing them here. Are you going to tell me that was a necessary evil?"

"There is no necessary evil," Auric said. "Evil by its very nature must be unnecessary. That's what makes it evil. Those people chose to be and do evil. Keep in mind that I'd already cured mental illness. Therefore, anyone remaining a wrongdoer on the Earth was exercising their free will to do so. I'm merely the cosmic consequence of their wrongdoing. Frankly, it should have been abundantly clear by that point that I would do something about them. The fact that they continued even when I served up the *Book of Don't* to them points to how unredeemable they are. There was no waiting for karmic retribution or some settling of accounts in a mythological afterlife; rather, I meted out punishment in real-time."

"How much evil is innate, versus, I don't know, bad circumstances?" I asked. "I mean, there aren't really any evil babies, right? That means evil must be learned."

Auric regarded me a moment, his face beautifully unreadable.

"Infants certainly aren't evil," Auric said. "And even have a basic sense of altruism. Cruelty and evil are learned behaviors over time."

"So, if evil's a learned behavior, it can be unlearned," I said. It wasn't like I was advocating for the evil people on Mars, but I did have sympathy for the devils here.

"I've filtered out those who are capable of learning that moral lesson from those who can't," Auric said. "The ones who might be redeemable are on Venus. The ones who cannot be redeemed are here. Everyone here is violent."

I didn't know what to think about that. Maybe I was an optimist, but I felt like the possibility of redemption had to be there, somewhere.

"It's not, Christian," Auric said. "Not with the people here. And you have to remember that they're a fraction of the overall human species. The remainder either are capable of understanding my Advisements or else can, over time, learn to understand them and work peacefully with each other toward larger, more worthwhile goals than simply not-killing each other."

As we floated over bloody Mars, I didn't know what to think. It was all too much to take in. I felt like I was playing devil's advocate for the human race. That's a lot to put on anybody's shoulders, especially mine.

We passed the Japanese Martian Prefecture, under the iron gauntlet of Emperor Hirowaru Takeda, who was apparently a crime boss who quickly took control of three of the towns, uniting them under a modified Japanese war flag banner that maintained the rising sun motif with rays, but with black and red in place of white and red. Members of the JMP saw us and began firing in coordinated volleys. Within the Prefecture, it appeared orderly to my eyes, with Japanese maples aplenty, and the houses looking well-maintained. There was a town square from which enemies of the Emperor were hanging, near well-guarded JMP bordellos.

"Yes, it is orderly. All of the women in those bordellos are in sexual bondage to the JMP Emperor, who is obsessed with reproducing himself," Auric said, as we heard bullets whizzing by. "The Chinese Cosmic Communists are very orderly, as well, with the added advantage of high numbers. They're in another quadrant and are likely to be very strong contenders for triumphing on Mars in the short run, at least until the absence of births begins to afflict them. There are three types of evil in residence on Mars—organized evil, disorganized evil, and opportunistic evil. Right now, I would guardedly say that the organized evil is vastly outperforming the other subsets. Groups can always outpace individuals—numbers matter."

We flew over countless battlefields, segmented according to ethnocultural differences, with groups from different countries banding together for lack of anything else to unify them.

"Beyond their universal hatred of me for putting them here, they are fractious in their affiliations," Auric said. "I'm at peace with that. Sometimes, the quality of one's enemies is a good gauge of one's own accomplishments. I'm fine with being an object of hatred for fascists, mass murderers, psychopaths, rapists, pedophiles, warlords, and so forth. Let them loathe me."

I wondered how it would play out, and then frightened myself with the understanding that I could, one day, see how it did end for them here. Depending on how long the fighting took, how long it took for some bloody order or détente to emerge on Mars, it could amount to a bunch of old enemies making peace with one another, or a graveyard planet, devoid of human life, with only the golden ghost towns of Auric remaining, along with the bones, to show that they'd ever been here. There was also the knowledge that whoever won would grow old and die here, knowing that the end of their regime had finally come.

"Civilization does not rule on Mars," Auric said. "The orderly among them are capable of organizing, but that's a reflection of the social instinct of your species, not anchored in any kind of higher morality on their part."

"Maybe that social instinct is part of our higher morality," I said, which made Auric chuckle.

"Ants are also highly social creatures," Auric said. "And entirely devoid of morality. One is possible without the other. The wars ants fight put humanity to shame. But ants are insects; humans aren't insects. The people here *could* choose to live peacefully and productively, but they are so hidebound in their hatreds that they cannot."

Auric teleported us to another place, a beautiful garden contained behind a golden dome. It was a place of peace and harmony, indirectly lit and inaccessible to the outside, with only the see-through dome above us. Within it, there was a gorgeous conservatory of plants and trees. It was beautiful and balmy, the most wonderful greenhouse I'd ever seen. It contrasted with the shadowy cold of Mars. It was a lovely, lush oasis.

There was a winding golden path through it, one that led to a glittery golden portal in the center of it, where there was an Auricle shrine. Outside, I could see some of the Martian exiles trying to get in, unable to breach the golden walls that contained it.

"What the hell is this place?" I asked.

The other Auric, the Martian Auric planetary protector, was here, in his male form. He wore a red suit and had a white shirt and a gold tie. He spoke, while my Auric didn't.

"This is the Sanctuary," Auric said. "You might, indeed, say it's an oasis of sorts; the only peaceful place upon war-torn Mars."

It was greenhouse-warm in here, and compared to the chilly climate of Mars, was very pleasant. The air smelled of good soil and the perfume of pollen.

"Why is this here?" I asked.

"This is the reward for the last surviving tribe of human exiles on Mars," Auric said.

"Reward?" I asked.

"Yes," Auric said. "The survival of the fittest. One day—I won't spoil it for you by telling you who or when—but one tribe will rise above all of the others. They will have successfully defeated all of the other tribes and factions here, exterminating them through their ruthlessness and evil. And when that happens, when they have conquered Mars, then, and only then, will the doors to this sanctuary open."

I looked at the golden portal at the center of the sanctuary, which was bathed in golden light.

"But I thought you said there was no getting off Mars," I said.

"And that's still true," Auric said. "That last tribe will enter this sanctuary and rejoice in their triumph over all of the others. They will be sure of their destiny as the conquerors of Mars. They will be the most perfect human evil your species has ever known. They will be battle-hardened and confident that they will be able to get back to Earth and conquer it. They will see *that* portal as their road to triumph."

All at once, I understood it. It was diabolical.

"It's another trap," I said. "This sanctuary is bait, and that portal is a trap."

"Yes," Auric said. "Any who pass through it will find themselves transformed."

"Into what?" I asked.

"Trees," Auric said. "They'll pass through the portal and a moment later, a new tree will sprout upon the surface of Mars. But nobody in the Sanctuary will notice this. They'll simply see them pass through the portal, vanishing from sight."

"You're annihilating them," I said.

"I'm reincarnating them. I'm giving them new and better life," Auric said. "They'll become a forest fueled by their own greed and rapacity. They will know lasting peace as trees. And Mars will be at peace again, but a peace of new life, and not death."

"Trees is weird," I said. "You said before how you decided against turning people into trees."

"Yes," Auric said. "But that was on Earth. On Mars, it's different."

That seemed incredibly cruel, too. Like a bad joke placed on this slice of mankind. Both Aurics looked at me with their benevolently godlike eyes and sad-smiled.

"I'm giving them the chance to live out their lives according to their true natures," both Aurics said at the same time, which was jarring for me. "It's the same gift I'm giving all of your species."

"But why not just simply turn them into a forest now?" I asked. "Why trick them at the end into annihilating themselves?"

"Evil's end result is always self-negation," the Aurics said. "Evil *is* annihilation. It's why nihilism is at the heart of all evil—evil stands for nothing beyond itself, and leads to oblivion. What reward is most suitable for the survivors of Mars? They would be a blight on the universe. Especially if anyone from Earth tried to rescue them from their banishment, which the kind hearts remaining there might be inclined to do, not realizing the peril they might face in doing so. I won't let that happen. Thus, I will have solved the problem they present. They will, propelled by their own ruthless ambition, hurl themselves into the portal and Mars will gain a great forest from that last, rapacious charge by those evil souls. Once the last of them is gone, I will inform the population of Earth that they are now free to colonize Mars as they see fit—that the evil exiles have extinguished themselves and Mars can progress."

"Nobody will ever know what happened to them," I said. "Just boneyards and cracked and broken crucifixes, empty gallows, broken forts."

"*You* will know their fate, Christian," the Aurics said. "You'll know. I'm allowing you to see this so that you can document it. And remember: it didn't have to be this way. They could have tried to be good to one another. But they were *unwilling* to be good. My Advisements are not difficult to follow, and yet proved quite beyond them. Their fate is the result of their actions."

"Aren't you worried that I'll tell people?" I asked. "That I'll warn them?"

"Who would you warn?" my Auric asked. "Who would believe you? And who would you save here on Mars? The murderers? The rapists? The terrorists? The fascists? The pedophiles? The serial killers? The psychopaths? Which group would you try to save, Christian?"

His logic was ironclad, of course. It was hard to argue with omniscience, let me tell you.

"You chronicle these things," Auric said. "I wanted you to see this. To understand."

I pointed to the other Auric.

"What'll he do? Will he lie to people about the portal?" I asked.

"I never lie," the other Auric said. "I will simply tell them that they should *not* go through that portal. That will be enough to propel them through it in droves. Your species loves to break rules, and the survivors of Mars will be inveterate rule-breakers."

"New Eden," I said. "You made this place like Eden on purpose. A paradise on Mars."

"Yes," Auric said. "Their greed will do the rest. And think of it this way—I'm not killing them. None of them will die when they pass through that portal. Rather, they will find another life, a peaceful life, as trees. They will know true peace for the first time in their entire lives. And they will be contributing to the wellbeing of this world in a far greater way than they ever would have as human beings."

"You've got it all figured out, don't you?" I asked.

Auric shrugged self-effacingly.

"What good would omniscience be if I hadn't?" Auric said. "Tell me, would you like to keep touring the slaughterhouses of Mars, or would you rather go back home to Earth? Would you like to meet Lady Bloodshed? She's been very busy since she's arrived."

I thought I'd inquire about Lady Bloodshed on my own. I couldn't bear to see more carnage. I wondered what point there was to staying here. Everyone would be desperate, hateful, angry, and afraid. It truly would be like touring Hell. Who would even do that?

"What about those HID agents? Skip and Reg?" I asked.

"We passed them already," Auric said. "Crucified. I didn't call them out to you, because I didn't want you to fret over it."

I didn't know what to think, honestly, given how they'd threatened me. I had somehow thought they might fare better than they had.

"They didn't die well," Auric said. "Secret police aren't nearly as effective without the power of a state behind them. They were adrift, and Willard Wilkins had captivated them into thinking he might prevail against Al Qatil. Alas, they chose poorly, and paid for it. Ironic, really, given their religiosity. Would you like to see more atrocities? As I said, the Americans here are not faring well—too disorganized to really take advantage of their new environment, and, weirdly, too corrupt."

"Too corrupt?" I asked.

"The moral bankruptcy of the GNP is absolute," Auric said. "And depended too heavily on the remaining wealth and power of the legacy CSA. Without the Polygon to protect them, the GNP has found itself at a decided disadvantage relative to their rivals here. Not to say there aren't plenty of American military personnel here, but they've allied with their military leaders, not partisan GNP hacks, televangelists, and talk show hosts. While they are well-armed and trained, they're not nearly as numerous as their rivals, and are finding they're having to lend their services out as mercenaries."

"Christ," I said. "I don't know what to say about that."

And I didn't. The Polygon was the most lavishly financed military apparatus in human history, with a level of funding that dwarfed those of dozens of nations. But without that infrastructure, boiling it down to the military personnel who were banished to Mars, my Auricle told me there were about 120,000 Polygon troops here.

"But no tanks, warplanes, aircraft carriers, submarines, bombers, missile launchers, nuclear weapons, etc.," Auric said. "Just boots on the ground. It poses problems in terms of battlefield supremacy."

Auric had thought it all through, of course. Mars deserved better than what it got, but when the Martian dust settled, and peace arrived at last, it would be a planet ready for proper colonization, with only the ghosts of past evils remaining, and a dark forest somewhere across its surface, the last charge of outright villainy. It gave me chills even within the warmth of the greenhouse sanctuary.

"No," I said. "Let's go home."

And we did, and it was good. I thought of that forest of the future, the Sea of Trees, the throngs of survivors who would find the Sanctuary and be tricked into their own oblivion. It felt strange to me that Auric would rig the game against them. Of course, Auric read my mind.

"Why should I reward those survivors for simply being the most successful at being evil?" Auric said. "That would be uncivilized. They'll be better trees than they ever were as humans. From my perspective, letting them be trees is the best reward they could hope for."

Still, the image of that Sea of Trees haunted me. The first honest colonists to Mars would see those forests and all the bones of the dead scattered throughout the planet, and what would they tell themselves? No one would ever know.

"Except for you, Chronicler," Auric said. "It's a burden you'll be entrusted to carry with you forever."

I wondered how long it would take.

"Not as long as you might think. Evil is corrupt, but it can be efficient at times, well-greased by its own immorality," Auric said. "Let's get you back where you belong."

CHAPTER

SIX

———

AURIC RODE THANATOS to Earth while the cameras rolled and the world freaked. Despite his assurances that he'd save the planet from it, when the sky lit up with the asteroid, people couldn't help but be afraid. Even I was afraid, Minerva and me watching it from my living room, on the big television screen.

I mean, it was a veritable mountain flying through the atmosphere, burning brightly, like a little star. And upon that asteroid, amid the friction-fueled fire, was golden Auric, standing there, like he was surfing. I mean, that's what it looked like.

He rode Thanatos all the way down to Streeterville, and when it got right to the point of impact, when the thing loomed over downtown Chicago, Auric slowed the fiery asteroid down until it stopped cold. The amount of force he'd dissipated was unimaginable. He broke physics in that moment and didn't even sweat it.

Arms upraised, golden Auric stood there atop Thanatos, having saved humankind from certain extinction yet again. It was like it was a magic trick, except that there was no magic, and he wasn't tricking us. He pivoted off it, gliding to the ground, while Thanatos hovered there, harmless, now, through his undeniable omnipotence. To see that space mountain standing there that way in the heart of Chicago, it was awe-inspiring and terrifying.

"As promised," Auric said, addressing the stunned reporters from around the world who'd gathered at ground zero, literally beneath the shadow of Thanatos. "I have saved your world from Thanatos. Nobody prayed it away. It wasn't a miracle. I stopped it. That's my covenant to your species. I'm not going to live your lives for you. And I'm not going to dictate how you live, beyond providing my Advisements on how you might become more civilized. I'm not an invader, although I am an alien. Your lives are your own, to live as you like. I'll be here, my Auricles will assist you, should you require it. I urge you to make the most of the reprieve I've given you. The breathing space you need to thrive as a species."

He gestured to the floating mountain of Thanatos. It was testament to the Aurician Era (as I and others saw it) that something like the stopping of Thanatos could have been a blasé event; we were becoming used to miracles. Of course Auric was true to his word. Of course he stopped it from destroying Earth.

"This asteroid is the universe," Auric said. "It traveled many billions of miles to get to your world, without intention, without malice, but with the capacity to annihilate your world. You are adrift on your little planet—your watery ball of air and rock—in a universe that's both unfathomably empty and packed with probabilistic missiles that will come, sooner or later. You owe it to yourselves to not give the last laugh to a ruthless universe. If you don't care for yourselves, no one will. I'm going to settle Thanatos offshore here in Chicago, creating an island. A monument to this moment. Any time you wonder whether there's some grand plan to the universe, just look at Thanatos Island. What you call 'God' didn't bring me here. I'm neither God nor a god. I'm just a fellow space traveler like yourselves, adrift in the universe. We all are. Let's make the most of the space-time that we have."

He didn't take questions, only floated Thanatos over Streeterville, taking it a mile out from the shore, and very gently deposited it into Lake Michigan.

Thanatos looked foreboding. I mean, it was a big-ass asteroid. It was impossible to ignore. Had Auric allowed it to strike Earth, we'd have all died horribly.

Auric settled it into the lake, and even going deep into the water, all the way in, Thanatos was dauntingly large. Auric buried it a mile into the lakebed and it still had several miles of vertical height.

And what a thing it was, this great asteroid, pockmarked and cratered, this celestial traveler. No one ever saw something like that. It was expected to smash into the planet and disintegrate from the physics of the heat and impact.

"Earth is under my protection, whether it wants to be or not," Auric said, when he'd returned to shore, the shadow of Thanatos behind him. "Go about your lives as you will. If you have questions of me, ask them. Live free in peace and prosperity. It's all I want for you."

"What about Mars? What about Venus?" some of the reporters asked, trying to shout over one another to be heard.

"They are living their own lives," Auric said. "Pursuing their own destinies."

"Did you send that asteroid?" another reporter asked.

"I did not," Auric said. "If the implication is that I did this as a kind of ploy, please understand that I'm far above and beyond such chicanery. Have you noticed that your prisons are empty? That the rogue regimes around the world have fallen? That's because they're on Venus and Mars, where they belong. They're not alone—many uncaught criminals, those who'd evaded your legal systems—were caught by me, as well. You can mourn for those on Mars and Venus, but they are where they belong. And there remains the possibility for rehabilitation and return, in the case of those on Venus. It's entirely in their hands."

"But not Mars," a reporter said.

"But not Mars," Auric said.

"I should be there," Minerva said. "I'm going there right now."

She stood up and touched the lapel pin she wore, but nothing happened. She touched it once, twice, thrice.

"Auricle," Minerva said. "Why aren't you taking me to Auric?"

She received an answer in her earpiece.

"What'd it say?" I asked.

"It said it was for my own self-protection that I *not* appear beside Auric," Minerva said. "He feels that people are still too hostile to the Auricians."

She cursed, paced, and watched the screen.

"It's brand poisoning, that's what it is," Minerva said. "They're hating on us for what Auric did."

Watching her pace, I wondered. I was always wondering.

"Who's 'they' in this context?" I asked. "The RAN and LAX News are both gutted when he purged their people. Who's saying it?"

"The other media channels," Minerva said. "They're not going on the air and calling us traitors, but the insinuation is there. They refer to us as 'Auric-adjacent' as if that's a bad thing."

The news broke in and the broadcaster declared that the UN General Assembly had voted on another measure, asking that Auric leave the Earth.

"Notice that the vote came through *after* he saved the Earth from Thanatos?" Minerva said. "How's that for gratitude?"

I was concerned about that, what it meant for Auric, for us, for the world. Would he abide by such a ruling? What would that mean for the things he'd created? Would they persist if he were gone?

"That's all I have time for right now," Auric said, vanishing in a flash of golden light. He reappeared in my living room, to the great relief of me and the consternation of Minerva.

"Auric," Minerva said, before I could. "Did you see the UN vote?"

"I'm aware of it," Auric said.

"And?"

"And nothing," Auric said. "I have a responsibility to protect the planet."

"But they're voting you off," I said. "You have to respect that, don't you?"

"Do I?" Auric asked. "They're afraid."

"They're ungrateful," Minerva said. "That's what they are. You literally just saved the world. Again."

She kept pacing, until Auric stopped her with a golden hand. He actually embraced her, hugged her, soothed her. I felt immediately jealous but told myself that Auric surely had a degree of intimacy with everyone close to him. The Cosmic Awesome loved freely.

"It's okay, Minerva," Auric said, releasing her, looking her in the eye. "I'm not going to abandon the planet."

"But we're all pariahs," Minerva said. "Your Auricians."

"Yes," Auric said. "That is a problem. But you're all protected."

"Protected, yes," Minerva said. "But they're shunning us, too. We're being shunned. Everywhere we go."

"I know," Auric said. "They can't attack me, so they're attacking you."

"It's not fair," Minerva said. "We've only been trying to live up to your ideals. All we did was try to help the way you've helped, on our own tiny levels."

I watched them and wondered if this was all part of Auric's plan, having me witness this and wonder. I could tell Minerva wasn't pretending or play-acting. She was sincerely upset. I felt like I needed to say something but wasn't sure what that should be.

"What if you renounced and denounced Auric?" I asked. Minerva turned on me, eyes flashing.

"I'd die before I did that," Minerva said. "I will *never* do that. I don't even know why you'd say that."

"If you wanted to be accepted, I mean. Just a thought," I said.

"A bad thought," Minerva said. "Auric *is* the savior of humanity."

Auric sighed because he knew it was true. We all knew it, but hearing Minerva say it that way, it was somehow unseemly. Auric didn't want to be seen that way, but the moral imperative to act had driven him to do the things he had done.

"Change management is difficult," Auric said. "I've foisted a tremendous amount of change onto people's plates these past months. Probably too much, too soon. But circumstances required timely and decisive action. The luxury of waiting was long gone."

"The Auricians need their own country," I said. "A place to call their own. That way, they can live in peace. And you can live there, Auric. It can be your excuse to remain on the planet."

Auric smiled at my suggestion, and I knew he'd already known I was going to say that. It was impossible to surprise Auric. The mention of a country startled Minerva into stopping her pacing.

"A country? Where?" Minerva asked.

"Anywhere," Auric said.

"Someplace temperate," I said. "Not too hot or cold."

"Atlantis," Minerva said. "That's basically what you're saying."

"It could be on the moon," Auric said. "Or in orbit. Or on Earth."

I saw a golden space station, a spaceship, another planet, even. Something otherworldly. Auric glanced at me, his blue eyes bright with divine light.

"So long as you remain on Earth, you're in danger, in some respect," Auric said. "I'll solve for that by building you a worldship."

He raised a hand and, in a moment, we were aboard a golden planet. Even being used to Auric's power, it was still a stunning thing. One moment, there was nothing. Another moment, we were aboard a planet he'd created out of nothing.

Like everything he created, it was beautiful. We walked to a grand window, the kind of thing one would never see in a terrestrial spaceship, but what you'd see in movies. Something that offered a stunning vista, in this case, the Earth, green and blue and white, healed and healthy, in the distance. Near us was a rolling landscape, a world Auric had made for us.

This golden world, this creation of Auric's, was a planetary paradise—pristine, verdant, full of trees and wildlife. The colors were typical of some of Auric's creations, being a blend of gold, white, and blue. It gave me chills, seeing this creation appear out of nothing. I touched the glass of the viewing room.

"It's not glass," Auric said, as if to reassure me. "It's a display panel. The planet is pure Auricanium—indestructible. Roughly the size of the Moon. We're a safe distance from the Earth, so as to avoid any gravitational concerns."

The interior of the viewing chamber, at least where we were, was ultramodernist white. I felt like we were on a Stanley Kubrick set—I remembered seeing some black market movies of his that my parents had secreted away. But there were plants growing in pots around us, and water burbling. This cavernous room was like an audience chamber.

"How many people can live on this world?" I asked.

"It can support all of the Auricians and their progeny," Auric said.

"So, how many?"

"All the ones he didn't banish," Minerva said, recovering herself. "And what about that, Auric? Why the hell did you banish those Auricians?"

"They were bad people," Auric said. "Someone's not good simply because they've called themselves an Aurician, Minerva. You know that. I had to be fair and impartial."

"Still, that's cruel," she said. "They're banished. They're dead."

Auric sighed. "It defeats the purpose of pointing to a better way if one exempts one's own followers from moral consideration. Therein resides the root of corruption. Those self-professed Auricians were filled with opportunists and fanatics who piled on to join when they thought I was going to take over the world. They joined up for the wrong reasons, thinking I wouldn't know the difference."

Brand management, Auric-style, as ever. I thought it through.

"This planet's able to carry 40,000 people?" I asked. "The original Auricians?"

"Yes," Auric said. "With the capacity for many more. It's a worldship—designed for multiple generations of passengers and travelers. A world unto itself."

Minerva thought about it, and I was thinking about it, too. I mean, originally, it was just going to be me traveling with Auric throughout the cosmos, but now I wondered if it would be me and the Auricians traveling the spaceways. Not like I wanted to have Auric all to myself, but it did kind of stick in my craw. Like it made it something else—I would just be one of many thousands of Auricians.

"I'm in," Minerva said, cocking an eyebrow at me. It looked like she'd found a way to get on board, after all.

"I don't want anyone following me to suffer for their loyalty," Auric said. "And you're right in that people detest you for your participation in what happened, in what I did."

"They already are," Minerva said. "But what about the people living in the Auric Towers?"

"They're not doctrinal Auricians per se," Auric said. "Merely beneficiaries of my celestial assistance."

"Won't they be treated that way, too?" Minerva asked. "With hostility and revulsion?"

"The Auric Towers remain," Auric said. "Remember, I'll leave a planetary protector there—one of me will remain on Earth as a steward."

"That's weird," I said. "I don't even know how you do that."

"Omnipresence is always harder to comprehend than omniscience and omnipotence," Auric said. "It's okay, you don't have to comprehend it. The reality is that the beneficiaries of the Auric Towers were already social misfits in your world—before I came to your planet, they were the homeless, the poor, the addicted, and the vulnerable. They were not well-treated in your country or throughout the world in some other countries. Since becoming part of the Auric Towers, they've been cured and cleansed of addictions, are enjoying skills training and life planning, and above all, they have safe shelter and ready access to healthy food and drink. The addition of the Volitionators on the premises offers them still more options. They understand the benefit they have with their association with me. I don't think they'll lightly cast that aside. The larger concern is for the majority, the ones who failed to care for them when they were able to—obviously, I've taken care of the worst of the lot, but we'll see what happens now that the *Book of Don't* is widely circulated and increasingly understood."

"Yeah, we'll see," I said.

I had wanted to travel with Auric as his Chronicler but had envisioned it as more of a one-on-one sort of thing. I hadn't imagined being a passenger on a planet, one I was fairly sure Minerva would be running as its queen or governess or whatever title it turned out to be.

"Where will the worldship go?" I asked.

"Anywhere it wants to," Auric said. "Out there. Exploring space. As an extension of me, it can cross interstellar and intergalactic distances quite readily. You won't have to worry about growing old and dying while transiting star systems, Christian. Besides, you don't have to worry about that."

Minerva pouted.

"Why should the Chronicler get *that* benefit, Auric?" Minerva asked. "Shouldn't we all get the benefit of immorality?"

"Is that what you want, Minerva? Immortality?" Auric asked. "It's not the boon you think it is."

Minerva looked positively peevish. Even that was charming on her face. She was a woman used to getting whatever she wanted. For her, immortality was just another accessory she wanted to add to her carefully-curated life.

"Still, it's not fair that Christian gets that, and others don't," Minerva said.

"The Chronicler has a specific role," Auric said. "It requires a long view."

"Yes, but I want that, too," Minerva said. "I don't want to grow old and die."

"You won't," Auric said. "Not for a long time. The improvements I've provided to health and lifestyle alone add considerably to one's life expectancy."

Minerva was not swayed.

"But it's *not* immortality," Minerva said, glaring at me even as she was addressing Auric.

"No, it's not," Auric said. "I'm sorry."

"So, you won't grant it to me," Minerva said.

"I gave you the capacity to teleport," Auric said. "That was your special boon."

"Ah," Minerva said. "One boon per follower? Is that it?"

"One shouldn't be greedy," Auric said. "Right?"

"Dammit," Minerva said, stomping a foot, before, reluctantly nodding. "Yes, I see your point."

"You are my Herald, Minerva," Auric said. "That's a critical role for which you are perfectly suited. Christian is my Chronicler. The same applies to him. You work together as a team. You can appear anywhere you like, in the blink of an eye. And Christian can live as long as he likes and appear where he needs to observe something. Those abilities allow you to perform the tasks integral to your respective roles. I have chosen you for those roles. If you wish to pass those duties on to others, you need only tell me, and I will do so."

"Still sounds like Christian has two abilities, not one," Minerva said.

"Immortality is not an ability," Auric said. "It is a state of being. And technically, you have another ability, in that you are protected from harm by me. You're functionally invulnerable."

"That makes three for Christian," Minerva said. "You love him."

"I love you all," Auric said.

Minerva swallowed her pride and nodded. I knew as well as she did that she'd never want to stop being Auric's Herald, whatever that precisely was. Moreover, she was known around the world for her work on Auric's behalf. There was no ordinary life for her to return to, even if she wanted to.

"Do all of the Auricians have chosen roles like that?" I asked.

"No," Auric said.

"We're *special*," Minerva said, smiling sarcastically at me. I could tell it still bothered her that I was the Chronicler, maybe because, in her mind, it was less work than being Auric's Herald.

"What does the Herald do, exactly?" I asked.

"I'm still Auric's PR person," Minerva said. "I'm there to represent him and his perspective in a manner that people can understand."

"Not to throw shade or anything, but Auric and the Auricians are in a really bad place right now, in terms of popular perception," I said. Minerva's eyes narrowed as she stared at me, hand on her hip.

"Are you saying I did a bad job, Christian?"

Auric interceded, golden hands upraised in that placating way he had.

"It's my fault," Auric said. "Minerva did an excellent job. But with all of the things I'd done, no one could have truly change managed all of it effectively. Minerva was outstanding, but I radically altered life on Earth in a very short amount of time, as I'd already said."

"Yeah," Minerva said. "Jesus, Christian. You have no idea how difficult it was. It's easy to be a critic from the comfort of your sectional."

"Alright," I said. "I wasn't suggesting anything."

"You kind of were," Minerva said.

Auric put his arms out and guided us from the grand viewing room.

"Let me take you both on a tour of the worldship," Auric said.

CHAPTER

SEVEN

THE WORLDSHIP WAS INSANE. It was a giant golden sphere, around 2000 miles in diameter, according to Auric. It was divided up into several key areas, internally and externally—there was a command deck at the equator, a massive hydroponic area—an internal forest habitat, really, enough passenger quarters to house around two million people in comfort, as well as a host of other resources and amenities.

The landscape was a perfect blend of land, lakes, rivers, and seas. Of golden-leafed forests, rolling hills, mountains, and plains. The climate ranged from cold, to temperate, to hot, and there were villages and cities in the Aurician style dotted throughout.

"Why not simply make a natural world?" I asked. Auric smiled at me, relishing my questions as much as ever.

"This is something else," Auric said. "It's not simply a rogue world. It's a new Aurician homeworld."

"What about light? It won't have its own Sun," I said.

"It will," Auric said. "Once it's underway and leaves this system behind."

There were dozens of to-be-opened restaurants, theaters, arcades, nightclubs, pools of unique configurations, three massive parks, an interactive holographic planetarium, an all-purpose sports stadium (seating capacity of 40,000), a library of over 25 million books, and a host of other amenities.

I wondered who would be working in the restaurants, clubs, and theaters. I'm sure Auric had an answer for it, but I still wondered, and didn't ask. He answered, anyway.

"The businesses are all co-ops," Auric said. "The restaurants will be serving food I've created for them, subdivided into casual and fine dining. All are welcome."

"Seems weird," I said. "Restaurants that serve your created food."

"There's an opportunity for diversification once the hydroponic gardens come into their own," Auric said. "There is a seed bank allowing for the growing of all terrestrial food crops."

"What about livestock?" I asked.

"The worldship is nominally vegetarian," Auric said. "There are meat substitutes."

"Of course there are," I said.

"You don't approve?" Auric asked.

"No, it's fine," I said. "You've thought of everything, as ever."

"It's what I do," Auric said, shrugging.

Everything was beautifully, classically rendered in those Auric sorts of combinations of gold and white and blue, with what looked like white marble prominently represented.

"The worldship has the capacity of a small moon," Auric said. "I want everyone aboard it to feel at home."

"It's incredible," I said. We were on a golden balcony that overlooked the Promenade, a long stretch that was envisioned as public meeting place, with comfortable seating nooks throughout and abundant trees.

"It's amazing," Minerva said. "Luxurious."

"And quite indestructible, as I'd told you," Auric said.

"Right," I said. "What's the purpose of this worldship, exactly?"

"It's a sanctuary for the first new Auricians," Auric said. "There's a portal at the end of the Promenade that's permanently linked to Earth. If people get homesick, they can simply step through it and they'll be transported to Earth. To get back to the worldship, they need merely step through the portal on the terrestrial side."

"What happens if they block that portal on the Earth side?" I asked. I was always thinking about those contingencies. Maybe it was part of trendscaping.

"I won't let that happen," Auric said. "Only Auricians can access the worldship. And you, of course, Christian."

"Of course," Minerva said. "Auric's favorite."

Auric smiled and patted Minerva's arm.

"There's no room for envy and jealousy aboard the worldship," Auric said.

Up on the balcony, gazing out across the empty Promenade, hearing the bubbling of the fountains, I was struck by the amazing beauty of the place, and how Auric had so effortlessly conjured it, the way he did everything.

"To be able to make such things, it's astounding," I said.

"I chose the original Auricians carefully," Auric said. "Every Aurician is very special—by my reckoning, some of the best humanity has to offer. With an even split of 20,000 females and 20,000 males, that's more than enough to repopulate any planet you encounter, with plenty to spare."

"It's another part of your experiment," I said. "All of this."

"I think of it as another branch of the tree of human life," Auric said. "There's legacy Earth—albeit vastly improved—and there's this worldship, consisting entirely of Auricians. There's also Venus and Mars, but you know that Mars is a literal dead end in my grand undertaking, and Venus won't entirely depopulate."

"All of this just because we mentioned how people hate the Auricians, now?" Minerva said. "We rate all of this?"

"While I'm fair, it doesn't mean I won't help those who were brave enough to embrace me early on," Auric said. "The true followers of my creed, versus the ones who tried to join the Aurician ranks for their own bad reasons."

"In other words, this is Paradise," I said.

Auric smirked at me, an alien look on his alien face.

"It's eminently more practical than paradise," Auric said. "It's more of a starting point than a destination. A chance for the Apostles of the Aurician creed to push out from your own solar system to colonize other planets."

"It's an insurance policy," I said. "In case the people on Earth blow it."

Auric treated me to another omniscient smile.

"It's the least I can do," Auric said. "Your world is your world. It's possible they'll make mistakes and still manage to exterminate themselves. Maybe they'll try to rescue the people on Venus and Mars and reintroduce evil people into their midst in a misguided attempt at justice or compassion."

Minerva shook her head, leaning on the golden railing.

"I don't see how that can happen if you're leaving behind a planetary protector," she said. "You won't let that happen."

Auric met her gaze evenly, his voice calm and soothing.

"My planetary protectors won't intervene. I've saved the planet, and I've saved not only your species, but many other species you share the world with," Auric said. "I'll protect the planet from extraplanetary threats, but I will respect the sovereignty of your species. While they can consult with me and ask questions of me, I won't interfere any more than I already have."

"Huh," Minerva said.

"Not even to save us from ourselves?" I asked.

"I already have," Auric said. "The question is whether I have to keep doing that. If I do, then I'm simply enabling ongoing bad behavior. I'd like to think that the *Book of Don't* will allow for people to coexist peacefully and civilly. But I think humans could still find a way to kill themselves. If that happens, well, I guess we'll see what happens."

"You already know," Minerva said. "You know our fate."

Auric looked at both of us in turn, his golden visage unreadable.

"Fate and probability are quantum cousins," Auric said. "But they are not siblings. If you step off a building, it's not fate that decides your fate; it's gravity, and your self-destructive urges. If you engage in risky behaviors, it's not your fate to die from them. Rather, you're increasing the probability that you will die from those risky behaviors. Strike the hornet's nest enough times, and you will eventually get stung."

"Alright," I said. "And the *Book of Don't* is your advising us not to strike that hornet's nest."

"Correct," Auric said. "It's not *that* hard, in truth, to be a good person."

I could see in Minerva's eyes that she was already transporting herself and the others aboard the worldship to someplace beyond.

"What're we using the worldship for? To colonize other worlds? To explore?" Minerva asked.

"Both," Auric said. "As I'd said, the worldship can comfortably hold up to around two million people. When it nears that carrying capacity, it will be necessary for some of the passengers to offload on a new world."

"How many?" Minerva asked.

"The bare minimum viable number, evolutionarily, would be anywhere from 2500 to 5000 people," Auric said. "That would be sufficient to populate a suitable planet."

As ever, where Auric was concerned, I was daunted by the logistics of it. I was envisioning this golden globe floating through space, or teleporting around the cosmos, spreading human beings like dandelion seeds.

Auric could see me brooding on it, and though I knew he already knew what I was brooding about, he spoke.

"What's the matter, Christian?" Auric asked.

"Okay, so let's say whoever's in command of the worldship guides it to Planet X," I said. "And they drop off 5000 colonists. Do you include one of you with them? One of your planetary protectors?"

"I would," Auric said. "To do otherwise would be uncivilized, akin to marooning people on an unfamiliar world without an ally."

"Sure," I said. "But what do you do? Hang back while people build a world from scratch? Or do you build Auricvilles like you did on Venus and Mars?"

"Auricvilles?" Minerva said. "You're so flippant, Christian."

Auric chuckled.

"No," Auric said. "Venus and Mars were special, unique cases. I wouldn't want to deprive the colonists of the worthwhile human challenge of settling a world."

I didn't want to shade the effort, but I had real concerns.

"We're talking alien worlds," I said. "No offense. It's not like hopping off a cruise ship for a bit of interstellar tourism. Unless the colonists are trained in homesteading, they're going to end up dead."

"I'll protect them," Auric said.

"Of course you will," I said. "But they're going to need that protection and they're going to need your help. It's like when the Pilgrims first arrived at the New World. They were starving to death. If not for the Native Americans—the ones who weren't yet killed by the introduction of smallpox and measles brought by the Europeans—showing the Pilgrims how to actually successfully grow crops, they'd have all died out."

"Jesus, Christian," Minerva said.

"I'm saying that they're going to be entirely dependent on you, Auric," I said. "The colonists will be leaning on you at every turn. Because they're not going to be xenobiologists, or electricians, or engineers, or physicians. I mean, you tapped 40,000 people as Auricians, but this worldship is going to have to have Colonist Training 101. You'll need a Minimum Viable Colony Unit in your consideration of the drop-offs."

Auric's smile stopped Minerva from shading me further, because he knew I was right, and maybe he'd already thought of that. Maybe his choice of Auricians had already taken that into account.

"The worldship will have the resources and time to train people in the necessary colonial functions for viability," Auric said. "I'd already preselected the 40,000 along those lines."

"Alright, so the medical personnel," I said. "Are we talking general practitioners or specialists? Because there's a lot of need for specialty care.

Or, again, since you healed us and cured us, we're okay? Or, further, if and when people get sick or injured, they just turn to you?"

"Thoughts and prayers," Minerva said. "It hardly matters, Christian. We have Auric. Auric is everything."

"We're going to need to solve those problems ourselves," I said. "If we're to make real progress. Progress comes through problem-solving. And Auric solved Earth's problems—or at least many of the ones we refused to solve ourselves. But do we really deserve to be the species colonizing the cosmos? If Auric hadn't come along, we'd have been part of the 99.9 percent of extinct species. We'd be one of those ruined civilizations he's said he's seen scattered throughout space."

"Way to kill the mood, Christian," Minerva said. "Auric's on our side. That's more than good enough for me."

Auric transported us to the Promenade floor and let us walk the length of it with him as he talked.

"You raise interesting points, Christian," Auric said, and, of course, I knew he'd already thought of them all. Maybe his saying as much was for Minerva's benefit.

"Christian the Cosmic Killjoy," Minerva said.

"If you want us to kill you, can't you just create something that would do it and show us how to use it?" I asked. "Why all of this celestial kabuki, having us tour the universe with you as cosmic conquistadors?"

"It's a far grander game than that, Christian," Auric replied. "While there's a certain pragmatism to your suggestion, it wouldn't work. I can't create the equivalent of a celestial noose and hang myself with it. Or even hand it to you and let you do that. It has to evolve."

Minerva hated me even bringing that up, I could tell.

"You shouldn't die, Auric," Minerva said. "You can't. We love you. I love you."

"I love you, too," Auric said. "The worldship can populate an infinite number of worlds, given enough time. It's self-sustaining. That will allow human beings to colonize widely and create independent civilizations. One of them may find the way to destroy me someday."

"And say that happens," Minerva said. "What about the rest of it? If one of you dies, does all of you die? Does the worldship vanish? Does all of it disappear?"

I could hear the plaintive nature of her questions, her concern. Minerva didn't want any of it to end. She did sincerely and truly love Auric. I did, too, in my own weird way. It was different, though.

"Despite my many incarnations, I'm a singleton," Auric said. "Were I to cease, the rest of me would become inert, yes. But the things I created would endure. The worldship would continue, although it would function more conventionally, would lose its portal linking ability, and would need to rely on its self-sustaining life support in the form of food crops and the like. But my demise isn't likely to happen anytime soon. You're wondering about something that's likely a billion years away from now, and even then, only if your species is incredibly successful and is still around to see it."

We walked through the empty Promenade, which looked majestic and forlorn at the same time, because no one was in it besides us. I imagined how it would appear with all the Auricians ambling through it, starry-eyed.

I didn't want to be an Aurician.

I *wasn't* an Aurician.

I wasn't a joiner.

I wanted to be with Auric and watch him do his thing, versus becoming a space colonist like the Auricians.

"And what about other alien civilizations?" I asked. "Supposing we find another living civilization? Then what? We come tooling up in our golden globe, with our golden god, and when what? Hand out the *Book of Don't* to them? It's from an anthropocentric perspective, for sure. What if the aliens are hostile to us? I mean, we lucked out that you're not hostile, but what if *they* are hostile? Then what? Do you destroy that civilization because you're protecting us?"

"Wow, Christian," Minerva said. "Are you always like this?"

"Trendscaper's gonna trendscape," I said.

"I had no idea you were such a catastrophist," Minerva said.

"I think about possibilities and contingencies," I said. "A few are great, some are good, most are bad."

Auric naturally had an answer. That was the thing about being omniscient—you always have an answer.

"If I were to use the Kardashev Scale parameters," Auric said. "Then it's at least conceivable that a powerful enough civilization could destroy me. It would have to be an extraordinarily powerful society to do that. It might be another singleton like myself, which could be interesting."

"A mate," I said.

"An intriguing idea, Christian. A peer, at the very least," Auric said. "Yes, that would be something. But if they were less advanced, it wouldn't particularly matter if they were warlike or hostile. Applying my Advisements, you'd be able to interact with them peacefully."

"And if they weren't peaceful, then what? You turn them into trees?" I asked. "You'd have to protect us—that'd be the civilized thing to do, right? Protect us from the alien barbarians? But what if they're not barbarians, but are merely very, very different from us and hostile? Then what?"

"In that case, I'd serve as a mediator between your two species," Auric said. "I'd facilitate and encourage cross-cultural dialogue and diplomacy. That would be the civilized thing to do."

Minerva scoffed as she walked with us.

"You're, what, a Kardashev Type IV, Auric? Effectively off the scales?" Minerva asked.

"Maybe I am," Auric said. "Or Type V."

"Why aren't you off hopping to other dimensions?" Minerva asked. "Why bother with us at all?"

"That sounds like a Christian question," Auric asked.

"He's rubbing off on me," Minerva said, managing to toss a smile my way.

"It would be inhumane to simply leave for another dimension," Auric said. "Besides, while there are intractable problems of tantalizing delight in other dimensions, it doesn't mean one can't find plenty to do in this dimension. Besides, who's to say I'm not in those other dimensions as well?"

"Are you?" I asked.

"No, believe it or not," Auric said. "I haven't fully explored this universe or dimension. I feel like I haven't earned extradimensionality, yet."

"So humble," Minerva said, and she meant it.

"There are so many dimensions to you already, Auric," I said, earning me a fresh scoff from Minerva and an all-knowing laugh from Auric.

"To go back to your earlier question," Auric said. "I won't be a weapon to destroy alien races for your species. I will defend you, but it'll still fall to your species to equitably and credibly represent yourselves to an alien audience. I'd like to think that I've chosen the original Auricians well enough that they won't simply go to war with anybody who's not like them."

The Promenade seemed to go forever, and part of me wondered if it was a circle, but because of the vagaries of gravity and what-not, it didn't feel like it. I looked behind us, and all I saw was the Promenade. Looking ahead of us, I saw the same thing.

"I wasn't talking about us attacking them so much as them attacking us," I said.

"I'll defend your species," Auric said. "But I won't commit xenocide."

"What if they're a *really* hostile species?" I asked. "Or, worse, like parasites or something?"

"I'll protect you," Auric said. "I really can't say that any other way. An unremittingly hostile alien species is, from my perspective, not unlike a rogue asteroid or comet, or a magnetar, or the equivalent. It's a threat that I'd fully protect you from."

"Nice that you have our backs, Auric," Minerva said.

"With all the bad and nasty people on Venus and Mars, how will we defend ourselves in the future?" I asked. "As unpleasant as psychopaths and evil people are, they are good at taking down enemies."

"You'll find newer, better ways of conflict resolution," Auric said. "You're right that there is survival value to some of those bad qualities. But only for the bad person at the expense of the rest of society. Bad people are bad actors. They operate with impunity and fail to accept responsibility for their actions. They lie constantly, both to themselves and to others. The harm they bring outweighs any benefit one can hope to glean from their relentless ruthlessness."

"Yeah," Minerva said. "We're better off without them, Christian."

"Although I still don't think we deserve you," I said. "Riding shotgun with you across the universe feels like a cheat. Like we're celestial missionaries or something, spreading the word."

"The comparison isn't apt," Auric said. "The missionaries of your past were cultural conquerors, fueled by greed for gold and land, bathed in bigotry, and justifying it through a fervent religious belief in their own righteousness. It was abetted by the early form of germ warfare that contributed to the death of over 90 percent of Native Americans—over 50 million people died because of the European invasion of the New World."

"There'll be culture clashes," I said. "We're still human. It's what we do. We clash with things."

"We'll be peaceful and civilized," Minerva said, a trifle annoyed at my line of inquiry. "With Auric, we'll be better than we ever were."

We reached the other end of the Promenade, which ended in another of those evocative windows—or meta-windows, since Auric talked about how dangerous windows actually were in spaceships. It offered a stellar view of the Earth. Everything Auric was stellar. He was interstellar.

"*The Book of Don't* is not culture- or species-specific," Auric said. "It can be applied successfully across the universe and leave the universe a more civilized place."

"I guess," I said.

"You guess?" Minerva said. "Come on, Christian."

"I guess we'll see," I said. "I'm an empiricist, not an imperialist."

Minerva rolled her eyes, while Auric only smiled.

The worldship was rotating, creating its own gravity, so the image of the Earth was sliding out of the frame, and we were turning slowly toward a view of space. The sea of darkness and the stars, it was lovely and frightening. The vastness of it all was overwhelming. The thought of this worldship traveling out there that way, it was weird to imagine. I didn't belong here. I certainly didn't want to be part of some Aurician crew, with Minerva running the show. No offense to her—she was a great and natural leader. The Auricians would go far with her. It's just that I wasn't an Aurician.

Despite it all, I simply wasn't.

And part of me tried to figure out why, like on my own, without asking my Auricle for insight. Auric knew I was thinking about this, and he didn't say anything.

I believed in Auric. There wasn't even an article of faith in it. Auric simply was. He was as incontrovertible and awesome as gravity. I understood that he was good by any human definition of the word. I was not afraid of him.

"I'm not going with you, Minerva," I said. "I'm staying with Auric."

Minerva was surprised by this, but Auric wasn't, of course.

"Why?" Minerva asked.

"It just feels right," I said. "I'll stay with Auric and see where he goes."

Minerva shook her head, unable to believe what she was hearing. She wanted me with her, jealously didn't like the idea of me being by Auric's side. Auric-Prime. However we chose to view it.

"I'll be with you as well, Minerva," Auric said. "Worldship Auric will be here."

"While you and Christian do what? Explore the universe?" Minerva asked, her heart wounded. Even I could see it.

"As Chronicler, I feel like I need to see that stuff, how it plays out. It's easy to walk with Auric. He makes everything better. I need to see things myself, unmediated," I said.

332 | DEAN VALE

"I respect your decision, Christian," Auric said. "And I'm always here if you need me, Minerva. And by 'here' I mean 'everywhere' of course."

Minerva pretended to be dismayed by my decision, but I think part of her was glad for it. Without me there, the Herald of Auric could carry out her own mission without feeling like she was being watched by the inquisitive, inactivist Chronicler. Her jealousy and envy would be mitigated by the prospect of leading the worldship.

Not that she was up to anything, but I think it suited her, somehow, to not have me there. The fact that I was the first person on the Earth to meet Auric always bothered her. I would always be a pain point with her.

"Good luck with the worldship," I said. "Incidentally, what are you going to name it?"

Minerva didn't waste a beat.

"The *Acropolis*," she said.

"Well, alright. That tracks," I said.

PART III

CHAPTER

EIGHT

———

I KNOW IT PROBABLY SEEMS like an anticlimax with everything that happened, but there it was. The Auricians were all transported up to the *Acropolis,* to the immense relief of any number of Auric's critics, and Minerva addressed the world with a message she was born to deliver, broadcast at the UN General Assembly, with the others standing with her—John, Yuko, Dan, Tessa, and dozens of other Apostles. I'm sorry I didn't get to spend more time with the other Apostles of Auric; I tried to focus on as much as I could.

"We understand that our work on behalf of Auric has caused considerable discontentment among you," Minerva said. "We're sorry that many of you consider us traitors to the species. But we only ever acted according to the moral Advisements of the *Book of Don't* that Auric gave us. We didn't kill anyone, and we helped everyone, as Auric wanted us to. We are leaving the solar system to peacefully colonize the galaxy aboard the worldship, *Acropolis.*"

At the mention of it, the screen showed cuts of life aboard the beautiful golden globe, where happy Auricians walked about, looking peaceful and contented in their white clothes. The loveliness of the ship was absolute and undeniable, like everything Auric. It looked like a cinematic science fiction paradise.

"You called us cultists," Minerva said. "Derided us as naïve and idealistic pawns of Auric. But we are leaving on our own volition, and in good faith. We wish the people of Earth the best of luck going forward. Auric will be with you, as he is with us. Auric is everywhere and everything good and civilized. The sooner you embrace that as a species, the better off you'll be. I'll keep you posted as we settle new worlds."

And like that, the broadcast ended. I imagine Minerva was happy not to have to take questions from reporters.

Members of the Anti-Auric Alliance spoke out as well, being offered time by the General Assembly, with none other than Angelina representing them as a spokesperson and self-proclaimed "Auric Survivor" straight from Venus. How the hell she'd already managed to free herself from exile on Venus was something I couldn't imagine, and I didn't ask my Auricle to tell me how she'd pulled that off.

"How convenient that these species-traitors are flying off in their golden mothership with their alien overlord, after making such a mess of our only home," Angelina said. "My own ex-boyfriend is fully captive to the Auric Agenda. Wherever you are, Christian, I hope you're pleased with yourself."

Her hateful eyes burned through the television.

"Earth belongs to humanity," Angelina said. "Not some alien superbeing pretending to be God. Only God is God. Auric's not God, and he's not a god. He's not divine. He's a usurper, and his actions—his 'Relief Beyond Belief'—has destroyed life as we knew it and cost us our sovereignty. Frankly, I'm glad that the *Acropolis* is flying away with those crazy Auricians. The world will be better off without them. And we'll be better off without Auric. Good riddance, I say."

Her followers hooted and jeered, wearing white baseball caps with the red circle on them, crossing out the Auric logo.

"The world deserves better than Auric," Angelina said. "A3 is leading a prayer vigil to pray Auric away this Sunday. I encourage everyone to join us in this, at 9:00 a.m. Central Standard Time. Let's see how Auric does when an entire planet of believers all prays at once for his elimination. On that day, we'll show Auric the power of thoughts and prayers. Join us and get this alien invader and would-be do-gooder off our world. Let's get the refugees from Venus and Mars brought back home, where they belong. Let's see Earth made whole again. Help us undo the damage he's done."

Questions arose around how Angelina had gotten off of Venus, and Angelina sputtered about the portal, how people could come back from Venus if they passed a kind of litmus test imposed by Auric. People asked her about her time on Venus, what was it like, and Angelina spoke to it, only stumbling when someone asked her how she was known as the Queen of the Assholes on Venus, and whether she intended to keep that title here on Earth.

I changed the channel, and then turned off the television, tossing the remote aside. The suites at the Auric Towers had balconies, and I walked out on my balcony, feeling the cooler, cleaner air. I mean, you could smell it, you could feel it even more now than before.

"Auricle, how the hell did Angelina get off of Venus?" I asked.

"You wanted her back," the Auricle said. "You felt bad about her being exiled. I didn't want you being preoccupied with that, so I brought her back. Compared to many on Venus, she's comparatively mild in her maleficence."

"You wanted to show the world that people could get off Venus," I said. "A path for hope. Even though she hates you. If the Queen of the Assholes could make it back to Earth, *anyone* can."

"Two birds, one stone," the Auricle said. *"Especially* because she hates me. If a rabid anti-Auric personality like Angelina could make her way back to Earth, it shows that I'm even-handed."

"Tricky," I said, turning off my intelliphone.

Auric appeared next to me, standing there as always in his perfect white suit, his golden metal skin catching the sunlight just right.

"I think you made the right call by staying with me," Auric said.

"Yeah," I said. "I'd only be in Minerva's way up there. She's pretty amazing."

"She really is," Auric said. "A born leader."

"Not me," I said. "I'm a born observer."

"I know," Auric said.

The balcony had some white chairs, and I sat down, Auric sitting beside me. It was peaceful, truly peaceful. But he brought peace with him, an aura as undeniable as everything else associated with him. He'd created a golden bucket that contained ice and a bottle of champagne and two blue, fluted crystal glasses.

"What's this for?" I asked.

"I thought we'd have a toast," Auric said. It occurred to me that I'd never seen Auric eat or drink anything before. I assumed he was only doing it for my benefit, as he popped the champagne and poured the golden bubbly in the glasses. He held out one to me, which I took.

"What are we toasting?" I asked.

"To a better, brighter future," Auric said. "To civilization's everlasting triumph in the face of constant adversity and challenges wrought by a perilous universe. The path of progress has plenty of twists and turns."

"Alright, I can drink to that," I said, clinking my glass. I drank the champagne, and saw that Auric drank it, too. A fresh thing for me to observe. The champagne was naturally exquisite, the top shelf of the top shelf. Auric could see me enjoying it.

"Nothing but the best," Auric said. "Always."

"Angelina's Prayerfest isn't going to get rid of you, is it?" I asked.

Auric shook his head, pursing his lips.

"They haven't got a prayer," Auric said, and we both chuckled. "But it'll be somewhat cathartic for them to try. People have to feel like they're doing something, even when that something they're doing is nothing."

"That's paradoxical," I said. "Even for an inactivist like me."

"That's human," Auric said.

"Enjoy the ride, because you're stuck with us, now," I said, raising my glass again. "To humanity, wherever exactly the hell we end up going. And *you're* stuck with me, too."

"I'll drink to that," Auric said, winking, draining his glass, his fiery hair dancing in the morning light, the divine sunlight gently kissing his golden face, his majestic, metallic, godlike profile.

The end of the world never looked so good.

FINIS

A NOTE ON THE TYPE

The text of this book is set in Aldine, designed by Robert Slimbach for Adobe Originals. Aldine is a contemporary interpretation of the humanist book types developed at the Aldine Press at the turn of the 15th century.

Robert Slimbach, who joined Adobe in 1987, began working seriously on type and calligraphy four years earlier in the type drawing department of Autologic in Newbury Park, California. Since then, he has concentrated primarily on designing text faces for digital technology, drawing inspiration from classical sources. In 1991, he received the Prix Charles Peignot from Association Typographique Internationale for excellence in type design. Slimbach now directs Adobe's type design program.

The chapter titles of this book are set in Lydian, a calligraphic humanist sans-serif typeface designed by Warren Chappell in 1938. It is available in bold, italic, and condensed, as well as in a cursive variant. The original foundry font was commissioned and cast by American Type Founders and included a stylistic alternate, a capital A with a cross bar. It was named after the designer's wife Lydia.

Warren Chappell (1904–March 26, 1991) was an American illustrator, book and type designer, and writer. Chappell was born in Richmond, Virginia. He was a graduate of the University of Richmond, and then studied at the Art Students League of New York, under Boardman Robinson, where he later taught. In 1931-2, he studied type design and punch-cutting under Rudolf Koch at the Design School Offenbach in Germany. In 1935, he studied illustration at the Colorado Springs Fine Arts Center. The University of Richmond awarded him an honorary D.F.A. in 1968. In 1970, his work in the graphic arts was recognized by the Rochester Institute of Technology, with the presentation of their Goudy Award.

Composed by Clever Crow Consulting and Design
Pittsburgh, Pennsylvania

ACKNOWLEDGMENTS

I would like to thank Christine Marie Scott of Clever Crow Consulting and Design in Pittsburgh for her wonderful cover art and her invaluable assistance with the layout and design of these pages.

ABOUT THE AUTHOR

Dean Vale lives and breathes Science Fiction at all hours in an early 20th-century brownstone, where he conjures up progressively more dystopian and utopian visions for the future of humankind. He is the author of *Sightseer, Farther,* and *The Charge of the Wolverhino.*

NOSETOUCH PRESS™

Nosetouch Press is an independent book publisher
tandemly based in Chicago and Pittsburgh.
We are dedicated to bringing some of today's most
energizing fiction to readers around the world.

Our commitment to classic book design in a digital
environment brings an innovative and authentic
approach to the traditions of literary excellence.

*We're Out There™
NOSETOUCHPRESS.COM

Horror | Science Fiction | Fantasy | Mystery
Supernatural | Gothic | Weird